THE COLLECTED WORKS OF
G. K. CHESTERTON

IV

THE COLLECTED WORKS OF G. K. CHESTERTON
IV

WHAT'S WRONG WITH THE WORLD
THE SUPERSTITION OF DIVORCE
EUGENICS AND OTHER EVILS
DIVORCE VERSUS DEMOCRACY
SOCIAL REFORM VERSUS BIRTH CONTROL

with Introduction by
James V. Schall, S.J.

IGNATIUS PRESS   SAN   FRANCISCO

© 1987 Ignatius Press, San Francisco
All rights reserved

ISBN 978-0-89870-147-0 (SB)
Library of Congress catalogue number 85-081511
Printed in the United States of America

CONTENTS

General Editors' Introduction   9

Introduction, by James V. Schall, S.J.   11

A Note on the Texts   31

WHAT'S WRONG WITH THE WORLD   33

PART ONE: THE HOMELESSNESS OF MAN

I	The Medical Mistake	39
II	Wanted: An Unpractical Man	42
III	The New Hypocrite	47
IV	The Fear of the Past	52
V	The Unfinished Temple	59
VI	The Enemies of Property	64
VII	The Free Family	67
VIII	The Wildness of Domesticity	71
IX	History of Hudge and Gudge	75
X	Oppression by Optimism	79
XI	The Homelessness of Jones	82

PART TWO: IMPERIALISM, OR THE MISTAKE ABOUT MAN

I	The Charm of Jingoism	89
II	Wisdom and the Weather	92
III	The Common Vision	97
IV	The Insane Necessity	100

PART THREE: FEMINISM, OR THE MISTAKE ABOUT WOMAN

I	The Unmilitary Suffragette	107
II	The Universal Stick	110
III	The Emancipation of Domesticity	115

CONTENTS

IV   The Romance of Thrift   120
V   The Coldness of Chloe   125
VI   The Pedant and the Savage   129
VII   The Modern Surrender of Woman   132
VIII   The Brand of the Fleur-de-Lis   135
IX   Sincerity and the Gallows   138
X   The Higher Anarchy   141
XI   The Queen and the Suffragettes   145
XII   The Modern Slave   147

PART FOUR: EDUCATION: OR THE MISTAKE ABOUT THE CHILD

I   The Calvinism of To-day   153
II   The Tribal Terror   155
III   The Tricks of Environment   158
IV   The Truth About Education   160
V   An Evil Cry   163
VI   Authority the Unavoidable   166
VII   The Humility of Mrs. Grundy   170
VIII   The Broken Rainbow   174
IX   The Need for Narrowness   178
X   The Case for the Public Schools   181
XI   The School for Hypocrites   186
XII   The Staleness of the New Schools   191
XIII   The Outlawed Parent   194
XIV   Folly and Female Education   197

PART FIVE: THE HOME OF MAN

I   The Empire of the Insect   203
II   The Fallacy of the Umbrella Stand   208
III   The Dreadful Duty of Gudge   212
IV   A Last Instance   214
V   Conclusion   215

THREE NOTES

I   On Female Suffrage   221

II	On Cleanliness in Education	223
III	On Peasant Proprietorship	224

THE SUPERSTITION OF DIVORCE

	Introductory Note	227
I	The Superstition of Divorce (1)	229
II	The Superstition of Divorce (2)	235
III	The Superstition of Divorce (3)	243
IV	The Superstition of Divorce (4)	248
V	The Story of the Family	252
VI	The Story of the Vow	262
VII	The Tragedies of Marriage	271
VIII	The Vista of Divorce	281
	Conclusion	289

EUGENICS AND OTHER EVILS

Part One: The False Theory

I	What is Eugenics?	297
II	The First Obstacles	303
III	The Anarchy from Above	309
IV	The Lunatic and the Law	315
V	The Flying Authority	325
VI	The Unanswered Challenge	335
VII	The Established Church of Doubt	343
VIII	A Summary of a False Theory	349

Part Two: The Real Aim

I	The Impotence of Impenitence	355
II	True History of a Tramp	362
III	True History of a Eugenist	370
IV	The Vengeance of the Flesh	378

CONTENTS

V   The Meanness of the Motive   385
VI   The Eclipse of Liberty   394
VII   The Transformation of Socialism   401
VIII   The End of the Household Gods   408
IX   A Short Chapter   416

DIVORCE VERSUS DEMOCRACY   419

SOCIAL REFORM VERSUS BIRTH CONTROL   433

GENERAL EDITORS' INTRODUCTION

Throughout his life, Gilbert Keith Chesterton staunchly opposed any assaults by the trend setters on the common man and his family. Chesterton possessed the genius to foresee the dangers if the modernist's proposals were implemented. He knew that relaxed moral standards, eugenics, behavioral psychology, divorce, the feminist movement, birth control, scientism and abortion would lead to the dehumanization of man and the annihilation of the family.

This volume will be the first of two devoted to G. K. C.'s political, sociological and economic writings. The present volume's subject matter encompasses "the family, its constituent elements, supports and character over against those ideas and institutions that would subvert it and thereby deliver man into the hands . . . of the servile state".

The prominent political philosopher James V. Schall, S.J., served as editor of Volume IV of the *Collected Works of G. K. Chesterton*. Father Schall, a professor in the Department of Government at Georgetown University, is a member of the Board of Consultors of the National Endowment for the Humanities. He is the author of over a dozen books including: *Christianity and Politics, Liberation Theology, The Politics of Heaven and Hell, Christianity and Life* and *Church, State and Society in the Thought of John Paul II*.

In his essay entitled "The Common Man", G. K. C. wrote:

> Progress, in the sense of the progress that has progressed since the sixteenth century, has upon every matter persecuted the Common Man; punished the gambling he enjoys and permitted the gambling he cannot follow . . . silenced the political quarrels that can be conducted among men and applauded the political stunts and syndicates that can only be conducted by millionaires; encouraged anybody who had anything to say against God, if it was said with a priggish and supercilious accent; but discouraged anybody who had anything to say in favour of Man, in his common relations to manhood and motherhood and the normal appetites of nature. Progress has been merely the persecution of the Common Man.

In the works included in this volume, Chesterton revealed to the public the sheer lunacy of the modernist's proposals because he had the great insight to recognize that this new progressive school of thought would ultimately lead to the persecution of the family and his beloved Common Man.

GEORGE J. MARLIN
RICHARD P. RABATIN
JOHN L. SWAN
  General Editors

JOSEPH SOBRAN
  Consulting Editor

PATRICIA AZAR
REV. RANDALL PAINE O.S.C.
  Associate Editors

BARBARA D. MARLIN
  Assistant

INTRODUCTION

By James V. Schall, S. J.

ON THINGS WORTH DOING BADLY

This is that insanely frivolous thing we call sanity. And the elegant female, drooping her ringlets over her water-colors, knew it and acted on it. She was juggling with frantic and flaming suns. She was maintaining the bold equilibrium of inferiorities which is the most mysterious of superiorities and perhaps the most unattainable. She was maintaining the prime truth of woman, the universal mother: that if a thing is worth doing, it is worth doing badly.

—G. K. Chesterton, "Female Education", in *What's Wrong with the World?*, p. 199.

Included in this volume of *The Collected Works of G. K. Chesterton* are three wonderfully contrary books: *What's Wrong with the World?* (1910), *The Superstition of Divorce* (1920) and *Eugenics and Other Evils* (1922)—together with two shorter essays, *Divorce Versus Democracy* (1916) and *Social Reform Versus Birth Control* (1927). It would be difficult to find a collection of incisive arguments more at odds with so many prevailing practices in contemporary civilization. Chesterton's refreshing argumentations make this present volume something of a defiance, a reminder of the higher things we are not often allowed or encouraged to reflect on, however central it is for us to do so.

Chesterton never hesitated, however, to challenge something because it was popular or widely accepted. Indeed, he suspected that a refusal to consider something as questionable because it was popular was itself a prejudice of the worst sort. These essays, make no doubt of it, challenge the very foundations of contemporary public life and the ideas on which they are based. Chesterton's ideal was quite different from the ideal of our era. But that very difference constitutes the reason why we might want to consider his ideal perhaps worthy to be put into effect. "There is only one really startling thing to be done with the ideal," he wrote in *What's Wrong with the World?*, " and that is to do it" (64).

The subject matter of these works, in other words, is the family, its constituent elements, supports and character over against those ideas and institutions that would subvert it and thereby deliver man into the hands of the modern state and those ideas that have formed it. "Without the family, we are helpless before the state, which in our modern case is the Servile State" (*SD*, 242).[1] Since most of the ideas from divorce to feminism to euthanasia to homosexuality to abortion have gained much of the day since Chesterton first wrote against them over a half century ago, these essays and reflections are even more remarkable. In them, we can see that what he was talking about did in fact come to pass, whereas he was mostly seeing these potential results in their incipient stages. In many ways, the actual consequences have been even worse than Chesterton anticipated.

In a humorous aside in *What's Wrong with the World?*, Chesterton remarked on the attitude and dangers one must endure to point out the problems with currently popular ideas.

> There is not really any courage at all in attacking hoary or antiquated things, any more than in offering to fight one's grandmother. The really courageous man is he who defies the tyrannies young as the morning and superstitions fresh as the first flowers. The only true free thinker is he whose intellect is as much free from the future as from the past (*WWW*, 57).

The fact that Chesterton was so blunt and contrary to many of today's basic and widely held ideas about the family and its members may be, for some, a reason not to consider him seriously again.

It is my view, however, that the opposite is the case. These

---

[1] On the subject of the Servile State, an expression which Chesterton got from Hilaire Belloc, see James V. Schall, "Freedom, Property, and the Servile State", *Chesterton Review*, XII (May, 1986), 185–94.

analyses of man, woman, child, home, education, divorce, birth control, property, the eugenic state and feminism are so remarkably perceptive that we can almost think they were written for today, almost as if Chesterton saw that our time would not be content to listen to his warnings. But he seemed to suspect that our era would insist on actually trying out the things that he knew would eventually destroy the foundations of human love and family.

Each of these books and essays is complete in itself, yet clearly they all support and ground the others at some basic point. Chesterton had a happy facility for summarizing and repeating himself in an original fashion that connected all his arguments together. His love of paradox shows itself here as always, but it is important to see that each paradox he used bore a definite truth which Chesterton clearly intended. His style was at the same time light and humorous, yet deadly serious and philosophical. Chesterton never doubted the primacy of ideas in the structure and nature of a social order.

We can long debate which of Gilbert K. Chesterton's books is the most profound or the most enduring. In one sense, of course, no one can doubt that *Orthodoxy* will ever remain the Chesterton book that strikes nearest to the heart of the reality *that is*, of which he spoke so well in *St. Thomas Aquinas*. Yet, I have long felt that *What's Wrong with the World?* and *Eugenics and Other Evils* have become more and more central to the key issues of our time.[2]

In these books, Chesterton discussed the perplexing issues of property, divorce and birth control, issues that connect intimately with Chesterton's arguments in *What's Wrong with the World?* about the man, the woman, the child and the home. To these must be added those specifically planned substitutes, both by science and the state, for begetting and human rearing that have subsequently arisen. We

[2] See James V. Schall, "The Rarest of All Revolutions: G. K. Chesterton on the Relation of Human Life to Christian Doctrine", *The American Benedictine Review* 32 (December, 1981), 304–26; "The Sanity of Gilbert Chesterton", *Social Survey*, Melbourne, 24 (October, 1977), 261–66; "On Doctrine and Dignity: From *Heretics* to *Orthodoxy*", *Homiletic and Pastoral Review* LXXXII (February, 1982), 16–25; Review of *Orthodoxy* (New York: Doubleday Image, 1972), in *Homiletic and Pastoral Review*, LXXIII (August–September, 1973), p. 89; Review of *A Chesterton Anthology* (San Francisco: Ignatius Press, 1985), in *Homiletic and Pastoral Review*, LXXXVI (October, 1986), pp. 80–84.

can begin to understand that Chesterton stood for the almost unbearable truth that something radically wrong was in practice *chosen*, the word is exact, by our civilization about the time he wrote
these books, in the period from 1910 to 1930.[3]

The Centrality of the Family

Yet, in an uncomprehending review of *What's Wrong with the World?*,
written by some uncourageous, "unsigned" reviewer in the London
Evening Standard, on June 28, 1910, we read, "We haven't the faintest
notion what's wrong with the world, and having read Mr. Chesterton's book — nearly 300 pages — have regretfully come to the conclusion
that he doesn't either." Well, this is, of course, marvelous puff and
controversy, the sort of wit Chesterton himself would love and no
doubt did.

But this early review shows an astonishing obtuseness about the
central theme of Chesterton concerning matters of familial and sexual activities as they relate to the foundations of society. Chesterton
himself was not in the slightest unclear about what he thought was
wrong with the world. This is, indeed, one of the pleasures in reading or rereading these lucid essays of G. K. Chesterton.

Chesterton simply held that what men and women really want is
what common sense and the Creeds have traditionally taught about
marriage and the family. "As every normal man desires a woman and
children born of a woman, every normal man desires a house of his own
to put them into . . ." (*WWW*, 73). The corollary to this is that any
violation of the fidelity demanded by the tradition about marriage
would end up not only in depriving our kind of what they would want,
but would lead them to evils that they definitely would find harmful.
Today, in retrospect, perhaps we can see Chesterton's point about what
is wrong with the world more clearly than the rather cynical reviewer
of 1910 because we see on all sides of us the experimental results of
choosing what Chesterton would have had us reject.

[3] See James V. Schall, *Human Dignity and Human Numbers* (Staten Island: Alba
House, 1971) and *Christianity and Life* (San Francisco: Ignatius Press, 1981).

Even though we admit on the basis of widely perceived evidence that there is something wrong with, say, divorce and its now commonly accepted frequency, we no longer have the courage to face the fact that our conception of divorce and marriage may itself be the problem. If divorce is some sort of civil right, so that its occurrence is something we might expect for most men and women because, well, long term fidelity is against statistics if not against nature, then it will sound simply unintelligible to maintain that it ought to cease because it violates what men and women really want.

"Well, if one happens to believe in democracy as I do", Chesterton wrote in *Divorce Versus Democracy*,

> as a large trust in the active and passive judgment of the human conscience, one can have no hesitation, no "impartiality", about one's view of divorce; and especially about one's view of the extension of divorce among the democracy. A democrat in any sense must regard that extension as the last and vilest of the insults offered by the modern rich to the modern poor. The rich do largely believe in divorce; the poor do mainly believe in fidelity (423).

But this latter notion of fidelity is what Chesterton held, and the considerations of the essays that follow contain his arguments to prove his case.

In *The Superstition of Divorce*, itself a title designed deliberately, I suppose, to challenge our very modern complacency, Chesterton wrote in 1920 that in considering divorce we are dealing with "the ultimate mystery and paradox of limitation and liberty" (229). And he went on to suggest, again with much humor, that really many people say they want divorce "without ever asking themselves whether they want marriage" (229). It is important, however, to recognize that Chesterton based his argument on a lucidly cold logic. In a sense, there was nothing religious in any of these books and essays, except that he suggested that traditional religion is in conformity with reason and that often, it is the only thing in the modern world that in fact upholds reason, especially in the area of the family. "It is the Christian Church which continues to hold strongly, when the world for some reason has weakened it, what others hold at other times" (*SD*, 232). But the argument itself is not one of faith.

The wonderful irony of these observations of Chesterton, the unforgivable chiding to our intellectual complacency, is that marriage itself is today in fact conceived to be something to be gotten out of, not something into which we use our freedom to bind ourselves — "liberty and limitation", to use Chesterton's phrase. That we can bind ourselves to one person is the only basis for romance and love that ever existed. Chesterton on divorce, then, is maddening to the modern mind, not because his view is a denial of romance and love, but because his anti-divorce view is their only sound affirmation. And no escape in logic is allowed to us in this matter.

We are today, even in religion, practically forbidden to say these things. Indeed, in the light of Chesterton's reflections on divorce, the prevalence of *de facto* divorce in the Church and the churches, in spite of the theories, is one of the major contemporary causes to doubt the truth of religion in the name of reason (*SD*, 232). For Chesterton himself, the Church's insistence on the durability of the marital vow was an argument for the truth of the claims of revelation, which did reflect the conclusions of reason and logic.

> The obvious thing to protect the ideal of marriage is the Christian religion. . . . I do not dream of denying, indeed I should take every opportunity of affirming, that monogamy and its domestic responsibilities can be defended on rational apart from religious grounds. But a religion is the practical protection of any moral idea which has to be popular and which has to be pugnacious. And our ideal, if it is to survive, has to be both (*EOE*, 412).

This is one reason why this republication of Chesterton allows us to argue some things otherwise almost culturally prohibited in our public order.

Chesterton's argument, as we have suggested, while clearly agreeing with classical Christianity, was not directly based upon it, but on reason and experience. Indeed, this reasonable basis is, from the religious point of view, the rather frightening thing about these reflections on marriage and family by Chesterton. He was against divorce, not so much because it was prohibited by the commandment, even though it was, but because it involved a clear intellectual contradiction, that of affirming and denying in the very same act something that was intended to be lasting. Chesterton thus wrote, "but the philosophic peculiarity of divorce and re-marriage, as compared with free love and no marriage, is that a man breaks and makes a promise at the same moment" (SD, 233). In Chesterton's view, men could not long live with such intrinsic contradictions in their actions.

Chesterton understood that there was one natural institution that stood outside the state and thereby limited the state. "It is not hard to see why the vow made most freely is the vow kept most firmly. There are attached to it, by the nature of things, consequences so tremendous that no contract can offer any comparison" (SD, 237). He saw that this institution was based upon the promise or vow of fidelity between two free persons, a man and a woman, a vow that alone enabled any real romance in the world to exist at all. "The shortest way of putting the problem is to ask whether being free includes being free to bind oneself" (SD, 233).

Upon this radical freedom and its intelligibility, Chesterton argued the case for the home and widely distributed property against eugenics, divorce, birth control and the modern state that sought to enlarge its power and moral authority by subsuming into itself the functions of the family, particularly those of schooling, nurturing and increasingly of begetting or allowing to be born. Chesterton's argument, his radicalism, was that the one true and vital social and political alternative to the modern state in its socialist or liberal absolutist forms was the classic family, the family with lasting promises, children, division of labor, home and freedom. This is the argument that we no longer see made even by the major religions, yet it remains the basic need of our society if we are indeed concerned about what it means for real men and women to be happy. Indeed, it is an idea whose time has come. "It is precisely those who have been conservative about the family who have been revolutionary about the state" (SD, 245).

Chesterton argued that the discussion of marriage, eugenics, divorce, birth control, property, children and home were part of the same discussion. These things belonged together in a unity so strict, so unbroken that any deviation from accurate argumentation would lead to the most dire consequences. Yet, the love of man and woman was to lead us to the most wondrous good, the good that was the child, for whom Chesterton had the most elevated affection.

Birth Control and Eugenics

The main discussion of birth control in Chesterton is probably found in *The Well and the Shallows* and *Social Reform Versus Birth Control*. However, it is important to know what Chesterton held here, since he saw eugenics and divorce to be related to mankind's attitude toward children and their begetting. He wrote at the time of the Lambeth Conference when the Anglican Church, first among the Christian churches, approved the practice of birth prevention. This was a move that Chesterton said was enough in itself to have caused him to reject its claim on truth—"one of the crises, which would in any case have driven me in the way I had gone already [to Catholicism], was the shilly-shallying and sham liberality of the famous Lambeth Report on what is quaintly called Birth Control."[4]

Chesterton clearly detested eugenics. His words for birth control were, perhaps unexpectedly, even more blunt. It is, he remarked, "a scheme for preventing birth in order to escape control".[5] Chesterton looked upon this Anglican ecclesiastical approval for birth control as a kind of "final surrender" in a long series of errors on the topic of sex by the church. Chesterton recalled that his own parents would have "regarded Birth-Prevention exactly as they would have regarded Infanticide".[6]

In a long series of instances wherein he noted how the exception to the rule has been used methodically to change the rule, Chesterton affirmed the importance of upholding the rule itself, even in the face of great hardship. Thus, "the weak and inconclusive pronouncement [Lambeth] upon Birth-Prevention was only the

---

[4] G. K. Chesterton, "The Surrender upon Sex", *The Well and the Shallows* (New York: Sheed & Ward, 1935), 37.

[5] Ibid., 37.

[6] Ibid., 41.

culmination of this long intellectual corruption."[7] The Church, then, "was right to refuse even the exemption" both in the case of divorce and birth control.

Chesterton stated quite forcefully that he had only "contempt" for the advocates of birth control.[8] This word "contempt" is, as I said, a strong word for Chesterton. He was especially annoyed, as he was in the case of divorce, at the abuse of word and idea. Birth control, he held, "does not control any birth. It only makes sure that there shall never be any birth to control."[9]

In the case of the eugenic argument for birth or population control, which purported to argue that only healthy or intelligent children should be conceived with all others prevented, Chesterton held rather that we ought not to kill or prevent births that "might" be unhealthy according to eugenic standards. A more "reasonable" policy would be, as he ironically put it, to let all the conceived children be born and then only kill the ones we do not want after taking a look at them.[10] This is really also the argument against the abortionist who acts on the grounds that a child "might" be defective. The only correct path, even in this deadly logic, would be to let the child be born and then kill it if it were in truth defective. Currently, this latter procedure has been, unfortunately, coming into use. But in Chesterton's parody, at least, the healthy fetus would not be killed to get at the presumably unhealthy one.

Chesterton, of course, had argued these "reductions to absurdity" because he never dreamed that anyone could seriously consider them. On the other hand, he understood that evil wins "through the strength of its splendid dupes", and that there has always been in this area a "disastrous alliance between abnormal innocence and abnormal sin" (*EOE*, 297). We can wonder, looking back on this observation, whether it has not been precisely this strange alliance of abnormal innocence and abnormal sin that has been instrumental in bringing about these threats to the family and marriage symbolized by

[7] Ibid., 43.
[8] "Babies and Distributism", ibid., 142.
[9] Ibid.
[10] Ibid., 144.

birth control, divorce, abortion and genetic engineering of human beings.

But for Chesterton, "a child is the very sign and sacrament of personal freedom. He is a fresh free will added to the wills of the world; he is something that his parents have freely chosen to produce and which they freely agree to produce."[11] Again the child is the result of a promise between a man and a woman who choose one another. And the ultimate notion of freedom is the freedom to bind oneself to this very result. This is why the breaking of the marriage vow is not an expression of "freedom" but the admission of its loss.

Chesterton's dislike of eugenics, almost as much as his dislike of birth control, derived from this same notion. If a man and a woman bind themselves together, what results from their relationship is their concern. The idea that it is the state's or science's concern to produce the "right" sort of child wholly ignores what it is that causes a child to come to be in the first place, that is, the relation of the parents to each other, and what it is that best cares for the particular child, namely, the parents.

The proper attitude of mankind with regard to the binding of a man and a woman, however, is to secure "the fidelity of the two sexes to each other and leave the rest to God."[12] This will mean that the children are not the responsibility of the state. But this latter depends upon the willingness and capacity of the sexes to enter into a real marriage in the first place. It is this possibility that was the primary concern of G. K. Chesterton. It was this possibility that he saw under attack not by our weakness but by our ideas about what it is we do when we marry.

Eugenics is presumably the "science of good birth". The very existence of such a so-called "science" was, in Chesterton's view, the result of a theory that the first concern in a marriage was not the relation of a man and a woman to each other, but the future condition of any possible children. This theory was what allowed the state and science directly into marriage. Thus, only if parents could be expected to bring forth a desired "product" could they be allowed to

[11] Ibid., 145.
[12] G. K. Chesterton, *Eugenics and Other Evils*, o.

marry and to have children. This view, of course, would make marriage depend not on the spiritual relations of man and woman but on the permission of science or the state. Yet, it is the love and fidelity of parents, whoever they are, that can alone provide the proper atmosphere for their child.

The moral basis of eugenics, Chesterton held, is that the "baby for whom we are principally and directly responsible is the child unborn" (*EOE*, 298). This is merely an application to the family of the more general idea that we should ground our thinking in the future not in the past, including the past of ourselves. And if the being of man itself is not based on something closed from political or scientific "re-construction", then "when once one begins to think of man as a shifting and alterable thing, it is always easy for the strong and crafty to twist him into new shapes for all kinds of unnatural purposes" (*WWW*, 204).

This is particularly easy when genetics comes to be applied to the formation of human beings, either in laboratories or in the act of begetting itself. The elevation of the relations of man and woman to a sphere beyond the direct control of state or science is the necessary step in protecting the possibility of romance and love with their products in the child that actually results from this specific love and fidelity.

Chesterton thus held that "the founding of a family is the personal adventure of a free man" (*EOE*, 301). This was an adventure essentially outside the state. The inner life of the family was simply beyond the public order and the public order was related to it as means to end. Chesterton understood the danger of conceiving the state after the manner of an organism. "In resisting this horrible theory of the Soul of the Hive, we of Christendom stand not for ourselves, but for all humanity; for the essential and distinctive human idea that one good and happy man is an end in himself, that a soul is worth saving" (*WWW*, 207).

This priority alone, then, was able to guarantee the right order of man to state. As he put it elsewhere, "If there are commands of God, then there must be rights of men"(*WWW*, 203). If there are no commands of God, nor any reason to think of man as an end in himself, but something subject to the betterment of the state, then there is nothing to protect the normal man from human experimentation, be it biological or social.

This transcendence of the child and the members of the family, this notion that each is an end in himself, grounds the thought of Chesterton in a reality which requires attention to each individual as such. The children of the future, he held, ought to be results of the adventure of the free man and free woman, fully bound, that is, people who want their freedom to be lasting because what they do is productive of what is itself lasting. A movement to restore such ideas was, in his mind, the first step back to sanity.

Chesterton held that today it is clearly not the Church that is using the "secular arm" in these biological areas to enforce its norms, but "the thing that is really trying to tyrannize through government is Science. The thing that really does use the secular arm is Science" (*EOE*, 345). The recent controversies over what is not allowed to be taught in the public schools because it is forbidden by "science" reveals the perception of Chesterton that "materialism is really our established church" (*EOE*, 345). We are only now beginning to realize that we have, by removing religion from public life, in fact established a non-theistic humanism as the only permitted doctrine taught in the state schools.

As Chesterton already understood, "they say that nowadays the creeds are crumbling; I doubt it, but at least the sects are increasing" (*WWW*, 178-179). That is to say, that when the secular arm enforces "science", when religion is removed, the "humanist" religion that results in eugenics or familial breakdown or state control becomes the established creed, a creed which refuses to call itself what it in fact is. It was against the incipient growth of this establishment that Chesterton wrote in defense of the family and what constituted it, since he understood that the sanctity of the family would be the main obstacle to prevent an all-embracing science, enforced by an all-powerful, all-caring state from controlling all of human life. The modern heresy, then, is to alter "the human soul to fit its conditions, instead of altering human conditions to fit the human soul" (*WWW*, 104).

The Pertinence of Ideals

Chesterton was an idealist, which in many ways is not a good word since idealists have often been responsible for destroying the very family he sought to defend. But Chesterton held that in the social sciences we needed to know what things were, particularly marriage, man, woman, and child, before we could decide what was wrong with them (*WWW*, 41). Progress ought not, then, to mean change for its own sake, but change to what was right. Chesterton was adamant in opposing the idea that, because we might have widespread, legal divorce, abortion, birth control or day care centers, we could not do anything to change the social order to what is right, a social order that would freely contain none of these things because we choose something better.

The determinism of the *status quo* with its established deformities was used to deny man's real freedom to construct a life men really wanted. "If I am to discuss what is wrong, one of the first things that are wrong is this: the deep and silent modern assumption that past things have become impossible" (*WWW*, 57). Thus, it was said that the vision Chesterton proposed was "impossible" because it could not be revivified. But Chesterton was a man of freedom. He did not think we had to have a society of eugenics, divorce and birth control, or a lack of homes for men and women with families. But such things as faithful families, property and children were possible only if we could begin to see why we ought to want them.

The first battles are always in the intellect. "The medieval system began to be broken to pieces intellectually, long before it showed the slightest hint of falling to pieces morally" (*WWW*, 60). Yet, Chesterton, in a famous passage, insisted that the refusal to embrace or live an ideal is no argument against it:

> . . .The great ideals of the past failed not by being outlived (which must mean over-lived), but by not being lived enough. Mankind has not passed through the Middle Ages. Rather mankind has retreated from the Middle Ages in reaction and rout. The Christian ideal has not been tried and found wanting. It has been found difficult; and left untried" (*WWW*, 60–61).

Chesterton refused to accept determinism of any sort, but he likewise refused to admit with the pessimists that a more human life was impossible.

"Heaven does not work; it plays. Men are most themselves when they are free . . ." (*WWW*, 99). If there is any common theme in all of these essays about the family, it is clearly the primacy of freedom, that radical freedom on which the family of man ought to be built in the first place. This is a freedom that, in its very structure, binds itself, a limited yet created freedom that recognizes that fidelity is the continuation of love, and love wants to possess, to be present once and for all, even in our weaknesses, especially in our children.

> God is that which can make something out of nothing. Man (it may be fairly said) is that which can make something out of anything. In other words, while the joy of God be unlimited creation, the special joy of man is limited creation, the continuation of creation with limitation (*WWW*, 65).

This extraordinary notion of "limited creativity" is the key to Chesterton's idea about the woman, the one creature free enough to do anything because her task ultimately is to teach everything to one person (*WWW*, 118). Speaking of the critics of women, he remarked, "How can it be broad to be the same thing to everyone, and narrow to be everything to someone?" (*WWW*, 119). Thus, "two people must be tied together to do themselves justice; for twenty minutes at a dance, for twenty years in a marriage" (*WWW*, 69). Without this intrinsic limitation, there can be no marriage, no freedom.

Property

The idea of limited freedom is likewise the key to understanding the place and attention Chesterton devoted in these essays to the deficiencies of "capitalism". By capitalism, of course, he meant *laissez faire* capitalism. He was opposed as much, if not more, to socialism, but he found both to be of the same origin.[13] Capitalism meant a very great concentration of wealth, whereas Chesterton's idea was based on a wide distribution of productive wealth so that each family could have some space for economic independence from the state and more especially for creative productivity. "Too much capitalism does not mean too many capitalists, but too few" (*SD*, 246).

Chesterton habitually posed these positions in terms of the crafts or peasant proprietorship. These ideas will seem outmoded today, but the principle he sought was sound and indeed, with the computer revolution, seems never closer to reality.[14] A revitalized notion of private productive property, small efficient organizations, if not smaller states, family-centered motivation, and policies to support each seems to be a political and economic idea waiting for someone to embrace it.

Man, Woman, Child, Home

No doubt the most memorable and remarkable aspect of these books of Chesterton, however, was what he said on the nature and relation of the sexes themselves. He left no doubt that the most romantic as well as the most desirable realities were the ones least attended to. He did not begin with any notion of the "equality" of the sexes, but with their radical difference. In a wonderfully quotable passage, he wrote:

> If Americans can be divorced for "incompatibility of temper", I cannot conceive why they are not all divorced. I have known many happy marriages, but never a compatible one. The whole aim of marriage is to fight through and survive the instant when incompatibility becomes unquestionable. For a man and a woman, as such, are incompatible (*WWW*, 70).

[13] For a marvelous discussion of the problems of socialism, see G. K. Chesterton, "Why I Am Not a Socialist", *Chesterton Review*, VII (no. 3, 1981).

[14] See James V. Schall, "The Future of Distributism", *Commonweal*, LXII (May 6, 1955), 123–25. Such reflections as George Gilder's *Wealth and Poverty*, E. F. Schumacher's *Small Is Beautiful*, P. T. Bauer's *Reality and Rhetoric*, and Thomas J. Peters and Robert H. Waterman's *In Search of Excellence* are books that touch in a contemporary way the ideas Chesterton had in mind.

This incompatibility, of course, lasts through all of life and all eternity as well. It is based on the very different realities that men and women are created to be. Chesterton held that men should be educated to be men, women to be women, that to confuse the two is to confuse man and woman, and through these, the child.

Chesterton argued that women should not normally work outside the home, and in fact that the vast majority of women did not want to do so, but were forced to do so either because of the economic system or because their husbands made them because of some deficiency. What he would have thought of modern divorce statistics which reveal that working women often work because they must is not difficult to surmise. He felt that women in jobs were a bad idea, not for the job, but because the nature of female loyalty caused them to be devoted to something quite unworthy of them, namely the factory or the office (*WWW*, 119).

Chesterton maintained, moreover, that the real place of woman's freedom was the home, and it was there that her capacity to do something of everything came to the fore because she had to teach someone all things. Chesterton was not being reactionary here, but defending a kind of freedom inherent in the very nature of females. "I would give woman, not more rights, but more privileges. Instead of sending her to seek such freedom as notoriously prevails in banks and factories, I would design especially a house in which she can be free"(*WWW*, 148).

Chesterton's ironic remarks about the originality of female education were that it was not original at all, but only an imitation of male education.

> I am often solemnly asked what I think of the new ideas about female education. But there are no new ideas about female education. There is not, there never has been, even the vestige of a new idea. All the educational reformers did was to ask what was being done to boys and then go and do it to girls . . . (*WWW*, 197).

This reflection can at least leave us with the suspicion that females are in fact not receiving the sort of education that they deserve, but the one that merely imitates what is normally given to men. Chesterton thought that women collapsed too easily in their desire to be educated and employed like men.

Chesterton held that the romance of the home made possible the romance of thrift. Real property could make it possible for each member of the family, with what all had individually and in common in terms of talent, work and goods, creatively to produce what he could. This could be a family grounding movement within a system of property and productive wealth. It seems an ideal that is well worth arguing. Certainly it is one that is not heard.

Chesterton likewise spoke memorably about the difference between love and comradeship as these are perceived by men and women. It is something at once so obvious and so unknown that it comes as something of a shock in our times. Yet, Chesterton pointed out that the differences between men and women, symbolized by the club and the home, were ones that ought to be fostered, not mitigated. A woman has the natural, mystical advantage that all males are born of her. "Nothing can overcome that one enormous sex superiority, that even the male child is born closer to his mother than to his father" (*WWW*, 143). And yet, a woman, in understanding the male, even the male child, will recognize that the mind of a man works in its own way, not superior to hers, but differently.

. . . These two necessary sanctities [of woman] of thrift and dignity are bound to come into collision with the wordiness, the wastefulness, and the perpetual pleasure-seeking of masculine companionship. Wise women allow for the thing; foolish women try to crush it; but all women try to counteract it, and they do well (*WWW*, 130-131).

These are wise words on a subject that it is almost forbidden to discuss in the public forum today.

Chesterton argued, then, for the home and for an education of children which respected their uniqueness. He recognized that education was not free, in spite of any popular rhetoric to the contrary. "All educationists are utterly dogmatic and authoritarian. You cannot have free education; for if you left a child free, you would not educate him at all" (*WWW*, 170). The issue is really over which set of dogmas, that is truths, we are going to teach. "There are no uneducated people. Everybody in England is educated; only most people are educated wrong" (*WWW*, 171).

Such words, no doubt, however true, go directly against the primary modern dogma that we cannot know or teach truths. Chesterton understood this to be merely the unadmitted endeavor to indoctrinate without admitting what we were doing. "Dogma is actually the only thing that cannot be separated from education. It *is* teaching. A teacher who is not dogmatic is simply a teacher who is not teaching" (*WWW*, 162).

Conclusion

These incisive observations of G. K. Chesterton on the human family, its varied members, and the condition of existence of each, with the kind of society in which it would flourish, are, in conclusion, quite unique and penetrating in a society which has deliberately chosen to follow an opposite route. We now have enough clear evidence that the present arrangements are not at all working at almost every level.

Yet the admission that the classic truths were in fact the better ones is something that we find difficult to accept. These reflections on divorce, marriage, property, education, eugenics, the sexes and the family are, however, trenchant ones, especially today. It is astonishing how pertinent they are in the light of the failures of their alternatives, failures not of theory but of practice.

"In most important matters," Chesterton wrote, "a man has always been free to ruin himself" (*WWW*, 142). This is a condition that is in principle unavoidable, one that we would not have otherwise. On the other hand, such ruin need not happen. This is the constant teaching of Chesterton in these pages, that we ought not to be, need not be determined to continue in the system we have chosen and created for ourselves. "The old tyrants invoked the past; the new tyrants will invoke the future" (*WWW*, 50-51). That is, the ideologies of our time are used to prevent us from reconsidering the values and institutions that we knew in the past, not perfectly knew, but knew enough to understand. Chesterton realized quite clearly that if we are ever to reinvent the ancient sanities, we must first convince ourselves that it is possible to achieve them even in our time, without at the same time invoking a kind of impossible utopia.

In the beautiful account of sanity and right order with which Chesterton ended *What's Wrong with the World?*, Chesterton wrote:

> Whatever else is evil, the pride of a good mother in the beauty of her daughter is good. . . . If other things are against it, other things must go down. . . . That little urchin with the gold-red hair, whom I have just watched toddling past my house, she shall not be lopped and lamed and altered; her hair shall not be cut short like a convict's; no, all the kingdoms of the earth shall be hacked about and mutilated to suit her. She is the human and sacred image; all around her the social fabric shall sway and split and fall; the pillars of society shall be shaken, and the roofs of ages come rushing down; and not one hair of her head shall be harmed (*WWW*, 217–218).

This is the spirit of Chesterton, his sense of the right order of things, beginning with the family of man in which a child is born.

We again can ask, with Chesterton, "What's wrong with the world?" And we can again answer with him that we cannot know what is wrong until we know what is right. This is a volume addressing itself to what is right. The real question is, can we listen? The beginning of change is the beginning of thought. But the beginning of thought is an act of intellectual bravery. It is the newer heresies that are the most difficult to contradict, even when we recognize that a G. K. Chesterton saw them at their beginning and where they might well end. "It is often essential to resist a tyranny before it exists", Chesterton wrote (*EOE*, 297). The fact that we did not so resist it means, however, that we now must deal with the consequences. This is the significance of these works of G. K. Chesterton, for they continue to present the ideal by which this can be done.

A NOTE ON THE TEXT

The first British edition of *What's Wrong with the World* was published by Cassell and Company, Ltd. on June 28, 1910. The text used here is taken from the Dodd, Mead and Company edition of 1910. This American edition contains very few variations from the Cassell publication.

The *Superstition of Divorce* appeared on January 20, 1920, and was published in Great Britain by Chatto and Windus. The American edition, which was brought out by the John Lane Company of New York in 1920, is used in this volume. The American edition contains very few variations from the English edition.

In February of 1922, Cassell and Company, Ltd. published the British edition of *Eugenics and Other Evils*. The American edition used in this text was published by Dodd, Mead & Company in 1927. Once again, there are very few changes from the English edition.

Divorce versus Democracy was brought out in pamphlet form in 1916 by the London Society of SS. Peter and Paul. York Books did the actual printing of the pamphlet. The original text is used this volume.

Social Reform versus Birth Control was also published in pamphlet form in 1927. It was sponsored by the League of National Life and printed in London by Simkin, Marshall, Hamilton, Kent and Company. The original text is used in this volume.

WHAT'S WRONG
WITH THE WORLD

1910

DEDICATION

To C. F. G. Masterman, M. P.[1]

My Dear Charles,

I originally called this book "What is Wrong," and it would have satisfied your sardonic temper to note the number of social misunderstandings that arose from the use of the title. Many a mild lady visitor opened her eyes when I remarked casually, "I have been doing 'What is Wrong' all this morning." And one minister of religion moved quite sharply in his chair when I told him (as he understood it) that I had to run upstairs and do what was wrong, but should be down again in a minute. Exactly of what occult vice they silently accused me I cannot conjecture, but I know of what I accuse myself; and that is, of having written a very shapeless and inadequate book, and one quite unworthy to be dedicated to you. As far as literature goes, this book is what is wrong, and no mistake.

It may seem a refinement of insolence to present so wild a composition to one who has recorded two or three of the really impressive visions of the moving millions of England. You are the only man alive who can make the map of England crawl with life; a most creepy and enviable accomplishment. Why then should I trouble you with a book which, even if it achieves its object (which is monstrously unlikely) can only be a thundering gallop of theory?

Well, I do it partly because I think you politicians are none the worse for a few inconvenient ideals; but more because you will recognise the many arguments we have had; those arguments which the most wonderful ladies in the world can never endure for very long. And, perhaps, you will agree with me that the thread of comradeship and conversation must be protected because it is so frivolous. It must be held sacred, it must not be snapped, because it is not worth tying together again. It is exactly because argument is idle that men (I mean males) must take it seriously; for when (we feel), until the crack of doom, shall we have so delightful a difference

---

[1] Charles F. G. Masterman (1873-1927), politician, author, Liberal Member of Parliament, 1906-1911.

again? But most of all I offer it to you because there exists not only comradeship, but a very different thing, called friendship; an agreement under all the arguments and a thread which, please God, will never break.

Yours always,

G. K. Chesterton.

PART ONE

THE HOMELESSNESS OF MAN

I

THE MEDICAL MISTAKE

A book of modern social inquiry has a shape that is somewhat sharply defined. It begins as a rule with an analysis, with statistics, tables of population, decrease of crime among Congregationalists, growth of hysteria among policemen, and similar ascertained facts; it ends with a chapter that is generally called "The Remedy." It is almost wholly due to this careful, solid, and scientific method that "The Remedy" is never found. For this scheme of medical question and answer is a blunder; the first great blunder of sociology. It is always called stating the disease before we find the cure. But it is the whole definition and dignity of man that in social matters we must actually find the cure before we find the disease.

The fallacy is one of the fifty fallacies that come from the modern madness for biological or bodily metaphors. It is convenient to speak of the Social Organism, just as it is convenient to speak of the British Lion. But Britain is no more an organism than Britain is a lion. The moment we begin to give a nation the unity and simplicity of an animal, we begin to think wildly. Because every man is a biped, fifty men are not a centipede. This has produced, for instance, the gaping absurdity of perpetually talking about "young nations" and "dying nations," as if a nation had a fixed and physical span of life. Thus people will say that Spain has entered a final senility; they might as well say that Spain is losing all her teeth. Or people will say that Canada should soon produce a literature; which is like saying that Canada must soon grow a mustache. Nations consist of people; the first generation may be decrepit, or the ten thousandth may be vigorous. Similar applications of the fallacy are made by those who see in the increasing size of national possessions, a simple increase in wisdom and stature, and in favor with God and man. These people, indeed, even fall short in subtlety of the parallel of a human body. They do not even ask whether an empire is growing taller in its youth, or only growing fatter in its old age. But of all the instances of error arising from this physical fancy, the worst is that we have before us: the

39

habit of exhaustively describing a social sickness, and then propounding a social drug.

Now we do talk first about the disease in cases of bodily breakdown; and that for an excellent reason. Because, though there may be doubt about the way in which the body broke down, there is no doubt at all about the shape in which it should be built up again. No doctor proposes to produce a new kind of man, with a new arrangement of eyes or limbs. The hospital, by necessity, may send a man home with one leg less: but it will not (in a creative rapture) send him home with one leg extra. Medical science is content with the normal human body, and only seeks to restore it.

But social science is by no means always content with the normal human soul; it has all sorts of fancy souls for sale. Man as a social idealist will say "I am tired of being a Puritan; I want to be a Pagan," or "Beyond this dark probation of Individualism I see the shining paradise of Collectivism." Now in bodily ills there is none of this difference about the ultimate ideal. The patient may or may not want quinine; but he certainly wants health. No one says "I am tired of this headache; I want some toothache," or "The only thing for this Russian influenza is a few German measles," or "Through this dark probation of catarrh I see the shining paradise of rheumatism." But exactly the whole difficulty in our public problems is that some men are aiming at cures which other men would regard as worse maladies; are offering ultimate conditions as states of health which others would uncompromisingly call states of disease. Mr. Belloc[1] once said that he would no more part with the idea of property than with his teeth; yet to Mr. Bernard Shaw property is not a tooth, but a toothache. Lord Milner[2] has sincerely attempted to introduce German efficiency; and many of us would as soon welcome German measles. Dr. Saleeby[3] would honestly like to have Eugenics; but I would rather have rheumatics.

[1] Hilaire Belloc (1870–1953), was an English essayist, historian, poet, and satirist who was born in France. He was Chesterton's colleague and friend.

[2] Sir Alfred Milner (1854–1925), English politician educated in Germany, member of war cabinet, former governor in South Africa.

[3] Caleb William Saleeby (1878–1940), obstetrician, Royal Institute Lecturer on Eugenics, writer.

This is the arresting and dominant fact about modern social discussion; that the quarrel is not merely about the difficulties, but about the aim. We agree about the evil; it is about the good that we should tear each other's eyes out. We all admit that a lazy aristocracy is a bad thing. We should not by any means all admit that an active aristocracy would be a good thing. We all feel angry with an irreligious priesthood; but some of us would go mad with disgust at a really religious one. Everyone is indignant if our army is weak, including the people who would be even more indignant if it were strong. The social case is exactly the opposite of the medical case. We do not disagree, like doctors, about the precise nature of the illness, while agreeing about the nature of health. On the contrary, we all agree that England is unhealthy, but half of us would not look at her in what the other half would call blooming health. Public abuses are so prominent and pestilent that they sweep all generous people into a sort of fictitious unanimity. We forget that, while we agree about the abuses of things, we should differ very much about the uses of them. Mr. Cadbury[4] and I would agree about the bad public-house. It would be precisely in front of the good public-house that our painful personal *fracas* would occur.

I maintain, therefore, that the common sociological method is quite useless: that of first dissecting abject poverty or cataloguing prostitution. We all dislike abject poverty; but it might be another business if we began to discuss independent and dignified poverty. We all disapprove of prostitution; but we do not all approve of purity. The only way to discuss the social evil is to get at once to the social ideal. We can all see the national madness; but what is national sanity? I have called this book "What Is Wrong with the World?" and the upshot of the title can be easily and clearly stated. What is wrong is that we do not ask what is right.

[4] George Cadbury (1829–1922), Chairman of Cadbury Brothers, Ltd., candy manufacturer. He was a known abstainer from alcohol and tobacco, probably due to the influence of his mother, an ardent Temperance worker.

II

WANTED, AN UNPRACTICAL MAN

There is a popular philosophical joke intended to typify the endless and useless arguments of philosophers; I mean the joke about which came first, the chicken or the egg? I am not sure that properly understood, it is so futile an inquiry after all. I am not concerned here to enter on those deep metaphysical and theological differences of which the chicken and egg debate is a frivolous, but a very felicitous, type. The evolutionary materialists are appropriately enough represented in the vision of all things coming from an egg, a dim and monstrous oval germ that had laid itself by accident. That other supernatural school of thought (to which I personally adhere) would be not unworthily typified in the fancy that this round world of ours is but an egg brooded upon by a sacred unbegotten bird; the mystic dove of the prophets. But it is to much humbler functions that I here call the awful power of such a distinction. Whether or no the living bird is at the beginning of our mental chain, it is absolutely necessary that it should be at the end of our mental chain. The bird is the thing to be aimed at—not with a gun, but a life-bestowing wand. What is essential to our right thinking is this: that the egg and the bird must not be thought of as equal cosmic occurrences recurring alternatively forever. They must not become a mere egg and bird pattern, like the egg and dart pattern. One is a means and the other an end; they are in different mental worlds. Leaving the complications of the human breakfast-table out of account, in an elemental sense, the egg only exists to produce the chicken. But the chicken does not exist only in order to produce another egg. He may also exist to amuse himself, to praise God, and even to suggest ideas to a French dramatist. Being a conscious life, he is, or may be, valuable in himself. Now our modern politics are full of a noisy forgetfulness; forgetfulness that the production of this happy and conscious life is after all the aim of all complexities and compromises. We talk of nothing but useful men and working institutions; that is, we only think of the chickens as things that will lay more eggs. Instead of seeking to breed our ideal bird, the eagle of Zeus or the Swan of Avon, or whatever we happen to want, we talk entirely in terms of the process and the embryo. The process itself, divorced from its divine object, becomes doubtful and even morbid; poison enters the embryo of everything; and our politics are rotten eggs.

Idealism is only considering everything in its practical essence. Idealism only means that we should consider a poker in reference to poking before we discuss its suitability for wife-beating; that we should ask if an egg is good enough for practical poultry-rearing before we decide that the egg is bad enough for practical politics. But I know that this primary pursuit of the theory (which is but pursuit of the aim) exposes one to the cheap charge of fiddling while Rome is burning. A school, of which Lord Rosebery[1] is representative, has endeavored to substitute for the moral or social ideals which have hitherto been the motive of politics a general coherency or complete-ness in the social system which has gained the nick-name of "effi-ciency." I am not very certain of the secret doctrine of this sect in the matter. But, as far as I can make out, "efficiency" means that we ought to discover everything about a machine except what it is for. There has arisen in our time a most singular fancy: the fancy that when things go very wrong we need a practical man. It would be far truer to say, that when things go very wrong we need an unpractical man. Certainly, at least, we need a theorist. A practical man means a man accustomed to mere daily practice, to the way things com-monly work. When things will not work, you must have the thinker, the man who has some doctrine about why they work at all. It is wrong to fiddle while Rome is burning; but it is quite right to study the theory of hydraulics while Rome is burning.

It is then necessary to drop one's daily agnosticism and attempt *rerum cognoscere causas*. If your aëroplane has a slight indisposition, a handy man may mend it. But, if it is seriously ill, it is all the more likely that some absent-minded old professor with wild white hair will have to be dragged out of a college or laboratory to analyze the

[1] Lord Rosebery, Archibald Philip Primrose, (1847–1929), British author and politician.

evil. The more complicated the smash, the whiter-haired and more absent-minded will be the theorist who is needed to deal with it; and in some extreme cases, no one but the man (probably insane) who invented your flying-ship could possibly say what was the matter with it.

"Efficiency," of course, is futile for the same reason that strong men, will-power and the superman are futile. That is, it is futile because it only deals with actions after they have been performed. It has no philosophy for incidents before they happen; therefore it has no power of choice. An act can only be successful or unsuccessful when it is over; if it is to begin, it must be, in the abstract, right or wrong. There is no such thing as backing a winner; for he cannot be a winner when he is backed. There is no such thing as fighting on the winning side; one fights to find out which is the winning side. If any operation has occurred, that operation was efficient. If a man is murdered, the murder was efficient. A tropical sun is as efficient in making people lazy as a Lancashire foreman bully in making them energetic. Maeterlinck[2] is as efficient in filling a man with strange spiritual tremors as Messrs. Crosse and Blackwell[3] are in filling a man with jam. But it all depends on what you want to be filled with. Lord Rosebery, being a modern skeptic, probably prefers the spiritual tremors. I, being an orthodox Christian, prefer the jam. But both are efficient when they have been effected; and inefficient until they are effected. A man who thinks much about success must be the drowsiest sentimentalist; for he must be always looking back. If he only likes victory he must always come late for the battle. For the man of action there is nothing but idealism.

This definite ideal is a far more urgent and practical matter in our existing English trouble than any immediate plans or proposals. For the present chaos is due to a sort of general oblivion of all that men were originally aiming at. No man demands what he desires; each man demands what he fancies he can get. Soon people forget what the man really wanted first; and after a successful and vigorous political life, he forgets it himself. The whole is an extravagant riot

[2] Comte Maurice Maeterlinck (1862–1947), Belgian poet, dramatist, and essayist.
[3] Thomas Francis Blackwell (1838–1907), British food manufacturer.

of second bests, a pandemonium of *pis-aller*. Now this sort of pliability does not merely prevent any heroic consistency; it also prevents any really practical compromise. One can only find the middle distance between two points if the two points will stand still. We may make an arrangement between two litigants who cannot both get what they want; but not if they will not even tell us what they want. The keeper of a restaurant would much prefer that each customer should give his order smartly, though it were for stewed ibis or boiled elephant, rather than that each customer should sit holding his head in his hands, plunged in arithmetical calculations about how much food there can be on the premises. Most of us have suffered from a certain sort of ladies who, by their perverse unselfishness, give more trouble than the selfish; who almost clamor for the unpopular dish and scramble for the worst seat. Most of us have known parties or expeditions full of this seething fuss of self-effacement. From much meaner motives than those of such admirable women, our practical politicians keep things in the same confusion through the same doubt about their real demands. There is nothing that so much prevents a settlement as a tangle of small surrenders. We are bewildered on every side by politicians who are in favor of secular education, but think it hopeless to work for it; who desire total prohibition, but are certain they should not demand it; who regret compulsory education, but resignedly continue it; or who want peasant proprietorship and therefore vote for something else. It is this dazed and floundering opportunism that gets in the way of everything. If our statesmen were visionaries something practical might be done. If we ask for something in the abstract we might get something in the concrete. As it is, it is not only impossible to get what one wants, but it is impossible to get any part of it, because nobody can mark it out plainly like a map. That clear and even hard quality that there was in the old bargaining has wholly vanished. We forget that the word "compromise" contains, among other things, the rigid and ringing word "promise." Moderation is not vague; it is as definite as perfection. The middle point is as fixed as the extreme point.

If I am made to walk the plank by a pirate, it is vain for me to offer, as a common-sense compromise, to walk along the plank for a reasonable distance. It is exactly about the reasonable distance that the pirate and I differ. There is an exquisite mathematical split second at which the plank tips up. My common-sense ends just before that instant; the pirate's common-sense begins just beyond it. But the point itself is as hard as any geometrical diagram; as abstract as any theological dogma.

III

THE NEW HYPOCRITE

But this new cloudy political cowardice has rendered useless the old English compromise. People have begun to be terrified of an improvement merely because it is complete. They call it utopian and revolutionary that anyone should really have his own way, or anything be really done, and done with. Compromise used to mean that half a loaf was better than no bread. Among modern statesmen it really seems to mean that half a loaf is better than a whole loaf.

As an instance to sharpen the argument, I take the one case of our everlasting education bills. We have actually contrived to invent a new kind of hyprocrite. The old hypocrite, Tartuffe[1] or Pecksniff,[2] was a man whose aims were really worldly and practical, while he pretended that they were religious. The new hypocrite is one whose aims are really religious, while he pretends that they are worldly and practical. The Rev. Brown, the Wesleyan minister, sturdily declares that he cares nothing for creeds, but only for education; meanwhile, in truth, the wildest Wesleyanism is tearing his soul. The Rev. Smith, of the Church of England, explains gracefully, with the Oxford manner, that the only question for him is the prosperity and efficiency of the schools; while in truth all the evil passions of a curate are roaring within him. It is a fight of creeds masquerading as policies. I think these reverend gentlemen do themselves wrong; I think they are more pious than they will admit. Theology is not (as some suppose) expunged as an error. It is merely concealed, like a sin. Dr. Clifford[3] really wants a theological atmosphere as much as Lord Halifax;[4] only it is a different one. If Dr. Clifford would ask

---

[1] The hypocritical hero of a play by Molière (1669).

[2] A character signifying hypocritical benevolence of high principles in Charles Dickens' *Martin Chuzzlewit* (1843).

[3] John Clifford (1836–1923), Baptist editor and author.

[4] Lord Halifax, Charles Lindley Wood (1839–1934), British churchman, leading Roman Catholic member of British nobility.

plainly for Puritanism and Lord Halifax ask plainly for Catholicism, something might be done for them. We are all, one hopes, imaginative enough to recognize the dignity and distinctness of another religion, like Islam or the cult of Apollo. I am quite ready to respect another man's faith; but it is too much to ask that I should respect his doubt, his worldly hesitations and fictions, his political bargain and make-believe. Most Nonconformists with an instinct for English history could see something poetic and national about the Archbishop of Canterbury as an Archbishop of Canterbury. It is when he does the rational British statesman that they very justifiably get annoyed. Most Anglicans with an eye for pluck and simplicity could admire Dr. Clifford as a Baptist minister. It is when he says that he is simply a citizen that nobody can possibly believe him.

But indeed the case is yet more curious than this. The one argument that used to be urged for our creedless vagueness was that at least it saved us from fanaticism. But it does not even do that. On the contrary, it creates and renews fanaticism with a force quite peculiar to itself. This is at once so strange and so true that I will ask the reader's attention to it with a little more precision.

Some people do not like the word "dogma." Fortunately they are free, and there is an alternative for them. There are two things, and two things only, for the human mind, a dogma and a prejudice. The Middle Ages were a rational epoch, an age of doctrine. Our age is, at its best, a poetical epoch, an age of prejudice. A doctrine is a definite point; a prejudice is a direction. That an ox may be eaten, while a man should not be eaten, is a doctrine. That as little as possible of anything should be eaten is a prejudice; which is also sometimes called an ideal. Now a direction is always far more fantastic than a plan. I would rather have the most archaic map of the road to Brighton than a general recommendation to turn to the left. Straight lines that are not parallel must meet at last; but curves may recoil forever. A pair of lovers might walk along the frontier of France and Germany, one on the one side and one on the other, so long as they were not vaguely told to keep away from each other. And this is a strictly true parable of the effect of our modern vagueness in losing and separating men as in a mist.

It is not merely true that a creed unites men. Nay, a difference of creed unites men—so long as it is a clear difference. A boundary unites. Many a magnanimous Moslem and chivalrous Crusader must have been nearer to each other, because they were both dogmatists, than any two homeless agnostics in a pew of Mr. Campbell's[5] chapel. "I say God is One," and "I say God is One but also Three," that is the beginning of a good quarrelsome, manly friendship. But our age would turn these creeds into tendencies. It would tell the Trinitarian to follow multiplicity as such (because it was his "temperament"), and he would turn up later with three hundred and thirty-three persons in the Trinity. Meanwhile, it would turn the Moslem into a Monist: a frightful intellectual fall. It would force that previously healthy person not only to admit that there was one God, but to admit that there was nobody else. When each had, for a long enough period, followed the gleam of his own nose (like the Dong)[6] they would appear again; the Christian a Polytheist, and the Moslem a Panegoist, both quite mad, and far more unfit to understand each other than before.

It is exactly the same with politics. Our political vagueness divides men, it does not fuse them. Men will walk along the edge of a chasm in clear weather, but they will edge miles away from it in a fog. So a Tory can walk up to the very edge of Socialism, *if he knows what is Socialism*. But if he is told that Socialism is a spirit, a sublime atmosphere, a noble, indefinable tendency, why, then he keeps out of its way; and quite right too. One can meet an assertion with argument; but healthy bigotry is the only way in which one can meet a tendency. I am told that the Japanese method of wrestling consists not of suddenly pressing, but of suddenly giving way. This is one of my many reasons for disliking the Japanese civilization. To use surrender as a weapon is the very worst spirit of the East. But

---

[5] Rev. Colin Campbell (1848–1933), Presbyterian minister, preacher, author.

[6] The Dong with the Luminous Nose is a character created by Edward Lear that appears in, among other works, *The Nonsense Songs* (1871). His nose, a container of vast proportions, is woven from the bark of a Twangum Tree and painted red. It protects a lamp that guides him as he searches through the dark for the Jumbly Girl he had loved and lost.

certainly there is no force so hard to fight as the force which it is easy
to conquer; the force that always yields and then returns. Such is the
force of a great impersonal prejudice, such as possesses the modern
world on so many points. Against this there is no weapon at all except a rigid and steely sanity, a resolution not to listen to fads, and
not to be infected by diseases.

   In short, the rational human faith must armor itself with prejudice in an age of prejudices, just as it armored itself with logic in an
age of logic. But the difference between the two mental methods is
marked and unmistakable. The essential of the difference is this: that
prejudices are divergent, whereas creeds are always in collision. Be-
lievers bump into each other; whereas bigots keep out of each
other's way. A creed is a collective thing, and even its sins are socia-
ble. A prejudice is a private thing, and even its tolerance is misan-
thropic. So it is with our existing divisions. They keep out of each
other's way; the Tory paper and the Radical paper do not answer
each other; they ignore each other. Genuine controversy, fair cut
and thrust before a common audience, has become in our special
epoch very rare. For the sincere controversialist is above all things a
good listener. The really burning enthusiast never interrupts; he lis-
tens to the enemy's arguments as eagerly as a spy would listen to the
enemy's arrangements. But if you attempt an actual argument with
a modern paper of opposite politics, you will find that no medium is
admitted between violence and evasion. You will have no answer
except slanging or silence. A modern editor must not have that eager
ear that goes with the honest tongue. He may be deaf and silent; and
that is called dignity. Or he may be deaf and noisy; and that is called
slashing journalism. In neither case is there any controversy; for the
whole object of modern party combatants is to charge out of earshot.

   The only logical cure for all this is the assertion of a human ideal.
In dealing with this, I will try to be as little transcendental as is consistent with reason; it is enough to say that unless we have some
doctrine of a divine man, all abuses may be excused, since evolution
may turn them into uses. It will be easy for the scientific plutocrat to
maintain that humanity will adapt itself to any conditions which we
now consider evil. The old tyrants invoked the past; the new tyrants

will invoke the future. Evolution has produced the snail and the owl; evolution can produce a workman who wants no more space than a snail, and no more light than an owl. The employer need not mind sending a Kaffir[7] to work underground; he will soon become an underground animal, like a mole. He need not mind sending a diver to hold his breath in the deep seas; he will soon be a deep-sea animal. Men need not trouble to alter conditions; conditions will so soon alter men. The head can be beaten small enough to fit the hat. Do not knock the fetters off the slave; knock the slave until he forgets the fetters. To all this plausible modern argument for oppression, the only adequate answer is, that there is a permanent human ideal that must not be either confused or destroyed. The most important man on earth is the perfect man who is not there. The Christian religion has specially uttered the ultimate sanity of Man, says Scripture, who shall judge the incarnate and human truth. Our lives and laws are not judged by divine superiority, but simply by human perfection. It is man, says Aristotle, who is the measure. It is the Son of Man, says Scripture, who shall judge the quick and the dead.

Doctrine, therefore, does not cause dissensions; rather a doctrine alone can cure our dissensions. It is necessary to ask, however, roughly, what abstract and ideal shape in state or family would fulfill the human hunger; and this apart from whether we can completely obtain it or not. But when we come to ask what is the need of normal men, what is the desire of all nations, what is the ideal house, or road, or rule, or republic, or king, or priesthood, then we are confronted with a strange and irritating difficulty peculiar to the present time; and we must call a temporary halt and examine that obstacle.

[7] A member of a Bantu-speaking South African race.

IV

THE FEAR OF THE PAST

The last few decades have been marked by a special cultivation of the romance of the future. We seem to have made up our minds to misunderstand what has happened; and we turn, with a sort of relief, to stating what will happen—which is (apparently) much easier. The modern man no longer preserves the memoirs of his great-grandfather; but he is engaged in writing a detailed and authoritative biography of his great-grandson. Instead of trembling before the specters of the dead, we shudder abjectly under the shadow of the babe unborn. This spirit is apparent everywhere, even to the creation of a form of futurist romance. Sir Walter Scott stands at the dawn of the nineteenth century for the novel of the past; Mr. H. G. Wells stands at the dawn of the twentieth century for the novel of the future. The old story, we know, was supposed to begin: "Late on a winter's evening two horsemen might have been seen—." The new story has to begin: "Late on a winter's evening two aviators will be seen—." The movement is not without its elements of charm; there is something spirited, if eccentric, in the sight of so many people fighting over again the fights that have not yet happened; of people still glowing with the memory of tomorrow morning. A man in advance of the age is a familiar phrase enough. An age in advance of the age is really rather odd.

But when full allowance has been made for this harmless element of poetry and pretty human perversity in the thing, I shall not hesitate to maintain here that this cult of the future is not only a weakness but a cowardice of the age. It is the peculiar evil of this epoch that even its pugnacity is fundamentally frightened; and the Jingo is contemptible not because he is impudent, but because he is timid. The reason why modern armaments do not inflame the imagination like the arms and emblazonments of the Crusades is a reason quite apart from optical ugliness or beauty. Some battleships are as beautiful as the sea; and many Norman nosepieces were as ugly as Norman noses.

The atmospheric ugliness that surrounds our scientific war is an emanation from that evil panic which is at the heart of it. The charge of the Crusades was a charge; it was charging towards God, the wild consolation of the braver. The charge of the modern armaments is not a charge at all. It is a rout, a retreat, a flight from the devil, who will catch the hindmost. It is impossible to imagine a mediaeval knight talking of longer and longer French lances, with precisely the quivering employed about larger and larger German ships. The man who called the Blue Water School[1] the "Blue Funk School" uttered a psychological truth which that school itself would scarcely essentially deny. Even the two-power standard, if it be a necessity, is in a sense a degrading necessity. Nothing has more alienated many magnanimous minds from Imperial enterprises than the fact that they are always exhibited as stealthy or sudden defenses against a world of cold rapacity and fear. The Boer War,[2] for instance, was colored not so much by the creed that we were doing something right, as by the creed that Boers and Germans were probably doing something wrong; driving us (as it was said) to the sea. Mr. Chamberlain, I think, said that the war was a feather in his cap; and so it was: a white feather.

Now this same primary panic that I feel in our rush towards patriotic armaments I feel also in our rush towards future visions of society. The modern mind is forced towards the future by a certain sense of fatigue, not unmixed with terror, with which it regards the past. It is propelled towards the coming time; it is, in the exact words of the popular phrase, knocked into the middle of next week. And the goad which drives it on thus eagerly is not an affectation for futurity. Futurity does not exist, because it is still future. Rather it is a fear of the past; a fear not merely of the evil in the past, but of the good in the past also. The brain breaks down under the unbearable virtue of mankind. There have been so many flaming faiths that we cannot hold; so many harsh heroisms that we cannot imitate; so many great efforts of monumental building or of military glory

[1] Diplomatic and military theory about the need to have access to high seas.
[2] A war in South Africa between Great Britain and the Dutch colonists (Boers), 1899–1902.

which seem to us at once sublime and pathetic. The future is a refuge from the fierce competition of our forefathers. The older generation, not the younger, is knocking at our door. It is agreeable to escape, as Henley said, into the Street of By-and-Bye, where stands the Hostelry of Never. It is pleasant to play with children, especially unborn children. The future is a blank wall on which every man can write his own name as large as he likes; the past I find already covered with illegible scribbles, such as Plato, Isaiah, Shakespeare, Michael Angelo, Napoleon. I can make the future as narrow as myself; the past is obliged to be as broad and turbulent as humanity. And the upshot of this modern attitude is really this: that men invent new ideals because they dare not attempt old ideals. They look forward with enthusiasm, because they are afraid to look back.

Now in history there is no Revolution that is not a Restoration. Among the many things that leave me doubtful about the modern habit of fixing eyes on the future, none is stronger than this: that all the men in history who have really done anything with the future have had their eyes fixed upon the past. I need not mention the Renaissance, the very word proves my case. The originality of Michael Angelo and Shakespeare began with the digging up of old vases and manuscripts. The mildnesss of poets absolutely arose out of the mildness of antiquaries. So the great mediaeval revival was a memory of the Roman Empire. So the Reformation looked back to the Bible and Bible times. So the modern Catholic movement has looked back to patristic times. But that modern movement which many would count the most anarchic of all is in this sense the most conservative of all. Never was the past more venerated by men than it was by the French Revolutionists. They invoked the little republics of antiquity with the complete confidence of one who invokes the gods. The Sans-culottes believed (as their name might imply) in a return to simplicity. They believed most piously in a remote past; some might call it a mythical past. For some strange reason man must always thus plant his fruit trees in a graveyard. Man can only find life among the dead. Man is a misshapen monster, with his feet set forward and his face turned back. He can make the future luxuriant and gigantic, so long as he is thinking about the past. When he tries to think about the future itself, his mind diminishes to a pin point with imbecility, which some call Nirvana. To-morrow is the Gorgon; a man must only see it mirrored in the shining shield of yesterday. If he sees it directly he is turned to stone. This has been the fate of all those who have really seen fate and futurity as clear and inevitable. The Calvinists, with their perfect creed of predestination, were turned to stone. The modern sociological scientists (with their excruciating Eugenics) are turned to stone. The only difference is that the Puritans make dignified, and the Eugenists somewhat amusing, statues.

But there is one feature in the past which more than all the rest defies and depresses the moderns and drives them towards this featureless future. I mean the presence in the past of huge ideals, unfulfilled and sometimes abandoned. The sight of these splendid failures is melancholy to a restless and rather morbid generation; and they maintain a strange silence about them — sometimes amounting to an unscrupulous silence. They keep them entirely out of their newspapers and almost entirely out of their history books. For example, they will often tell you (in their praises of the coming age) that we are moving on towards a United States of Europe. But they carefully omit to tell you that we are moving away from a United States of Europe; that such a thing existed literally in Roman and essentially in mediaeval times. They never admit that the international hatreds (which they call barbaric) are really very recent, the mere breakdown of the ideal of the Holy Roman Empire. Or again, they will tell you that there is going to be a social revolution, a great rising of the poor against the rich; but they never rub it in that France made that magnificent attempt, unaided, and that we and all the world allowed it to be trampled out and forgotten. I say decisively that nothing is so marked in modern writing as the prediction of such ideals in the future combined with the ignoring of them in the past. Anyone can test this for himself. Read any thirty or forty pages of pamphlets advocating peace in Europe and see how many of them praise the old Popes or Emperors for keeping the peace in Europe. Read any armful of essays and poems in praise of social democracy, and see how many of them praise the old Jacobins who created democracy and died for it. These colossal ruins are to the modern only enormous eyesores. He looks back along the valley of the past and sees a perspective of splendid but unfinished cities. They are unfinished, not always through enmity or accident, but often through fickleness, mental fatigue, and the lust for alien philosophies. We have not only left undone those things that we ought to have done, but we have even left undone those things that we wanted to do.

It is very currently suggested that the modern man is the heir of all the ages, that he has got the good out of these successive human experiments. I know not what to say in answer to this, except to ask the reader to look at the modern man, as I have just looked at the modern man — in the looking-glass. Is it really true that you and I are two starry towers built up of all the most towering visions of the past? Have we really fulfilled all the great historic ideals one after the other, from our naked ancestor who was brave enough to kill a mammoth with a stone knife, through the Greek citizen and the Christian saint to our own grandfather or great-grandfather, who may have been sabred by the Manchester Yeomanry or shot in the '48? Are we still strong enough to spear mammoths, but now tender enough to spare them? Does the cosmos contain any mammoth that we have either speared or spared? When we decline (in a marked manner) to fly the red flag and fire across a barricade like our grandfathers, are we really declining in deference to sociologists — or to soldiers? Have we indeed outstripped the warrior and passed the ascetical saint? I fear we only outstrip the warrior in the sense that we should probably run away from him. And if we have passed the saint, I fear we have passed him without bowing.

This is, first and foremost, what I mean by the narrowness of the new ideas, the limiting effect of the future. Our modern prophetic idealism is narrow because it has undergone a persistent process of elimination. We must ask for new things because we are not allowed to ask for old things. The whole position is based on this idea that we have got all the good that can be got out of the ideas of the past. But we have not got all the good out of them, perhaps at this moment not any of the good out of them. And the need here is a need of complete freedom for restoration as well as revolution.

We often read nowadays of the valor or audacity with which some rebel attacks a hoary tyranny or an antiquated superstition. There is not really any courage at all in attacking hoary or antiquated things, any more than in offering to fight one's grandmother. The really courageous man is he who defies tyrannies young as the morning and superstitions fresh as the first flowers. The only true free-thinker is he whose intellect is as much free from the future as from the past. He cares as little for what will be as for what has been; he cares only for what ought to be. And for my present purpose I specially insist on this abstract independence. If I am to discuss what is wrong, one of the first things that are wrong is this: the deep and silent modern assumption that past things have become impossible. There is one metaphor of which the moderns are very fond; they are always saying, "You can't put the clock back." The simple and obvious answer is "You can." A clock, being a piece of human construction, can be restored by the human finger to any figure or hour. In the same way society, being a piece of human construction, can be reconstructed upon any plan that has ever existed.

There is another proverb, "As you have made your bed, so you must lie on it"; which again is simply a lie. If I have made my bed uncomfortable, please God I will make it again. We could restore the Heptarchy or the stage coaches if we chose. It might take some time to do, and it might be very inadvisable to do it; but certainly it is not impossible as bringing back last Friday is impossible. This is, as I say, the first freedom that I claim: the freedom to restore. I claim a right to propose as a solution the old patriarchal system of a Highland clan, if that should seem to eliminate the largest number of evils. It certainly would eliminate some evils; for instance, the unnatural sense of obeying cold and harsh strangers, mere bureaucrats and policemen. I claim the right to propose the complete independence of the small Greek or Italian towns, a sovereign city of Brixton or Brompton, if that seems the best way out of our troubles. It would be a way out of some of our troubles; we could not have in a small state, for instance, those enormous illusions about men or measures which are nourished by the great national or international newspapers. You could not persuade a city state that Mr. Beit[3] was an Englishman, or Mr. Dillon[4] a desperado, any more than you could persuade a Hampshire village that the village drunkard was a teetotaler or the village idiot a statesman. Nevertheless, I do not as a fact propose that the Browns and the Smiths should be collected under separate tartans. Nor do I even propose that Clapham should declare its independence. I merely declare my independence. I merely claim my choice of all the tools in the universe; and I shall not admit that any of them are blunted merely because they have been used.

[3] Alfred Beit (1853–1906), German-born governor of DeBeers Consolidated Mines in South Africa.

[4] Conrad Dillon (1854–1901), Chairman of National Temperance League.

V

THE UNFINISHED TEMPLE

The task of modern idealists indeed is made much too easy for them by the fact that they are always taught that if a thing has been defeated it has been disproved. Logically, the case is quite clearly the other way. The lost causes are exactly those which might have saved the world. If a man says that the Young Pretender would have made England happy, it is hard to answer him. If anyone says that the Georges made England happy, I hope we all know what to answer. That which was prevented is always impregnable; and the only perfect King of England was he who was smothered. Exactly because Jacobitism[1] failed we cannot call it a failure. Precisely because the Commune collapsed as a rebellion we cannot say that it collapsed as a system. But such outbursts were brief or incidental. Few people realize how many of the largest efforts, the facts that will fill history, were frustrated in their full design and come down to us as gigantic cripples. I have only space to allude to the two largest facts of modern history: the Catholic Church and that modern growth rooted in the French Revolution.

When four knights scattered the blood and brains of St. Thomas of Canterbury, it was not only a sign of anger but of a sort of black admiration. They wished for his blood, but they wished even more for his brains. Such a blow will remain forever unintelligible unless we realize what the brains of St. Thomas were thinking about just before they were distributed over the floor. They were thinking about the great mediaeval conception that the church is the judge of the world. Becket objected to a priest being tried even by the Lord Chief Justice. And his reason was simple: because the Lord Chief Justice was being tried by the priest. The judiciary was itself *sub-judice*. The kings were themselves in the dock. The idea was to create an invisible kingdom, without armies or prisons, but with

---

[1] The movement after 1688 to promote the defeated Stuart cause.

complete freedom to condemn publicly all the kingdoms of the earth. Whether such a supreme church would have cured society we cannot affirm definitely; because the church never was a supreme church. We only know that in England at any rate the princes conquered the saints. What the world wanted we see before us; and some of us call it a failure. But we cannot call what the church wanted a failure, simply because the church failed. Tracy[2] struck a little too soon. England had not yet made the great Protestant discovery that the king can do no wrong. The king was whipped in the cathedral; a performance which I recommend to those who regret the unpopularity of church-going. But the discovery was made; and Henry VIII. scattered Becket's bones as easily as Tracy had scattered his brains.

Of course, I mean that Catholicism was not tried; plenty of Catholics were tried, and found guilty. My point is that the world did not tire of the church's ideal, but of its reality. Monasteries were impugned not for the chastity of monks, but for the unchastity of monks. Christianity was unpopular not because of the humility, but of the arrogance of Christians. Certainly, if the church failed it was largely through the churchmen. But at the same time hostile elements had certainly begun to end it long before it could have done its work. In the nature of things it needed a common scheme of life and thought in Europe. Yet the mediaeval system began to be broken to pieces intellectually, long before it showed the slightest hint of falling to pieces morally. The huge early heresies, like the Albigenses, had not the faintest excuse in moral superiority. And it is actually true that the Reformation began to tear Europe apart before the Catholic Church had had time to pull it together. The Prussians, for instance, were not converted to Christianity at all until quite close to the Reformation. The poor creatures hardly had time to become Catholics before they were told to become Protestants. This explains a great deal of their subsequent conduct. But I have only taken this as the first and most evident case of the general truth: that the great ideals of the past failed not by being outlived (which must mean over-lived), but by not being lived enough. Mankind has

---

[2] William Tracy (d. 1173), assisted at the murder of St. Thomas of Canterbury.

not passed through the Middle Ages. Rather mankind has retreated from the Middle Ages in reaction and rout. The Christian ideal has not been tried and found wanting. It has been found difficult; and left untried.

It is, of course, the same in the case of the French Revolution. A great part of our present perplexity arises from the fact that the French Revolution has half succeeded and half failed. In one sense, Valmy was the decisive battle of the West, and in another Trafalgar. We have, indeed, destroyed the largest territorial tyrannies, and created a free peasantry in almost all Christian countries except England; of which we shall say more anon. But representative government, the one universal relic, is a very poor fragment of the full republican idea. The theory of the French Revolution presupposed two things in government, things which it achieved at the time, but which it has certainly not bequeathed to its imitators in England, Germany, and America. The first of these was the idea of honorable poverty; that a statesman must be something of a stoic; the second was the idea of extreme publicity. Many imaginative English writers, including Carlyle, seem quite unable to imagine how it was that men like Robespierre and Marat were ardently admired. The best answer is that they were admired for being poor — poor when they might have been rich.

No one will pretend that this ideal exists at all in the *haute politique* of this country. Our national claim to political incorruptibility is actually based on exactly the opposite argument; it is based on the theory that wealthy men in assured positions will have no temptation to financial trickery. Whether the history of the English aristocracy, from the spoliation of the monasteries to the annexation of the mines, entirely supports this theory I am not now inquiring; but certainly it is our theory, that wealth will be a protection against political corruption. The English statesman is bribed not to be bribed. He is born with a silver spoon in his mouth, so that he may never afterwards be found with the silver spoons in his pocket. So strong is our faith in this protection by plutocracy, that we are more and more trusting our empire in the hands of families which inherit wealth without either blood or manners. Some of our political houses are parvenue by pedigree; they hand on vulgarity like a coat-of-arms. In the case of many a modern statesman to say that he is born with a silver spoon in his mouth, is at once inadequate and excessive. He is born with a silver knife in his mouth. But all this only illustrates the English theory that poverty is perilous for a politician.

It will be the same if we compare the conditions that have come about with the Revolution legend touching publicity. The old democratic doctrine was that the more light that was let in to all departments of State, the easier it was for a righteous indignation to move promptly against wrong. In other words, monarchs were to live in glass houses, that mobs might throw stones. Again, no admirer of existing English politics (if there is any admirer of existing English politics) will really pretend that this ideal of publicity is exhausted, or even attempted. Obviously public life grows more private every day. The French have, indeed, continued the tradition of revealing secrets and making scandals; hence they are more flagrant and palpable than we, not in sin, but in the confession of sin. The first trial of Dreyfus[3] might have happened in England; it is exactly the second trial that would have been legally impossible. But, indeed, if we wish to realize how far we fall short of the original republican outline, the sharpest way to test it is to note how far we fall short even of the republican element in the older régime. Not only are we less democratic than Danton and Condorcet, but we are in many ways less democratic than Choiseul and Marie Antoinette. The richest nobles before the revolt were needy middle-class people compared with our Rothschilds and Roseberys. And in the matter of publicity the old French monarchy was infinitely more democratic than any of the monarchies of to-day. Practically anybody who chose could walk into the palace and see the king playing with his children, or paring his nails. The people possessed the monarch, as the people possess Primrose Hill; that is, they cannot move it, but they can sprawl all over it. The old French monarchy was founded on the excellent principle that a cat may look at a king. But nowadays a cat may not look at a king; unless it is a very tame cat. Even where the press is free for criticism it is only used for adulation. The substantial difference

---

[3] Alfred Dreyfus (1859–1935), French army officer of Jewish descent convicted of treason in 1894 and 1899, then acquitted in 1906.

comes to something uncommonly like this: Eighteenth century tyranny meant that you could say "The K—— of Br——rd is a profligate." Twentieth century liberty really means that you are allowed to say "The King of Brentford is a model family man."

But we have delayed the main argument too long for the parenthetical purpose of showing that the great democratic dream, like the great mediaeval dream, has in a strict and practical sense been a dream unfulfilled. Whatever is the matter with modern England it is not that we have carried out too literally, or achieved with disappointing completeness, either the Catholicism of Becket or the equality of Marat. Now I have taken these two cases merely because they are typical of ten thousand other cases; the world is full of these unfulfilled ideas, these uncompleted temples. History does not consist of completed and crumbling ruins; rather it consists of half-built villas abandoned by a bankrupt-builder. This world is more like an unfinished suburb than a deserted cemetery.

VI

THE ENEMIES OF PROPERTY

But it is for this especial reason that such an explanation is necessary on the very threshold of the definition of ideals. For owing to that historic fallacy with which I have just dealt, numbers of readers will expect me, when I propound an ideal, to propound a new ideal. Now I have no notion at all of propounding a new ideal. There is no new ideal imaginable by the madness of modern sophists, which will be anything like so startling as fulfilling any one of the old ones. On the day that any copybook maxim is carried out there will be something like an earthquake on the earth. There is only one thing new that can be done under the sun; and that is to look at the sun. If you attempt it on a blue day in June, you will know why men do not look straight at their ideals. There is only one really startling thing to be done with the ideal, and that is to do it. It is to face the flaming logical fact, and its frightful consequences. Christ knew that it would be a more stunning thunderbolt to fulfill the law than to destroy it. It is true of both the cases I have quoted, and of every case. The pagans had always adored purity: Athene, Artemis, Vesta. It was when the virgin martyrs began defiantly to practice purity that they rent them with wild beasts, and rolled them on red-hot coals. The world had always loved the notion of the poor man uppermost; it can be proved by every legend from Cinderella to Whittington,[1] by every poem from the Magnificat to the Marseillaise. The kings went mad against France not because she idealized this ideal, but because she realized it. Joseph of Austria and Catherine of Russia quite agreed that the people should rule; what horrified them was that the people did. The French Revolution, therefore, is the type of all true revolutions, because its ideal is as old as the Old Adam, but its fulfillment almost as fresh, as miraculous, and as new as the New Jerusalem.

[1] Richard Wittington (d. 1423), Mayor of London, subsequently became a legendary hero, embodying a rags-to-riches philosophy.

But in the modern world we are primarily confronted with the extraordinary spectacle of people turning to new ideals because they have not tried the old. Men have not got tired of Christianity; they have never found enough Christianity to get tired of. Men have never wearied of political justice; they have wearied of waiting for it.

Now, for the purpose of this book, I propose to take only one of these old ideals; but one that is perhaps the oldest. I take the principle of domesticity: the ideal house; the happy family, the holy family of history. For the moment it is only necessary to remark that it is like the church and like the republic, now chiefly assailed by those who have never known it, or by those who have failed to fulfill it. Numberless modern women have rebelled against domesticity in theory because they have never known it in practice. Hosts of the poor are driven to the workhouse without ever having known the house. Generally speaking, the cultured class is shrieking to be let out of the decent home, just as the working class is shouting to be let into it.

Now if we take this house or home as a test, we may very generally lay the simple spiritual foundations of the idea. God is that which can make something out of nothing. Man (it may truly be said) is that which can make something out of anything. In other words, while the joy of God be unlimited creation, the special joy of man is limited creation, the combination of creation with limits. Man's pleasure, therefore, is to possess conditions, but also to be partly possessed by them; to be half-controlled by the flute he plays or by the field he digs. The excitement is to get the utmost out of given conditions; the conditions will stretch, but not indefinitely. A man can write an immortal sonnet on an old envelope, or hack a hero out of a lump of rock. But hacking a sonnet out of a rock would be a laborious business, and making a hero out of an envelope is almost out of the sphere of practical politics. This fruitful strife with limitations, when it concerns some airy entertainment of an educated class, goes by the name of Art. But the mass of men have neither time nor aptitude for the invention of invisible or abstract beauty. For the mass of men the idea of artistic creation can only be expressed by an idea unpopular in present discussions—the idea of property.

The average man cannot cut clay into the shape of a man; but he can cut earth into the shape of a garden; and though he arranges it with red geraniums and blue potatoes in alternate straight lines, he is still an artist; because he has chosen. The average man cannot paint the sunset whose colors he admires; but he can paint his own house with what color he chooses, and though he paints it pea green with pink spots, he is still an artist; because that is his choice. Property is merely the art of the democracy. It means that every man should have something that he can shape in his own image, as he is shaped in the image of heaven. But because he is not God, but only a graven image of God, his self-expression must deal with limits; properly with limits that are strict and even small.

I am well aware that the word "property" has been defied in our time by the corruption of the great capitalists. One would think, to hear people talk, that the Rothchilds and the Rockefellers were on the side of property. But obviously they are the enemies of property; because they are enemies of their own limitations. They do not want their own land; but other people's. When they remove their neighbor's landmark, they also remove their own. A man who loves a little triangular field ought to love it because it is triangular; anyone who destroys the shape, by giving him more land, is a thief who has stolen a triangle. A man with the true poetry of possession wishes to see the wall where his garden meets Smith's garden; the hedge where his farm touches Brown's. He cannot see the shape of his own land unless he sees the edges of his neighbor's. It is the negation of property that the Duke of Sutherland should have all the farms in one estate; just as it would be the negation of marriage if he had all our wives in one harem.

VII

THE FREE FAMILY

As I have said, I propose to take only one central instance; I will take the institution called the private house or home; the shell and organ of the family. We will consider cosmic and political tendencies simply as they strike that ancient and unique roof. Very few words will suffice for all I have to say about the family itself. I leave alone the speculations about its animal origin and the details of its social reconstruction; I am concerned only with its palpable omnipresence. It is a necessity for mankind; it is (if you like to put it so) a trap for mankind. Only by the hypocritical ignoring of a huge fact can anyone contrive to talk of "free love"; as if love were an episode like lighting a cigarette, or whistling a tune. Suppose whenever a man lit a cigarette, a towering genie arose from the rings of smoke and followed him everywhere as a huge slave. Suppose whenever a man whistled a tune he "drew an angel down" and had to walk about forever with a seraph on a string. These catastrophic images are but faint parallels to the earthquake consequences that Nature has attached to sex; and it is perfectly plain at the beginning that a man cannot be a free lover; he is either a traitor or a tied man. The second element that creates the family is that its consequences, though colossal, are gradual; the cigarette produces a baby giant, the song only an infant seraph. Thence arises the necessity for some prolonged system of co-operation; and thence arises the family in its full educational sense.

It may be said that this institution of the home is the one anarchist institution. That is to say, it is older than law, and stands outside the State. By its nature it is refreshed or corrupted by indefinable forces of custom or kinship. This is not to be understood as meaning that the State has no authority over families; that State authority is invoked and ought to be invoked in many abnormal cases. But in most normal cases of family joys and sorrows, the State has no mode of entry. It is not so much that the law should not interfere, as that the law cannot. Just as there are fields too far off for law, so there are fields too near; as a man may see the North Pole before he sees his own backbone. Small and near matters escape control at least as much as vast and remote ones; and the real pains and pleasures of the family form a strong instance of this. If a baby cries for the moon, the policeman cannot procure the moon—but neither can he stop the baby. Creatures so close to each other as husband and wife, or a mother and children, have powers of making each other happy or miserable with which no public coercion can deal. If a marriage could be dissolved every morning it would not give back his night's rest to a man kept awake by a curtain lecture; and what is the good of giving a man a lot of power where he only wants a little peace? The child must depend on the most imperfect mother; the mother may be devoted to the most unworthy children; in such relations legal revenges are vain. Even in the abnormal cases where the law may operate, this difficulty is constantly found; as many a bewildered magistrate knows. He has to save children from starvation by taking away their breadwinner. And he often has to break a wife's heart because her husband has already broken her head. The State has no tool delicate enough to deracinate the rooted habits and tangled affections of the family; the two sexes, whether happy or unhappy, are glued together too tightly for us to get the blade of a legal penknife in between them. The man and the woman are one flesh—yes, even when they are not one spirit. Man is a quadruped. Upon this ancient and anarchic intimacy, types of government have little or no effect; it is happy or unhappy, by its own sexual wholesomeness and genial habit, under the republic of Switzerland or the despotism of Siam. Even a republic in Siam would not have done much towards freeing the Siamese Twins.

The problem is not in marriage, but in sex; and would be felt under the freest concubinage. Nevertheless, the overwhelming mass of mankind has not believed in freedom in this matter, but rather in a more or less lasting tie. Tribes and civilizations differ about the occasions on which we may loosen the bond, but they all agree that there is a bond to be loosened, not a mere universal detachment. For the purposes of this book I am not concerned to discuss that mystical view of marriage in which I myself believe: the great European tradition which has made marriage a sacrament. It is enough to say here that heathen and Christian alike have regarded marriage as a tie; a thing not normally to be sundered. Briefly, this human belief in a sexual bond rests on a principle of which the modern mind has made a very inadequate study. It is, perhaps, most nearly paralleled by the principle of the second wind in walking.

The principle is this: that in everything worth having, even in every pleasure, there is a point of pain or tedium that must be survived, so that the pleasure may revive and endure. The joy of battle comes after the first fear of death; the joy of reading Virgil comes after the bore of learning him; the glow of the sea-bather comes after the icy shock of the sea bath; and the success of the marriage comes after the failure of the honeymoon. All human vows, laws, and contracts are so many ways of surviving with success this breaking point, this instant of potential surrender.

In everything on this earth that is worth doing, there is a stage when no one would do it, except for necessity or honor. It is then that the Institution upholds a man and helps him on to the firmer ground ahead. Whether this solid fact of human nature is sufficient to justify the sublime dedication of Christian marriage is quite another matter, it is amply sufficient to justify the general human feeling of marriage as a fixed thing, dissolution of which is a fault or, at least, an ignominy. The essential element is not so much duration as security. Two people must be tied together in order to do themselves justice; for twenty minutes at a dance, or for twenty years in a marriage. In both cases the point is, that if a man is bored in the first five minutes he must go on and force himself to be happy. Coercion is a kind of encouragement; and anarchy (or what some call liberty) is essentially oppressive, because it is essentially discouraging. If we all floated in the air like bubbles, free to drift anywhere at any instant, the practical result would be that no one would have the courage to begin a conversation. It would be so embarrassing to start a sentence in a friendly whisper, and then have to shout the last half of it because the other party was floating away into the free and formless ether. The two must hold each other to do justice to each other.

If Americans can be divorced for "incompatibility of temper" I cannot conceive why they are not all divorced. I have known many happy marriages, but never a compatible one. The whole aim of marriage is to fight through and survive the instant when incompatibility becomes unquestionable. For a man and a woman, as such, are incompatible.

VIII

THE WILDNESS OF DOMESTICITY

In the course of this crude study we shall have to touch on what is called the problem of poverty, especially the dehumanized poverty of modern industrialism. But in this primary matter of the ideal the difficulty is not the problem of poverty, but the problem of wealth. It is the special psychology of leisure and luxury that falsifies life. Some experience of modern movements of the sort called "advanced" has led me to the conviction that they generally repose upon some experience peculiar to the rich. It is so with that fallacy of free love of which I have already spoken; the idea of sexuality as a string of episodes. That implies a long holiday in which to get tired of one woman, and a motor car in which to wander looking for others; it also implies money for maintenances. An omnibus conductor has hardly time to love his own wife, let alone other people's. And the success with which nuptial estrangements are depicted in modern "problem plays" is due to the fact that there is only one thing that a drama cannot depict—that is a hard day's work. I could give many other instances of this plutocratic assumption behind progressive fads. For instance, there is a plutocratic assumption behind the phrase "Why should woman be economically dependent upon man?" The answer is that among poor and practical people she isn't; except in the sense in which he is dependent upon her. A hunter has to tear his clothes; there must be somebody to mend them. A fisher has to catch fish; there must be somebody to cook them. It is surely quite clear that this modern notion that woman is a mere "pretty clinging parasite," "a plaything," etc., arose through the somber contemplation of some rich banking family, in which the banker, at least, went to the city and pretended to do something, while the banker's wife went to the Park and did not pretend to do anything at all. A poor man and his wife are a business partnership. If one partner in a firm of publishers interviews the authors while the other interviews the clerks, is one of them economically dependent? Was Hodder a

71

pretty parasite clinging to Stoughton? Was Marshall a mere plaything for Snelgrove?[1]

But of all the modern notions generated by mere wealth the worst is this: the notion that domesticity is dull and tame. Inside the home (they say) is dead decorum and routine; outside is adventure and variety. This is indeed a rich man's opinion. The rich man knows that his own house moves on vast and soundless wheels of wealth, is run by regiments of servants, by a swift and silent ritual. On the other hand, every sort of vagabondage of romance is open to him in the streets outside. He has plenty of money and can afford to be a tramp. His wildest adventure will end in a restaurant, while the yokel's tamest adventure may end in a police-court. If he smashes a window he can pay for it; if he smashes a man he can pension him. He can (like the millionaire in the story) buy an hotel to get a glass of gin. And because he, the luxurious man, dictates the tone of nearly all "advanced" and "progressive" thought, we have almost forgotten what a home really means to the overwhelming millions of mankind.

For the truth is, that to the moderately poor the home is the only place of liberty. Nay, it is the only place of anarchy. It is the only spot on the earth where a man can alter arrangements suddenly, make an experiment or indulge in a whim. Everywhere else he goes he must accept the strict rules of the shop, inn, club, or museum that he happens to enter. He can eat his meals on the floor in his own house if he likes. I often do it myself; it gives a curious, childish, poetic, picnic feeling. There would be considerable trouble if I tried to do it in an A. B. C. tea-shop. A man can wear a dressing-gown and slippers in his house; while I am sure that this would not be permitted at the Savoy, though I never actually tested the point. If you go to a restaurant you must drink some of the wines on the wine list, all of them if you insist, but certainly some of them. But if you have a house and garden you can try to make hollyhock tea or convolvulus wine if you like. For a plain, hard-working man the home is not the one tame place in the world of adventure. It is the one wild place in the world of rules and set tasks. The home is the

[1] Hodder and Stoughton are English publishers; Marshall and Snelgrove are a chain of British stores.

one place where he can put the carpet on the ceiling or the slates on the floor if he wants to. When a man spends every night staggering from bar to bar or from music-hall to music-hall, we say that he is living an irregular life. But he is not; he is living a highly regular life, under the dull, and often oppressive, laws of such places. Sometimes he is not allowed even to sit down in the bars; and frequently he is not allowed to sing in the music-halls. Hotels may be defined as places where you are forced to dress; and theaters may be defined as places where you are forbidden to smoke. A man can only picnic at home.

Now I take, as I have said, this small human omnipotence, this possession of a definite cell or chamber of liberty, as the working model for the present inquiry. Whether we can give every Englishman a free home of his own or not, at least we should desire it; and he desires it. For the moment we speak of what he wants, not of what he expects to get. He wants, for instance, a separate house; he does not want a semi-detached house. He may be forced in the commercial race to share one wall with another man. Similarly he might be forced in a three-legged race to share one leg with another man; but it is not so that he pictures himself in his dreams of elegance and liberty. Again, he does not desire a flat. He can eat and sleep and praise God in a flat; he can eat and sleep and praise God in a railway train. But a railway train is not a house, because it is a house on wheels. And a flat is not a house, because it is a house on stilts. An idea of earthy contact and foundation, as well as an idea of separation and independence, is a part of this instructive human picture.

I take, then, this one institution as a test. As every normal man desires a woman, and children born of a woman, every normal man desires a house of his own to put them into. He does not merely want a roof above him and a chair below him; he wants an objective and visible kingdom; a fire at which he can cook what food he likes, a door he can open to what friends he chooses. This is the normal appetite of men; I do not say there are not exceptions. There may be saints above the need and philanthropists below it. Opalstein, now he is a duke, may have got used to more than this; and when he was a convict may have got used to less. But the normality of the thing is enormous. To give nearly everybody ordinary houses would please nearly everybody; that is what I assert without apology. Now in modern England (as you eagerly point out) it is very difficult to give nearly everybody houses. Quite so; I merely set up the *desideratum*; and ask the reader to leave it standing there while he turns with me to a consideration of what really happens in the social wars of our time.

IX

HISTORY OF HUDGE AND GUDGE

There is, let us say, a certain filthy rookery in Hoxton, dripping with disease and honeycombed with crime and promiscuity. There are, let us say, two noble and courageous young men, of pure intentions and (if you prefer it) noble birth; let us call them Hudge and Gudge. Hudge, let us say, is of a bustling sort; he points out that the people must at all costs be got out of this den; he subscribes and collects money, but he finds (despite the large financial interests of the Hudges) that the thing will have to be done on the cheap if it is to be done on the spot. He, therefore, runs up a row of tall bare tenements like beehives; and soon has all the poor people bundled into their little brick cells, which are certainly better than their old quarters, in so far as they are weather proof, well ventilated and supplied with clean water. But Gudge has a more delicate nature. He feels a nameless something lacking in the little brick boxes; he raises numberless objections; he even assails the celebrated Hudge Report, with the Gudge Minority Report; and by the end of a year or so has come to telling Hudge heatedly that the people were much happier where they were before. As the people preserve in both places precisely the same air of dazed amiability, it is very difficult to find out which is right. But at least one might safely say that no people ever liked stench or starvation as such, but only some peculiar pleasures entangled with them. Not so feels the sensitive Gudge. Long before the final quarrel (Hudge *v.* Gudge and Another), Gudge has succeeded in persuading himself that slums and stinks are really very nice things; that the habit of sleeping fourteen in a room is what has made our England great; and that the smell of open drains is absolutely essential to the rearing of a viking breed.

But, meanwhile, has there been no degeneration in Hudge? Alas, I fear there has. Those maniacally ugly buildings which he originally put up as unpretentious sheds barely to shelter human life, grow every day more and more lovely to his deluded eye. Things he would never have dreamed of defending, except as crude necessities, things like common kitchens or infamous asbestos stoves, begin to shine quite sacredly before him, merely because they reflect the wrath of Gudge. He maintains, with the aid of eager little books by Socialists, that man is really happier in a hive than in a house. The practical difficulty of keeping total strangers out of your bedroom he describes as Brotherhood; and the necessity for climbing twenty-three flights of cold stone stairs, I dare say he calls Effort. The net result of their philanthropic adventure is this: that one has come to defending indefensible slums and still more indefensible slum-landlords; while the other has come to treating as divine the sheds and pipes which he only meant as desperate. Gudge is now a corrupt and apoplectic old Tory in the Carlton Club; if you mention poverty to him he roars at you in a thick, hoarse voice something that is conjectured to be "Do 'em good!" Nor is Hudge more happy; for he is a lean vegetarian with a gray, pointed beard and an unnaturally easy smile, who goes about telling everybody that at last we shall all sleep in one universal bedroom; and he lives in a Garden City, like one forgotten of God.

Such is the lamentable history of Hudge and Gudge; which I merely introduce as a type of an endless and exasperating misunderstanding which is always occurring in modern England. To get men out of a rookery men are put into a tenement; and at the beginning the healthy human soul loathes them both. A man's first desire is to get away as far as possible from the rookery, even should his mad course lead him to a model dwelling. The second desire is, naturally, to get away from the model dwelling, even if it should lead a man back to the rookery. But I am neither a Hudgian nor a Gudgian; and I think the mistakes of these two famous and fascinating persons arose from one simple fact. They arose from the fact that neither Hudge nor Gudge had ever thought for an instant what sort of house a man might probably like for himself. In short, they did not begin with the ideal; and, therefore, were not practical politicians.

We may now return to the purpose of our awkward parenthesis about the praise of the future and the failures of the past. A house of his own being the obvious ideal for every man, we may now ask (taking this need as typical of all such needs) why he hasn't got it; and whether it is in any philosophical sense his own fault. Now, I think that in some philosophical sense it is his own fault; I think in a yet more philosophical sense it is the fault of his philosophy. And this is what I have now to attempt to explain.

Burke, a fine rhetorician, who rarely faced realities, said, I think, that an Englishman's house is his castle. This is honestly entertaining; for as it happens the Englishman is almost the only man in Europe whose house is not his castle. Nearly everywhere else exists the assumption of peasant proprietorship; that a poor man may be a landlord, though he is only lord of his own land. Making the landlord and the tenant the same person has certain trivial advantages, as that the tenant pays no rent, while the landlord does a little work. But I am not concerned with the defense of small proprietorship, but merely with the fact that it exists almost everywhere except in England. It is also true, however, that this estate of small possession is attacked everywhere today; it has never existed among ourselves, and it may be destroyed among our neighbors. We have, therefore, to ask ourselves what it is in human affairs generally, and in this domestic ideal in particular, that has really ruined the natural human creation, especially in this country.

Man has always lost his way. He has been a tramp ever since Eden; but he always knew, or thought he knew, what he was looking for. Every man has a house somewhere in the elaborate cosmos; his house waits for him waist deep in slow Norfolk rivers or sunning itself upon Sussex downs. Man has always been looking for that home which is the subject matter of this book. But in the bleak and blinding hail of skepticism to which he has been now so long subjected, he has begun for the first time to be chilled, not merely in his hopes, but in his desires. For the first time in history he begins really to doubt the object of his wanderings on the earth. He has always lost his way; but now he has lost his address.

Under the pressure of certain upper-class philosophies (or in other words, under the pressure of Hudge and Gudge) the average man has really become bewildered about the goal of his efforts; and his efforts, therefore, grow feebler and feebler. His simple notion of having a home of his own is derided as bourgeois, as sentimental, or as despicably Christian. Under various verbal forms he is recommended to go on to the streets—which is called Individualism; or to the work-house—which is called Collectivism. We shall consider this process somewhat more carefully in a moment. But it may be said here that Hudge and Gudge, or the governing class generally, will never fail for lack of some modern phrase to cover their ancient predominance. The great lords will refuse the English peasant his three acres and a cow on advanced grounds, if they cannot refuse it longer on reactionary grounds. They will deny him the three acres on grounds of State Ownership. They will forbid him the cow on grounds of humanitarianism.

And this brings us to the ultimate analysis of this singular influence that has prevented doctrinal demands by the English people. There are, I believe, some who still deny that England is governed by an oligarchy. It is quite enough for me to know that a man might have gone to sleep some thirty years ago over the day's newspaper and woke up last week over the later newspaper, and fancied he was reading about the same people. In one paper he would have found a Lord Robert Cecil, a Mr. Gladstone, a Mr. Lyttleton, a Churchill, a Chamberlain, a Trevelyan, an Acland. In the other paper he would find a Lord Robert Cecil, a Mr. Gladstone, a Mr. Lyttleton, a Churchill, a Chamberlain, a Trevelyan, an Acland. If this is not being governed by families I cannot imagine what it is. I suppose it is being governed by extraordinary democratic coincidences.

X

OPPRESSION BY OPTIMISM

But we are not here concerned with the nature and existence of the aristocracy, but with the origin of its peculiar power; why is it the last of the true oligarchies of Europe; and why does there seem no very immediate prospect of our seeing the end of it? The explanation is simple though it remains strangely unnoticed. The friends of aristocracy often praise it for preserving ancient and gracious traditions. The enemies of aristocracy often blame it for clinging to cruel or antiquated customs. Both its enemies and its friends are wrong. Generally speaking the aristocracy does not preserve either good or bad traditions; it does not preserve anything except game. Who would dream of looking among aristocrats anywhere for an old custom? One might as well look for an old costume! The god of the aristocrats is not tradition, but fashion, which is the opposite of tradition. If you wanted to find an old-world Norwegian headdress, would you look for it in the Scandinavian Smart Set? No; the aristocrats never have customs; at the best they have habits, like the animals. Only the mob has customs.

The real power of the English aristocrats has lain in exactly the opposite of tradition. The simple key to the power of our upper classes is this: that they have always kept carefully on the side of what is called Progress. They have always been up to date, and this comes quite easy to an aristocracy. For the aristocracy are the supreme instances of that frame of mind of which we spoke just now. Novelty is to them a luxury verging on a necessity. They, above all, are so bored with the past and with the present, that they gape, with a horrible hunger, for the future.

But whatever else the great lords forgot they never forgot that it was their business to stand for the new things, for whatever was being most talked about among university dons or fussy financiers. Thus they were on the side of the Reformation against the Church, of the Whigs against the Stuarts, of the Baconian science against the old philosophy, of the manufacturing system against the operatives, and (to-day) of the increased power of the State against the old-fashioned individualists. In short, the rich are always modern; it is their business. But the immediate effect of this fact upon the question we are studying is somewhat singular.

In each of the separate holes or quandaries in which the ordinary Englishman has been placed, he has been told that his situation is, for some particular reason, all for the best. He woke up one fine morning and discovered that the public things, which for eight hundred years he had used at once as inns and sanctuaries, had all been suddenly and savagely abolished, to increase the private wealth of about six or seven men. One would think he might have been annoyed at that; in many places he was, and was put down by the soldiery. But it was not merely the army that kept him quiet. He was kept quiet by the sages as well as the soldiers; the six or seven men who took away the inns of the poor told him that they were not doing it for themselves, but for the religion of the future, the great dawn of Protestantism and truth. So whenever a seventeenth century noble was caught pulling down a peasant's fence and stealing his field, the noble pointed excitedly at the face of Charles I. or James II. (which at that moment, perhaps, wore a cross expression) and thus diverted the simple peasant's attention. The great Puritan lords created the Commonwealth, and destroyed the common land. They saved their poorer countrymen from the disgrace of paying Ship Money, by taking from them the plow money and spade money which they were doubtless too weak to guard. A fine old English rhyme has immortalized this easy aristocratic habit—

> You prosecute the man or woman
> Who steals the goose from off the common,
> But leave the larger felon loose
> Who steals the common from the goose.

But here, as in the case of the monasteries, we confront the strange problem of submission. If they stole the common from the goose, one can only say that he was a great goose to stand it. The truth is that they reasoned with the goose; they explained to him that all this was needed to get the Stuart fox over seas. So in the nineteenth century the great nobles who became mine-owners and railway directors earnestly assured everybody that they did not do this from preference, but owing to a newly discovered Economic Law. So the prosperous politicians of our own generation introduce bills to prevent poor mothers from going about with their own babies; or they calmly forbid their tenants to drink beer in public inns. But this insolence is not (as you would suppose) howled at by everybody as outrageous feudalism. It is gently rebuked as Socialism. For an aristocracy is always progressive; it is a form of going the pace. Their parties grow later and later at night; for they are trying to live to-morrow.

XI

THE HOMELESSNESS OF JONES

Thus the Future of which we spoke at the beginning has (in England at least) always been the ally of tyranny. The ordinary Englishman has been duped out of his old possessions, such as they were, and always in the name of progress. The destroyers of the abbeys took away his bread and gave him a stone, assuring him that it was a precious stone, the white pebble of the Lord's elect. They took away his maypole and his original rural life and promised him instead the Golden Age of Peace and Commerce inaugurated at the Crystal Palace. And now they are taking away the little that remains of his dignity as a householder and the head of a family, promising him instead Utopias which are called (appropriately enough) "Anticipations" or "News from Nowhere." We come back, in fact, to the main feature which has already been mentioned. The past is communal: the future must be individualist. In the past are all the evils of democracy, variety and violence and doubt, but the future is pure despotism, for the future is pure caprice. Yesterday, I know I was a human fool, but to-morrow I can easily be the Superman.

The modern Englishman, however, is like a man who should be perpetually kept out, for one reason after another, from the house in which he had meant his married life to begin. This man (Jones let us call him) has always desired the divinely ordinary things; he has married for love, he has chosen or built a small house that fits like a coat; he is ready to be a great grandfather and a local god. And just as he is moving in, something goes wrong. Some tyranny, personal or political, suddenly debars him from the home; and he has to take his meals in the front garden. A passing philosopher (who is also, by a mere coincidence, the man who turned him out) pauses, and leaning elegantly on the railings, explains to him that he is now living that bold life upon the bounty of nature which will be the life of the sublime future. He finds life in the front garden more bold than bountiful, and has to move into mean lodgings in the next spring. The philosopher (who turned him out), happening to call at these lodgings, with the probable intention of raising the rent, stops to explain to him that he is now in the real life of mercantile endeavor; the economic struggle between him and the landlady is the only thing out of which, in the sublime future, the wealth of nations can come. He is defeated in the economic struggle, and goes to the workhouse. The philosopher who turned him out (happening at that very moment to be inspecting the workhouse) assures him that he is now at last in that golden republic which is the goal of mankind; he is in an equal, scientific, Socialistic commonwealth, owned by the State and ruled by public officers; in fact, the commonwealth of the sublime future.

Nevertheless, there are signs that the irrational Jones still dreams at night of his old idea of having an ordinary home. He asked for so little, and he has been offered so much. He has been offered bribes of worlds and systems; he has been offered Eden and Utopia and the New Jerusalem, and he only wanted a house; and that has been refused him.

Such an apologue is literally no exaggeration of the facts of English history. The rich did literally turn the poor out of the old guest house on to the road, briefly telling them that it was the road of progress. They did literally force them into factories and the modern wage-slavery, assuring them all the time that this was the only way to wealth and civilization. Just as they had dragged the rustic from the convent food and ale by saying that the streets of heaven were paved with gold, so now they dragged him from the village food and ale by telling him that the streets of London were paved with gold. As he entered the gloomy porch of Puritanism, so he entered the gloomy porch of Industrialism, being told that each of them was the gate of the future. Hitherto he has only gone from prison to prison, nay, into darkening prisons, for Calvinism opened one small window upon heaven. And now he is asked, in the same educated and authoritative tones, to enter another dark porch, at which he has to surrender, into unseen hands, his children, his small possessions and all the habits of his fathers.

Whether this last opening be in truth any more inviting than the old openings of Puritanism and Industrialism can be discussed later. But there can be little doubt, I think, that if some form of Collectivism is imposed upon England it will be imposed, as everything else has been, by an instructed political class upon a people partly apathetic and partly hypnotized. The aristocracy will be as ready to "administer" Collectivism as they were to administer Puritanism or Manchesterism; in some ways such a centralized political power is necessarily attractive to them. It will not be so hard as some innocent Socialists seem to suppose to induce the Honorable Tomnoddy to take over the milk supply as well as the stamp supply — at an increased salary. Mr. Bernard Shaw has remarked that rich men are better than poor men on parish councils because they are free from "financial timidity." Now, the English ruling class is quite free from financial timidity. The Duke of Sussex will be quite ready to be Administrator of Sussex at the same screw. Sir William Harcourt, that typical aristocrat, put it quite correctly. "We" (that is, the aristocracy) "are all Socialists now."

But this is not the essential note on which I desire to end. My main contention is that, whether necessary or not, both Industrialism and Collectivism have been accepted as necessities — not as naked ideals or desires. Nobody liked the Manchester School; it was endured as the only way of producing wealth. Nobody likes the Marxian school; it is endured as the only way of preventing poverty. Nobody's real heart is in the idea of preventing a free man from owning his own farm, or an old woman from cultivating her own garden, any more than anybody's real heart was in the heartless battle of the machines. The purpose of this chapter is sufficiently served in indicating that this proposal also is a *pis aller*, a desperate second best — like teetotalism. I do not propose to prove here that Socialism is a poison; it is enough if I maintain that it is a medicine and not a wine.

The idea of private property universal but private, the idea of families free but still families, of domesticity democratic but still domestic, of one man one house — this remains the real vision and magnet of mankind. The world may accept something more official and general, less human and intimate. But the world will be like a broken-hearted woman who makes a humdrum marriage because she may not make a happy one; Socialism may be the world's deliverance, but it is not the world's desire.

PART TWO

IMPERIALISM, OR THE
MISTAKE ABOUT MAN

I

THE CHARM OF JINGOISM

I have cast about widely to find a title for this section; and I confess
that the word "Imperialism" is a clumsy version of my meaning. But
no other word came nearer; "Militarism" would have been even
more misleading, and "The Superman" makes nonsense of any discussion that he enters. Perhaps, upon the whole, the word "Caesarism" would have been better; but I desire a popular word; and
Imperialism (as the reader will perceive) does cover for the most part
the men and theories that I mean to discuss.

This small confusion is increased, however, by the fact that I do
also disbelieve in Imperialism in its popular sense, as a mode or
theory of the patriotic sentiment of this country. But popular Imperialism in England has very little to do with the sort of Caesarean
Imperialism I wish to sketch. I differ from the Colonial idealism of
Rhodes[1] and Kipling; but I do not think, as some of its opponents
do, that it is an insolent creation of English harshness and rapacity.
Imperialism, I think, is a fiction created, not by English hardness,
but by English softness; nay, in a sense, even by English kindness.

The reasons for believing in Australia are mostly as sentimental as
the most sentimental reasons for believing in heaven. New South
Wales is quite literally regarded as a place where the wicked cease
from troubling and the weary are at rest; that is, a paradise for uncles
who have turned dishonest and for nephews who are born tired.
British Columbia is in strict sense a fairyland; it is a world where a
magic and irrational luck is supposed to attend the youngest sons.
This strange optimism about the ends of the earth is an English
weakness; but to show that it is not a coldness or a harshness it is
quite sufficient to say that no one shared it more than that gigantic
English sentimentalist—the great Charles Dickens. The end of
"David Copperfield" is unreal not merely because it is an optimistic

[1] Cecil John Rhodes (1853–1902), English colonial capitalist and government administrator in South Africa. The famous scholarships at Oxford were named after him.

ending, but because it is an Imperialistic ending. The decorous British happiness planned out for David Copperfield and Agnes would be embarrassed by the perpetual presence of the hopeless tragedy of Emily, or the more hopeless farce of Micawber. Therefore, both Emily and Micawber are shipped off to a vague colony where changes come over them with no conceivable cause, except the climate. The tragic woman becomes contented and the comic man becomes responsible, solely as the result of a sea voyage and the first sight of a kangaroo.

To Imperialism in the light political sense, therefore, my only objection is that it is an illusion of comfort; that an Empire whose heart is failing should be specially proud of the extremities, is to me no more sublime a fact than that an old dandy whose brain is gone should still be proud of his legs. It consoles men for the evident ugliness and apathy of England with legends of fair youth and heroic strenuousness in distant continents and islands. A man can sit amid the squalor of Seven Dials[2] and feel that life is innocent and godlike in the bush or on the veldt. Just so a man might sit in the squalor of Seven Dials and feel that life was innocent and godlike in Brixton and Surbiton. Brixton and Surbiton are "new"; they are expanding; they are "nearer to nature," in the sense that they have eaten up nature mile by mile. The only objection is the objection of fact. The young men of Brixton are not young giants. The lovers of Surbiton are not all pagan poets, singing with the sweet energy of the spring. Nor are the people of the Colonies when you meet them young giants or pagan poets. They are mostly Cockneys who have lost their last music of real things by getting out of the sound of Bow Bells. Mr. Rudyard Kipling, a man of real though decadent genius, threw a theoretic glamour over them which is already fading. Mr. Kipling is, in a precise and rather startling sense, the exception that proves the rule. For he has imagination, of an oriental and cruel kind, but he has it, not because he grew up in a new country, but precisely because he grew up in the oldest country upon earth. He is rooted in a past—an Asiatic past. He might never have written "Kabul River" if he had been born in Melbourne.

[2] A district originally named for its Doric column adorned with sun-dials. This area came to be notorious for squalor, vice, crime and degradation.

I say frankly, therefore (lest there should be any air of evasion), that Imperialism in its common patriotic pretensions appears to me both weak and perilous. It is the attempt of a European country to create a kind of sham Europe which it can dominate, instead of the real Europe, which it can only share. It is a love of living with one's inferiors. The notion of restoring the Roman Empire by oneself and for oneself is a dream that has haunted every Christian nation in a different shape and in almost every shape as a snare. The Spanish are a consistent and conservative people; therefore they embodied that attempt at Empire in long and lingering dynasties. The French are a violent people, and therefore they twice conquered that Empire by violence of arms. The English are above all a poetical and optimistic people; and therefore their Empire is something vague and yet sympathetic, something distant and yet dear. But this dream of theirs of being powerful in the uttermost places, though a native weakness, is still a weakness in them; much more of a weakness than gold was to Spain or glory to Napoleon. If ever we were in collision with our real brothers and rivals we should leave all this fancy out of account. We should no more dream of pitting Australian armies against German than of pitting Tasmanian sculpture against French. I have thus explained, lest anyone should accuse me of concealing an unpopular attitude, why I do not believe in Imperialism as commonly understood. I think it not merely an occasional wrong to other peoples, but a continuous feebleness, a running sore, in my own. But it is also true that I have dwelt on this Imperialism that is an amiable delusion partly in order to show how different it is from the deeper, more sinister and yet more persuasive thing that I have been forced to call Imperialism for the convenience of this chapter. In order to get to the root of this evil and quite un-English Imperialism we must cast back and begin anew with a more general discussion of the first needs of human intercourse.

II

WISDOM AND THE WEATHER

It is admitted, one may hope, that common things are never commonplace. Birth is covered with curtains precisely because it is a staggering and monstrous prodigy. Death and first love, though they happen to everybody, can stop one's heart with the very thought of them. But while this is granted, something further may be claimed. It is not merely true that these universal things are strange; it is moreover true that they are subtle. In the last analysis most common things will be found to be highly complicated. Some men of science do indeed get over the difficulty by dealing only with the easy part of it: thus, they will call first love the instinct of sex, and the awe of death the instinct of self-preservation. But this is only getting over the difficulty of describing peacock green by calling it blue. There is blue in it. That there is a strong physical element in both romance and the *Memento Mori* makes them if possible more baffling than if they had been wholly intellectual. No man could say exactly how much his sexuality was colored by a clean love of beauty, or by the mere boyish itch for irrevocable adventures, like running away to sea. No man could say how far his animal dread of the end was mixed up with mystical traditions touching morals and religion. It is exactly because these things are animal, but not quite animal, that the dance of all the difficulties begins. The materialists analyze the easy part, deny the hard part and go home to their tea.

It is complete error to suppose that because a thing is vulgar therefore it is not refined; that is, subtle and hard to define. A drawing-room song of my youth which began "In the gloaming, O, my darling," was vulgar enough as a song; but the connection between human passion and the twilight is none the less an exquisite and even inscrutable thing. Or to take another obvious instance: the jokes about a mother-in-law are scarcely delicate, but the problem of a mother-in-law is extremely delicate. A mother-in-law is subtle because she is a thing like the twilight. She is a mystical blend of two inconsistent things — law and a mother. The caricatures misrepresent her; but they arise out of a real human enigma. "Comic Cuts" deals with the difficulty wrongly, but it would need George Meredith[1] at his best to deal with the difficulty rightly. The nearest statement of the problem perhaps is this: it is not that a mother-in-law must be nasty, but that she must be very nice.

But it is best perhaps to take in illustration some daily custom we have all heard despised as vulgar or trite. Take, for the sake of argument, the custom of talking about the weather. Stevenson calls it "the very nadir and scoff of good conversationalists." Now there are very deep reasons for talking about the weather, reasons that are delicate as well as deep; they lie in layer upon layer of stratified sagacity. First of all it is a gesture of primeval worship. The sky must be invoked; and to begin everything with the weather is a sort of pagan way of beginning everything with prayer. Jones and Brown talk about the weather: but so do Milton and Shelley. Then it is an expression of that elementary idea in politeness — equality. For the very word politeness is only the Greek for citizenship. The word politeness is akin to the word policeman: a charming thought. Properly understood, the citizen should be more polite than the gentleman; perhaps the policeman should be the most courtly and elegant of the three. But all good manners must obviously begin with the sharing of something in a simple style. Two men should share an umbrella; if they have not got an umbrella, they should at least share the rain, with all its rich potentialities of wit and philosophy. "For He maketh His sun to shine. . . ." This is the second element in the weather; its recognition of human equality in that we all have our hats under the dark blue spangled umbrella of the universe. Arising out of this is the third wholesome strain in the custom; I mean that it begins with the body and with our inevitable bodily brotherhood. All true friendliness begins with fire and food and drink and the recognition of rain or frost. Those who will not *begin* at the bodily end of things are already prigs and may soon be Christian Scientists. Each human soul has in a sense to enact for itself

[1] George Meredith (1828–1909), a well-known British writer.

the gigantic humility of the Incarnation. Every man must descend into the flesh to meet mankind.

Briefly, in the mere observation "a fine day" there is the whole great human idea of comradeship. Now, pure comradeship is another of those broad and yet bewildering things. We all enjoy it; yet when we come to talk about it we almost always talk nonsense, chiefly because we suppose it to be a simpler affair than it is. It is simple to conduct; but it is by no means simple to analyze. Comradeship is at the most only one half of human life; the other half is Love, a thing so different that one might fancy it had been made for another universe. And I do not mean mere sex love; any kind of concentrated passion, maternal love, or even the fiercer kinds of friendship are in their nature alien to pure comradeship. Both sides are essential to life; and both are known in differing degrees to everybody of every age or sex. But very broadly speaking it may still be said that women stand for the dignity of love and men for the dignity of comradeship. I mean that the institution would hardly be expected if the males of the tribe did not mount guard over it. The affections in which women excel have so much more authority and intensity that pure comradeship would be washed away if it were not rallied and guarded in clubs, corps, colleges, banquets and regiments. Most of us have heard the voice in which the hostess tells her husband not to sit too long over the cigars. It is the dreadful voice of Love, seeking to destroy Comradeship.

All true comradeship has in it those three elements which I have remarked in the ordinary exclamation about the weather. First, it has a sort of broad philosophy like the common sky, emphasizing that we are all under the same cosmic conditions. We are all in the same boat, the "winged rock" of Mr. Herbert Trench.[2] Secondly, it recognizes this bond as the essential one; for comradeship is simply humanity seen in that one aspect in which men are really equal. The old writers were entirely wise when they talked of the equality of men; but they were also very wise in not mentioning women. Women are always authoritarian; they are always above or below;

[2] Herbert Trench (1865–1923), an English poet.

that is why marriage is a sort of poetical see-saw. There are only three things in the world that women do not understand; and they are Liberty, Equality, and Fraternity. But men (a class little understood in the modern world) find these things the breath of their nostrils; and our most learned ladies will not even begin to understand them until they make allowance for this kind of cool camaraderie. Lastly, it contains the third quality of the weather, the insistence upon the body and its indispensable satisfaction. No one has even begun to understand comradeship who does not accept with it a certain hearty eagerness in eating, drinking, or smoking, an uproarious materialism which to many women appears only hoggish. You may call the thing an orgy or a sacrament; it is certainly an essential. It is at root a resistance to the superciliousness of the individual. Nay, its very swaggering and howling are humble. In the heart of its rowdiness there is a sort of mad modesty; a desire to melt the separate soul into the mass of unpretentious masculinity. It is a clamorous confession of the weakness of all flesh. No man must be superior to the things that are common to men. This sort of equality must be bodily and gross and comic. Not only are we all in the same boat, but we are all seasick.

The word comradeship just now promises to become as fatuous as the word "affinity." There are clubs of a Socialist sort where all the members, men and women, call each other "Comrade." I have no serious emotions, hostile or otherwise, about this particular habit: at the worst it is conventionality, and at the best flirtation. I am convinced here only to point out a rational principle. If you choose to lump all flowers together, lilies and dahlias and tulips and chrysanthemums and call them all daisies, you will find that you have spoiled the very fine word daisy. If you choose to call every human attachment comradeship, if you include under that name the respect of a youth for a venerable prophetess, the interest of a man in a beautiful woman who baffles him, the pleasure of a philosophical old fogy in a girl who is impudent and innocent, the end of the meanest quarrel or the beginning of the most mountainous love; if you are going to call all these comradeship, you will gain nothing; you will only lose a word. Daisies are obvious and universal and open; but they are only one kind of flower. Comradeship is obvious and universal and open; but it is only one kind of affection; it has characteristics that would destroy any other kind. Anyone who has known true comradeship in a club or in a regiment, knows that it is impersonal. There is a pedantic phrase used in debating clubs which is strictly true to the masculine emotion; they call it "speaking to the question." Women speak to each other; men speak to the subject they are speaking about. Many an honest man has sat in a ring of his five best friends under heaven and forgotten who was in the room while he explained some system. This is not peculiar to intellectual men; men are all theoretical, whether they are talking about God or about golf. Men are all impersonal; that is to say, republican. No one remembers after a really good talk who has said the good things. Every man speaks to a visionary multitude; a mystical cloud, that is called the club.

It is obvious that this cool and careless quality which is essential to the collective affection of males involves disadvantages and dangers. It leads to spitting; it leads to coarse speech; it must lead to these things so long as it is honorable; comradeship must be in some degree ugly. The moment beauty is mentioned in male friendship, the nostrils are stopped with the smell of abominable things. Friendship must be physically dirty if it is to be morally clean. It must be in its shirt sleeves. The chaos of habits that always goes with males when left entirely to themselves has only one honorable cure; and that is the strict discipline of a monastery. Anyone who has seen our unhappy young idealists in East End Settlements losing their collars in the wash and living on tinned salmon will fully understand why it was decided by the wisdom of St. Bernard or St. Benedict, that if men were to live without women, they must not live without rules. Something of the same sort of artificial exactitude, of course, is obtained in an army; and an army also has to be in many ways monastic; only that it has celibacy without chastity. But these things do not apply to normal married men. These have a quite sufficient restraint on their instinctive anarchy in the savage common-sense of the other sex. There is only one very timid sort of man that is not afraid of women.

III

THE COMMON VISION

Now this masculine love of an open and level camaraderie is the life within all democracies and attempts to govern by debate; without it the republic would be a dead formula. Even as it is, of course, the spirit of democracy frequently differs widely from the letter, and a pothouse is often a better test than a Parliament. Democracy in its human sense is not arbitrament by the majority; it is not even arbitrament by everybody. It can be more nearly defined as arbitrament by anybody. I mean that it rests on that club habit of taking a total stranger for granted, of assuming certain things to be inevitably common to yourself and him. Only the things that anybody may be presumed to hold have the full authority of democracy. Look out of the window and notice the first man who walks by. The Liberals may have swept England with an over-whelming majority; but you would not stake a button that the man is a Liberal. The Bible may be read in all schools and respected in all law courts; but you would not bet a straw that he believes in the Bible. But you would bet your week's wages, let us say, that he believes in wearing clothes. You would bet that he believes that physical courage is a fine thing, or that parents have authority over children. Of course, he might be the millionth man who does not believe these things; if it comes to that, he might be the Bearded Lady dressed up as a man. But these prodigies are quite a different thing from any mere calculation of numbers. People who hold these views are not a minority, but a monstrosity. But of these universal dogmas that have full democratic authority the only test is this test of anybody. What you would observe before any newcomer in a tavern—that is the real English law. The first man you see from the window, he is the King of England.

The decay of taverns, which is but a part of the general decay of democracy, has undoubtedly weakened this masculine spirit of equality. I remember that a roomful of Socialists literally laughed when I

97

told them that there were no two nobler words in all poetry than
Public House. They thought it was a joke. Why *they* should think it
a joke, since they want to make all houses public houses, I cannot
imagine. But if anyone wishes to see the real rowdy egalitarianism
which is necessary (to males, at least) he can find it as well as anywhere in the great old tavern disputes which come down to us in
such books as Boswell's Johnson. It is worth while to mention that
one name especially because the modern world in its morbidity has
done it a strange injustice. The demeanor of Johnson, it is said, was
"harsh and despotic." It was occasionally harsh, but it was never
despotic. Johnson was not in the least a despot; Johnson was a demagogue, he shouted against a shouting crowd. The very fact that he
wrangled with other people is proof that other people were allowed
to wrangle with him. His very brutality was based on the idea of an
equal scrimmage, like that of football. It is strictly true that he bawled
and banged the table because he was a modest man. He was honestly
afraid of being overwhelmed or even overlooked. Addison had exquisite manners and was the king of his company; he was polite to
everybody; but superior to everybody; therefore he has been handed
down forever in the immortal insult of Pope—

> "Like Cato, give his little Senate laws
> And sit attentive to his own applause."

Johnson, so far from being king of his company, was a sort of Irish
Member in his own Parliament. Addison was a courteous superior
and was hated. Johnson was an insolent equal and therefore was loved
by all who knew him, and handed down in a marvelous book,
which is one of the mere miracles of love.

   This doctrine of equality is essential to conversation; so much may
be admitted by anyone who knows what conversation is. Once arguing at a table in a tavern the most famous man on earth would wish to
be obscure, so that his brilliant remarks might blaze like the stars on
the background of his obscurity. To anything worth calling a man
nothing can be conceived more cold or cheerless than to be king of
your company. But it may be said that in masculine sports and games,
other than the great game of debate, there is definite emulation

and eclipse. There is indeed emulation, but this is only an ardent sort of equality. Games are competitive, because that is the only way of making them exciting. But if anyone doubts that men must forever return to the ideal of equality, it is only necessary to answer that there is such a thing as a handicap. If men exulted in mere superiority, they would seek to see how far such superiority could go; they would be glad when one strong runner came in miles ahead of all the rest. But what men like is not the triumph of superiors, but the struggle of equals; and, therefore, they introduce even into their competitive sports an artificial equality. It is sad to think how few of those who arrange our sporting handicaps can be supposed with any probability to realize that they are abstract and even severe republicans.

No; the real objection to equality and self-rule has nothing to do with any of these free and festive aspects of mankind; all men are democrats when they are happy. The philosophic opponent of democracy would substantially sum up his position by saying that it "will not work." Before going further, I will register in passing a protest against the assumption that working is the one test of humanity. Heaven does not work; it plays. Men are most themselves when they are free; and if I find that men are snobs in their work but democrats on their holidays, I shall take the liberty to believe their holidays. But it is this question of work which really perplexes the question of equality; and it is with that that we must now deal. Perhaps the truth can be put most pointedly thus: that democracy has one real enemy, and that is civilization. Those utilitarian miracles which science has made are anti-democratic, not so much in their perversion, or even in their practical result, as in their primary shape and purpose. The Frame-Breaking Rioters were right; not perhaps in thinking that machines would make fewer men workmen; but certainly in thinking that machines would make fewer men masters. More wheels do mean fewer handles; fewer handles do mean fewer hands. The machinery of science must be individualistic and isolated. A mob can shout round a palace; but a mob cannot shout down a telephone. The specialist appears and democracy is half spoiled at a stroke.

IV

THE INSANE NECESSITY

The common conception among the dregs of Darwinian culture is that men have slowly worked their way out of inequality into a state of comparative equality. The truth is, I fancy, almost exactly the opposite. All men have normally and naturally begun with the idea of equality; they have only abandoned it late and reluctantly, and always for some material reason of detail. They have never naturally felt that one class of men was superior to another; they have always been driven to assume it through certain practical limitations of space and time.

For example, there is one element which must always tend to oligarchy—or rather to despotism; I mean the element of hurry. If the house has caught fire a man must ring up the fire engines; a committee cannot ring them up. If a camp is surprised by night somebody must give the order to fire; there is no time to vote it. It is solely a question of the physical limitations of time and space; not at all of any mental limitations in the mass of men commanded. If all the people in the house were men of destiny it would still be better that they should not all talk into the telephone at once; nay, it would be better that the silliest man of all should speak uninterrupted. If an army actually consisted of nothing but Hanibals and Napoleons, it would still be better in the case of a surprise that they should not all give orders together. Nay, it would be better if the stupidest of them all gave the orders. Thus, we see that merely military subordination, so far from resting on the inequality of men, actually rests on the equality of men. Discipline does not involve the Carlylean notion that somebody is always right when everybody is wrong, and that we must discover and crown that somebody. On the contrary, discipline means that in certain frightfully rapid circumstances, one can trust anybody so long as he is not everybody. The military spirit does not mean (as Carlyle fancied) obeying the strongest and wisest man. On the contrary, the military spirit means, if anything, obeying the weakest and stupidest man, obeying him merely because he is a man, and not a thousand men. Submission to a weak man is discipline. Submission to a strong man is only servility.

Now it can be easily shown that the thing we call aristocracy in Europe is not in its origin and spirit an aristocracy at all. It is not a system of spiritual degrees and distinctions like, for example, the caste system of India, or even like the old Greek distinction between free-men and slaves. It is simply the remains of a military organization, framed partly to sustain the sinking Roman Empire, partly to break and avenge the awful onslaught of Islam. The word Duke simply means Colonel, just as the word Emperor simply means Commander-in-Chief. The whole story is told in the single title of Counts of the Holy Roman Empire, which merely means officers in the European army against the contemporary Yellow Peril. Now in an army nobody ever dreams of supposing that difference of rank represents a difference of moral reality. Nobody ever says about a regiment, "Your Major is very humorous and energetic; your Colonel, of course, must be even more humorous and yet more energetic." No one ever says, in reporting a mess-room conversation, "Lieutenant Jones was very witty, but was naturally inferior to Captain Smith." The essence of an army is the idea of official inequality, founded on unofficial equality. The Colonel is not obeyed because he is the best man, but because he is the Colonel. Such was probably the spirit of the system of dukes and counts when it first arose out of the military spirit and military necessities of Rome. With the decline of those necessities it has gradually ceased to have meaning as a military organization, and become honeycombed with unclean plutocracy. Even now it is not a spiritual aristocracy — it is not so bad as all that. It is simply an army without an enemy — billeted upon the people.

Man, therefore, has a specialist as well as comrade-like aspect; and the case of militarism is not the only case of such specialist submission. The tinker and tailor, as well as the soldier and sailor, require a certain rigidity or rapidity of action: at least, if the tinker is not organized that is largely why he does not tink on any large scale. The tinker and tailor often represent the two nomadic races in Europe: the Gipsy and the Jew; but the Jew alone has influence because he alone accepts some sort of discipline. Man, we say, has two sides, the specialist side where he must have subordination, and the social side where he must have equality. There is a truth in the saying that ten tailors go to make a man; but we must remember also that ten Poets Laureate or ten Astronomers Royal go to make a man, too. Ten million tradesmen go to make Man himself; but humanity consists of tradesmen when they are not talking shop. Now the peculiar peril of our time, which I call for argument's sake Imperialism or Caesarism, is the complete eclipse of comradeship and equality by specialism and domination.

There are only two kinds of social structure conceivable — personal government and impersonal government. If my anarchic friends will not have rules — they will have rulers. Preferring personal government, with its tact and flexibility, is called Royalism. Preferring impersonal government, with its dogmas and definitions, is called Republicanism. Objecting broadmindedly both to kings and creeds is called Bosh; at least, I know no more philosophic word for it. You can be guided by the shrewdness or presence of mind of one ruler, or by the equality and ascertained justice of one rule; but you must have one or the other, or you are not a nation, but a nasty mess. Now men in their aspect of equality and debate adore the idea of rules; they develop and complicate them greatly to excess. A man finds far more regulations and definitions in his club, where there are rules, than in his home, where there is a ruler. A deliberate assembly, the House of Commons, for instance, carries this mummery to the point of a methodical madness. The whole system is stiff with rigid unreason; like the Royal Court in Lewis Carroll. You would think the Speaker would speak; therefore he is mostly silent. You would think a man would take off his hat to stop and put it on to go away; therefore he takes off his hat to walk out and puts it on to stop in. Names are forbidden, and a man must call his own father "my right honorable friend the member for West Birmingham." These are, perhaps, fantasies of decay: but fundamentally they answer a masculine appetite. Men feel that rules, even if irrational, are universal; men feel that law is equal, even when it is not equitable. There is a wild fairness in the thing — as there is in tossing up.

Again, it is gravely unfortunate that when critics do attack such cases as the Commons it is always on the points (perhaps the few points) where the Commons are right. They denounce the House as the Talking-Shop, and complain that it wastes time in wordy mazes. Now this is just one respect in which the Commons are actually like the Common People. If they love leisure and long debate, it is because all men love it; that they really represent England. There the Parliament does approach to the virile virtues of the pothouse.

The real truth is that adumbrated in the introductory section, when we spoke of the sense of home and property, as now we speak of the sense of counsel and community. All men do naturally love the idea of leisure, laughter, loud and equal argument; but there stands a specter in our hall. We are conscious of the towering modern challenge that is called specialism or cut-throat competition — Business. Business will have nothing to do with leisure; business will have no truck with comradeship; business will pretend to no patience with all the legal fictions and fantastic handicaps by which comradeship protects its egalitarian ideal. The modern millionaire, when engaged in the agreeable and typical task of sacking his own father, will certainly not refer to him as the right honorable clerk from the Laburnum Road, Brixton. Therefore there has arisen in modern life a literary fashion devoting itself to the romance of business, to great demigods of greed and to the fairyland of finance. This popular philosophy is utterly despotic and anti-democratic; this fashion is the flower of that Caesarism against which I am concerned to protest. The ideal millionaire is strong in the possession of a brain of steel. The fact that the real millionaire is rather more often strong in the possession of a head of wood, does not alter the spirit and trend of the idolatry. The essential argument is "Specialists must be despots; men must be specialists. You cannot have equality in a soap factory; so you cannot have it anywhere. You cannot have comradeship in a wheat corner; so you cannot have it at all. We must have commercial civilization; therefore we must destroy democracy." I know that plutocrats have seldom sufficient fancy to soar to such examples as soap or wheat. They generally confine themselves, with fine freshness of mind, to a comparison between the state and a ship.

One anti-democratic writer remarked that he would not like to sail in a vessel in which the cabin-boy had an equal vote with the captain. It might easily be urged in answer that many a ship (the *Victoria*,[1] for instance) was sunk because an admiral gave an order which a cabin-boy could see was wrong. But this is a debating reply; the essential fallacy is both deeper and simpler. The elementary fact is that we were all born in a state; we were not all born on a ship; like some of our great British bankers. A ship still remains a specialist experiment, like a diving-bell or a flying ship: in such peculiar perils the need for promptitude constitutes the need for autocracy. But we live and die in the vessel of the state; and if we cannot find freedom, camaraderie and the popular element in the state, we cannot find it at all. And the modern doctrine of commercial despotism means that we shall not find it at all. Our specialist trades in their highly civilized state cannot (it says) be run without the whole brutal business of bossing and sacking, "too old at forty" and all the rest of the filth. And they must be run, and therefore we call on Caesar. Nobody but the Superman could descend to do such dirty work.

Now (to reiterate my title) this is what is wrong. This is the huge modern heresy of altering the human soul to fit its conditions, instead of altering human conditions to fit the human soul. If soap-boiling is really inconsistent with brotherhood, so much the worst for soap-boiling, not for brotherhood. If civilization really cannot get on with democracy, so much the worse for civilization, not for democracy. Certainly, it would be far better to go back to village communes, if they really are communes. Certainly, it would be better to do without soap rather than to do without society. Certainly, we would sacrifice all our wires, wheels, systems, specialties, physical science and frenzied finance for one half-hour of happiness such as has often come to us with comrades in a common tavern. I do not say the sacrifice will be necessary; I only say it will be easy.

[1] The *Victoria* is the name of the British flagship which sank in 1893 when she collided with another ship in her fleet; the collision was due to the blatant judgment error of her captain, Sir George Tryon. Three hundred and fifty-nine men drowned as a result of the mishap, including Captain Tryon.

PART THREE

FEMINISM, OR THE MISTAKE ABOUT WOMAN

I

THE UNMILITARY SUFFRAGETTE

It will be better to adopt in this chapter the same process that appeared a piece of mental justice in the last. My general opinions on the feminine question are such as many suffragists would warmly approve; and it would be easy to state them without any open reference to the current controversy. But just as it seemed more decent to say first that I was not in favor of Imperialism even in its practical and popular sense, so it seems more decent to say the same of Female Suffrage, in its practical and popular sense. In other words, it is only fair to state, however hurriedly, the superficial objection to the Suffragettes before we go on to the really subtle questions behind the Suffrage.

Well, to get this honest but unpleasant business over, the objection to the Suffragettes is not that they are Militant Suffragettes. On the contrary, it is that they are not militant enough. A revolution is a military thing; it has all the military virtues; one of which is that it comes to an end. Two parties fight with deadly weapons, but under certain rules of arbitrary honor; the party that wins becomes the government and proceeds to govern. The aim of civil war, like the aim of all war, is peace. Now the Suffragettes cannot raise civil war in this soldierly and decisive sense; first, because they are women; and, secondly, because they are very few women. But they can raise something else; which is altogether another pair of shoes. They do not create revolution; what they do create is anarchy; and the difference between these is not a question of violence, but a question of fruitfulness and finality. Revolution of its nature produces government; anarchy only produces more anarchy. Men may have what opinions they please about the beheading of King Charles or King Louis, but they cannot deny that Bradshaw[1] and Cromwell ruled, that Carnot[2] and Napoleon

[1] John Bradshaw (1602–1659), presided at the trials of Charles I and other of his followers.
[2] Lazare Carnot (1753–1823), French general and statesman.

governed. Someone conquered; something occurred. You can only knock off the King's head once. But you can knock off the King's hat any number of times. Destruction is finite; obstruction is infinite: so long as rebellion takes the form of mere disorder (instead of an attempt to enforce a new order) there is no logical end to it; it can feed on itself and renew itself forever. If Napoleon had not wanted to be a Consul, but only wanted to be a nuisance, he could, possibly, have prevented any government arising successfully out of the Revolution. But such a proceeding would not have deserved the dignified name of rebellion.

It is exactly this unmilitant quality in the Suffragettes that makes their superficial problem. The problem is that their action has none of the advantages of ultimate violence; it does not afford a test. War is a dreadful thing; but it does prove two points sharply and unanswerably—numbers, and an unnatural valor. One does discover the two urgent matters; how many rebels there are alive, and how many are ready to be dead. But a tiny minority, even an interested minority, may maintain mere disorder forever. There is also, of course, in the case of these women, the further falsity that is introduced by their sex. It is false to state the matter as a mere brutal question of strength. If his muscles give a man a vote, then his horse ought to have two votes and his elephant five votes. The truth is more subtle than that; it is that bodily outbreak is a man's instinctive weapon, like the hoofs to the horse or the tusks to the elephant. All riot is a threat of war; but the woman is brandishing a weapon she can never use. There are many weapons that she could and does use. If (for example) all the women nagged for a vote they would get it in a month. But there again, one must remember, it would be necessary to get all the women to nag. And that brings us to the end of the political surface of the matter. The working objection to the Suffragette philosophy is simply that overmastering millions of women do not agree with it. I am aware that some maintain that women ought to have votes whether the majority wants them or not; but this is surely a strange and childish case of setting up formal democracy to the destruction of actual democracy. What should the mass of women decide if they do not decide their general place in the

State? These people practically say that females may vote about everything except about Female Suffrage.

But having again cleared my conscience of my merely political and possibly unpopular opinion, I will again cast back and try to treat the matter in a slower and more sympathetic style; attempt to trace the real roots of woman's position in the western state, and the causes of our existing traditions or perhaps prejudices upon the point. And for this purpose it is again necessary to travel far from the modern topic, the mere Suffragette of today, and to go back to subjects which, though much more old, are, I think, considerably more fresh.

II

THE UNIVERSAL STICK

Cast your eye round the room in which you sit, and select some three or four things that have been with man almost since his beginning; which at least we hear of early in the centuries and often among the tribes. Let me suppose that you see a knife on the table, a stick in the corner, or a fire on the hearth. About each of these you will notice one specialty; that not one of them is special. Each of these ancestral things is a universal thing; made to supply many different needs; and while tottering pedants nose about to find the cause and origin of some old custom, the truth is that it had fifty causes or a hundred origins. The knife is meant to cut wood, to cut cheese, to cut pencils, to cut throats; for a myriad ingenious or innocent human objects. The stick is meant partly to hold a man up, partly to knock a man down; partly to point with like a finger-post, partly to balance with like a balancing pole, partly to trifle with like a cigarette, partly to kill with like a club of a giant; it is a crutch and a cudgel; an elongated finger and an extra leg. The case is the same, of course, with the fire; about which the strangest modern views have arisen. A queer fancy seems to be current that a fire exists to warm people. It exists to warm people, to light their darkness, to raise their spirits, to toast their muffins, to air their rooms, to cook their chestnuts, to tell stories to their children, to make checkered shadows on their walls, to boil their hurried kettles, and to be the red heart of a man's house and that hearth for which, as the great heathens said, a man should die.

Now it is the great mark of our modernity that people are always proposing substitutes for these old things; and these substitutes always answer one purpose where the old thing answered ten. The modern man will wave a cigarette instead of a stick; he will cut his pencil with a little screwing pencil-sharpener instead of a knife; and he will even boldly offer to be warmed by hot water pipes instead of a fire. I have my doubts about pencil-sharpeners even for sharpening pencils; and about hot water pipes even for heat. But when we think of all those other requirements that these institutions answered, there opens before us the whole horrible harlequinade of our civilization. We see as in a vision a world where a man tries to cut his throat with a pencil-sharpener; where a man must learn single-stick with a cigarette; where a man must try to toast muffins at electric lamps, and see red and golden castles in the surface of hot water pipes.

The principle of which I speak can be seen everywhere in a comparison between the ancient and universal things and the modern and specialist things. The object of a theodolite is to lie level; the object of a stick is to swing loose at any angle; to whirl like the very wheel of liberty. The object of a lancet is to lance; when used for slashing, gashing, ripping, lopping off heads and limbs, it is a disappointing instrument. The object of an electric light is merely to light (a despicable modesty); and the object of an asbestos stove . . . I wonder what is the object of an asbestos stove? If a man found a coil of rope in a desert he could at least think of all the things that can be done with a coil of rope; and some of them might even be practical. He could tow a boat or lasso a horse. He could play cat's-cradle, or pick oakum. He could construct a rope-ladder for an eloping heiress, or cord her boxes for a traveling maiden aunt. He could learn to tie a bow, or he could hang himself. Far otherwise with the unfortunate traveler who should find a telephone in the desert. You can telephone with a telephone; you cannot do anything else with it. And though this is one of the wildest joys of life, it falls by one degree from its full delirium when there is nobody to answer you. The contention is, in brief, that you must pull up a hundred roots, and not one, before you uproot any of these hoary and simple expedients. It is only with great difficulty that a modern scientific sociologist can be got to see that any old method has a leg to stand on. But almost every old method has four or five legs to stand on. Almost all the old institutions are quadrupeds; and some of them are centipedes.

Consider these cases, old and new, and you will observe the operation of a general tendency. Everywhere there was one big thing that served six purposes; everywhere now there are six small things; or, rather (and there is the trouble), there are just five and a half. Nevertheless, we will not say that this separation and specialism is entirely useless or inexcusable. I have often thanked God for the telephone; I may any day thank God for the lancet; and there is none of these brilliant and narrow inventions (except, of course, the asbestos stove) which might not be at some moment necessary and lovely. But I do not think the most austere upholder of specialism will deny that there is in these old, many-sided institutions an element of unity and universality which may well be preserved in its due proportion and place. Spiritually, at least, it will be admitted that some all-round balance is needed to equalize the extravagance of experts. It would not be difficult to carry the parable of the knife and stick into higher regions. Religion, the immortal maiden, has been a maid-of-all-work as well as a servant of mankind. She provided men at once with the theoretic laws of an unalterable cosmos; and also with the practical rules of the rapid and thrilling game of morality. She taught logic to the student and told fairy tales to the children; it was her business to confront the nameless gods whose fears are on all flesh, and also to see the streets were spotted with silver and scarlet, that there was a day for wearing ribbons or an hour for ringing bells. The large uses of religion have been broken up into lesser specialties, just as the uses of the hearth have been broken up into hot water pipes and electric bulbs. The romance of ritual and colored emblem has been taken over by that narrowest of all trades, modern art (the sort called art for art's sake), and men are in modern practice informed that they may use all symbols so long as they mean nothing by them. The romance of conscience has been dried up into the science of ethics; which may well be called decency for decency's sake, decency unborn of cosmic energies and barren of artistic flower. The cry to the dim gods, cut off from ethics and cosmology, has become mere Psychical Research. Everything has been sundered from everything else, and everything has grown cold. Soon we shall hear of specialists dividing the tune from the words of a song, on the ground that they spoil each other; and I did once meet a man who openly advocated the separation of almonds and raisins. This world is all one wild divorce court; nevertheless, there are many who still hear in their souls the thunder of authority of human habit; those whom Man hath joined let no man sunder.

This book must avoid religion, but there must (I say) be many, religious and irreligious, who will concede that this power of answering many purposes was a sort of strength which should not wholly die out of our lives. As a part of personal character, even the moderns will agree that many-sidedness is a merit and a merit that may easily be overlooked. This balance and universality has been the vision of many groups of men in many ages. It was the Liberal Education of Aristotle; the jack-of-all-trades artistry of Leonardo da Vinci and his friends; the august amateurishness of the Cavalier Person of Quality like Sir William Temple[1] or the great Earl of Dorset.[2] It has appeared in literature in our time in the most erratic and opposite shapes, set to almost inaudible music by Walter Pater and enunciated through a foghorn by Walt Whitman. But the great mass of men have always been unable to achieve this literal universality, because of the nature of their work in the world. Not, let it be noted, because of the existence of their work. Leonardo da Vinci must have worked pretty hard; on the other hand, many a government office clerk, village constable or elusive plumber may do (to all human appearance) no work at all, and yet show no signs of the Aristotelian universalism. What makes it difficult for the average man to be a universalist is that the average man has to be a specialist; he has not only to learn one trade, but to learn it so well as to uphold him in a more or less ruthless society. This is generally true of males from the first hunter to the last electrical engineer; each has not merely to act, but to excel. Nimrod has not only to be a mighty hunter before the Lord, but also a mighty hunter before the other hunters. The electrical engineer has to be a very electrical engineer, or he is outstripped by engineers yet more electrical. Those very miracles of the human mind on which the modern world prides itself,

[1] Sir William Temple (1628–1699), English statesman and author; his writings are chiefly valuable for the picture they afford of the cultured gentlemen of the period.

[2] Probably Sir Edward Sackville, fourth Earl of Dorset (1591–1652), a man of varied accomplishments. He was, among others, a barrister, a poet, an actor, privy councillor, and Lord Treasurer.

and rightly in the main, would be impossible without a certain concentration which disturbs the pure balance of reason more than does religious bigotry. No creed can be so limiting as that awful adjuration that the cobbler must not go beyond his last. So the largest and wildest shots of our world are but in one direction and with a defined trajectory: the gunner cannot go beyond his shot, and his shot so often falls short; the astronomer cannot go beyond his telescope, and his telescope goes such a little way. All these are like men who have stood on the high peak of a mountain and seen the horizon like a single ring and who then descend down different paths towards different towns, traveling slow or fast. It is right; there must be people traveling to different towns; there must be specialists; but shall no one behold the horizon? Shall all mankind be specialist surgeons or peculiar plumbers; shall all humanity be monomaniac? Tradition has decided that only half of humanity shall be monomaniac. It has decided that in every home there shall be a tradesman and a Jack-of-all-trades. But it has also decided, among other things, that the Jack-of-all-trades shall be a Gill-of-all-trades. It has decided, rightly or wrongly, that this specialism and this universalism shall be divided between the sexes. Cleverness shall be left for men and wisdom for women. For cleverness kills wisdom; that is one of the few sad and certain things.

But for women this ideal of comprehensive capacity (or commonsense) must long ago have been washed away. It must have melted in the frightful furnaces of ambition and eager technicality. A man must be partly a one-idead man, because he is a one-weaponed man—and he is flung naked into the fight. The world's demand comes to him direct; to his wife indirectly. In short, he must (as the books on Success say) give "his best"; and what a small part of a man "his best" is! His second and third best are often much better. If he is the first violin he must fiddle for life; he must not remember that he is a fine fourth bagpipe, a fair fifteenth billiard-cue, a foil, a fountain-pen, a hand at whist, a gun, and an image of God.

III

THE EMANCIPATION OF DOMESTICITY

And it should be remarked in passing that this force upon a man to develop one feature has nothing to do with what is commonly called our competitive system, but would equally exist under any rationally conceivable kind of Collectivism. Unless the Socialists are frankly ready for a fall in the standard of violins, telescopes and electric lights, they must somehow create a moral demand on the individual that he shall keep up his present concentration on these things. It was only by men being in some degree specialist that there ever were any telescopes; they must certainly be in some degree specialist in order to keep them going. It is not by making a man a State wage-earner that you can prevent him thinking principally about the very difficult way he earns his wages. There is only one way to preserve in the world that high levity and that more leisurely outlook which fulfills the old vision of universalism. That is, to permit the existence of a partly protected half of humanity; a half which the harassing industrial demand troubles indeed, but only troubles indirectly. In other words, there must be in every center of humanity one human being upon a larger plan; one who does not "give her best," but gives her all.

Our old analogy of the fire remains the most workable one. The fire need not blaze like electricity nor boil like boiling water; its point is that it blazes more than water and warms more than light. The wife is like the fire, or to put things in their proper proportion, the fire is like the wife. Like the fire, the woman is expected to cook: not to excel in cooking, but to cook; to cook better than her husband who is earning the coke by lecturing on botany or breaking stones. Like the fire, the woman is expected to tell tales to the children, not original and artistic tales, but tales—better tales than would probably be told by a first-class cook. Like the fire, the woman is expected to illuminate and ventilate, not by the most startling revelations or the wildest winds of thought, but better than a man can do it after breaking stones or lecturing. But she cannot be expected to endure anything like this universal duty if she is also to endure the direct cruelty of competitive or bureaucratic toil. Woman must be a cook, but not a competitive cook; a school-mistress, but not a competitive schoolmistress; a house-decorator, but not a competitive house-decorator; a dressmaker, but not a competitive dressmaker. She should have not one trade but twenty hobbies; she, unlike the man, may develop all her second bests. This is what has been really aimed at from the first in what is called the seclusion, or even the oppression, of women. Women were not kept at home in order to keep them narrow; on the contrary, they were kept at home in order to keep them broad. The world outside the home was one mass of narrowness, a maze of cramped paths, a madhouse of monomaniacs. It was only by partly limiting and protecting the woman that she was enabled to play at five or six professions and so come almost as near to God as the child when he plays at a hundred trades. But the woman's professions, unlike the child's, were all truly and almost terribly fruitful; so tragically real that nothing but her universality and balance prevented them being merely morbid. This is the substance of the contention I offer about the historic female position. I do not deny that women have been wronged and even tortured; but I doubt if they were ever tortured so much as they are tortured now by the absurd modern attempt to make them domestic empresses and competitive clerks at the same time. I do not deny that even under the old tradition women had a harder time than men; that is why we take off our hats. I do not deny that all these various female functions were exasperating; but I say that there was some aim and meaning in keeping them various. I do not pause even to deny that woman was a servant; but at least she was a general servant.

The shortest way of summarizing the position is to say that woman stands for the idea of Sanity; that intellectual home to which the mind must return after every excursion on extravagance. The mind that finds its way to wild places is the poet's; but the mind that never finds its way back is the lunatic's. There must in every machine be a part that moves and a part that stands still; there must be in everything that changes a part that is unchangeable. And many of the phenomena which moderns hastily condemn are really parts of this position of the woman as the center and pillar of health. Much of what is called her subservience, and even her pliability, is merely the subservience and pliability of a universal remedy; she varies as medicines vary, with the disease. She has to be an optimist to the morbid husband, a salutary pessimist to the happy-go-lucky husband. She has to prevent the Quixote from being put upon, and the bully from putting upon others. The French King wrote—

"Toujours femme varie
Bien fol qui s'y fie,"[1]

but the truth is that woman always varies, and that is exactly why we always trust her. To correct every adventure and extravagance with its antidote in common-sense is not (as the moderns seem to think) to be in the position of a spy or a slave. It is to be in the position of Aristotle or (at the lowest) Herbert Spencer,[2] to be a universal morality, a complete system of thought. The slave flatters; the complete moralist rebukes. It is, in short, to be a Trimmer in the true sense of that honorable term; which for some reason or other is always used in a sense exactly opposite to its own. It seems really to be supposed that a Trimmer means a cowardly person who always goes over to the stronger side. It really means a highly chivalrous person who always goes over to the weaker side; like one who trims a boat by sitting where there are few people seated. Woman is a trimmer; and it is a generous, dangerous and romantic trade.

The final fact which fixes this is a sufficiently plain one. Supposing it to be conceded that humanity has acted at least not unnaturally in dividing itself into two halves, respectively typifying the ideals of special talent and of general sanity (since they are genuinely difficult to combine completely in one mind), it is not difficult to see why the line of cleavage has followed the line of sex, or why the female became the emblem of the universal and the male of the special and

[1] "Woman always varies; quite foolish he who trusts her."
[2] Herbert Spencer (1820–1903), English philosopher whose system was based on evolutionary theory.

superior. Two gigantic facts of nature fixed it thus: first, that the woman who frequently fulfilled her functions literally could not be specially prominent in experiment and adventure; and second, that the same natural operation surrounded her with very young children, who require to be taught not so much anything as everything. Babies need not to be taught a trade, but to be introduced to a world. To put the matter shortly, woman is generally shut up in a house with a human being at the time when he asks all the questions that there are, and some that there aren't. It would be odd if she retained any of the narrowness of a specialist. Now if anyone says that this duty of general enlightenment (even when freed from modern rules and hours, and exercised more spontaneously by a more protected person) is in itself too exacting and oppressive, I can understand the view. I can only answer that our race has thought it worth while to cast this burden on women in order to keep common-sense in the world. But when people begin to talk about this domestic duty as not merely difficult but trivial and dreary, I simply give up the question. For I cannot with the utmost energy of imagination conceive what they mean. When domesticity, for instance, is called drudgery, all the difficulty arises from a double meaning in the word. If drudgery only means dreadfully hard work, I admit the woman drudges in the home, as a man might drudge at the Cathedral of Amiens or drudge behind a gun at Trafalgar. But if it means that the hard work is more heavy because it is trifling, colorless and of small import to the soul, then as I say, I give it up; I do not know what the words mean. To be Queen Elizabeth within a definite area, deciding sales, banquets, labors and holidays; to be Whiteley[3] within a certain area, providing toys, boots, sheets, cakes, and books, to be Aristotle within a certain area, teaching morals, manners, theology, and hygiene; I can understand how this might exhaust the mind, but I cannot imagine how it could narrow it. How can it be a large career to tell other people's children

[3] William Whiteley (1831–1907) began his career by opening a small draper's shop which he expanded into the first general goods store in London owned and operated by a single man. He described himself as the "Universal Provider" and boasted that there was nothing his stores could not provide.

about the Rule of Three, and a small career to tell one's own children about the universe? How can it be broad to be the same thing to everyone, and narrow to be everything to someone? No; a woman's function is laborious, but because it is gigantic, not because it is minute. I will pity Mrs. Jones for the hugeness of her task; I will never pity her for its smallness.

But though the essential of the woman's task is universality, this does not, of course, prevent her from having one or two severe though largely wholesome prejudices. She has, on the whole, been more conscious than man that she is only one half of humanity; but she has expressed it (if one may say so of a lady) by getting her teeth into the two or three things which she thinks she stands for. I would observe here in parenthesis that much of the recent official trouble about women has arisen from the fact that they transfer to things of doubt and reason that sacred stubbornness only proper to the primary things which a woman was set to guard. One's own children, one's own altar, ought to be a matter of principle—or if you like, a matter of prejudice. On the other hand, who wrote Junius's Letters ought not to be a principle or a prejudice, it ought to be a matter of free and almost indifferent inquiry. But make an energetic modern girl secretary to a league to show that George III. wrote Junius,[4] and in three months she will believe it, too, out of mere loyalty to her employers. Modern women defend their office with all the fierceness of domesticity. They fight for desk and typewriter as for hearth and home, and develop a sort of wolfish wifehood on behalf of the invisible head of the firm. That is why they do office work so well; and that is why they ought not to do it.

[4] Junius, the pen name of an unidentified author of a series of letters published in a London newspaper (1769–1772), attacking the English King and his ministers' abuse of royal prerogative in denying John Wilkes his seat in Parliament.

IV

THE ROMANCE OF THRIFT

The larger part of womankind, however, have had to fight for things slightly more intoxicating to the eye than the desk or the type-writer; and it cannot be denied that in defending these, women have developed the quality called prejudice to a powerful and even menacing degree. But these prejudices will always be found to fortify the main position of the woman, that she is to remain a general overseer, an autocrat within small compass but on all sides. On the one or two points on which she really misunderstands the man's position, it is almost entirely in order to preserve her own. The two points on which woman, actually and of herself, is most tenacious may be roughly summarized as the ideal of thrift and the ideal of dignity.

Unfortunately for this book it is written by a male, and these two qualities, if not hateful to a man, are at least hateful in a man. But if we are to settle the sex question at all fairly, all males must make an imaginative attempt to enter into the attitude of all good women toward these two things. The difficulty exists especially, perhaps, in the thing called thrift; we men have so much encouraged each other in throwing money right and left, that there has come at last to be a sort of chivalrous and poetical air about losing sixpence. But on a broader and more candid consideration the case scarcely stands so.

Thrift is the really romantic thing; economy is more romantic than extravagance. Heaven knows I for one speak disinterestedly in the matter; for I cannot clearly remember saving a half-penny ever since I was born. But the thing is true; economy, properly understood, is the more poetic. Thrift is poetic because it is creative; waste is unpoetic because it is waste. It is prosaic to throw money away, because it is prosaic to throw anything away; it is negative; it is a confession of indifference, that is, it is a confession of failure. The most prosaic thing about the house is the dustbin, and the one great objection to the new fastidious and aesthetic homestead is simply that in such a moral *ménage* the dustbin must be bigger than the house. If a man could undertake to make use of all things in his dustbin he would be a broader genius than Shakespeare. When science began to use by-products; when science found that colors could be made out of coaltar, she made her greatest and perhaps her only claim on the real respect of the human soul. Now the aim of the good woman is to use the by-products, or, in other words, to rummage in the dustbin.

A man can only fully comprehend it if he thinks of some sudden joke or expedient got up with such materials as may be found in a private house on a rainy day. A man's definite daily work is generally run with such rigid convenience of modern science that thrift, the picking up of potential helps here and there, has almost become unmeaning to him. He comes across it most (as I say) when he is playing some game within four walls; when in charades, a hearthrug will just do for a fur coat, or a tea-cozy just do for a cocked hat; when a toy theater needs timber and cardboard, and the house has just enough firewood and just enough bandboxes. This is the man's occasional glimpse and pleasing parody of thrift. But many a good housekeeper plays the same game every day with ends of cheese and scraps of silk, not because she is mean, but on the contrary, because she is magnanimous; because she wishes her creative mercy to be over all her works, that not one sardine should be destroyed, or cast as rubbish to the void, when she has made the pile complete.

The modern world must somehow be made to understand (in theology and other things) that a view may be vast, broad, universal, liberal and yet come into conflict with another view that is vast, broad, universal and liberal also. There is never a war between two sects, but only between two universal Catholic Churches. The only possible collision is the collision of one cosmos with another. So in a smaller way it must be first made clear that this female economic ideal is a part of that female variety of outlook and all-round art of life which we have already attributed to the sex: thrift is not a small or timid or provincial thing; it is part of that great idea of the woman watching on all sides out of all the windows of the soul and being answerable for everything. For in the average human house there is one hole by which money comes in and a hundred by which it goes out; man has to do with the one hole, woman with the hundred. But though the very stinginess of a woman is a part of her spiritual breadth, it is none the less true that it brings her into conflict with the special kind of spiritual breadth that belongs to the males of the tribe. It brings her into conflict with that shapeless cataract of Comradeship, of chaotic feasting and deafening debate, which we noted in the last section. The very touch of the eternal in the two sexual tastes brings them the more into antagonism; for one stands for a universal vigilance and the other for an almost infinite output. Partly through the nature of his moral weakness, and partly through the nature or his physical strength, the male is normally prone to expand things into a sort of eternity; he always thinks of a dinner party as lasting all night; and he always thinks of a night as lasting forever. When the working women in the poor districts come to the doors of the public houses and try to get their husbands home, simple-minded "social workers" always imagine that every husband is a tragic drunkard and every wife a broken-hearted saint. It never occurs to them that the poor woman is only doing under coarser conventions exactly what every fashionable hostess does when she tries to get the men from arguing over the cigars to come and gossip over the teacups. These women are not exasperated merely at the amount of money that is wasted in beer; they are exasperated also at the amount of time that is wasted in talk. It is not merely what goeth into the mouth but what cometh out of the mouth that, in their opinion, defileth a man. They will raise against an argument (like their sisters of all ranks) the ridiculous objection that nobody is convinced by it; as if a man wanted to make a body-slave of anybody with whom he had played single-stick. But the real female prejudice on this point is not without a basis; the real feeling is this, that the most masculine pleasures have a quality of the ephemeral. A duchess may ruin a duke for a diamond necklace; but there is the necklace. A coster may ruin his wife for a pot of beer; and where is the beer? The duchess quarrels with another duchess in order to crush her, to produce a result; the coster does not argue with another coster in order to convince him, but in order to enjoy at once the sound of his own voice, the clearness of his own opinions and the sense of masculine society. There is this element of a fine fruitlessness about the male enjoyments; wine is poured into a bottomless bucket; thought plunges into a bottomless abyss. All this has set woman against the Public House—that is, against the Parliament House. She is there to prevent waste; and the "pub" and the parliament are the very palaces of waste. In the upper classes the "pub" is called the club, but that makes no more difference to the reason than it does to the rhyme. High and low, the woman's objection to the Public House is perfectly definite and rational, it is that the Public House wastes the energies that could be used on the private house.

As it is about feminine thrift against masculine waste, so it is about feminine dignity against masculine rowdiness. The woman has a fixed and very well-founded idea that if she does not insist on good manners nobody else will. Babies are not always strong on the point of dignity, and grown-up men are quite unpresentable. It is true that there are many very polite men, but none that I ever heard of who were not either fascinating women or obeying them. But indeed the female ideal of dignity, like the female ideal of thrift, lies deeper and may easily be misunderstood. It rests ultimately on a strong idea of spiritual isolation; the same that makes women religious. They do not like being melted down; they dislike and avoid the mob. That anonymous quality we have remarked in the club conversation would be common impertinence in a case of ladies. I remember an artistic and eager lady asking me in her grand green drawing-room whether I believed in comradeship between the sexes, and why not. I was driven back on offering the obvious and sincere answer "Because if I were to treat you for two minutes like a comrade you would turn me out of the house." The only certain rule on this subject is always to deal with woman and never with women. "Women" is a profligate word; I have used it repeatedly in this chapter; but it always has a blackguard sound. It smells of oriental cynicism and hedonism. Every woman is a captive queen. But every crowd of women is only a harem broken loose.

I am not expressing my own views here, but those of nearly all the women I have known. It is quite unfair to say that a woman hates other women individually; but I think it would be quite true to say that she detests them in a confused heap. And this is not because she despises her own sex, but because she respects it; and respects especially that sanctity and separation of each item which is represented in manners by the idea of dignity and in morals by the idea of chastity.

V

THE COLDNESS OF CHLOE

We hear much of the human error which accepts what is sham and what is real. But it is worth while to remember that with unfamiliar things we often mistake what is real for what is sham. It is true that a very young man may think the wig of an actress is her hair. But it is equally true that a child yet younger may call the hair of a negro his wig. Just because the woolly savage is remote and barbaric he seems to be unnaturally neat and tidy. Everyone must have noticed the same thing in the fixed and almost offensive color of all unfamiliar things, tropic birds and tropic blossoms. Tropic birds look like staring toys out of a toy-shop. Tropic flowers simply look like artificial flowers, like things cut out of wax. This is a deep matter, and, I think, not unconnected with divinity; but anyhow it is the truth that when we see things for the first time we feel instantly that they are fictive creations; we feel the finger of God. It is only when we are thoroughly used to them and our five wits are wearied, that we see them as wild and objectless; like the shapeless tree-tops or the shifting cloud. It is the design in Nature that strikes us first; the sense of the crosses and confusions in that design only comes afterwards through experience and an almost eerie monotony. If a man saw the stars abruptly by accident he would think them as festive and as artificial as a firework. We talk of the folly of painting the lily; but if we saw the lily without warning we should think that it was painted. We talk of the devil not being so black as he is painted; but that very phrase is a testimony to the kinship between what is called vivid and what is called artificial. If the modern sage had only one glimpse of grass and sky, he would say that grass was not as green as it was painted; that sky was not as blue as it was painted. If one could see the whole universe suddenly, it would look like a bright-colored toy, just as the South American hornbill looks like a bright-colored toy. And so they are—both of them, I mean.

But it was not with this aspect of the startling air of artifice about all strange objects that I meant to deal. I mean merely, as a guide to history, that we should not be surprised if things wrought in fashions remote from ours seem artificial; we should convince ourselves that nine times out of ten these things are nakedly and almost indecently honest. You will hear men talk of the frosted classicism of Corneille or of the powdered pomposities of the eighteenth century, but all these phrases are very superficial. There never was an artificial epoch. There never was an age of reason. Men were always men and women women: and their two generous appetites always were the expression of passion and the telling of truth. We can see something stiff and quaint in their mode of expression, just as our descendants will see something stiff and quaint in our coarsest slum sketch or our most naked pathological play. But men have never talked about anything but important things; and the next force in femininity which we have to consider can be considered best perhaps in some dusty old volume of verses by a person of quality.

The eighteenth century is spoken of as the period of artificiality, in externals at least; but, indeed, there may be two words about that. In modern speech one uses artificiality as meaning indefinitely a sort of deceit; and the eighteenth century was far too artificial to deceive. It cultivated that completest art that does not conceal the art. Its fashions and costumes positively revealed nature by avowing artifice; as in that obvious instance of a barbering that frosted every head with the same silver. It would be fantastic to call this a quaint humility that concealed youth; but, at least, it was not one with the evil pride that conceals old age. Under the eighteenth century fashion people did not so much all pretend to be young, as all agree to be old. The same applies to the most odd and unnatural of their fashions; they were freakish, but they were not false. A lady may or may not be as red as she is painted, but plainly she was not so black as she was patched.

But I only introduce the reader into this atmosphere of the older and franker fictions that he may be induced to have patience for a moment with a certain element which is very common in the decoration and literature of that age and of the two centuries preceding it. It is necessary to mention it in such a connection because it is exactly one of those things that look as superficial as powder, and are really as rooted as hair.

In all the old flowery and pastoral love-songs, those of the seventeenth and eighteenth centuries especially, you will find a perpetual reproach against woman in the matter of her coldness; ceaseless and stale similes that compare her eyes to northern stars, her heart to ice, or her bosom to snow. Now most of us have always supposed these old and iterant phrases to be a mere pattern of dead words, a thing like a cold wall-paper. Yet I think those old cavalier poets who wrote about the coldness of Chloe had hold of a psychological truth missed in nearly all the realistic novels of today. Our psychological romancers perpetually represent wives as striking terror into their husbands by rolling on the floor, gnashing their teeth, throwing about the furniture or poisoning the coffee; all this upon some strange fixed theory that women are what they call emotional. But in truth the old and frigid form is much nearer to the vital fact. Most men if they spoke with any sincerity would agree that the most terrible quality in women, whether in friendship, courtship or marriage, was not so much being emotional as being unemotional.

There is an awful armor of ice which may be the legitimate protection of a more delicate organism; but whatever be the psychological explanation there can surely be no question of the fact. The instinctive cry of the female in anger is *noli me tangere*. I take this as the most obvious and at the same time the least hackneyed instance of a fundamental quality in the female tradition, which has tended in our time to be almost immeasurably misunderstood, both by the cant of moralists and the cant of immoralists. The proper name for the thing is modesty; but as we live in an age of prejudice and must not call things by their right names, we will yield to a more modern nomenclature and call it dignity. Whatever else it is, it is the thing which a thousand poets and a million lovers have called the coldness of Chloe. It is akin to the classical, and is at least the opposite of the grotesque. And since we are talking here chiefly in types and symbols, perhaps as good an embodiment as any of the idea may be found in the mere fact of a woman wearing a skirt. It is highly typical of the rabid plagiarism which now passes everywhere for emancipation, that a little while ago it was common for an "advanced" woman to claim the right to wear trousers; a right about as grotesque as the right to wear a false nose. Whether female liberty is much advanced by the act of wearing a skirt on each leg I do not know; perhaps Turkish women might offer some information on the point. But if the western woman walks about (as it were) trailing the curtains of the harem with her, it is quite certain that the woven mansion is meant for a perambulating palace, not for a perambulating prison. It is quite certain that the skirt means female dignity, not female submission; it can be proved by the simplest of all tests. No ruler would deliberately dress up in the recognized fetters of a slave; no judge would appear covered with broad arrows. But when men wish to be safely impressive, as judges, priests or kings, they do wear skirts, the long, trailing robes of female dignity. The whole world is under petticoat government; for even men wear petticoats when they wish to govern.

VI

THE PEDANT AND THE SAVAGE

We say then that the female holds up with two strong arms these two pillars of civilization; we say also that she could do neither, but for her position; her curious position of private omnipotence, universality on a small scale. The first element is thrift; not the destructive thrift of the miser, but the creative thrift of the peasant; the second element is dignity, which is but the expression of sacred personality and privacy. Now I know the question that will be abruptly and automatically asked by all that know the dull tricks and turns of the modern sexual quarrel. The advanced person will at once begin to argue about whether these instincts are inherent and inevitable in woman or whether they are merely prejudices produced by her history and education. Now I do not propose to discuss whether woman could now be educated out of her habits touching thrift and dignity; and that for two excellent reasons. First it is a question which cannot conceivably ever find any answer: that is why modern people are so fond of it. From the nature of the case it is obviously impossible to decide whether any of the peculiarities of civilized man have been strictly necessary to his civilization. It is not self-evident (for instance), that even the habit of standing upright was the only path of human progress. There might have been a quadrupedal civilization, in which a city gentleman put on four boots to go to the city every morning. Or there might have been a reptilian civilization, in which he rolled up to the office on his stomach; it is impossible to say that intelligence might not have developed in such creatures. All we can say is that man as he is walks upright; and that woman is something almost more upright than uprightness.

And the second point is this: that upon the whole we rather prefer women (nay, even men) to walk upright; so we do not waste much of our noble lives in inventing any other way for them to walk. In short, my second reason for not speculating upon whether woman might get rid of these peculiarities, is that I do not want her to get rid of them; nor does she. I will not exhaust my intelligence by inventing ways in which mankind might unlearn the violin or forget how to ride horses; and the art of domesticity seems to me as special and as valuable as all the ancient arts of our race. Nor do I propose to enter at all into those formless and floundering speculations about how woman was or is regarded in the primitive times that we cannot remember, or in the savage countries which we cannot understand. Even if these people segregated their women for low or barbaric reasons it would not make our reasons barbaric; and I am haunted with a tenacious suspicion that these people's feelings were really, under other forms, very much the same as ours. Some impatient trader, some superficial missionary, walks across an island and sees the squaw digging in the fields while the man is playing a flute; and immediately says that the man is a mere lord of creation and the woman a mere serf. He does not remember that he might see the same thing in half the back gardens in Brixton, merely because women are at once more conscientious and more impatient, while men are at once more quiescent and more greedy for pleasure. It may often be in Hawaii simply as it is in Hoxton. That is, the woman does not work because the man tells her to work and she obeys. On the contrary, the woman works because she has told the man to work and he hasn't obeyed. I do not affirm that this is the whole truth, but I do affirm that we have too little comprehension of the souls of savages to know how far it is untrue. It is the same with the relations of our hasty and surface science, with the problem of sexual dignity and modesty. Professors find all over the world fragmentary ceremonies in which the bride affects some sort of reluctance, hides from her husband, or runs away from him. The professor then pompously proclaims that this is a survival of Marriage by Capture. I wonder he never says that the veil thrown over the bride is really a net. I gravely doubt whether women ever were married by capture. I think they pretended to be; as they do still.

It is equally obvious that these two necessary sanctities of thrift and dignity are bound to come into collision with the wordiness, the wastefulness, and the perpetual pleasure-seeking of masculine companionship. Wise women allow for the thing; foolish women try to crush it; but all women try to counteract it, and they do well. In many a home all round us at this moment, we know that the nursery rhyme is reversed. The queen is in the counting-house, counting out the money. The king is in the parlor, eating bread and honey. But it must be strictly understood that the king has captured the honey in some heroic wars. The quarrel can be found in moldering Gothic carvings and in crabbed Greek manuscripts. In every age, in every land, in every tribe and village, has been waged the great sexual war between the Private House and the Public House. I have seen a collection of mediaeval English poems, divided into sections such as "Religious Carols," "Drinking Songs," and so on; and the section headed, "Poems of Domestic Life" consisted entirely (literally, entirely) of the complaints of husbands who were bullied by their wives. Though the English was archaic, the words were in many cases precisely the same as those which I have heard in the streets and public houses of Battersea, protests on behalf of an extension of time and talk, protests against the nervous impatience and the devouring utilitarianism of the female. Such, I say, is the quarrel; it can never be anything but a quarrel; but the aim of all morals and all society is to keep it a lovers' quarrel.

VII

THE MODERN SURRENDER OF WOMAN

But in this corner called England, at this end of the century, there
has happened a strange and startling thing. Openly and to all appearance, this ancestral conflict has silently and abruptly ended; one of
the two sexes has suddenly surrendered to the other. By the beginning
of the twentieth century, within the last few years, the woman has in
public surrendered to the man. She has seriously and officially owned
that the man has been right all along; that the public house (or Parliament) is really more important than the private house; that politics are
not (as woman had always maintained) an excuse for pots of beer, but
are a sacred solemnity to which new female worshipers may kneel;
that the talkative patriots in the tavern are not only admirable but enviable; that talk is not a waste of time, and therefore (as a consequence, surely) that taverns are not a waste of money. All we men had
grown used to our wives and mothers, and grandmothers, and great
aunts all pouring a chorus of contempt upon our hobbies of sport,
drink and party politics. And now comes Miss Pankhurst[1] with tears
in her eyes, owning that all the women were wrong and all the men
were right; humbly imploring to be admitted into so much as an
outer court, from which she may catch a glimpse of those masculine
merits which her erring sisters had so thoughtlessly scorned.

Now this development naturally perturbs and even paralyzes us.
Males, like females, in the course of that old fight between the public and private house, had indulged in overstatement and extravagance, feeling that they must keep up their end of the see-saw.
We told our wives that Parliament had sat late on most essential
business; but it never crossed our minds that our wives would
believe it. We said that everyone must have a vote in the country;
similarly our wives said that no one must have a pipe in the drawing-
room. In both cases the idea was the same. "It does not matter much,
but if you let those things slide there is chaos." We said that Lord

[1] Emmeline Pankhurst (1858–1928), English suffragist leader.

Huggins or Mr. Buggins was absolutely necessary to the country. We knew quite well that nothing is necessary to the country except that the men should be men and the women women. We knew this; we thought the women knew it even more clearly; and we thought the women would say it. Suddenly, without warning, the women have begun to say all the nonsense that we ourselves hardly believed when we said it. The solemnity of politics; the necessity of votes; the necessity of Huggins; the necessity of Buggins; all these flow in a pellucid stream from the lips of all the suffragette speakers. I suppose in every fight, however old, one has a vague aspiration to conquer; but we never wanted to conquer women so completely as this. We only expected that they might leave us a little more margin for our nonsense; we never expected that they would accept it seriously as sense. Therefore I am all at sea about the existing situation; I scarcely know whether to be relieved or enraged by this substitution of the feeble platform lecture for the forcible curtain-lecture. I am lost without the trenchant and candid Mrs. Caudle.[2] I really do not know what to do with the prostrate and penitent Miss Pankhurst. This surrender of the modern woman has taken us all so much by surprise that it is desirable to pause a moment, and collect our wits about what she is really saying.

As I have already remarked, there is one very simple answer to all this; these are not the modern women, but about one in two thousand of the modern women. This fact is important to a democrat; but it is of very little importance to the typically modern mind. Both the characteristic modern parties believed in a government by the few; the only difference is whether it is the Conservative few or Progressive few. It might be put, somewhat coarsely perhaps, by saying that one believes in any minority that is rich and the other in any minority that is mad. But in this state of things the democratic argument obviously falls out for the moment; and we are bound to take the prominent minority, merely because it is prominent. Let us

[2] Mrs. Caudle's Curtain Lectures were a series of sketches written by Douglas Jerrold that appeared in *Punch* (1845). The sketches consisted of discourses on domestic subjects that Mrs. Caudle inflicted upon Mr. Caudle after they had gone to bed and the curtains had been drawn for the night.

eliminate altogether from our minds the thousands of women who detest this cause, and the millions of women who have hardly heard of it. Let us concede that the English people itself is not and will not be for a very long time within the sphere of practical politics. Let us confine ourselves to saying that these particular women want a vote and to asking themselves what a vote is. If we ask these ladies ourselves what a vote is, we shall get a very vague reply. It is the only question, as a rule, for which they are not prepared. For the truth is that they go mainly by precedent; by the mere fact that men have votes already. So far from being a mutinous movement, it is really a very Conservative one; it is in the narrowest rut of the British Constitution. Let us take a little wider and freer sweep of thought and ask ourselves what is the ultimate point and meaning of this odd business called voting.

VIII

THE BRAND OF THE FLEUR-DE-LIS

Seemingly from the dawn of man all nations have had governments; and all nations have been ashamed of them. Nothing is more openly fallacious than to fancy that in ruder or simpler ages ruling, judging and punishing appeared perfectly innocent and dignified. These things were always regarded as the penalties of the Fall; as part of the humiliation of mankind, as bad in themselves. That the king can do no wrong was never anything but a legal fiction; and it is a legal fiction still. The doctrine of Divine Right was not a piece of idealism, but rather a piece of realism, a practical way of ruling amid the ruin of humanity; a very pragmatist piece of faith. The religious basis of government was not so much that people put their trust in princes, as that they did not put their trust in any child of man. It was so with all the ugly institutions which disfigure human history. Torture and slavery were never talked of as good things; they were always talked of as necessary evils. A pagan spoke of one man owning ten slaves just as a modern business man speaks of one merchant sacking ten clerks: "It's very horrible; but how else can society be conducted?" A mediaeval scholastic regarded the possibility of a man being burned to death just as a modern business man regards the possibility of a man being starved to death: "It is a shocking torture; but can you organize a painless world?" It is possible that a future society may find a way of doing without the question by hunger as we have done without the question by fire. It is equally possible, for the matter of that, that a future society may reestablish legal torture with the whole apparatus of rack and fagot. The most modern of countries, America, has introduced with a vague savor of science, a method which it calls "the third degree." This is simply the extortion of secrets by nervous fatigue; which is surely uncommonly close to their extortion by bodily pain. And this is legal and scientific America. Amateur ordinary America, of course, simply burns people alive in broad daylight, as they did in the Reformation Wars.

But though some punishments are more inhuman than others there is no such thing as humane punishment. As long as nineteen men claim the right in any sense or shape to take hold of the twentieth man and make him even mildly uncomfortable, so long the whole proceeding must be a humiliating one for all concerned. And the proof of how poignantly men have always felt this lies in the fact that the headsman and the hangman, the jailors and the torturers, were always regarded not merely with fear but with contempt; while all kinds of careless smiters, bankrupt knights and swashbucklers and outlaws, were regarded with indulgence or even admiration. To kill a man lawlessly was pardoned. To kill a man lawfully was unpardonable. The most bare-faced duelist might almost brandish his weapon. But the executioner was always masked.

This is the first essential element in government; coercion; a necessary but not a noble element. I may remark in passing that when people say that government rests on force they give an admirable instance of the foggy and muddled cynicism of modernity. Government does not rest on force. Government is force; it rests on consent or a conception of justice. A king or a community holding a certain thing to be abnormal, evil, uses the general strength to crush it out; the strength is his tool, but the belief is his only sanction. You might as well say that glass is the real reason for telescopes. But arising from whatever reason the act of government is coercive and is burdened with all the coarse and painful qualities of coercion. And if anyone asks what is the use of insisting on the ugliness of this task of state violence since all mankind is condemned to employ it, I have a simple answer to that. It would be useless to insist on it if all humanity were condemned to it. But it is not irrelevant to insist on its ugliness so long as half of humanity is kept out of it.

All government then is coercive; we happen to have created a government which is not only coercive; but collective. There are only two kinds of government, as I have already said, the despotic and the democratic. Aristocracy is not a government, it is a riot; that most effective kind of riot, a riot of the rich. The most intelligent apologists of aristocracy, sophists like Burke and Nietzsche, have never claimed for aristocracy any virtues but the virtues of a riot, the accidental virtues, courage, variety and adventure. There is no case anywhere of aristocracy having established a universal and applicable order, as despots and democracies have often done; as the last Caesars created the Roman law, as the last Jacobins created the Code Napoleon. With the first of these elementary forms of government, that of the king or chieftain, we are not in this matter of the sexes immediately concerned. We shall return to it later when we remark how differently mankind has dealt with female claims in the despotic as against the democratic field. But for the moment the essential point is that in self-governing countries this coercion of criminals is a collective coercion. The abnormal person is theoretically thumped by a million fists and kicked by a million feet. If a man is flogged we all flogged him; if a man is hanged, we all hanged him. That is the only possible meaning of democracy, which can give any meaning to the first two syllables and also to the last two. In this sense each citizen has the high responsibility of a rioter. Every statute is a declaration of war, to be backed by arms. Every tribunal is a revolutionary tribunal. In a republic all punishment is as sacred and solemn as lynching.

IX

SINCERITY AND THE GALLOWS

When, therefore, it is said that the tradition against Female Suffrage keeps women out of activity, social influence and citizenship, let us a little more soberly and strictly ask ourselves what it actually does keep her out of. It does definitely keep her out of the collective act of coercion; the act of punishment by a mob. The human tradition does say that, if twenty men hang a man from a tree or a lamp-post, they shall be twenty men and not women. Now I do not think any reasonable Suffragist will deny that exclusion from this function, to say the least of it, might be maintained to be a protection as well as a veto. No candid person will wholly dismiss the proposition that the idea of having a Lord Chancellor but not a Lady Chancellor may at least be connected with the idea of having a headsman but not a headswoman, a hangman but not a hangwoman. Nor will it be adequate to answer (as is so often answered to this contention) that in modern civilization women would not really be required to capture, to sentence, or to slay; that all this is done indirectly, that specialists kill our criminals as they kill our cattle. To urge this is not to urge the reality of the vote, but to urge its unreality. Democracy was meant to be a more direct way of ruling, not a more indirect way; and if we do not feel that we are all jailers, so much the worse for us, and for the prisoners. If it is really an unwomanly thing to lock up a robber or a tyrant, it ought to be no softening of the situation that the woman does not feel as if she were doing the thing that she certainly is doing. It is bad enough that men can only associate on paper who could once associate in the street; it is bad enough that men have made a vote very much of a fiction. It is much worse that a great class should claim the vote because it is a fiction, who would be sickened by it if it were a fact. If votes for women do not mean mobs for women they do not mean what they were meant to mean. A woman can make a cross on a paper as well as a man; a child could do it as well as a woman; and a chimpanzee after a few lessons could do it as well as a child. But no-body ought to regard it merely as making a cross on paper; everyone ought to regard it as what it ultimately is, branding the fleur-de-lis, marking the broad arrow, signing the death warrant. Both men and women ought to face more fully the things they do or cause to be done; face them or leave off doing them.

On that disastrous day when public executions were abolished, private executions were renewed and ratified, perhaps forever. Things grossly unsuited to the moral sentiment of a society cannot be safely done in broad daylight; but I see no reason why we should not still be roasting heretics alive, in a private room. It is very likely (to speak in the manner foolishly called Irish) that if there were pub-lic executions there would be no executions. The old open-air punishments, the pillory and the gibbet, at least fixed responsibility upon the law; and in actual practice they gave the mob an oppor-tunity of throwing roses as well as rotten eggs; of crying "Hosan-nah" as well as "Crucify." But I do not like the public executioner being turned into the private executioner. I think it is a crooked ori-ental, sinister sort of business, and smells of the harem and the divan rather than of the forum and the market place. In modern times the official has lost all the social honor and dignity of the common hangman. He is only the bearer of the bowstring.

Here, however, I suggest a plea for a brutal publicity only in order to emphasize the fact that it is this brutal publicity and nothing else from which women have been excluded. I also say it to emphasize the fact that the mere modern veiling of the brutality does not make the situation different, unless we openly say that we are giving the suffrage, not because it is power but because it is not; or in other words, that women are not so much to vote as to play voting. No suffragist, I suppose, will take up that position; and a few suf-fragists will wholly deny that this human necessity of pains and penalties is an ugly, humiliating business, and that good motives as well as bad may have helped to keep women out of it. More than once I have remarked in these pages that female limitations may be the limits of a temple as well as of a prison, the disabilities of a priest and not of a pariah. I noted it, I think, in the case of the pontifical feminine dress. In the same way it is not evidently irrational, if men decided that a woman, like a priest, must not be a shedder of blood.

X

THE HIGHER ANARCHY

But there is a further fact; forgotten also because we moderns forget that there is a female point of view. The woman's wisdom stands partly, not only for a wholesome hesitation about punishment, but even for a wholesome hesitation about absolute rules. There was something feminine and perversely true in that phrase of Wilde's, that people should not be treated as the rule, but all of them as exceptions. Made by a man the remark was a little effeminate; for Wilde did lack the masculine power of dogma and of democratic cooperation. But if a woman had said it it would have been simply true; a woman does treat each person as a peculiar person. In other words, she stands for Anarchy; a very ancient and arguable philosophy; not anarchy in the sense of having no customs in one's life (which is inconceivable), but anarchy in the sense of having no rules for one's mind. To her, almost certainly, are due all those working traditions that cannot be found in books, especially those of education; it was she who first gave a child a stuffed stocking for being good or stood him in the corner for being naughty. This unclassified knowledge is sometimes called rule of thumb and sometimes motherwit. The last phrase suggests the whole truth, for none ever called it fatherwit.

Now anarchy is only tact when it works badly. Tact is only anarchy when it works well. And we ought to realize that in one half of the world—the private house—it does work well. We modern men are perpetually forgetting that the case for clear rules and crude penalties is not self-evident, that there is a great deal to be said for the benevolent lawlessness of the autocrat, especially on a small scale; in short, that government is only one side of life. The other half is called Society, in which women are admittedly dominant. And they have always been ready to maintain that their kingdom is better governed than ours, because (in the logical and legal sense) it is not governed at all. "Whenever you have a real difficulty," they say, "when a boy is bumptious or an aunt is stingy, when a silly girl will marry somebody, or a wicked man won't marry somebody, all your lumbering Roman Law and British Constitution come to a standstill. A snub from a duchess or a slanging from a fish-wife are much more likely to put things straight." So, at least, rang the ancient female challenge down the ages until the recent female capitulation. So streamed the red standard of the higher anarchy until Miss Pankhurst hoisted the white flag.

It must be remembered that the modern world has done deep treason to the eternal intellect by believing in the swing of the pendulum. A man must be dead before he swings. It has substituted an idea of fatalistic alternation for the mediaeval freedom of the soul seeking truth. All modern thinkers are reactionaries; for their thought is always a reaction from what went before. When you meet a modern man he is always coming from a place, not going to it. Thus, mankind has in nearly all places and periods seen that there is a soul and a body as plainly as that there is a sun and moon. But because a narrow Protestant sect called Materialists declared for a short time that there was no soul, another narrow Protestant sect called Christian Science is now maintaining that there is no body. Now just in the same way the unreasonable neglect of government by the Manchester School has produced, not a reasonable regard for government, but an unreasonable neglect of everything else. So that to hear people talk to-day one would fancy that every important human function must be organized and avenged by law; that all education must be state education, and all employment state employment; that everybody and everything must be brought to the foot of the august and prehistoric gibbet. But a somewhat more liberal and sympathetic examination of mankind will convince us that the cross is even older than the gibbet, that voluntary suffering was before and independent of compulsory; and in short that in most important matters a man has always been free to ruin himself if he chose. The huge fundamental function upon which all anthropology turns, that of sex and childbirth, has never been inside the political state, but always outside of it. The state concerned itself with the trivial question of killing people, but wisely left alone the whole business of getting them born. A Eugenist might indeed plausibly say that the government is an absent-minded and inconsistent person who occupies himself with providing for the old age of people who have never been infants. I will not deal here in any detail with the fact that some Eugenists have in our time made the maniacal answer that the police ought to control marriage and birth as they control labor and death. Except for this inhuman handful (with whom I regret to say I shall have to deal with later) all the Eugenists I know divide themselves into two sections: ingenious people who once meant this, and rather bewildered people who swear they never meant it—nor anything else. But if it be conceded (by a breezier estimate of men) that they do mostly desire marriage to remain free from government, it does not follow that they desire it to remain free from everything. If man does not control the marriage market by law, is it controlled at all? Surely the answer is broadly that man does not control the marriage market by law, but the woman does control it by sympathy and prejudice. There was until lately a law forbidding a man to marry his deceased wife's sister; yet the thing happened constantly. There was no law forbidding a man to marry his deceased wife's scullery-maid; yet it did not happen nearly so often. It did not happen because the marriage market is managed in the spirit and by the authority of women; and women are generally conservative where classes are concerned. It is the same with that system of exclusiveness by which ladies have so often contrived (as by a process of elimination) to prevent marriages that they did not want and even sometimes procure those they did. There is no need of the broad arrow and the fleur-de-lis, the turnkey's chains or the hangman's halter. You need not strangle a man if you can silence him. The branded shoulder is less effective and final than the cold shoulder; and you need not trouble to lock a man in when you can lock him out.

The same, of course, is true of the colossal architecture which we call infant education: an architecture reared wholly by women. Nothing can ever overcome that one enormous sex superiority, that even the male child is born closer to his mother than to his father. No one, staring at that frightful female privilege, can quite believe in the equality of the sexes. Here and there we read of a girl brought up like a tom-boy; but every boy is brought up like a tame girl. The flesh and spirit of femininity surround him from the first like the four walls of a house; and even the vaguest or most brutal man has been womanized by being born. Man that is born of a woman has short days and full of misery; but nobody can picture the obscenity and bestial tragedy that would belong to such a monster as man that was born of a man.

XI

THE QUEEN AND THE SUFFRAGETTES

But, indeed, with this educational matter I must of necessity em-
broil myself later. The fourth section of discussion is supposed to be
about the child, but I think it will be mostly about the mother. In
this place I have systematically insisted on the large part of life that is
governed, not by man with his vote, but by woman with her voice,
or more often, with her horrible silence. Only one thing remains to
be added. In a sprawling and explanatory style has been traced out
the idea that government is ultimately coercion, that coercion must
mean cold definitions as well as cruel consequences, and that
therefore there is something to be said for the old human habit of
keeping one-half of humanity out of so harsh and dirty a business.
But the case is stronger still.

Voting is not only coercion, but collective coercion. I think
Queen Victoria would have been yet more popular and satisfying if
she had never signed a death warrant. I think Queen Elizabeth
would have stood out as more solid and splendid in history if she had
not earned (among those who happen to know her history) the nick-
name of Bloody Bess. I think, in short, that the great historic
woman is more herself when she is persuasive rather than coercive.
But I feel all mankind behind me when I say that if a woman has this
power it should be despotic power—not democratic power. There is
a much stronger historic argument for giving Miss Pankhurst a
throne than for giving her a vote. She might have a crown, or at
least a coronet, like so many of her supporters; for these old powers
are purely personal and therefore female. Miss Pankhurst as a despot
might be as virtuous as Queen Victoria, and she certainly would find
it difficult to be as wicked as Queen Bess; but the point is that, good
or bad, she would be irresponsible—she would not be governed by a
rule and by a ruler. There are only two ways of governing: by a rule
and by a ruler. And it is seriously true to say of a woman, in education and domesticity, that the freedom of the autocrat appears to be

necessary to her. She is never responsible until she is irresponsible. In case this sounds like an idle contradiction, I confidently appeal to the cold facts of history. Almost every despotic or oligarchic state has admitted women to its privileges. Scarcely one democratic state has ever admitted them to its rights. The reason is very simple: that something female is endangered much more by the violence of the crowd. In short, one Pankhurst is an exception, but a thousand Pankhursts are a nightmare, a Bacchic orgie, a Witches Sabbath. For in all legends men have thought of women as sublime separately but horrible in a herd.

XII

THE MODERN SLAVE

Now I have only taken the test case of Female Suffrage because it is topical and concrete; it is not of great moment for me as a political proposal. I can quite imagine anyone substantially agreeing with my view of woman as universalist and autocrat in a limited area; and still thinking that she would be none the worse for a ballot paper. The real question is whether this old ideal of woman as the great amateur is admitted or not. There are many modern things which threaten it much more than suffragism; notably the increase of self-supporting women, even in the most severe or the most squalid employments. If there be something against nature in the idea of a horde of wild women governing, there is something truly intolerable in the idea of a herd of tame women being governed. And there are elements in human psychology that make this situation particularly poignant or ignominious. The ugly exactitudes of business, the bells and clocks the fixed hours and rigid departments, were all meant for the male: who, as a rule, can only do one thing and can only with the greatest difficulty be induced to do that. If clerks do not try to shirk their work, our whole great commercial system breaks down. It *is* breaking down, under the inroad of women who are adopting the un- precedented and impossible course of taking the system seriously and doing it well. Their very efficiency is the definition of their slavery. It is generally a very bad sign when one is trusted very much by one's employers. And if the evasive clerks have a look of being blackguards, the earnest ladies are often something very like blacklegs. But the more immediate point is that the modern work- ing woman bears a double burden, for she endures both the grinding officialism of the new office and the distracting scrupulosity of the old home. Few men understand what conscientiousness is. They understand duty, which generally means one duty; but conscien- tiousness is the duty of the universalist. It is limited by no work days or holidays; it is a lawless, limitless, devouring decorum. If women are to be subjected to the dull rule of commerce, we must find some way of emancipating them from the wild rule of conscience. But I rather fancy you will find it easier to leave the conscience and knock off the commerce. As it is, the modern clerk or secretary exhausts herself to put one thing straight in the ledger and then goes home to put everything straight in the house.

This condition (described by some as emancipated) is at least the reverse of my ideal. I would give woman, not more rights, but more privileges. Instead of sending her to seek such freedom as notoriously prevails in banks and factories, I would design specially a house in which she can be free. And with that we come to the last point of all; the point at which we can perceive the needs of women, like the rights of men, stopped and falsified by something which it is the object of this book to expose.

The Feminist (which means, I think, one who dislikes the chief feminine characteristics) has heard my loose monologue, bursting all the time with one pent-up protest. At this point he will break out and say, "But what are we to do? There is modern commerce and its clerks; there is the modern family with its unmarried daughters; specialism is expected everywhere; female thrift and conscientiousness are demanded and supplied. What does it matter whether we should in the abstract prefer the old human and housekeeping woman; we might prefer the Garden of Eden. But since women have trades they ought to have trades unions. Since women work in factories, they ought to vote on factory-acts. If they are unmarried they must be commercial; if they are commercial they must be political. We must have new rules for a new world—even if it be not a better one." I said to a Feminist once: "The question is not whether women are good enough for votes: it is whether votes are good enough for women." He only answered: "Ah, you go and say that to the women chain-makers on Cradley Heath."

Now this is the attitude which I attack. It is the huge heresy of Precedent. It is the view that because we have got into a mess we must grow messier to suit it; that because we have taken a wrong turn some time ago we must go forward and not backwards; that because we have lost our way we must lose our map also; and because we have missed our ideal, we must forget it. There are numbers of excellent people who do not think votes unfeminine; and there may be enthusiasts for our beautiful modern industry who do not think factories unfeminine. But if these things are unfeminine it is no answer to say that they fit into each other. I am not satisfied with the statement that my daughter must have unwomanly powers because she has unwomanly wrongs. Industrial soot and political printer's ink are two blacks which do not make a white. Most of the Feminists would probably agree with me that womanhood is under shameful tyranny in the shops and mills. But I want to destroy the tyranny. They want to destroy womanhood. That is the only difference.

Whether we can recover the clear vision of woman as a tower with many windows, the fixed eternal feminine from which her sons, the specialists, go forth; whether we can preserve the tradition of a central thing which is even more human than democracy and even more practical than politics; whether, in a word, it is possible to re-establish the family, freed from the filthy cynicism and cruelty of the commercial epoch, I shall discuss in the last section of this book. But meanwhile do not talk to me about the poor chain-makers on Cradley Heath. I know all about them and what they are doing. They are engaged in a very wide-spread and flourishing industry of the present age. They are making chains.

PART FOUR

EDUCATION: OR THE MISTAKE ABOUT THE CHILD

I

THE CALVINISM OF TO-DAY

When I wrote a little volume on my friend Mr. Bernard Shaw, it is needless to say that he reviewed it. I naturally felt tempted to answer and to criticise the book from the same disinterested and impartial standpoint from which Mr. Shaw had criticised the subject of it. I was not withheld by any feeling that the joke was getting a little obvious; for an obvious joke is only a successful joke; it is only the unsuccessful clowns who comfort themselves with being subtle. The real reason why I did not answer Mr. Shaw's amusing attack was this: that one simple phrase in it surrendered to me all that I have ever wanted, or could want from him to all eternity. I told Mr. Shaw (in substance) that he was a charming and clever fellow, but a common Calvinist. He admitted that this was true; and there (so far as I am concerned) is an end of the matter. He said that, of course, Calvin was quite right in holding that "if once a man is born it is too late to damn or save him." That is the fundamental and subterranean secret; that is the last lie in hell.

The difference between Puritanism and Catholicism is not about whether some priestly word or gesture is significant and sacred. It is about whether any word or gesture is significant and sacred. To the Catholic every other daily act is a dramatic dedication to the service of good or of evil. To the Calvinist no act can have that sort of solemnity, because the person doing it has been dedicated from eternity, and is merely filling up his time until the crack of doom. The difference is something subtler than plum-puddings or private theatricals; the difference is that to a Christian of my kind this short earthly life is intensely thrilling and precious; to a Calvinist like Mr. Shaw it is confessedly automatic and uninteresting. To me these threescore years and ten are the battle. To the Fabian[1] Calvinist (by his own confession) they are only a long procession of the victors in laurels and the vanquished in chains. To me earthly life is the drama;

[1] A reference to the British Fabian Society, which sought to find a gradual way to socialism.

to him it is the epilogue. Shavians think about the embryo; Spir-
itualists about the ghost; Christians about the man. It is as well to
have these things clear.

Now all our sociology and eugenics and the rest of it are not so
much materialist as confusedly Calvinist; they are chiefly occupied in
educating the child before he exists. The whole movement is full of a
singular depression about what one can do with the populace, combined with a strange disembodied gayety about what may be done
with posterity. These essential Calvinists have, indeed, abolished
some of the more liberal and universal parts of Calvinism, such as
the belief in an intellectual design or an everlasting happiness. But
though Mr. Shaw and his friends admit it is a superstition that a man
is judged after death, they stick to their central doctrine, that he is
judged before he is born.

In consequence of this atmosphere of Calvinism in the cultured
world of to-day, it is apparently necessary to begin all arguments on
education with some mention of obstetrics and the unknown world
of the prenatal. All I shall have to say, however, on heredity will be
very brief, because I shall confine myself to what is known about it,
and that is very nearly nothing. It is by no means self-evident, but it
is a current modern dogma, that nothing actually enters the body at
birth except a life derived and compounded from the parents. There
is at least quite as much to be said for the Christian theory that an
element comes from God, or the Buddhist theory that such an element comes from previous existences. But this is not a religious
work, and I must submit to those very narrow intellectual limits
which the absence of theology always imposes. Leaving the soul on
one side, let us suppose for the sake of argument that the human
character in the first case comes wholly from parents; and then let us
curtly state our knowledge rather than our ignorance.

II

THE TRIBAL TERROR

Popular science, like that of Mr. Blatchford,[1] is in this matter as mild as old wives' tales. Mr. Blatchford, with colossal simplicity, explained to millions of clerks and workingmen that the mother is like a bottle of blue beads and the father is like a bottle of yellow beads; and so the child is like a bottle of mixed blue beads and yellow. He might just as well have said that if the father has two legs and the mother has two legs, the child will have four legs. Obviously it is not a question of simple addition or simple division of a number of hard detached "qualities," like beads. It is an organic crisis and transformation of the most mysterious sort; so that even if the result is unavoidable, it will still be unexpected. It is not like blue beads mixed with yellow beads; it is like blue mixed with yellow; the result of which is *green*, a totally novel and unique experience, a new emotion. A man might live in a complete cosmos of blue and yellow, like the "Edinburgh Review"[2]; a man might never have seen anything but a golden cornfield and a sapphire sky; and still he might never have had so wild a fancy as green. If you paid a sovereign for a bluebell; if you spilled the mustard on the blue-books; if you married a canary to a blue baboon; there is nothing in any of these wild weddings that contains even a hint of green. Green is not a mental combination, like addition; it is a physical result like birth. So, apart from the fact that nobody ever really understands parents or children either, yet even if we could understand the parents, we could not make any conjecture about the children. Each time the force works in a different way; each time the constituent colors combine into a different spectacle. A girl may actually inherit her ugliness from her mother's good looks. A boy may actually get his weakness from his father's strength. Even if we admit it is really a fate, for us it must remain a fairy tale. Considered in

[1] Robert Blatchford (1851–1943), Editor of *The Clarion*, English writer.
[2] An outstanding quarterly magazine founded at Edinburgh in 1802; it was originally published in the buff and blue colors of the Whig party.

regard to its causes, the Calvinists and materialists may be right or wrong; we leave them their dreary debate. But considered in regard to its results there is no doubt about it. The thing is always a new color; a strange star. Every birth is as lonely as a miracle. Every child is as uninvited as a monstrosity.

On all such subjects there is no science, but only a sort of ardent ignorance; and nobody has ever been able to offer any theories of moral heredity which justified themselves in the only scientific sense; that is that one could calculate on them beforehand. There are six cases, say, of a grandson having the same twitch of mouth or vice of character as his grandfather; or perhaps there are sixteen cases, or perhaps sixty. But there are not two cases, there is not one case, there are no cases at all, of anybody betting half a crown that the grandfather will have a grandson with the twitch or the vice. In short, we deal with heredity as we deal with omens, affinities and the fulfillment of dreams. The things do happen, and when they happen we record them; but not even a lunatic ever reckons on them. Indeed, heredity, like dreams and omens, is a barbaric notion; that is, not necessarily an untrue, but a dim, groping and unsystematized notion. A civilized man feels himself a little more free from his family. Before Christianity these tales of tribal doom occupied the savage north; and since the Reformation and the revolt against Christianity (which is the religion of a civilized freedom) savagery is slowly creeping back in the form of realistic novels and problem plays. The curse of Rougon-Macquart[3] is as heathen and superstitious as the curse of Ravenswood;[4] only not so well written. But in this twilight barbaric sense the feeling of a racial fate is not irrational, and may be allowed like a hundred other half emotions that make life whole. The only essential of tragedy is that one should take it lightly. But even when the barbarian deluge rose to its highest in the madder novels of Zola (such as that called "The Human Beast"; a gross libel on beasts as well as humanity), even then the application of the

[3] A reference to a family in a series of novels by French novelist Emile Zola based on the thesis of the connection of character and heredity.

[4] This probably refers to Edgar, the Master of Ravenswood in Sir Walter Scott's novel *The Bride of Lammermoor*.

hereditary idea to practice is avowedly timid and fumbling. The students of heredity are savages in this vital sense; that they stare back at marvels, but they dare not stare forward to schemes. In practice no one is mad enough to legislate or educate upon dogmas of physical inheritance; and even the language of the thing is rarely used except for special modern purposes, such as the endowment of research or the oppression of the poor.

III

THE TRICKS OF ENVIRONMENT

After all the modern clatter of Calvinism, therefore, it is only with the born child that anybody dares to deal; and the question is not eugenics but education. Or again, to adopt that rather tiresome terminology of popular science, it is not a question of heredity but of environment. I will not needlessly complicate this question by urging at length that environment also is open to some of the objections and hesitations which paralyze the employment of heredity. I will merely suggest in passing that even about the effect of environment modern people talk much too cheerfully and cheaply. The idea that surroundings will mold a man is always mixed up with the totally different idea that they will mold him in one particular way. To take the broadest case, landscape no doubt affects the soul; but how it affects it is quite another matter. To be born among pine-trees might mean loving pine-trees. It might mean loathing pine-trees. It might quite seriously mean never having seen a pine-tree. Or it might mean any mixture of these or any degree of any of them. So that the scientific method here lacks a little in precision. I am not speaking without the book; on the contrary, I am speaking with the blue-book, with the guide-book and the atlas. It may be that the Highlanders are poetical because they inhabit mountains; but are the Swiss prosaic because they inhabit mountains? It may be the Swiss have fought for freedom because they had hills; did the Dutch fight for freedom because they hadn't? Personally I should think it quite likely. Environment might work negatively as well as positively. The Swiss may be sensible, not in spite of their wild skyline, but because of their wild skyline. The Flemings may be fantastic artists, not in spite of their dull skyline, but because of it.

I only pause on this parenthesis to show that, even in matters admittedly within its range, popular science goes a great deal too fast, and drops enormous links of logic. Nevertheless, it remains the working reality that what we have to deal with in the case of children is, for all practical purposes, environment; or, to use the older word, education. When all such deductions are made, education is at least a form of will-worship; not of cowardly fact-worship; it deals with a department that we can control; it does not merely darken us with the barbarian pessimism of Zola and the heredity-hunt. We shall certainly make fools of ourselves; that is what is meant by philosophy. But we shall not merely make beasts of ourselves; which is the nearest popular definition for merely following the laws of Nature and cowering under the vengeance of the flesh. Education contains much moonshine; but not of the sort that makes mere mooncalves and idiots, the slaves of a silver magnet, the one eye of the world. In this decent arena there are fads, but not frenzies. Doubtless we shall often find a mare's nest; but it will not always be the nightmare's.

IV

THE TRUTH ABOUT EDUCATION

When a man is asked to write down what he really thinks on education, a certain gravity grips and stiffens his soul, which might be mistaken by the superficial for disgust. If it be really true that men sickened of sacred words and wearied of theology, if this largely unreasoning irritation against "dogma" did arise out of some ridiculous excess of such things among priests in the past, then I fancy we must be laying up a fine crop of cant for our descendants to grow tired of. Probably the word "education" will some day seem honestly as old and objectless as the word "justification" now seems in a Puritan folio. Gibbon thought it frightfully funny that people should have fought about the difference between the "Homoousion"[1] and the "Homoiousion."[2] The time will come when somebody will laugh louder to think that men thundered against Sectarian Education and also against Secular Education; that men of prominence and position actually denounced the schools for teaching a creed and also for not teaching a faith. The two Greek words in Gibbon look rather alike; but they really mean quite different things. Faith and creed do not look alike, but they mean exactly the same thing. Creed happens to be the Latin for faith.

Now having read numberless newspaper articles on education, and even written a good many of them, and having heard deafening and indeterminate discussion going on all around me almost ever since I was born, about whether religion was part of education, about whether hygiene was an essential of education, about whether militarism was inconsistent with true education, I naturally pondered much on this recurring substantive, and I am ashamed to say that it was comparatively late in life that I saw the main fact about it.

Of course, the main fact about education is that there is no such

[1] "Homoousion" means "of one nature", from the Council of Nicea (325).

[2] "Homoiousion" means "of like substance", the semi-Arian word in Greek to deny the divinity of Christ.

thing. It does not exist, as theology or soldiering exist. Theology is a word like geology, soldiering is a word like soldering; these sciences may be healthy or no as hobbies; but they deal with stone and kettles, with definite things. But education is not a word like geology or kettles. Education is a word like "transmission" or "inheritance"; it is not an object, but a method. It must mean the conveying of certain facts, views or qualities, to the last baby born. They might be the most trivial facts or the most preposterous views or the most offensive qualities; but if they are handed on from one generation to another they are education. Education is not a thing like theology; it is not an inferior or superior thing; it is not a thing in the same category of terms. Theology and education are to each other like a love-letter to the General Post Office. Mr. Fagin[3] was quite as educational as Dr. Strong;[4] in practice probably more educational. It is giving something—perhaps poison. Education is tradition, and tradition (as its name implies) can be treason.

This first truth is frankly banal; but it is so perpetually ignored in our political prosing that it must be made plain. A little boy in a little house, son of a little tradesman, is taught to eat his breakfast, to take his medicine, to love his country, to say his prayers, and to wear his Sunday clothes. Obviously Fagin, if he found such a boy, would teach him to drink gin, to lie, to betray his country, to blaspheme and to wear false whiskers. But so also Mr. Salt the vegetarian would abolish the boy's breakfast; Mrs. Eddy would throw away his medicine; Count Tolstoi would rebuke him for loving his country; Mr. Blatchford would stop his prayers, and Mr. Edward Carpenter[5] would theoretically denounce Sunday clothes, and perhaps all clothes. I do not defend any of these advanced views, not even Fagin's. But I do ask what, between the lot of them, has become of the abstract entity called education. It is not (as commonly supposed) that the tradesman teaches education plus Christianity; Mr. Salt, education plus vegetarianism; Fagin, education plus crime. The truth is, that there is nothing in common at all between these

[3] The villainous teacher of petty crime in Charles Dickens' novel *Oliver Twist*.

[4] Herbert A. Strong (d. 1918), British educator and writer.

[5] Edward Carpenter (1844–1929), British writer, socialist and ethicist.

teachers, except that they teach. In short, the only thing they share is the one thing they profess to dislike: the general idea of authority. It is quaint that people talk of separating dogma from education. Dogma is actually the only thing that cannot be separated from education. It *is* education. A teacher who is not dogmatic is simply a teacher who is not teaching.

V

AN EVIL CRY

The fashionable fallacy is that by education we can give people something that we have not got. To hear people talk one would think it was some sort of magic chemistry, by which, out of a laborious hotchpotch of hygienic meals, baths, breathing exercises, fresh air and freehand drawing, we can produce something splendid by accident; we can create what we cannot conceive. These pages have, of course, no other general purpose than to point out that we cannot create anything good until we have conceived it. It is odd that these people, who in the matter of heredity are so sullenly attached to law, in the matter of environment seem almost to believe in miracle. They insist that nothing but what was in the bodies of the parents can go to make the bodies of the children. But they seem somehow to think that things can get into the heads of the children which were not in the heads of the parents, or, indeed, anywhere else.

There has arisen in this connection a foolish and wicked cry typical of the confusion. I mean the cry, "Save the children." It is, of course, part of that modern morbidity that insists on treating the State (which is the home of man) as a sort of desperate expedient in time of panic. This terrified opportunism is also the origin of the Socialist and other schemes. Just as they would collect and share all the food as men do in a famine, so they would divide the children from their fathers, as men do in a shipwreck. That a human community might conceivably not be in a condition of famine or shipwreck never seems to cross their minds. This cry of "Save the children" has in it the hateful implication that it is impossible to save the fathers; in other words, that many millions of grown-up, sane, responsible and self-supporting Europeans are to be treated as dirt or débris and swept away out of the discussion; called dipsomaniacs because they drink in public houses instead of private houses; called unemployables because nobody knows how to get them work; called dullards if they still adhere to conventions, and called loafers if they still love liberty. Now I am concerned, first and last, to maintain that unless you can save the fathers, you cannot save the children; that at present we cannot save others, for we cannot save ourselves. We cannot teach citizenship if we are not citizens; we cannot free others if we have forgotten the appetite of freedom. Education is only truth in a state of transmission; and how can we pass on truth if it has never come into our hand? Thus we find that education is of all the cases the clearest for our general purpose. It is vain to save children; for they cannot remain children. By hypothesis we are teaching them to be men; and how can it be so simple to teach an ideal manhood to others if it is so vain and hopeless to find one for ourselves?

I know that certain crazy pedants have attempted to counter this difficulty by maintaining that education is not instruction at all, does not teach by authority at all. They present the process as coming, not from the outside, from the teacher, but entirely from inside the boy. Education, they say, is the Latin for leading out or drawing out the dormant faculties of each person. Somewhere far down in the dim boyish soul is a primordial yearning to learn Greek accents or to wear clean collars; and the schoolmaster only gently and tenderly liberates this imprisoned purpose. Sealed up in the newborn babe are the intrinsic secrets of how to eat asparagus and what was the date of Bannockburn.[1] The educator only draws out the child's own unapparent love of long division; only leads out the child's slightly veiled preference for milk pudding to tarts. I am not sure that I believe in the derivation; I have heard the disgraceful suggestion that "educator," if applied to a Roman schoolmaster, did not mean leading out young functions into freedom; but only meant taking out little boys for a walk. But I am much more certain that I do not agree with the doctrine; I think it would be about as sane to say that the baby's milk comes from the baby as to say that the baby's educational merits do. There is, indeed, in each living creature a collection of forces and functions; but education means producing these in particular shapes and training them to particular purposes, or it means nothing at all. Speaking is the most practical instance

[1] A village in Central Scotland which was the site of the defeat (in 1314) of the English by the Scots under Robert the Bruce.

of the whole situation. You may indeed "draw out" squeals and grunts from the child by simply poking him and pulling him about, a pleasant but cruel pastime to which many psychologists are addicted. But you will wait and watch very patiently indeed before you draw the English language out of him. That you have got to put into him; and there is an end of the matter.

VI

AUTHORITY THE UNAVOIDABLE

But the important point here is only that you cannot anyhow get rid of authority in education; it is not so much (as poor Conservatives say) that parental authority ought to be preserved, as that it cannot be destroyed. Mr. Bernard Shaw once said that he hated the idea of forming a child's mind. In that case Mr. Bernard Shaw had better hang himself; for he hates something inseparable from human life. I only mentioned *educere* and the drawing out of the faculties in order to point out that even this mental trick does not avoid the inevitable idea of parental or scholastic authority. The educator drawing out is just as arbitrary and coercive as the instructor pouring in; for he draws out what he chooses. He decides what in the child shall be developed and what shall not be developed. He does not (I suppose) draw out the neglected faculty of forgery. He does not (so far at least) lead out, with timid steps, a shy talent for torture. The only result of all this pompous and precise distinction between the educator and the instructor is that the instructor pokes where he likes and the educator pulls where he likes. Exactly the same intellectual violence is done to the creature who is poked and pulled. Now we must all accept the responsibility of this intellectual violence. Education is violent; because it is creative. It is creative because it is human. It is as reckless as playing on the fiddle; as dogmatic as drawing a picture; as brutal as building a house. In short, it is what all human action is; it is an interference with life and growth. After that it is a trifling and even a jocular question whether we say of this tremendous tormentor, the artist Man, that he puts things into us like an apothecary, or draws things out of us, like a dentist.

The point is that Man does what he likes. He claims the right to take his mother Nature under his control; he claims the right to make his child the Superman, in his image. Once flinch from this creative authority of man, and the whole courageous raid which we call civilization wavers and falls to pieces. Now most modern

freedom is at root fear. It is not so much that we are too bold to endure rules; it is rather that we are too timid to endure responsibilities. And Mr. Shaw and such people are especially shrinking from that
awful and ancestral responsibility to which our fathers committed us
when they took the wild step of becoming men. I mean the responsibility of affirming the truth of our human tradition and handing
it on with a voice of authority, an unshaken voice. That is the one
eternal education; to be sure enough that something is true that you
dare to tell it to a child. From this high audacious duty the moderns
are fleeing on every side; and the only excuse for them is, (of course,)
that their modern philosophies are so half-baked and hypothetical that
they cannot convince themselves enough to convince even a newborn
babe. This, of course, is connected with the decay of democracy; and
is somewhat of a separate subject. Suffice it to say here that when I say
that we should instruct our children, I mean that we should do it, not
that Mr. Sully[1] or Professor Earl Barnes[2] should do it. The trouble in
too many of our modern schools is that the State, being controlled so
specially by the few, allows cranks and experiments to go straight to
the schoolroom when they have never passed through the Parliament,
the public house, the private house, the church, or the marketplace.
Obviously, it ought to be the oldest things that are taught to the
youngest people; the assured and experienced truths that are put first
to the baby. But in a school to-day the baby has to submit to a system
that is younger than himself. The flopping infant of four actually has
more experience, and has weathered the world longer, than the
dogma to which he is made to submit. Many a school boasts of having
the last ideas in education, when it has not even the first idea; for the
first idea is that even innocence, divine as it is, may learn something
from experience. But this, as I say, is all due to the mere fact that we
are managed by a little oligarchy; my system presupposes that men
who govern themselves will govern their children. To-day we all use
Popular Education as meaning education of the people. I wish I could
use it as meaning education by the people.

[1] James Sully (1842–1923), English philosopher and psychologist.
[2] Earl Barnes (1861–1935), American educator, lecturer, writer and professor of
education at Stanford University (1891–1897).

The urgent point at present is that these expansive educators do not avoid the violence of authority an inch more than the old schoolmasters. Nay, it might be maintained that they avoid it less. The old village schoolmaster beat a boy for not learning grammar and sent him out into the playground to play at anything he liked; or at nothing, if he liked that better. The modern scientific schoolmaster pursues him into the playground and makes him play at cricket, because exercise is so good for the health. The modern Dr. Busby[3] is a doctor of medicine as well as a doctor of divinity. He may say that the good of exercise is self-evident; but *he* must say it, and say it with authority. It cannot really be self-evident or it never could have been compulsory. But this is in modern practice a very mild case. In modern practice the free educationists forbid far more things than the old-fashioned educationists. A person with a taste for paradox (if any such shameless creature could exist) might with some plausibility maintain concerning all our expansion since the failure of Luther's frank paganism and its replacement by Calvin's Puritanism, that all this expansion has not been an expansion, but the closing in of a prison, so that less and less beautiful and humane things have been permitted. The Puritans destroyed images; the Rationalists forbade fairy tales. Count Tolstoi practically issued one of his papal encyclicals against music; I have heard of modern educationists who forbid children to play with tin soldiers. I remember a meek little madman who came up to me at some Socialist soiree or other, and asked me to use my influence (have I any influence?) against adventure stories for boys. It seems they breed an appetite for blood. But never mind that; one must keep one's temper in this madhouse. I need only insist here that these things, even if a just deprivation, are a deprivation. I do not deny that the old vetoes and punishments were often idiotic and cruel; though they are much more so in a country like England (where in practice only a rich man decrees the punishment and only a poor man receives it) than in countries with a clearer popular tradition—such as Russia. In Russia flogging is

---

[3] Richard Busby (1606–1695), English clergyman and head master of Westminster school. He had a great reputation as an instructor, and among his more illustrious pupils are included South, Dryden and Locke.

often inflicted by peasants on a peasant. In modern England flogging can only in practice be inflicted by a gentleman on a very poor man. Thus only a few days ago as I write a small boy (a son of the poor, of course) was sentenced to flogging and imprisonment for five years for having picked up a small piece of coal which the experts value at 5d. I am entirely on the side of such liberals and humanitarians as have protested against this almost bestial ignorance about boys. But I do think it a little unfair that these humanitarians, who excuse boys for being robbers, should denounce them for playing at robbers. I do think that those who understand a guttersnipe playing with a piece of coal might, by a sudden spurt of imagination, understand him playing with a tin soldier. To sum it up in one sentence: I think my meek little madman might have understood that there is many a boy who would rather be flogged, and unjustly flogged, than have his adventure story taken away.

VII

THE HUMILITY OF MRS. GRUNDY

In short, the new education is as harsh as the old, whether or no it is as high. The freest fad, as much as the strictest formula, is stiff with authority. It is because the humane father thinks soldiers wrong that they are forbidden; there is no pretense, there can be no pretense, that the boy would think so. The average boy's impression certainly would be simply this: "If your father is a Methodist you must not play with soldiers on Sunday. If your father is a Socialist you must not play with them even on week days." All educationists are utterly dogmatic and authoritarian. You cannot have free education; for if you left a child free you would not educate him at all. Is there, then, no distinction or difference between the most hide-bound conventionalists and the most brilliant and bizarre innovators? Is there no difference between the heaviest heavy father and the most reckless and speculative maiden aunt? Yes; there is. The difference is that the heavy father, in his heavy way, is a democrat. He does not urge a thing merely because to his fancy it should be done; but, because (in his own admirable republican formula) "Everybody does it." The conventional authority does claim some popular mandate; the unconventional authority does not. The Puritan who forbids soldiers on Sunday is at least expressing Puritan opinion; not merely his own opinion. He is not a despot; he is a democracy, a tyrannical democracy, a dingy and local democracy perhaps; but one that could do and has done the two ultimate virile things—fight and appeal to God. But the veto of the new educationist is like the veto of the House of Lords; it does not pretend to be representative. These innovators are always talking about the blushing modesty of Mrs. Grundy. I do not know whether Mrs. Grundy is more modest than they are; but I am sure she is more humble.

But there is a further complication. The more anarchic modern may again attempt to escape the dilemma by saying that education should only be an enlargement of the mind, an opening of all the

organs of receptivity. Light (he says) should be brought into darkness; blinded and thwarted existences in all our ugly corners should
merely be permitted to perceive and expand; in short, enlightenment should be shed over darkest London. Now here is just the
trouble; that, in so far as this is involved, there is no darkest London. London is not dark at all; not even at night. We have said that
if education is a solid substance, then there is none of it. We may
now say that if education is an abstract expansion there is no lack of
it. There is far too much of it. In fact, there is nothing else.

There are no uneducated people. Everybody in England is educated; only most people are educated wrong. The state schools were
not the first schools, but among the last schools to be established;
and London had been educating Londoners long before the London
School Board. The error is a highly practical one. It is persistently
assumed that unless a child is civilized by the established schools, he
must remain a barbarian. I wish he did. Every child in London becomes
a highly civilized person. But there are so many different civilizations,
most of them born tired. Anyone will tell you that the trouble with
the poor is not so much that the old are still foolish, but rather that
the young are already wise. Without going to school at all, the
gutter-boy would be educated. Without going to school at all, he
would be over-educated. The real object of our schools should be
not so much to suggest complexity as solely to restore simplicity.
You will hear venerable idealists declare we must make war on the
ignorance of the poor; but, indeed, we have rather to make war on
their knowledge. Real educationists have to resist a kind of roaring
cataract of culture. The truant is being taught all day. If the children
do not look at the large letters in the spelling-book, they need only
walk outside and look at the large letters on the poster. If they do
not care for the colored maps provided by the school, they can gape
at the colored maps provided by the *Daily Mail*. If they tire of electricity, they can take to electric trams. If they are unmoved by music, they can take to drink. If they will not work so as to get a prize
from their school, they may work to get a prize from *Prizy Bits*. If
they cannot learn enough about law and citizenship to please the
teacher, they learn enough about them to avoid the policeman.

If they will not learn history forwards from the right end in the history books, they will learn it backwards from the wrong end in the party newspapers. And this is the tragedy of the whole affair: that the London poor, a particularly quick-witted and civilized class, learn everything tail foremost, learn even what is right in the way of what is wrong. They do not see the first principles of law in a law book; they only see its last results in the police news. They do not see the truths of politics in a general survey. They only see the lies of politics, at a General Election.

But whatever be the pathos of the London poor, it has nothing to do with being uneducated. So far from being without guidance, they are guided constantly, earnestly, excitedly; only guided wrong. The poor are not at all neglected, they are merely oppressed; nay, rather they are persecuted. There are no people in London who are not appealed to by the rich; the appeals of the rich shriek from every hoarding and shout from every hustings. For it should always be remembered that the queer, abrupt ugliness of our streets and costumes are not the creation of democracy, but of aristocracy. The House of Lords objected to the Embankment being disfigured by trams. But most of the rich men who disfigure the street-walls with their wares are actually in the House of Lords. The peers make the country seats beautiful by making the town streets hideous. This, however, is parenthetical. The point is, that the poor in London are not left alone, but rather deafened and bewildered with raucous and despotic advice. They are not like sheep without a shepherd. They are more like one sheep whom twenty-seven shepherds are shouting at. All the newspapers, all the new advertisements, all the new medicines and new theologies, all the glare and blare of the gas and brass of modern times—it is against these that the national school must bear up if it can. I will not question that our elementary education is better than barbaric ignorance. But there is no barbaric ignorance. I do not doubt that our schools would be good for uninstructed boys. But there are no uninstructed boys. A modern London school ought not merely to be clearer, kindlier, more clever and more rapid than ignorance and darkness. It must also be clearer than a picture postcard, cleverer than a Limerick competition, quicker than the tram, and kindlier than the tavern. The school, in fact, has the responsibility of universal rivalry. We need not deny that everywhere there is a light that must conquer darkness. But here we demand a light that can conquer light.

VIII

THE BROKEN RAINBOW

I will take one case that will serve both as symbol and example: the case of color. We hear the realists (those sentimental fellows) talking about the gray streets and the gray lives of the poor. But whatever the poor streets are they are not gray; but motley, striped, spotted, piebald and patched like a quilt. Hoxton is not aesthetic enough to be monochrome; and there is nothing of the Celtic twilight about it. As a matter of fact, a London gutter-boy walks unscathed among furnaces of color. Watch him walk along a line of hoardings, and you will see him now against glowing green, like a traveler in a tropic forest; now black like a bird against the burning blue of the Midi; now *passant* across a field gules, like the golden leopards of England. He ought to understand the irrational rapture of that cry of Mr. Stephen Phillips[1] about "that bluer blue, that greener green." There is no blue much bluer than Reckitt's[2] Blue and no blacking blacker than Day and Martin's; no more emphatic yellow than that of Colman's Mustard. If, despite this chaos of color, like a shattered rainbow, the spirit of the small boy is not exactly intoxicated with art and culture, the cause certainly does not lie in universal grayness or the mere starving of his senses. It lies in the fact that the colors are presented in the wrong connection, on the wrong scale, and, above all, from the wrong motive. It is not colors he lacks, but a philosophy of colors. In short, there is nothing wrong with Reckitt's Blue except that it is not Reckitt's. Blue does not belong to Reckitt, but to the sky; black does not belong to Day and Martin, but to the abyss. Even the finest posters are only very little things on a very large scale. There is something specially irritant in this way about the iteration of advertisements of mustard: a condiment, a small luxury; a thing in its nature not to be taken in quantity. There is a special irony

[1] Stephen Phillips (d. 1915), English poet.
[2] Sir James Reckitt (1838–1924), prosperous English merchant. References to contemporary food products.

in these starving streets to see such a great deal of mustard to such very little meat. Yellow is a bright pigment; mustard is a pungent pleasure. But to look at these seas of yellow is to be like a man who should swallow gallons of mustard. He would either die, or lose the taste of mustard altogether.

Now suppose we compare these gigantic trivialities on the hoardings with those tiny and tremendous pictures in which the mediaevals recorded their dreams; little pictures where the blue sky is hardly longer than a single sapphire, and the fires of judgment only a pigmy patch of gold. The difference here is not merely that poster art is in its nature more hasty than illumination art; it is not even merely that the ancient artist was serving the Lord while the modern artist is serving the lords. It is that the old artist contrived to convey an impression that colors really were significant and precious things, like jewels and talismanic stones. The color was often arbitrary; but it was always authoritative. If a bird was blue, if a tree was golden, if a fish was silver, if a cloud was scarlet, the artist managed to convey that these colors were important and almost painfully intense; all the red red-hot and all the gold tried in the fire. Now that is the spirit touching color which the schools must recover and protect if they are really to give the children any imaginative appetite or pleasure in the thing. It is not so much an indulgence in color; it is rather, if anything, a sort of fiery thrift. It fenced in a green field in heraldry as straitly as a green field in peasant proprietorship. It would not fling away gold leaf any more than gold coin; it would not heedlessly pour out purple or crimson, any more than it would spill good wine or shed blameless blood. That is the hard task before educationists in this special matter; they have to teach people to relish colors like liquors. They have the heavy business of turning drunkards into wine tasters. If even the twentieth century succeeds in doing these things, it will almost catch up with the twelfth.

The principle covers, however, the whole of modern life. Morris[3] and the merely aesthetic mediaevalists always indicated that a crowd in the time of Chaucer would have been brightly clad and glittering,

[3] William Morris (1834–1896), English painter, designer, poet and socialist writer.

compared with a crowd in the time of Queen Victoria. I am not so sure that the real distinction is here. There would be brown frocks of friars in the first scene as well as brown bowlers of clerks in the second. There would be purple plumes of factory girls in the second scene as well as purple lenten vestments in the first. There would be white waistcoats against white ermine; gold watch chains against gold lions. The real difference is this: that the brown earth-color of the monk's coat was instinctively chosen to express labor and humility, whereas the brown color of the clerk's hat was not chosen to express anything. The monk did mean to say that he robed himself in dust. I am sure the clerk does not mean to say that he crowns himself with clay. He is not putting dust on his head, as the only diadem of man. Purple, at once rich and somber, does suggest a triumph temporarily eclipsed by a tragedy. But the factory girl does not intend her hat to express a triumph temporarily eclipsed by a tragedy; far from it. White ermine was meant to express moral purity; white waistcoats were not. Gold lions do suggest a flaming magnanimity; gold watch chains do not. The point is not that we have lost the material hues, but that we have lost the trick of turning them to the best advantage. We are not like children who have lost their paint-box and are left alone with a gray lead-pencil. We are like children who have mixed all the colors in the paint-box together and lost the paper of instructions. Even then (I do not deny) one has some fun.

Now this abundance of colors and loss of a color scheme is a pretty perfect parable of all that is wrong with our modern ideals and especially with our modern education. It is the same with ethical education, economic education, every sort of education. The growing London child will find no lack of highly controversial teachers who will teach him that geography means painting the map red; that economics means taxing the foreigner; that patriotism means the peculiarly un-English habit of flying a flag on Empire Day. In mentioning these examples specially I do not mean to imply that there are no similar crudities and popular fallacies upon the other political side. I mention them because they constitute a very special and arresting feature of the situation. I mean this, that there were always Radical revolutionists; but now there are Tory revolutionists also.

The modern Conservative no longer conserves. He is avowedly an innovator. Thus all the current defenses of the House of Lords which describe it as a bulwark against the mob, are intellectually done for; the bottom has fallen out of them; because on five or six of the most turbulent topics of the day, the House of Lords is a mob itself; and exceedingly likely to behave like one.

IX

THE NEED FOR NARROWNESS

Through all this chaos, then we come back once more to our main conclusion. The true task of culture to-day is not a task of expansion, but very decidedly of selection—and rejection. The educationist must find a creed and teach it. Even if it be not a theological creed, it must still be as fastidious and as firm as theology. In short, it must be orthodox. The teacher may think it antiquated to have to decide precisely between the faith of Calvin and of Laud,[1] the faith of Aquinas and of Swedenborg; but he still has to choose between the faith of Kipling and of Shaw, between the world of Blatchford and of General Booth.[2] Call it, if you will, a narrow question whether your child shall be brought up by the vicar or the minister or the popish priest. You have still to face that larger, more liberal, more highly civilized question, of whether he shall be brought up by Harmsworth[3] or by Pearson,[4] by Mr. Eustace Miles[5] with his Simple Life or Mr. Peter Keary[6] with his Strenuous Life; whether he shall most eagerly read Miss Annie S. Swan[7] or Mr. Bart Kennedy;[8] in short, whether he shall end up in the mere violence of the S. D. F.,[9] or in the mere vulgarity of the Primrose League.[10] They say that nowadays

[1] William Laud (1573–1645), Archbishop of Canterbury during the reign of Charles I.

[2] William Booth (1829–1913), English founder of the Salvation Army.

[3] Hildebrand A. Harmsworth (d. 1929), English politician and newspaperman.

[4] Karl Pearson (1857–1936), Eugenics professor and writer.

[5] Eustace Miles (1868–1948), English writer and athletic promoter of healthy life.

[6] Peter Keary (1865–1915), publisher and successful business promoter.

[7] Annie S. Swan (Mrs. Burnett-Smith) (1860–1943), English novelist who contributed to *The Woman at Home* (1883) and the *People's Friend*, and who wrote many popular stories.

[8] Bart Kennedy (1861–1930), English author, lecturer and traveller whose works include *The German Danger* (1907), *A Tramp in Spain, from Andalusia to Andorra* (1904), *The Human Compass* (1912) and *A Sailor Tramp* (1913).

[9] Social Democratic Federation, a socialist organization founded in 1881.

[10] Conservative club followers of the principles of Disraeli.

the creeds are crumbling; I doubt it, but at least the sects are increasing; and education must now be sectarian education, merely for practical purposes. Out of all this throng of theories it must somehow select a theory; out of all these thundering voices it must manage to hear a voice; out of all this awful and aching battle of blinding lights, without one shadow to give shape to them, it must manage somehow to trace and to track a star.

I have spoken so far of popular education, which began too vague and vast and which therefore has accomplished little. But as it happens there is in England something to compare it with. There is an institution, or class of institutions, which began with the same popular object, which has since followed a much narrower object; but which had the great advantage that it did follow some object, unlike our modern elementary schools.

In all these problems I should urge the solution which is positive, or, as silly people say, "optimistic." I should set my face, that is, against most of the solutions that are solely negative and abolitionist. Most educators of the poor seem to think that they have to teach the poor man not to drink. I should be quite content if they teach him to drink; for it is mere ignorance about how to drink and when to drink that is accountable for most of his tragedies. I do not propose (like some of my revolutionary friends) that we should abolish the public schools. I propose the much more lurid and desperate experiment that we should make them public. I do not wish to make Parliament stop working, but rather to make it work; not to shut up churches, but rather to open them; not to put out the lamp of learning or destroy the hedge of property, but only to make some rude effort to make universities fairly universal and property decently proper.

In many cases, let it be remembered, such action is not merely going back to the old ideal, but is even going back to the old reality. It would be a great step forward for the gin shop to go back to the inn. It is incontrovertibly true that to mediaevalize the public schools would be to democratize the public schools. Parliament did once really mean (as its name seems to imply) a place where people were allowed to talk. It is only lately that the general increase of efficiency, that is, of the Speaker, has made it mostly a place where people are prevented from talking. The poor do not go to the modern church, but they went to the ancient church all right; and if the common man in the past had a grave respect for property, it may conceivably have been because he sometimes had some of his own. I therefore can claim that I have no vulgar itch of innovation in anything I say about any of these institutions. Certainly I have none in that particular one which I am now obliged to pick out of the list; a type of institution to which I have genuine and personal reasons for being friendly and grateful: I mean the great Tudor foundations, the public schools of England. They have been praised for a great many things, mostly, I am sorry to say, praised by themselves and their children. And yet for some reason no one has ever praised them for the one really convincing reason.

X

THE CASE FOR THE PUBLIC SCHOOLS

The word success can of course be used in two senses. It may be used with reference to a thing serving its immediate and peculiar purpose, as of a wheel going around; or it can be used with reference to a thing adding to the general welfare, as of a wheel being a useful discovery. It is one thing to say that Smith's flying machine is a failure, and quite another to say that Smith has failed to make a flying machine. Now this is very broadly the difference between the old English public schools and the new democratic schools. Perhaps the old public schools are (as I personally think they are) ultimately weakening the country rather than strengthening it, and are therefore, in that ultimate sense, inefficient. But there is such a thing as being efficiently inefficient. You can make your flying ship so that it flies, even if you also make it so that it kills you. Now the public-school system may not work satisfactorily, but it works; the public schools may not achieve what we want, but they achieve what they want. The popular elementary schools do not in that sense achieve anything at all. It is very difficult to point to any guttersnipe in the street and say that he embodies the ideal for which popular education has been working, in the sense that the fresh-faced, foolish boy in "Etons" does embody the ideal for which the headmasters of Harrow and Winchester have been working. The aristocratic educationists have the positive purpose of turning out gentlemen; and they do turn out gentlemen, even when they expel them. The popular educationists would say that they had the far nobler idea of turning out citizens. I concede that it is a much nobler idea, but where are the citizens? I know that the boy in "Etons" is stiff with a rather silly and sentimental stoicism, called being a man of the world. I do not fancy that the errand-boy is rigid with that republican stoicism that is called being a citizen. The schoolboy will really say with fresh and innocent *hauteur*, "I am an English gentleman." I cannot so easily picture the errand-boy drawing up his head to the stars and answering,

"Romanus civis sum." Let it be granted that our elementary teachers are teaching the very broadest code of morals, while our great headmasters are teaching only the narrowest code of manners. Let it be granted that both these things are being taught. But only one of them is being learned.

It is always said that great reformers or masters of events can manage to bring about some specific and practical reforms, but that they never fulfill their visions or satisfy their souls. I believe there is a real sense in which this apparent platitude is quite untrue. By a strange inversion the political idealist often does not get what he asks for, but does get what he wants. The silent pressure of his ideal lasts much longer and reshapes the world much more than the actualities by which he attempted to suggest it. What perishes is the letter, which he thought so practical. What endures is the spirit, which he felt to be unattainable and even unutterable. It is exactly his schemes that are not fulfilled; it is exactly his vision that is fulfilled. Thus the ten or twelve paper constitutions of the French Revolution, which seemed so business-like to the framers of them, seem to us to have flown away on the wind as the wildest fancies. What has not flown away, what is a fixed fact in Europe, is the ideal and vision. The Republic, the idea of a land full of mere citizens all with some minimum of manners and minimum of wealth, the vision of the eighteenth century, the reality of the twentieth. So I think it will generally be with the creator of social things, desirable or undesirable. All his schemes will fail, all his tools break in his hands. His compromises will collapse, his concessions will be useless. He must brace himself to bear his fate; he shall have nothing but his heart's desire.

Now if one may compare very small things with very great, one may say that the English aristocratic schools can claim something of the same sort of success and solid splendor as the French democratic politics. At least they can claim the same sort of superiority over the distracted and fumbling attempts of modern England to establish democratic education. Such success as has attended the public schoolboy throughout the Empire, a success exaggerated indeed by himself, but still positive and a fact of a certain indisputable shape and size, has been due to the central and supreme circumstance that the managers of our public schools did know what sort of boy they liked. They wanted something and they got something; instead of going to work in the broad-minded manner and wanting everything and getting nothing.

The only thing in question is the quality of the thing they got. There is something highly maddening in the circumstance that when modern people attack an institution that really does demand reform, they always attack it for the wrong reasons. Thus many opponents of our public schools, imagining themselves to be very democratic, have exhausted themselves in an unmeaning attack upon the study of Greek. I can understand how Greek may be regarded as useless, especially by those thirsting to throw themselves into the cut-throat commerce which is the negation of citizenship; but I do not understand how it can be considered undemocratic. I quite understand why Mr. Carnegie has a hatred of Greek. It is obscurely founded on the firm and sound impression that in any self-governing Greek city he would have been killed. But I cannot comprehend why any chance democrat, say Mr. Quelch, or Mr. Will Crooks,[1] or Mr. John M. Robertson,[2] should be opposed to people learning the Greek alphabet, which was the alphabet of liberty. Why should Radicals dislike Greek? In that language is written all the earliest and, Heaven knows, the most heroic history of the Radical party. Why should Greek disgust a democrat, when the very word democrat is Greek?

A similar mistake, though a less serious one, is merely attacking the athletics of public schools as something promoting animalism and brutality. Now brutality, in the only immoral sense, is not a vice of the English public schools. There is much moral bullying, owing to the general lack of moral courage in the public-school atmosphere. These schools do, upon the whole, encourage physical courage; but they do not merely discourage moral courage, they forbid it. The ultimate result of the thing is seen in the egregious English officer who cannot even endure to wear a bright uniform except when it is blurred and hidden in the smoke of battle. This,

[1] Will Crooks (1852–1921), British local politician.
[2] John M. Robertson (d. 1926), Scottish labor leader.

like all the affectations of our present plutocracy, is an entirely modern thing. It was unknown to the old aristocrats. The Black Prince[3] would certainly have asked that any knight who had the courage to lift his crest among his enemies, should also have the courage to lift it among his friends. As regards moral courage, then, it is not so much that the public schools support it feebly, as that they suppress it firmly. But physical courage they do, on the whole, support; and physical courage is a magnificent fundamental. The one great, wise Englishman of the eighteenth century said truly that if a man lost that virtue he could never be sure of keeping any other. Now it is one of the mean and morbid modern lies that physical courage is connected with cruelty. The Tolstoian and Kiplingite are nowhere more at one than in maintaining this. They have, I believe, some small sectarian quarrel with each other, the one saying that courage must be abandoned because it is connected with cruelty, and the other maintaining that cruelty is charming because it is a part of courage. But it is all, thank God, a lie. An energy and boldness of body may make a man stupid or reckless or dull or drunk or hungry, but it does not make him spiteful. And we may admit heartily (without joining in that perpetual praise which public-school men are always pouring upon themselves) that this does operate to the removal of mere evil cruelty in the public schools. English public-school life is extremely like English public life, for which it is the preparatory school. It is like it specially in this, that things are either very open, common and conventional, or else are very secret indeed. Now there is cruelty in public schools, just as there is kleptomania and secret drinking and vices without a name. But these things do not flourish in the full daylight and common consciousness of the school; and no more does cruelty. A tiny trio of sullen-looking boys gather in corners and seem to have some ugly business always; it may be indecent literature, it may be the beginning of drink, it may occasionally be cruelty to little boys. But on this stage the bully is not a braggart. The proverb says that bullies are always cowardly, but these bullies are more than cowardly; they are shy.

[3] The prince of Wales, Duke of Cornwall, 1330–1376.

As a third instance of the wrong form of revolt against the public schools, I may mention the habit of using the word aristocracy with a double implication. To put the plain truth as briefly as possible, if aristocracy means rule by a rich ring, England has aristocracy and the English public schools support it. If it means rule by ancient families or flawless blood, England has not got aristocracy, and the public schools systematically destroy it. In these circles real aristocracy, like real democracy, has become bad form. A modern fashionable host dare not praise his ancestry; it would so often be an insult to half the other oligarchs at table, who have no ancestry. We have said he has not the moral courage to wear his uniform; still less has he the moral courage to wear his coat-of-arms. The whole thing now is only a vague hotch-potch of nice and nasty gentlemen. The nice gentleman never refers to anyone else's father, the nasty gentleman never refers to his own. That is the only difference; the rest is the public-school manner. But Eton and Harrow have to be aristocratic because they consist so largely of parvenues. The public school is not a sort of refuge for aristocrats, like an asylum, a place where they go in and never come out. It is a factory for aristocrats; they come out without ever having perceptibly gone in. The poor little private schools, in their old-world, sentimental, feudal style, used to stick up a notice, "For the Sons of Gentlemen only." If the public schools stuck up a notice it ought to be inscribed, "For the Fathers of Gentlemen only." In two generations they can do the trick.

XI

THE SCHOOL FOR HYPOCRITES

These are the false accusations; the accusation of classicism, the accusation of cruelty, and the accusation of an exclusiveness based on perfection of pedigree. English public-school boys are not pedants, they are not torturers; and they are not, in the vast majority of cases, people fiercely proud of their ancestry, or even people with any ancestry to be proud of. They are taught to be courteous, to be good tempered, to be brave in a bodily sense, to be clean in a bodily sense; they are generally kind to animals, generally civil to servants, and to anyone in any sense their equal, the jolliest companions on earth. Is there then anything wrong in the public-school ideal? I think we all feel there is something very wrong in it, but a blinding network of newspaper phraseology obscures and entangles us; so that it is hard to trace to its beginning, beyond all words and phrases, the faults in this great English achievement.

Surely, when all is said, the ultimate objection to the English public school is its utterly blatant and indecent disregard of the duty of telling the truth. I know there does still linger among maiden ladies in remote country houses a notion that English schoolboys are taught to tell the truth, but it cannot be maintained seriously for a moment. Very occasionally, very vaguely, English schoolboys are told not to tell lies, which is a totally different thing. I may silently support all the obscene fictions and forgeries in the universe, without once telling a lie. I may wear another man's coat, steal another man's wit, apostatize to another man's creed, or poison another man's coffee, all without ever telling a lie. But no English school-boy is ever taught to tell the truth, for the very simple reason that he is never taught to desire the truth. From the very first he is taught to be totally careless about whether a fact is a fact; he is taught to care only whether the fact can be used on his "side" when he is engaged in "playing the game." He takes sides in his Union debating society to settle whether Charles I. ought to have been killed, with the same solemn and pompous frivolity with which he takes sides in the cricket field to decide whether Rugby or Westminster shall win. He is never allowed to admit the abstract notion of the truth, that the match is a matter of what may happen, but that Charles I. is a matter of what did happen—or did not. He is Liberal or Tory at the general election exactly as he is Oxford or Cambridge at the boat-race. He knows that sport deals with the unknown; he has not even a notion that politics should deal with the known. If anyone really doubts this self-evident proposition, that the public schools definitely discourage the love of truth, there is one fact which I should think would settle him. England is the country of the Party System, and it has always been chiefly run by public-school men. Is there anyone out of Hanwell[1] who will maintain that the Party System, whatever its conveniences or inconveniences, could have been created by people particularly fond of truth?

The very English happiness on this point is itself a hypocrisy. When a man really tells the truth, the first truth he tells is that he himself is a liar. David said in his haste, that is, in his honesty, that all men are liars. It was afterwards, in some leisurely official explanation, that he said that Kings of Israel at least told the truth. When Lord Curzon[2] was Viceroy he delivered a moral lecture to the Indians on their reputed indifference to veracity, to actuality and intellectual honor. A great many people indignantly discussed whether orientals deserved to receive this rebuke; whether Indians were indeed in a position to receive such severe admonition. No one seemed to ask, as I should venture to ask, whether Lord Curzon was in a position to give it. He is an ordinary party politician; a party politician means a politician who might have belonged to either party. Being such a person, he must again and again, at every twist and turn of party strategy, either have deceived others or grossly deceived himself. I do not know the East; nor do I like what I know. I am quite ready to believe that when Lord Curzon went out he found a very false atmosphere. I only say it must have been something startlingly and chokingly false if it was falser than that English atmosphere

[1] An English asylum.
[2] Lord Curzon (1859–1925), British statesman, Viceroy of India, 1899–1905.

from which he came. The English Parliament actually cares for everything except veracity. The public-school man is kind, courageous, polite, clean, companionable; but, in the most awful sense of the words, the truth is not in him.

This weakness of untruthfulness in the English public schools, in the English political system, and to some extent in the English character, is a weakness which necessarily produces a curious crop of superstitions, of lying legends, of evident delusions clung to through low spiritual self-indulgence. There are so many of these public-school superstitions that I have here only space for one of them, which may be called the superstition of soap. It appears to have been shared by the ablutionary Pharisees, who resembled the English public-school aristocrats in so many respects: in their care about club rules and traditions, in their offensive optimism at the expense of other people, and above all in their unimaginative plodding patriotism in the worst interests of their country. Now the old human common sense about washing is that it is a great pleasure. Water (applied externally) is a splendid thing, like wine. Sybarites bathe in wine, and Nonconformists drink water; but we are not concerned with these frantic exceptions. Washing being a pleasure, it stands to reason that rich people can afford it more than poor people, and as long as this was recognized all was well; and it was very right that rich people should offer baths to poor people, as they might offer any other agreeable thing—a drink or a donkey ride. But one dreadful day, somewhere about the middle of the nineteenth century, somebody discovered (somebody pretty well off) the two great modern truths, that washing is a virtue in the rich and therefore a duty in the poor. For a duty is a virtue that one can't do. And a virtue is generally a duty that one can do quite easily; like the bodily cleanliness of the upper classes. But in the public-school tradition of public life, soap has become creditable simply because it is pleasant. Baths are represented as a part of the decay of the Roman Empire; but the same baths are represented as part of the energy and rejuvenation of the British Empire. There are distinguished public-school men, bishops, dons, headmasters, and high politicians, who, in the course of the eulogies which from time to time they pass upon themselves, have actually identified physical cleanliness with moral purity. They say (if I remember rightly) that a public-school man is clean inside and out. As if everyone did not know that while saints can afford to be dirty, seducers have to be clean. As if everyone did not know that the harlot must be clean, because it is her business to captivate, while the good wife may be dirty, because it is her business to clean. As if we did not all know that whenever God's thunder cracks above us, it is very likely indeed to find the simplest man in a muck cart and the most complex blackguard in a bath.

There are other instances, of course, of this oily trick of turning the pleasures of a gentleman into the virtues of an Anglo-Saxon. Sport, like soap, is an admirable thing, but, like soap, it is an agreeable thing. And it does not sum up all mortal merits to be a sportsman playing the game in a world where it is so often necessary to be a workman doing the work. By all means let a gentleman congratulate himself that he has not lost his natural love of pleasure, as against the *blasé*, and unchildlike. But when one has the childlike joy it is best to have also the childlike unconsciousness; and I do not think we should have special affection for the little boy who everlastingly explained that it was his duty to play Hide and Seek and one of his family virtues to be prominent in Puss in the Corner.

Another such irritating hypocrisy is the oligarchic attitude towards mendicity as against organized charity. Here again, as in the case of cleanliness and of athletics, the attitude would be perfectly human and intelligible if it were not maintained as a merit. Just as the obvious thing about soap is that it is a convenience, so the obvious thing about beggars is that they are an inconvenience. The rich would deserve very little blame if they simply said that they never dealt directly with beggars, because in modern urban civilization it is impossible to deal directly with beggars; or if not impossible, at least very difficult. But these people do not refuse money to beggars on the ground that such charity is difficult. They refuse it on the grossly hypocritical ground that such charity is easy. They say, with the most grotesque gravity, "Anyone can put his hand in his pocket and give a poor man a penny; but we, philanthropists, go home and brood and travail over the poor man's troubles until we have discovered exactly what jail, reformatory, workhouse, or lunatic asylum it will really be best for him to go to." This is all sheer lying. They do not brood about the man when they get home, and if they did it would not alter the original fact that their motive for discouraging beggars is the perfectly rational one that beggars are a bother. A man may easily be forgiven for not doing this or that incidental act of charity, especially when the question is as genuinely difficult as is the case of mendicity. But there is something quite pestilently Pecksniffian about shrinking from a hard task on the plea that it is not hard enough. If any man will really try talking to the ten beggars who come to his door he will soon find out whether it is really so much easier than the labor of writing a check for a hospital.

XII

THE STALENESS OF THE NEW SCHOOLS

For this deep and disabling reason therefore, its cynical and abandoned indifference to the truth, the English public school does not provide us with the ideal that we require. We can only ask its modern critics to remember that right or wrong the thing can be done; the factory is working, the wheels are going around, the gentlemen are being produced, with their soap, cricket and organized charity all complete. And in this, as we have said before, the public school really has an advantage over all the other educational schemes of our time. You can pick out a public-school man in any of the many companies into which they stray, from a Chinese opium den to a German-Jewish dinner-party. But I doubt if you could tell which little match girl had been brought up by undenominational religion and which by secular education. The great English aristocracy which has ruled us since the Reformation is really, in this sense, a model to the moderns. It did have an ideal, and therefore it has produced a reality.

We may repeat here that these pages propose mainly to show one thing: that progress ought to be based on principle, while our modern progress is mostly based on precedent. We go, not by what may be affirmed in theory, but by what has been already admitted in practice. That is why the Jacobites are the last Tories in history with whom a high-spirited person can have much sympathy. They wanted a specific thing; they were ready to go forward for it, and so they were also ready to go back for it. But modern Tories have only the dullness of defending situations that they had not the excitement of creating. Revolutionists make a reform, Conservatives only conserve the reform. They never reform the reform, which is often very much wanted. Just as the rivalry of armaments is only a sort of sulky plagiarism, so the rivalry of parties is only a sort of sulky inheritance. Men have votes, so women must soon have votes; poor children are taught by force, so they must soon be fed by force; the police shut public houses by twelve o'clock, so soon they must shut them by eleven o'clock; children stop at school till they are fourteen, so soon they will stop till they are forty. No gleam of reason, no momentary return to first principles, no abstract asking of any obvious question, can interrupt this mad and monotonous gallop of mere progress by precedent. It is a good way to prevent real revolution. By this logic of events, the Radical gets as much into a rut as the Conservative. We meet one hoary old lunatic who says his grandfather told him to stand by one stile. We meet another hoary old lunatic who says his grandfather told him only to walk along one lane.

I say we may repeat here this primary part of the argument, because we have just now come to the place where it is most startlingly and strongly shown. The final proof that our elementary schools have no definite ideal of their own is the fact that they so openly imitate the ideals of the public schools. In the elementary schools we have all the ethical prejudices and exaggerations of Eton and Harrow carefully copied for people to whom they do not even roughly apply. We have the same wildly disproportionate doctrine of the effect of physical cleanliness on moral character. Educators and educational politicians declare, amid warm cheers, that cleanliness is far more important than all the squabbles about moral and religious training. It would really seem that so long as a little boy washes his hands it does not matter whether he is washing off his mother's jam or his brother's gore. We have the same grossly insincere pretense that sport always encourages a sense of honor, when we know that it often ruins it. Above all, we have the same great upperclass assumption that things are done best by large institutions handling large sums of money and ordering everybody about; and that trivial and impulsive charity is in some way contemptible. As Mr. Blatchford says, "The world does not want piety, but soap—and Socialism." Piety is one of the popular virtues, whereas soap and Socialism are two hobbies of the upper middle class.

These "healthy" ideals, as they are called, which our politicians and schoolmasters have borrowed from the aristocratic schools and applied to the democratic, are by no means particularly appropriate to an impoverished democracy. A vague admiration for organized government and a vague distrust of individual aid cannot be made to fit in at all into the lives of people among whom kindness means lending a saucepan and honor means keeping out of the workhouse. It resolves itself either into discouraging that system of prompt and patchwork generosity which is a daily glory of the poor, or else into hazy advice to people who have no money not to give it recklessly away. Nor is the exaggerated glory of athletics, defensible enough in dealing with the rich who, if they did not romp and race, would eat and drink unwholesomely, by any means so much to the point when applied to people, most of whom will take a great deal of exercise anyhow, with spade or hammer, pickax or saw. And for the third case, of washing, it is obvious that the same sort of rhetoric about corporeal daintiness which is proper to an ornamental class cannot, merely as it stands, be applicable to a dustman. A gentleman is expected to be substantially spotless all the time. But it is no more discreditable for a scavenger to be dirty than for a deep-sea diver to be wet. A sweep is no more disgraced when he is covered with soot than Michael Angelo when he is covered with clay, or Bayard[1] when he is covered with blood. Nor have these extenders of the public-school tradition done or suggested anything by way of a substitute for the present snobbish system which makes cleanliness almost impossible to the poor; I mean the general ritual of linen and the wearing of the cast-off clothes of the rich. One man moves into another man's clothes as he moves into another man's house. No wonder that our educationists are not horrified at a man picking up the aristocrat's second-hand trousers, when they themselves have only taken up the aristocrat's second-hand ideas.

[1] Pierre Bayard (1473–1524), heroic French soldier.

XIII

THE OUTLAWED PARENT

There is one thing at least of which there is never so much as a whisper inside the popular schools; and that is the opinion of the people. The only persons who seem to have nothing to do with the education of the children are the parents. Yet the English poor have very definite traditions in many ways. They are hidden under embarrassment and irony; and those psychologists who have disentangled them talk of them as very strange, barbaric and secretive things. But, as a matter of fact, the traditions of the poor are mostly simply the traditions of humanity, a thing which many of us have not seen for some time. For instance, workingmen have a tradition that if one is talking about a vile thing it is better to talk of it in coarse language; one is the less likely to be seduced into excusing it. But mankind had this tradition also, until the Puritans and their children, the Ibsenites, started the opposite idea, that it does not matter what you say so long as you say it with long words and a long face. Or again, the educated classes have tabooed most jesting about personal appearance; but in doing this they taboo not only the humor of the slums, but more than half the healthy literature of the world; they put polite nose-bags on the noses of Punch[1] and Bardolph,[2] Stiggins[3] and Cyrano de Bergerac.[4] Again, the educated classes have adopted a hideous and heathen custom of considering death as too dreadful to talk about, and letting it remain a secret for each person, like some private malformation. The poor, on the contrary, make a great gossip and display about bereavement; and they are right. They have hold of a truth of psychology which is at the back of all the funeral

---

[1] A traditional puppet with a violent temper and a sly character.

[2] A sharp, acerbic character in Shakespeare's plays *Henry V, Henry VI* and the *Merry Wives of Windsor.*

[3] A hypocritical and intemperate character in Charles Dickens' *Pickwick Papers.*

[4] Cyrano de Bergerac (1619–1655), French soldier, swordsman and hero of a play by Rostand.

customs of the children of men. The way to lessen sorrow is to make a lot of it. The way to endure a painful crisis is to insist very much that it is a crisis; to permit people who must feel sad at least to feel important. In this the poor are simply the priests of the universal civilization; and in their stuffy feasts and solemn chattering there is the smell of the baked meats of Hamlet and the dust and echo of the funeral games of Patroclus.

The things philanthropists barely excuse (or do not excuse) in the life of the laboring classes are simply the things we have to excuse in all the greatest monuments of man. It may be that the laborer is as gross as Shakespeare or as garrulous as Homer; that if he is religious he talks nearly as much about hell as Dante; that if he is worldly he talks nearly as much about drink as Dickens. Nor is the poor man without historic support if he thinks less of that ceremonial washing which Christ dismissed, and rather more of that ceremonial drinking which Christ specially sanctified. The only difference between the poor man of to-day and the saints and heroes of history is that which in all classes separates the common man who can feel things from the great man who can express them. What he feels is merely the heritage of man. Now nobody expects of course that the cabmen and coal-heavers can be complete instructors of their children any more than the squires and colonels and tea merchants are complete instructors of their children. There must be an educational specialist *in loco parentis.* But the master at Harrow is *in loco parentis;* the master in Hoxton is rather *contra parentum.* The vague politics of the squire, the vaguer virtues of the colonel, the soul and spiritual yearnings of a tea merchant, are, in veritable practice, conveyed to the children of these people at the English public schools. But I wish here to ask a very plain and emphatic question. Can anyone alive even pretend to point out any way in which these special virtues and traditions of the poor are reproduced in the education of the poor? I do not wish the costers' irony to appear as coarsely in the school as it does in the tap-room; but does it appear at all? Is the child taught to sympathize at all with his father's admirable cheerfulness and slang? I do not expect the pathetic, eager *pietas* of the mother, with her funeral clothes and funeral baked meats, to be exactly imitated in the educational system; but has it any influence at all on the educational system? Does any elementary schoolmaster accord it even an instant's consideration or respect? I do not expect the schoolmaster to hate hospitals and C.O.S.[5] centers so much as the schoolboy's father; but does he hate them at all? Does he sympathize in the least with the poor man's point of honor against official institutions? Is it not quite certain that the ordinary elementary schoolmaster will think it not merely natural but simply conscientious to eradicate all these rugged legends of a laborious people, and on principle to preach soap and Socialism against beer and liberty? In the lower classes the schoolmaster does not work for the parent, but against the parent. Modern education means handing down the customs of the minority, and rooting out the customs of the majority. Instead of their Christlike charity, their Shakespearean laughter and their high Homeric reverence for the dead, the poor have imposed on them mere pedantic copies of the prejudices of the remote rich. They must think a bathroom a necessity because to the lucky it is a luxury; they must swing Swedish clubs because their masters are afraid of English cudgels; and they must get over their prejudice against being fed by the parish, because aristocrats feel no shame about being fed by the nation.

[5] Charity Organization Society.

XIV

FOLLY AND FEMALE EDUCATION

It is the same in the case of girls. I am often solemnly asked what I
think of the new ideas about female education. But there are no new
ideas about female education. There is not, there never has been, even
the vestige of a new idea. All the educational reformers did was to ask
what was being done to boys and then go and do it to girls; just as
they asked what was being taught to young squires and then taught it
to young chimney-sweeps. What they call new ideas are very old ideas
in the wrong place. Boys play football, why shouldn't girls play football; boys have school-colors, why shouldn't girls have school-colors;
boys go in hundreds to day-schools, why shouldn't girls go in hundreds to day-schools; boys go to Oxford, why shouldn't girls go to
Oxford—in short, boys grow mustaches, why shouldn't girls grow
mustaches—that is about their notion of a new idea. There is no
brain-work in the thing at all; no root query of what sex is, of whether
it alters this or that, and why, any more than there is any imaginative
grip of the humor and heart of the populace in the popular education.
There is nothing but plodding, elaborate, elephantine imitation. And
just as in the case of elementary teaching, the cases are of a cold and
reckless inappropriateness. Even a savage could see that bodily things, at
least, which are good for a man are very likely to be bad for a woman.
Yet there is no boy's game, however brutal, which these mild lunatics
have not promoted among girls. To take a stronger case, they give girls
very heavy home-work; never reflecting that all girls have home-work
already in their homes. It is all a part of the same silly subjugation; there
must be a hard stick-up collar round the neck of a woman, because it is
already a nuisance round the neck of a man. Though a Saxon serf, if he
wore that collar of cardboard, would ask for his collar of brass.

It will then be answered, not without a sneer, "And what would
you prefer? Would you go back to the elegant early Victorian female, with ringlets and smelling-bottle, doing a little in water-
colors, dabbling a little in Italian, playing a little on the harp,

writing in vulgar albums and painting on senseless screens? Do you prefer that?" To which I answer, "Emphatically, yes." I solidly prefer it to the new female education, for this reason, that I can see in it an intellectual design, while there is none in the other. I am by no means sure that even in point of practical fact that elegant female would not have been more than a match for most of the inelegant females. I fancy Jane Austen was stronger, sharper and shrewder than Charlotte Brontë; I am quite certain she was stronger, sharper and shrewder than George Eliot. She could do one thing neither of them could do: she could coolly and sensibly describe a man. I am not sure that the old great lady who could only smatter Italian was not more vigorous than the new great lady who can only stammer American; nor am I certain that the bygone duchesses who were scarcely successful when they painted Melrose Abbey, were so much more weak-minded than the modern duchesses who paint only their own faces, and are bad at that. But that is not the point. What was the theory, what was the idea, in their old, weak water-colors and their shaky Italian? The idea was the same which in a ruder rank expressed itself in home-made wines and hereditary recipes; and which still, in a thousand unexpected ways, can be found clinging to the women of the poor. It was the idea I urged in the second part of this book: that the world must keep one great amateur, lest we all become artists and perish. Somebody must renounce all specialist conquests, that she may conquer all the conquerors. That she may be a queen of life, she must not be a private soldier in it. I do not think the elegant female with her bad Italian was a perfect product, any more than I think the slum woman talking gin and funerals is a perfect product; alas! there are few perfect products. But they come from a comprehensible idea; and the new woman comes from nothing and nowhere. It is right to have an ideal, it is right to have the right ideal, and these two have the right ideal. The slum mother with her funerals is the degenerate daughter of Antigone, the obstinate priestess of the household gods. The lady talking bad Italian was the decayed tenth cousin of Portia, the great and golden Italian lady, the Renascence amateur of life, who could be a barrister because she could be anything. Sunken and neglected in the sea of modern monotony and imitation, the types hold tightly to their original truths. Antigone, ugly, dirty and often drunken, will still bury her father. The elegant female, vapid and fading away to nothing, still feels faintly the fundamental difference between herself and her husband: that he must be Something in the City, that she may be everything in the country.

There was a time when you and I and all of us were all very close to God; so that even now the color of a pebble (or a paint), the smell of a flower (or a firework), comes to our hearts with a kind of authority and certainty; as if they were fragments of a muddled message, or features of a forgotten face. To pour that fiery simplicity upon the whole of life is the only real aim of education; and closest to the child comes the woman—she understands. To say what she understands is beyond me; save only this, that it is not a solemnity. Rather it is a towering levity, an uproarious amateurishness of the universe, such as we felt when we were little, and would as soon sing as garden, as soon paint as run. To smatter the tongues of men and angels, to dabble in the dreadful sciences, to juggle with pillars and pyramids and toss up the planets like balls, this is that inner audacity and indifference which the human soul, like a conjurer catching oranges, must keep up forever. This is that insanely frivolous thing we call sanity. And the elegant female, drooping her ringlets over her water-colors, knew it and acted on it. She was juggling with frantic and flaming suns. She was maintaining the bold equilibrium of inferiorities which is the most mysterious of superiorities and perhaps the most unattainable. She was maintaining the prime truth of woman, the universal mother: that if a thing is worth doing, it is worth doing badly.

PART FIVE

THE HOME OF MAN

THE EMPIRE OF THE INSECT

A cultivated Conservative friend of mine once exhibited great distress because in a gay moment I once called Edmund Burke an atheist. I need scarcely say that the remark lacked something of biographical precision; it was meant to. Burke was certainly not an atheist in his conscious cosmic theory, though he had not a special and flaming faith in God, like Robespierre. Nevertheless, the remark had reference to a truth which it is here relevant to repeat. I mean that in the quarrel over the French Revolution, Burke did stand for the atheistic attitude and mode of argument, as Robespierre stood for the theistic. The Revolution appealed to the idea of an abstract and eternal justice, beyond all local custom or convenience. If there are commands of God, then there must be rights of man. Here Burke made his brilliant diversion; he did not attack the Robespierre doctrine with the old mediaeval doctrine of *jus divinum* (which, like the Robespierre doctrine, was theistic), he attacked it with the modern argument of scientific relativity; in short, the argument of evolution. He suggested that humanity was everywhere molded by or fitted to its environment and institutions; in fact, that each people practically got, not only the tyrant it deserved, but the tyrant it ought to have. "I know nothing of the rights of men," he said, "but I know something of the rights of Englishmen." There you have the essential atheist. His argument is that we have got some protection by natural accident and growth; and why should we profess to think beyond it, for all the world as if we were the images of God! We are born under a House of Lords, as birds under a house of leaves; we live under a monarchy as niggers live under a tropic sun; it is not their fault if they are slaves, and it is not ours if we are snobs. Thus, long before Darwin struck his great blow at democracy, the essential of the Darwinian argument had been already urged against the French Revolution. Man, said Burke in effect, must adapt himself to everything, like an animal; he must not try to alter everything, like an angel. The last weak cry of the pious, pretty, half-artificial optimism and deism of

the eighteenth century came in the voice of Sterne,[1] saying, "God
tempers the wind to the shorn lamb." And Burke, the iron evolutionist, essentially answered, "No; God tempers the shorn lamb to
the wind." It is the lamb that has to adapt himself. That is, he either
dies or becomes a particular kind of lamb who likes standing in a
draught.

The subconscious popular instinct against Darwinism was not a
mere offense at the grotesque notion of visiting one's grandfather in
a cage in the Regent's Park. Men go in for drink, practical jokes and
many other grotesque things; they do not much mind making beasts
of themselves, and would not much mind having beasts made of
their forefathers. The real instinct was much deeper and much more
valuable. It was this: that when once one begins to think of man as a
shifting and alterable thing, it is always easy for the strong and
crafty to twist him into new shapes for all kinds of unnatural purposes. The popular instinct sees in such developments the possibility
of backs bowed and hunch-backed for their burden, or limbs twisted
for their task. It has a very well-grounded guess that whatever is
done swiftly and systematically will mostly be done by a successful
class and almost solely in their interests. It has therefore a vision of
inhuman hybrids and half-human experiments much in the style of
Mr. Wells's "Island of Dr. Moreau." The rich man may come to
breeding a tribe of dwarfs to be his jockeys, and a tribe of giants to be
his hall-porters. Grooms might be born bow-legged and tailors born
cross-legged; perfumers might have long, large noses and a crouching
attitude, like hounds of scent; and professional wine-tasters might
have the horrible expression of one tasting wine stamped upon their
faces as infants. Whatever wild image one employs it cannot keep
pace with the panic of the human fancy, when once it supposes that
the fixed type called man could be changed. If some millionaire
wanted arms, some porter must grow ten arms like an octopus; if he
wants legs, some messenger-boy must go with a hundred trotting legs
like a centipede. In the distorted mirror of hypothesis, that is, of the
unknown, men can dimly see such monstrous and evil shapes; men

[1] Laurence Sterne (1713–1768), English novelist.

run all to eye, or all to fingers, with nothing left but one nostril or one ear. That is the nightmare with which the mere notion of adaptation threatens us. That is the nightmare that is not so very far from the reality.

It will be said that not the wildest evolutionist really asks that we should become in any way unhuman or copy any other animal. Pardon me, that is exactly what not merely the wildest evolutionists urge, but some of the tamest evolutionists, too. There has risen high in recent history an important *cultus* which bids fair to be the religion of the future—which means the religion of those few weak-minded people who live in the future. It is typical of our time that it has to look for its god through a microscope; and our time has marked a definite adoration of the insect. Like most things we call new, of course, it is not at all new as an idea; it is only new as an idolatry. Virgil takes bees seriously, but I doubt if he would have kept bees as carefully as he wrote about them. The wise king told the sluggard to watch the ant, a charming occupation—for a sluggard. But in our own time has appeared a very different tone, and more than one great man, as well as numberless intelligent men, have in our time seriously suggested that we should study the insect because we are his inferiors. The old moralists merely took the virtues of man and distributed them quite decoratively and arbitrarily among the animals. The ant was an almost heraldic symbol of industry, as the lion was of courage, or, for the matter of that, the pelican of charity. But if the mediaevals had been convinced that a lion was not courageous, they would have dropped the lion and kept the courage; if the pelican is not charitable, they would say, so much the worse for the pelican. The old moralists, I say, permitted the ant to enforce and typify man's morality; they never allowed the ant to upset it. They used the ant for industry as the lark for punctuality; they looked up at the flapping birds and down at the crawling insects for a homely lesson. But we have lived to see a sect that does not look down at the insects, but looks up at the insects; that asks us essentially to bow down and worship beetles, like ancient Egyptians.

Maurice Maeterlinck is a man of unmistakable genius, and genius always carries a magnifying glass. In the terrible crystal of his lens we have seen the bees not as a little yellow swarm, but rather in golden armies and hierarchies of warriors and queens. Imagination perpetually peers and creeps further down the avenues and vistas in the tubes of science, and one fancies every frantic reversal of proportions; the earwig striding across the echoing plain like an elephant, or the grasshopper coming roaring above our roofs like a vast aëroplane, as he leaps from Hertfordshire to Surrey. One seems to enter in a dream a temple of enormous entomology, whose architecture is based on something wilder than arms or backbones; in which the ribbed columns have the half-crawling look of dim and monstrous caterpillars; or the dome is a starry spider hung horribly in the void. There is one of the modern works of engineering that gives one something of this nameless fear of the exaggerations of an underworld; and that is the curious curved architecture of the underground railway, commonly called the Twopenny Tube. Those squat archways, without any upright line or pillar, look as if they had been tunneled by huge worms who have never learned to lift their heads. It is the very underground palace of the Serpent, the spirit of changing shape and color, that is the enemy of man.

But it is not merely by such strange aesthetic suggestions that writers like Maeterlinck have influenced us in the matter; there is also an ethical side to the business. The upshot of M. Maeterlinck's book on bees is an admiration, one might also say an envy, of their collective spirituality; of the fact that they live only for something which he calls the Soul of the Hive. And this admiration for the communal morality of insects is expressed in many other modern writers in various quarters and shapes; in Mr. Benjamin Kidd's[2] theory of living only for the evolutionary future of our race, and in the great interest of some Socialists in ants, which they generally prefer to bees, I suppose, because they are not so brightly colored. Not least among the hundred evidences of this vague insectolatry are the floods of flattery poured by modern people on that energetic

[2] Benjamin Kidd (1858–1916), English novelist. His most successful book, *Social Evolution* (1894), argues that moral progress consists in subordinating individual selfishness to the common good.

nation of the Far East of which it has been said that "Patriotism is its only religion"; or, in other words, that it lives only for the Soul of the Hive. When at long intervals of the centuries Christendom grows weak, morbid or skeptical, and mysterious Asia begins to move against us her dim populations and to pour them westward like a dark movement of matter, in such cases it has been very common to compare the invasion to a plague of lice or incessant armies of locusts. The Eastern armies were indeed like insects; in their blind, busy destructiveness, in their black nihilism of personal outlook, in their hateful indifference to inidividual life and love, in their base belief in mere numbers, in their pessimistic courage and their atheistic patriotism, the riders and raiders of the East are indeed like all the creeping things of the earth. But never before, I think, have Christians called a Turk a locust and meant it as a compliment. Now for the first time we worship as well as fear; and trace with adoration that enormous form advancing vast and vague out of Asia, faintly discernible amid the mystic clouds of winged creatures hung over the wasted lands, thronging the skies like thunder and discoloring the skies like rain; Beelzebub, the Lord of Flies.

In resisting this horrible theory of the Soul of the Hive, we of Christendom stand not for ourselves, but for all humanity; for the essential and distinctive human idea that one good and happy man is an end in himself, that a soul is worth saving. Nay, for those who like such biological fancies it might well be said that we stand as chiefs and champions of a whole section of nature, princes of the house whose cognizance is the backbone, standing for the milk of the individual mother and the courage of the wandering cub, representing the pathetic chivalry of the dog, the humor and perversity of cats, the affection of the tranquil horse, the loneliness of the lion. It is more to the point, however, to urge that this mere glorification of society as it is in the social insects is a transformation and a dissolution in one of the outlines which have been specially the symbols of man. In the cloud and confusion of the flies and bees is growing fainter and fainter, as if finally disappearing, the idea of the human family. The hive has become larger than the house, the bees are destroying their captors; what the locust hath left, the caterpillar hath eaten; and the little house and garden of our friend Jones is in a bad way.

II

THE FALLACY OF THE UMBRELLA STAND

When Lord Morley[1] said that the House of Lords must be either mended or ended, he used a phrase which has caused some confusion; because it might seem to suggest that mending and ending are somewhat similar things. I wish specially to insist on the fact that mending and ending are opposite things. You mend a thing because you like it; you end a thing because you don't. To mend is to strengthen. I, for instance, disbelieve in oligarchy; so I would no more mend the House of Lords than I would mend a thumbscrew. On the other hand, I do believe in the family; therefore I would mend the family as I would mend a chair; and I will never deny for a moment that the modern family is a chair that wants mending. But here comes in the essential point about the mass of modern advanced sociologists. Here are two institutions that have always been fundamental with mankind, the family and the state. Anarchists, I believe, disbelieve in both. It is quite unfair to say that Socialists believe in the state, but do not believe in the family; thousands of Socialists believe more in the family than any Tory. But it is true to say that while anarchists would end both, Socialists are specially engaged in mending (that is, strengthening and renewing) the state; and they are not specially engaged in strengthening and renewing the family. They are not doing anything to define the functions of father, mother, and child, as such; they are not tightening the machine up again; they are not blackening in again the fading lines of the old drawing. With the state they are doing this; they are sharpening its machinery, they are blackening in its black dogmatic lines, they are making mere government in every way stronger and in some ways harsher than before. While they leave the home in ruins, they restore the hive, especially the stings. Indeed, some schemes of labor and Poor Law reform recently

[1] John Morley (1838–1923), English statesman and writer.

208

advanced by distinguished Socialists, amount to little more than putting the largest number of people in the despotic power of Mr. Bumble. Apparently, progress means being moved on—by the police.

The point it is my purpose to urge might perhaps be suggesed thus: that Socialists and most social reformers of their color are vividly conscious of the line between the kind of things that belong to the state and the kind of things that belong to mere chaos or uncoercible nature; they may force children to go to school before the sun rises, but they will not try to force the sun to rise; they will not, like Canute, banish the sea, but only the sea-bathers. But inside the outline of the state their lines are confused, and entities melt into each other. They have no firm instinctive sense of one thing being in its nature private and another public, of one thing being necessarily bond and another free. That is why piece by piece, and quite silently, personal liberty is being stolen from Englishmen, as personal land has been silently stolen ever since the sixteenth century.

I can only put it sufficiently curtly in a careless simile. A Socialist means a man who thinks a walking-stick like an umbrella because they both go into the umbrella-stand. Yet they are as different as a battle-ax and a bootjack. The essential idea of an umbrella is breadth and protection. The essential idea of a stick is slenderness and, partly, attack. The stick is the sword, the umbrella is the shield, but it is a shield against another and more nameless enemy—the hostile but anonymous universe. More properly, therefore, the umbrella is the roof; it is a kind of collapsible house. But the vital difference goes far deeper than this; it branches off into two kingdoms of man's mind, with a chasm between. For the point is this: that the umbrella is a shield against an enemy so actual as to be a mere nuisance; whereas the stick is a sword against enemies so entirely imaginary as to be a pure pleasure. The stick is not merely a sword, but a court sword; it is a thing of purely ceremonial swagger. One cannot express the emotion in any way except by saying that a man feels more like a man with a stick in his hand, just as he feels more like a man with a sword at his side. But nobody ever had any swelling sentiments about an umbrella; it is a convenience, like a door scraper.

An umbrella is a necessary evil. A walking-stick is a quite un-necessary good. This, I fancy, is the real explanation of the perpetual losing of umbrellas; one does not hear of people losing walking-sticks. For a walking-stick is a pleasure, a piece of real personal property; it is missed even when it is not needed. When my right hand forgets its stick may it forget its cunning. But anybody may forget an umbrella, as anybody might forget a shed that he has stood up in out of the rain. Anybody can forget a necessary thing.

If I might pursue the figure of speech, I might briefly say that the whole Collectivist error consists in saying that because two men can share an umbrella, therefore two men can share a walking-stick. Umbrellas might possibly be replaced by some kind of common awnings covering certain streets from particular showers. But there is nothing but nonsense in the notion of swinging a communal stick; it is as if one spoke of twirling a communal mustache. It will be said that this is a frank fantasia and that no sociologists suggest such follies. Pardon me, they do. I will give a precise parallel to the case of confusion of sticks and umbrellas, a parallel from a perpetu-ally reiterated suggestion of reform. At least sixty Socialists out of a hundred, when they have spoken of common laundries, will go on at once to speak of common kitchens. This is just as mechanical and unintelligent as the fanciful case I have quoted. Sticks and umbrellas are both stiff rods that go into holes in a stand in the hall. Kitchens and washhouses are both large rooms full of heat and damp and steam. But the soul and function of the two things are utterly oppo-site. There is only one way of washing a shirt; that is, there is only one right way. There is no taste and fancy in tattered shirts. Nobody says, "Tompkins likes five holes in his shirt, but I must say, give me the good old four holes." Nobody says, "This washerwoman rips up the left leg of my pyjamas; now if there is one thing I insist on it is the *right* leg ripped up." The ideal washing is simply to send a thing back washed. But it is by no means true that the ideal cooking is simply to send a thing back cooked. Cooking is an art; it has in it personality, and even perversity, for the definition of an art is that which must be personal and may be perverse. I know a man, not otherwise dainty, who cannot touch common sausages unless they are almost burned to a coal. He wants his sausages fried to rags, yet he does not insist on his shirts being boiled to rags. I do not say that such points of culinary delicacy are of high importance. I do not say that the communal ideal must give way to them. What I say is that the communal ideal is not conscious of their existence, and therefore goes wrong from the very start, mixing a wholly public thing with a highly individual one. Perhaps we ought to accept communal kitchens in the social crisis, just as we should accept communal cat's-meat in a siege. But the cultured Socialist, quite at his ease, by no means in a siege, talks about communal kitchens as if they were the same kind of thing as communal laundries. This shows at the start that he misunderstands human nature. It is as different as three men singing the same chorus from three men playing three tunes on the same piano.

III

THE DREADFUL DUTY OF GUDGE

In the quarrel earlier alluded to between the energetic Progressive and the obstinate Conservative (or, to talk a tenderer language, between Hudge and Gudge), the state of cross-purposes is at the present moment acute. The Tory says he wants to preserve family life in Cindertown; the Socialist very reasonably points out to him that in Cindertown at present there isn't any family life to preserve. But Hudge, the Socialist, in his turn, is highly vague and mysterious about whether he would preserve the family life if there were any; or whether he will try to restore it where it has disappeared. It is all very confusing. The Tory sometimes talks as if he wanted to tighten the domestic bonds that do not exist; the Socialist as if he wanted to loosen the bonds that do not bind anybody. The question we all want to ask of both of them is the original ideal question, "Do you want to keep the family at all?" If Hudge, the Socialist, does want the family he must be prepared for the natural restraints, distinctions and divisions of labor in the family. He must brace himself up to bear the idea of the woman having a preference for the private house and a man for the public house. He must manage to endure somehow the idea of a woman being womanly, which does not mean soft and yielding, but handy, thrifty, rather hard, and very humorous. He must confront without a quiver the notion of a child who shall be childish, that is, full of energy, but without an idea of independence; fundamentally as eager for authority as for information and butter-scotch. If a man, a woman and a child live together any more in free and sovereign households, these ancient relations will recur; and Hudge must put up with it. He can only avoid it by destroying the family, driving both sexes into sexless hives and hordes, and bringing up all children as the children of the state—like Oliver Twist. But if these stern words must be addressed to Hudge, neither shall Gudge escape a somewhat severe admonition. For the plain truth to be told pretty sharply to the Tory is this, that if *he* wants the family to remain, if he wants to be strong enough to resist the rending forces of our essentially savage commerce, he must make some very big sacrifices and try to equalize property. The over-whelming mass of the English people at this particular instant are simply too poor to be domestic. They are as domestic as they can manage; they are much more domestic than the governing class; but they cannot get what good there was originally meant to be in this institution, simply because they have not got enough money. The man ought to stand for a certain magnanimity, quite lawfully ex-pressed in throwing money away; but if under given circumstances he can only do it by throwing the week's food away, then he is not magnanimous, but mean. The woman ought to stand for a certain wisdom which is well expressed in valuing things rightly and guard-ing money sensibly; but how is she to guard money if there is no money to guard? The child ought to look on his mother as a foun-tain of natural fun and poetry; but how can he unless the fountain, like other fountains, is allowed to play? What chance have any of these ancient arts and functions in a house so hideously topsy-turvy; a house where the woman is out working and the man isn't; and the child is forced by law to think his schoolmaster's requirements more important than his mother's? No, Gudge and his friends in the House of Lords and the Carlton Club must make up their minds on this mat-ter, and that very quickly. If they are content to have England turned into a beehive and an ant-hill, decorated here and there with a few faded butterflies playing at an old game called domesticity in the inter-vals of the divorce court, then let them have their empire of insects; they will find plenty of Socialists who will give it to them. But if they want a domestic England, they must "shell out," as the phrase goes, to a vastly greater extent than any Radical politician has yet dared to suggest; they must endure burdens much heavier than the Budget and strokes much deadlier than the death duties; for the thing to be done is nothing more nor less than the distribution of the great fortunes and the great estates. We can now only avoid Socialism by a change as vast as Socialism. If we are to save property, we must distribute prop-erty, almost as sternly and sweepingly as did the French Revolution. If we are to preserve the family we must revolutionize the nation.

IV

A LAST INSTANCE

And now, as this book is drawing to a close, I will whisper in the reader's ear a horrible suspicion that has sometimes haunted me: the suspicion that Hudge and Gudge are secretly in partnership. That the quarrel they keep up in public is very much of a put-up job, and that the way in which they perpetually play into each other's hands is not an everlasting coincidence. Gudge, the plutocrat, wants an anarchic industrialism; Hudge, the idealist, provides him with lyric praises of anarchy. Gudge wants women-workers because they are cheaper; Hudge calls the woman's work "freedom to live her own life." Gudge wants steady and obedient workmen; Hudge preaches teetotalism—to workmen, not to Gudge. Gudge wants a tame and timid population who will never take arms against tyranny; Hudge proves from Tolstoi that nobody must take arms against anything. Gudge is naturally a healthy and well-washed gentleman; Hudge earnestly preaches the perfection of Gudge's washing to people who can't practice it. Above all, Gudge rules by a coarse and cruel system of sacking and sweating and bi-sexual toil which is totally inconsistent with the free family and which is bound to destroy it; therefore Hudge, stretching out his arms to the universe with a prophetic smile, tells us that the family is something that we shall soon gloriously outgrow.

I do not know whether the partnership of Hudge and Gudge is conscious or unconscious. I only know that between them they still keep the common man homeless. I only know I still meet Jones walking the streets in the gray twilight, looking sadly at the poles and barriers and low red goblin lanterns which still guard the house which is none the less his because he has never been in it.

V

CONCLUSION

Here, it may be said, my book ends just where it ought to begin. I have said that the strong centers of modern English property must swiftly or slowly be broken up, if even the idea of property is to remain among Englishmen. There are two ways in which it could be done, a cold administration by quite detached officials, which is called Collectivism, or a personal distribution, so as to produce what is called Peasant Proprietorship. I think the latter solution the finer and more fully human, because it makes each man as somebody blamed somebody for saying of the Pope, a sort of small god. A man on his own turf tastes eternity or, in other words, will give ten minutes more work than is required. But I believe I am justified in shutting the door on this vista of argument, instead of opening it. For this book is not designed to prove the case for Peasant Proprietorship, but to prove the case against modern sages who turn reform to a routine. The whole of this book has been a rambling and elaborate urging of one purely ethical fact. And if by any chance it should happen that there are still some who do not quite see what that point is, I will end with one plain parable, which is none the worse for being also a fact.

A little while ago certain doctors and other persons permitted by modern law to dictate to their shabbier fellow-citizens, sent out an order that all little girls should have their hair cut short. I mean, of course, all little girls whose parents were poor. Many very unhealthy habits are common among rich little girls, but it will be long before any doctors interfere forcibly with them. Now, the case for this particular interference was this, that the poor are pressed down from above into such stinking and suffocating underworlds of squalor, that poor people must not be allowed to have hair, because in their case it must mean lice in the hair. Therefore, the doctors propose to abolish the hair. It never seems to have occurred to them to abolish the lice. Yet it could be done. As is common in most modern discussions the unmentionable thing is the pivot of the whole discusssion. It is obvious to any Christian man (that is, to any man with a free soul) that any coercion applied to a cabman's daughter ought, if possible, to be applied to a Cabinet Minister's daughter. I will not ask why the doctors do not, as a matter of fact apply their rule to a Cabinet Minister's daughter. I will not ask, because I know. They do not because they dare not. But what is the excuse they would urge, what is the plausible argument they would use, for thus cutting and clipping poor children and not rich? Their argument would be that the disease is more likely to be in the hair of poor people than of rich. And why? Because the poor children are forced (against all the instincts of the highly domestic working classes) to crowd together in close rooms under a wildly inefficient system of public instruction; and because in one out of the forty children there may be offense. And why? Because the poor man is so ground down by the great rents of the great ground landlords that his wife often has to work as well as he. Therefore she has no time to look after the children; therefore one in forty of them is dirty. Because the workingman has these two persons on top of him, the landlord sitting (literally) on his stomach, and the schoolmaster sitting (literally) on his head, the workingman must allow his little girl's hair, first to be neglected from poverty, next to be poisoned by promiscuity, and, lastly, to be abolished by hygiene. He, perhaps, was proud of his little girl's hair. But he does not count.

Upon this simple principle (or rather precedent) the sociological doctor drives gayly ahead. When a crapulous tyranny crushes men down into the dirt, so that their very hair is dirty, the scientific course is clear. It would be long and laborious to cut off the heads of the tyrants; it is easier to cut off the hair of the slaves. In the same way, if it should ever happen that poor children, screaming with toothache, disturbed any schoolmaster or artistic gentleman, it would be easy to pull out all the teeth of the poor; if their nails were disgustingly dirty, their nails could be plucked out; if their noses were indecently blown, their noses could be cut off. The appearance of our humbler fellow-citizen could be quite strikingly simplified before we had done with him. But all this is not a bit wilder than the brute fact that a doctor can walk into the house of a free man, whose daughter's hair may be as clean as spring flowers, and order him to cut it off. It never seems to strike these people that the lesson of lice in the slums is the wrongness of slums, not the wrongness of hair. Hair is, to say the least of it, a rooted thing. Its enemy (like the other insects and oriental armies of whom we have spoken) sweep upon us but seldom. In truth, it is only by eternal institutions like hair that we can test passing institutions like empires. If a house is so built as to knock a man's head off when he enters it, it is built wrong.

The mob can never rebel unless it is conservative, at least enough to have conserved some reasons for rebelling. It is the most awful thought in all our anarchy, that most of the ancient blows struck for freedom would not be struck at all to-day, because of the obscuration of the clean, popular customs from which they came. The insult that brought down the hammer of Wat Tyler[1] might now be called a medical examination. That which Virginius[2] loathed and avenged as foul slavery might now be praised as free love. The cruel taunt of Foulon,[3] "Let them eat grass," might now be represented as the dying cry of an idealistic vegetarian. Those great scissors of science that would snip off the curls of the poor little school children are ceaselessly snapping closer and closer to cut off all the corners and fringes of the arts and honors of the poor. Soon they will be twisting necks to suit clean collars, and hacking feet to fit new boots. It never seems to strike them that the body is more than raiment; that the Sabbath was made for man; that all institutions shall be judged and damned by whether they have fitted the normal flesh and spirit. It is the test of political sanity to keep your head. It is the test of artistic sanity to keep your hair on.

Now the whole parable and purpose of these last pages, and indeed of all these pages, is this: to assert that we must instantly begin all over again, and begin at the other end. I begin with a little girl's hair. That I know is a good thing at any rate. Whatever else is evil,

[1] Wat Tyler (d. 1381), English rebel, leader of Peasants Revolt in 1381.

[2] The Roman centurion who sacrificed his daughter rather than let her fall in the hands of a Decimvir.

[3] Joseph François Foulon (Foullon) (1717–1789), French revolutionary bureaucrat.

the pride of a good mother in the beauty of her daughter is good. It is one of those adamantine tendernesses which are the touchstones of every age and race. If other things are against it, other things must go down. If landlords and laws and sciences are against it, landlords and laws and sciences must go down. With the red hair of one she-urchin in the gutter I will set fire to all modern civilization. Because a girl should have long hair, she should have clean hair; because she should have clean hair, she should not have an unclean home: because she should not have an unclean home, she should have a free and leisured mother; because she should have a free mother, she should not have an usurious landlord; because there should not be an usurious landlord, there should be a redistribution of property, because there should be a redistribution of property, there shall be a revolution. That little urchin with the gold-red hair, whom I have just watched toddling past my house, she shall not be lopped and lamed and altered; her hair shall not be cut short like a convict's; no, all the kingdoms of the earth shall be hacked about and mutilated to suit her. She is the human and sacred image; all around her the social fabric shall sway and split and fall; the pillars of society shall be shaken, and the roofs of ages come rushing down; and not one hair of her head shall be harmed.

THREE NOTES

I

ON FEMALE SUFFRAGE

Not wishing to overload this long essay with too many parentheses, apart from its thesis of progress and precedent, I append here three notes on points of detail that may possibly be misunderstood.

The first refers to the female controversy. It may seem to many that I dismiss too curtly the contention that all women should have votes, even if most women do not desire them. It is constantly said in this connection that males have received the vote (the agricultural laborers for instance) when only a minority of them were in favor of it. Mr. Galsworthy,[1] one of the few fine fighting intellects of our time, has talked this language in the "Nation." Now, broadly, I have only to answer here, as everywhere in this book, that history is not a toboggan slide, but a road to be reconsidered and even retraced. If we really forced General Elections upon free laborers who definitely disliked General Elections, then it was a thoroughly undemocratic thing to do; if we are democrats we ought to undo it. We want the will of the people, not the votes of the people; and to give a man a vote against his will is to make voting more valuable than the democracy it declares.

But this analogy is false, for a plain and particular reason. Many voteless women regard a vote as unwomanly. Nobody says that most voteless men regarded a vote as unmanly. Nobody says that any voteless men regarded it as unmanly. Not in the stillest hamlet or the most stagnant fen could you find a yokel or a tramp who thought he lost his sexual dignity by being part of a political mob. If he did not care about a vote it was solely because he did not know about a vote; he did not understand the word any better than Bimetallism. His opposition, if it existed, was merely negative. His indifference to a vote was really indifference.

But the female sentiment against the franchise, whatever its size, is positive. It is not negative; it is by no means indifferent. Such women

---

[1] John Galsworthy (1867–1933), English novelist.

as are opposed to the change regard it (rightly or wrongly) as unfeminine. That is, as insulting certain affirmative traditions to which they are attached. You may think such a view prejudiced; but I violently deny that any democrat has a right to override such prejudices, if they are popular and positive. Thus he would not have a right to make millions of Moslems vote with a cross if they had a prejudice in favor of voting with a crescent. Unless this is admitted, democracy is a farce we need scarcely keep up. If it is admitted, the Suffragists have not merely to awaken an indifferent, but to convert a hostile majority.

II

ON CLEANLINESS IN EDUCATION

On re-reading my protest, which I honestly think much needed, against our heathen idolatry of mere ablution, I see that it may possibly be misread. I hasten to say that I think washing a most important thing to be taught both to rich and poor. I do not attack the positive but the relative position of soap. Let it be insisted on even as much as now; but let other things be insisted on much more. I am even ready to admit that cleanliness is next to godliness; but the moderns will not even admit godliness to be next to cleanliness. In their talk about Thomas Becket and such saints and heroes they make soap more important than soul; they reject godliness whenever it is not cleanliness. If we resent this about remote saints and heroes, we should resent it more about the many saints and heroes of the slums, whose unclean hands cleanse the world. Dirt is evil chiefly as evidence of sloth; but the fact remains that the classes that wash most are those that work least. Concerning these, the practical course is simple; soap should be urged on them and advertised as what it is—a luxury. With regard to the poor also the practical course is not hard to harmonize with our thesis. If we want to give poor people soap we must set out deliberately to give them luxuries. If we will not make them rich enough to be clean, then emphatically we must do what we did with the saints. We must reverence them for being dirty.

III

ON PEASANT PROPRIETORSHIP

I have not dealt with any details touching distributed ownership, or its possibility in England, for the reason stated in the text. This book deals with what is wrong, wrong in our root of argument and effort. This wrong is, I say, that we will go forward because we dare not go back. Thus the Socialist says that property is already concentrated into Trusts and Stores: the only hope is to concentrate it further in the State. I say the only hope is to unconcentrate it; that is, to repent and return; the only step forward is the step backward.

But in connection with this distribution I have laid myself open to another potential mistake. In speaking of a sweeping redistribution, I speak of decision in the aim, not necessarily of abruptness in the means. It is not at all too late to restore an approximately rational state of English possessions without any mere confiscation. A policy of buying out landlordism, steadily adopted in England as it has already been adopted in Ireland (notably in Mr. Wyndham's[1] wise and fruitful Act), would in a very short time release the lower end of the seesaw and make the whole plank swing more level. The objection to this course is not at all that it would not do, only that it will not be done. If we leave things as they are, there will almost certainly be a crash of confiscation. If we hesitate, we shall soon have to hurry. But if we start doing it quickly we have still time to do it slowly.

This point, however, is not essential to my book. All I have to urge between these two boards is that I dislike the big Whiteley shop,[2] and that I dislike Socialism because it will (according to Socialists) be so like that shop. It is its fulfilment, not its reversal. I do not object to Socialism because it will revolutionize our commerce, but because it will leave it so horribly the same.

[1] George Wyndham (1863–1913), British politician and writer, sometime Secretary for Ireland.

[2] See Part II, Chapter III, footnote 3.

THE SUPERSTITION
OF DIVORCE

1920

INTRODUCTORY NOTE

The earlier part of this book appeared in the form of five articles which came out in the "New Witness" at the crisis of the recent controversy in the Press on the subject of divorce. Crude and sketchy as they confessedly were, they had a certain rude plan of their own, which I find it very difficult to recast even in order to expand. I have therefore decided to reprint the original articles as they stood, save for a few introductory words; and then, at the risk of repetition, to add a few further chapters, explaining more fully any conceptions that may seem to have been too crudely assumed or dismissed. I have set forth the original matter as it appeared, under a general heading, without dividing it into chapters.

G. K. C.

I

THE SUPERSTITION OF DIVORCE (1)

It is futile to talk of reform with reference to form. To take a case from my own taste and fancy, there is nothing I feel to be so beautiful and wonderful as a window. All casements are magic casements, whether they open on the foam or the front-garden; they lie close to the ultimate mystery and paradox of limitation and liberty. But if I followed my instinct towards an infinite number of windows, it would end in having no walls. It would also (it may be added incidentally) end in having no windows either; for a window makes a picture by making a picture-frame. But there is a simpler way of stating my more simple and fatal error. It is that I have wanted a window, without considering whether I wanted a house. Now many appeals are being made to us to-day on behalf of that light and liberty that might well be symbolised by windows; especially as so many of them concern the enlightenment and liberation of the house, in the sense of the home. Many quite disinterested people urge many quite reasonable considerations in the case of divorce, as a type of domestic liberation; but in the journalistic and general discussion of the matter there is far too much of the mind that works backwards and at random, in the manner of all windows and no walls. Such people say they want divorce, without asking themselves whether they want marriage. Even in order to be divorced it has generally been found necessary to go through the preliminary formality of being married; and unless the nature of this initial act be considered, we might as well be discussing haircutting for the bald or spectacles for the blind. To be divorced is to be in the literal sense unmarried; and there is no sense in a thing being undone when we do not know if it is done.

There is perhaps no worse advice, nine times out of ten, than the advice to do the work that's nearest. It is especially bad when it means, as it generally does, removing the obstacle that's nearest. It means that men are not to behave like men but like mice; who nibble at the thing that's nearest. The man, like the mouse, undermines what he cannot understand. Because he himself bumps into a thing, he calls it the nearest obstacle; though the obstacle may happen to be the pillar that holds up the whole roof over his head. He industriously removes the obstacle; and in return the obstacle removes him, and much more valuable things than he. This opportunism is perhaps the most unpractical thing in this highly unpractical world. People talk vaguely against destructive criticism; but what is the matter with this criticism is not that it destroys, but that it does not criticise. It is destruction without design. It is taking a complex machine to pieces bit by bit, in any order, without even knowing what the machine is for. And if a man deals with a deadly dynamic machine on the principle of touching the knob that's nearest, he will find out the defects of that cheery philosophy. Now leaving many sincere and serious critics of modern marriage on one side for the moment, great masses of modern men and women, who write and talk about marriage, are thus nibbling blindly at it like an army of mice. When the reformers propose, for instance, that divorce should be obtainable after an absence of three years (the absence actually taken for granted in the first military arrangements of the late European War) their readers and supporters could seldom give any sort of logical reason for the period being three years, and not three months or three minutes. They are like people who should say "Give me three feet of dog"; and not care where the cut came. Such persons fail to see a dog as an organic entity; in other words, they cannot make head or tail of it. And the chief thing to say about such reformers of marriage is that they cannot make head or tail of it. They do not know what it is, or what it is meant to be, or what its supporters suppose it to be; they never look at it, even when they are inside it. They do the work that's nearest; which is poking holes in the bottom of a boat under the impression that they are digging in a garden. This question of what a thing is, and whether it is a garden or a boat, appears to them abstract and academic. They have no notion of how large is the idea they attack; or how relatively small appear the holes that they pick in it.

Thus, Sir Arthur Conan Doyle, an intelligent man in other matters, says that there is only a "theological" opposition to divorce, and that it is entirely founded on "certain texts" in the Bible about marriages. This is exactly as if he said that a belief in the brotherhood of men was only founded on certain texts in the Bible, about all men being the children of Adam and Eve. Millions of peasants and plain people all over the world assume marriage to be static, without having ever clapped eyes on any text. Numbers of more modern people, especially after the recent experiments in America, think divorce is a social disease, without having ever bothered about any text. It may be maintained that even in these, or in any one, the idea of marriage is ultimately mystical; and the same may be maintained about the idea of brotherhood. It is obvious that a husband and wife are not visibly one flesh, in the sense of being one quadruped. It is equally obvious that Paderewski[1] and Jack Johnson[2] are not twins, and probably have not played together at their mother's knee. There is indeed a very important admission, or addition, to be realised here. What is true is this: that if the nonsense of Nietzsche or some such sophist submerged current culture, so that it was the fashion to deny the duties of fraternity; then indeed it might be found that the group which still affirmed fraternity was the original group in whose sacred books was the text about Adam and Eve. Suppose some Prussian professor has opportunely discovered that Germans and lesser men are respectively descended from two such very different monkeys that they are in no sense brothers, but barely cousins (German) any number of times removed. And suppose he proceeds to remove them even further with a hatchet; suppose he bases on this a repetition of the conduct of Cain, saying not so much "Am I my brother's keeper?" as "Is he really my brother?" And suppose this higher philosophy of the hatchet becomes prevalent in colleges and cultivated circles, as even more foolish philosophies have done. Then I agree it probably will be the Christian, the man who preserves the text about Cain, who will continue to assert that he is still the professor's brother; that he is still the professor's keeper. He may possibly add that, in his opinion, the professor seems to require a keeper.

[1] Ignacy Paderewski (1860–1941), Polish pianist and patriot.
[2] Jack Johnson (1878–1946), U.S. heavyweight prize fighter, World Champion, 1905–1915.

And that is doubtless the situation in the controversies about divorce and marriage to-day. It is the Christian church which continues to hold strongly, when the world for some reason has weakened on it, what many others hold at other times. But even then it is barely picking up the shreds and scraps of the subject to talk about a reliance on texts. The vital point in the comparison is this: that human brotherhood means a whole view of life, held in the light of life, and defended, rightly or wrongly, by constant appeals to every aspect of life. The religion that holds it most strongly will hold it when nobody else holds it; that is quite true, and that some of us may be so perverse as to think a point in favour of the religion. But anybody who holds it at all will hold it as a philosophy, not hung on one text but on a hundred truths. Fraternity may be a sentimental metaphor; I may be suffering a delusion when I hail a Montenegrin[3] peasant as my long lost brother. As a fact, I have my own suspicions about which of us it is that has got lost. But my delusion is not a deduction from one text, or from twenty; it is the expression of a relation that to me at least seems a reality. And what I should say about the idea of a brother, I should say about the idea of a wife.

It is supposed to be very unbusinesslike to begin at the beginning. It is called "abstract and academic principles with which we English, etc., etc." It is still in some strange way considered unpractical to open up inquiries about anything by asking what it is. I happen to have, however, a fairly complete contempt for that sort of practicality; for I know that it is not even practical. My ideal business man would not be one who planked down fifty pounds and said "Here is hard cash; I am a plain man; it is quite indifferent to me whether I am paying a debt, or giving alms to a beggar, or buying a wild bull or a bathing machine." Despite the infectious heartiness of his tone, I should still, in considering the hard cash, say (like a cabman) "What's this?" I should continue to insist, priggishly, that it was a highly practical point what the money *was*; what it was supposed to stand for, to aim at or to declare; what was the nature of the transaction; or, in short, what the devil the man supposed he was doing. I

[3] Montenegro, a former kingdom, is part of present day Yugoslavia.

shall therefore begin by asking, in an equally mystical manner, what in the name of God and the angels a man getting married supposes he is doing. I shall begin by asking what marriage is; and the mere question will probably reveal that the act itself, good or bad, wise or foolish, is of a certain kind; that it is not an inquiry or an experiment or an accident; it may probably dawn on us that it is a promise. It can be more fully defined by saying it is a vow.

Many will immediately answer that it is a rash vow. I am content for the moment to reply that all vows are rash vows. I am not now defending but defining vows; I am pointing out that this is a discussion about vows; first, of whether there ought to be vows; and second, of what vows ought to be. Ought a man to break a promise? Ought a man to make a promise? These are philosophic questions; but the philosophic peculiarity of divorce and re-marriage, as compared with free love and no marriage, is that a man breaks and makes a promise at the same moment. It is a highly German philosophy; and recalls the way in which the enemy wishes to celebrate his successful destruction of all treaties by signing some more. If I were breaking a promise, I would do it without promises. But I am very far from minimising the momentous and disputable nature of the vow itself. I shall try to show, in a further article, that this rash and romantic operation is the only furnace from which can come the plain hardware of humanity, the cast-iron resistance of citizenship or the cold steel of common sense; but I am not denying that the furnace is a fire. The vow is a violent and unique thing; though there have been many besides the marriage vow; vows of chivalry, vows of poverty, vows of celibacy, pagan as well as Christian. But modern fashion has rather fallen out of the habit; and men miss the type for the lack of the parallels. The shortest way of putting the problem is to ask whether being free includes being free to bind oneself. For the vow is a tryst with oneself.

I may be misunderstood if I say, for brevity, that marriage is an affair of honour. The sceptic will be delighted to assent, by saying it is a fight. And so it is, if only with oneself; but the point here is that it necessarily has the touch of the heroic, in which virtue can be translated by *virtus*. Now about fighting, in its nature, there is an implied infinity, or at least a potential infinity. I mean that loyalty in war is loyalty in defeat or even disgrace; it is due to the flag precisely at the moment when the flag nearly falls. We do already apply this to the flag of the nation; and the question is whether it is wise or unwise to apply it to the flag of the family. Of course, it is tenable that we should apply it to neither; that misgovernment in the nation or misery in the citizen would make the desertion of the flag an act of reason and not treason. I will only say here that, if this were really the limit of national loyalty, some of us would have deserted our nation long ago.

THE SUPERSTITION OF DIVORCE (2)

To the two or three articles appearing here on this subject I have given the title of the Superstition of Divorce; and the title is not taken at random. While free love seems to me a heresy, divorce does really seem to me a superstition. It is not only more of a superstition than free love, but much more of a superstition than strict sacramental marriage; and this point can hardly be made too plain. It is the partisans of divorce, not the defenders of marriage, who attach a stiff and senseless sanctity to a mere ceremony, apart from the meaning of the ceremony. It is our opponents, and not we, who hope to be saved by the letter of ritual, instead of the spirit of reality. It is they who hold that vow or violation, loyalty or disloyalty, can all be disposed of by a mysterious and magic rite, performed first in a law-court and then in a church or a registry office. There is little difference between the two parts of the ritual; except that the law court is much more ritualistic. But the plainest parallels will show anybody that all this is sheer barbarous credulity. It may or may not be superstition for a man to believe he must kiss the Bible to show he is telling the truth. It is certainly the most grovelling superstition for him to believe that, if he kisses the Bible, anything he says will come true. It would surely be the blackest and most benighted Bible-worship to suggest that the mere kiss on the mere book alters the moral quality of perjury. Yet this is precisely what is implied in saying that formal re-marriage alters the moral quality of conjugal infidelity. It may have been a mark of the Dark Ages that Harold should swear on a relic, though he were afterwards forsworn. But surely those ages would have been at their darkest, if he had been content to be sworn on a relic and forsworn on another relic. Yet this is the new altar these reformers would erect for us, out of the mouldy and meaningless relics of their dead law and their dying religion.

Now we, at any rate, are talking about an idea, a thing of the intellect and the soul; which we feel to be unalterable by legal antics.

We are talking about the idea of loyalty; perhaps a fantastic, perhaps only an unfashionable idea, but one we can explain and defend as an idea. Now I have already pointed out that most sane men do admit our ideal in such a case as patriotism or public spirit; the necessity of saving the state to which we belong. The patriot may revile but must not renounce his country; he must curse it to cure it, but not to wither it up. The old pagan citizens felt thus about the city; and modern nationalists feel thus about the nation. But even mere modern internationalists feel it about something; if it is only the nation of mankind. Even the humanitarian does not become a misanthrope and live in a monkey-house. Even a disappointed Collectivist or Communist does not retire into the exclusive society of beavers, because beavers are all communists of the most class-conscious solidarity. He admits the necessity of clinging to his fellow creatures, and begging them to abandon the use of the possessive pronoun; heartbreaking as his efforts must seem to him after a time. Even a Pacifist does not prefer rats to men, on the ground that the rat community is so pure from the taint of Jingoism as always to leave the sinking ship. In short, everybody recognises that there is *some* ship, large and small, which he ought not to leave, even when he thinks it is sinking.

We may take it then that there are institutions to which we are attached finally; just as there are others to which we are attached temporarily. We go from shop to shop trying to get what we want; but we do not go from nation to nation doing this; unless we belong to a certain group now heading very straight for Pogroms. In the first case it is the threat that we shall withdraw our custom; in the second it is the threat that we shall never withdraw ourselves; that we shall be part of the institution to the last. The time when the shop loses its customers is the time when the city needs its citizens; but it needs them as critics who will always remain to criticise. I need not now emphasise the deadly need of this double energy of internal reform and external defence; the whole towering tragedy which has eclipsed our earth in our time is but one terrific illustration of it. The hammer-strokes are coming thick and fast now;[1] and filling the world with infernal thunders; and there is still the iron

[1] Written at the time of the last great German assaults.

sound of something unbreakable deeper and louder than all the things that break. We may curse the kings, we may distrust the captains, we may murmur at the very existence of the armies; but we know that in the darkest days that may come to us, no man will desert the flag.

Now when we pass from loyalty to the nation to loyalty to the family, there can be no doubt about the first and plainest difference. The difference is that the family is a thing far more free. The vow is a voluntary loyalty; and the marriage vow is marked among ordinary oaths of allegiance by the fact that the allegiance is also a choice. The man is not only a citizen of the city, but also the founder and builder of the city. He is not only a soldier serving the colours, but he has himself artistically selected and combined the colours, like the colours of an individual dress. If it be admissible to ask him to be true to the commonwealth that has made him, it is at least not more illiberal to ask him to be true to the commonwealth he has himself made. If civic fidelity be, as it is, a necessity, it is also in a special sense a constraint. The old joke against patriotism, the Gilbertian irony, congratulated the Englishman on his fine and fastidious taste in being born in England. It made a plausible point in saying "For he might have been a Russian"; though indeed we have lived to see some persons who seemed to think they could be Russians when the fancy took them. If commonsense considers even such involuntary loyalty natural, we can hardly wonder if it thinks voluntary loyalty still more natural. And the small state founded on the sexes is at once the most voluntary and the most natural of all self-governing states. It is not true of Mr. Brown that he might have been a Russian; but it may be true of Mrs. Brown that she might have been a Robinson.

Now it is not at all hard to see why this small community, so specially free touching its cause, should yet be specially bound touching its effects. It is not hard to see why the vow made most freely is the vow kept most firmly. There are attached to it, by the nature of things, consequences so tremendous that no contract can offer any comparison. There is no contract, unless it be that said to be signed in blood, that can call spirits from the vasty deep; or bring cherubs (or goblins) to inhabit a small modern villa. There is no stroke of the pen which creates real bodies and souls, or makes the characters in a novel come to life. The institution that puzzles intellectuals so much can be explained by the mere material fact (perceptible even to intellectuals) that children are, generally speaking, younger than their parents. "Till death do us part" is not an irrational formula, for those will almost certainly die before they see more than half of the amazing (or alarming) thing they have done.

Such is, in a curt and crude outline, this obvious thing for those to whom it is not obvious. Now I know there are thinking men among those who would tamper with it; and I shall expect some of these to reply to my questions. But for the moment I only ask this question: whether the parliamentary and journalistic divorce movement shows even a shadowy trace of these fundamental truths, regarded as tests. Does it even discuss the nature of a vow, the limits and objects of loyalty, the survival of the family as a small and free state? The writers are content to say that Mr. Brown is uncomfortable with Mrs. Brown, and the last emancipation, for separated couples, seems only to mean that he is still uncomfortable without Mrs. Brown. These are not days in which being uncomfortable is felt as the final test of public action. For the rest, the reformers show statistically that families are in fact so scattered in our industrial anarchy, that they may as well abandon hope of finding their way home again. I am acquainted with that argument for making bad worse and I see it everywhere leading to slavery. Because London Bridge is broken down, we must assume that bridges are not meant to bridge. Because London commercialism and capitalism have copied hell, we are to continue to copy them. Anyhow, some will retain the conviction that the ancient bridge built between the two towers of sex is the worthiest of the great works of the earth.

It is exceedingly characteristic of the dreary decades before the War that the forms of freedom in which they seemed to specialise were suicide and divorce. I am not at the moment pronouncing on the moral problem of either; I am merely noting, as signs of those times, those two true or false counsels of despair; the end of life and the end of love. Other forms of freedom were being increasingly curtailed. Freedom indeed was the one thing that progressives and conservatives alike contemned. Socialists were largely concerned to prevent strikes, by State arbitration; that is, by adding another rich man to give the casting vote between rich and poor. Even in claiming what they called the right to work they tacitly surrendered the right to leave off working. Tories were preaching conscription, not so much to defend the independence of England as to destroy the independence of Englishmen. Liberals, of course, were chiefly interested in eliminating liberty, especially touching beer and betting. It was wicked to fight, and unsafe even to argue; for citing any certain and contemporary fact might land one in a libel action. As all these doors were successfully shut in our faces along the chilly and cheerless corridor of progress (with its glazed tiles) the doors of death and divorce alone stood open, or rather opened wider and wider. I do not expect the exponents of divorce to admit any similarity in the two things; yet the passing parallel is not irrelevant. It may enable them to realise the limits within which our moral instincts can, even for the sake of argument, treat this desperate remedy as a normal object of desire. Divorce is for us at best a failure, of which we are more concerned to find and cure the cause than to complete the effects; and we regard a system that produces many divorces as we do a system that drives men to drown and shoot themselves. For instance, it is perhaps the commonest complaint against the existing law that the poor cannot afford to avail themselves of it. It is an argument to which normally I should listen with special sympathy. But while I should condemn the law being a luxury, my first thought will naturally be that divorce and death are only luxuries in a rather rare sense. I should not primarily condole with the poor man on the high price of prussic acid; or on the fact that all precipices of suitable suicidal height were the private property of the landlords. There are other high prices and high precipices I should attack first. I should admit in the abstract that what is sauce for the goose is sauce for the gander; that what is good for the rich is good for the poor; but my first and strongest impression would be that prussic acid sauce is not good for anybody. I fear I should, on the impulse of the moment, pull a poor clerk or artisan back by the coat-tails, if he were jumping over Shakespeare's Cliff, even if Dover sands were strewn with the remains of the dukes and bankers who had already taken the plunge.

But in one respect, I will heartily concede, the cult of divorce has differed from the mere cult of death. The cult of death is dead. Those I knew in my youth as young pessimists are now aged optimists. And, what is more to the point at present, even when it was living it was limited; it was a thing of one clique in one class. We know the rule in the old comedy, that when the heroine went mad in white satin, the confidante went mad in white muslin. But when, in some tragedy of the artistic temperament, the painter committed suicide in velvet, it was never implied that the plumber must commit suicide in corduroy. It was never held that Hedda Gabler's[2] housemaid must die in torments on the carpet (trying as her term of service may have been); or that Mrs. Tanqueray's[3] butler must play the Roman fool and die on his own carving knife. That particular form of playing the fool, Roman or otherwise, was an oligarchic privilege in the decadent epoch; and even as such has largely passed with that epoch. Pessimism, which was never popular, is no longer even fashionable. A far different fate has awaited the other fashion; the other somewhat dismal form of freedom. If divorce is a disease, it is no longer to be a fashionable disease like appendicitis; it is to be made an epidemic like small-pox. As we have already seen, papers and public men to-day make a vast parade of the necessity of setting the poor man free to get a divorce. Now why are they so mortally anxious that he should be free to get a divorce, and not in the least anxious that he should be free to get anything else? Why are the same people happy, nay almost hilarious, when he gets a divorce, who are horrified when he gets a drink? What becomes of his money, what becomes of his children, where he works, when he ceases to work, are less and less under his personal control. Labour Exchanges, Insurance Cards, Welfare Work, and a hundred forms of police inspection and supervision, have combined for good or evil to fix him more and more strictly to a certain place in society. He is less

[2] *Hedda Gabler*, a play by Henrich Ibsen (1828–1906), Norwegian dramatist.

[3] Paula Ray Tanqueray is the second wife of Aubrey Tanqueray in Arthur Pinero's play *The Second Mrs. Tanqueray* (1893). Paula is a younger woman of questionable character who commits suicide when she learns that her ex-lover is her stepdaughter's suitor and that she stands in the way of her stepdaughter's marriage.

and less allowed to go to look for a new job; why is he allowed to go to look for a new wife? He is more and more compelled to recognise a Moslem code about liquor; why is it made so easy for him to escape from his old Christian code about sex? What is the meaning of this mysterious immunity, this special permit for adultery; and why is running away with his neighbour's wife to be the only exhilaration still left open to him? Why must he love as he pleases; when he may not even live as he pleases?

The answer is, I regret to say, that this social campaign, in most though by no means all of its most prominent campaigners, relies in this matter on a very smug and pestilent piece of cant. There are some advocates of democratic divorce who are really advocates of general democratic freedom; but they are the exceptions; I might say, with all respect, that they are the dupes. The omnipresence of the thing in the press and in political society is due to a motive precisely opposite to the motive professed. The modern rulers, who are simply the rich men, are really quite consistent in their attitude to the poor man. It is the same spirit which takes away his children under the pretence of order, which takes away his wife under the pretence of liberty. That which wishes, in the words of the comic song, to break up the happy home, is primarily anxious not to break up the much more unhappy factory. Capitalism, of course, is at war with the family, for the same reason which has led to its being at war with the Trade Union. This indeed is the only sense in which it is true that capitalism is connected with individualism. Capitalism believes in collectivism for itself and individualism for its enemies. It desires its victims to be individuals, or (in other words) to be atoms. For the word atom, in its clearest meaning (which is none too clear) might be translated as "individual." If there be any bond, if there be any brotherhood, if there be any class loyalty or domestic discipline, by which the poor can help the poor, these emancipators will certainly strive to loosen that bond or lift that discipline in the most liberal fashion. If there be such a brotherhood, these individualists will redistribute it in the form of individuals; or in other words smash it to atoms.

The masters of modern plutocracy know what they are about. They are making no mistake; they can be cleared of the slander of inconsistency. A very profound and precise instinct has led them to single out the human household as the chief obstacle to their inhuman progress. Without the family we are helpless before the State, which in our modern case is the Servile State. To use a military metaphor, the family is the only formation in which the charge of the rich can be repulsed. It is a force that forms twos as soldiers form fours; and, in every peasant country, has stood in the square house or the square plot of land as infantry have stood in squares against cavalry. How this force operates thus, and why, I will try to explain in the last of these articles. But it is when it is most nearly ridden down by the horsemen of pride and privilege, as in Poland or Ireland, when the battle grows most desperate and the hope most dark, that men begin to understand why that wild oath in its beginnings was flung beyond the bonds of the world; and what would seem as passing as a vision is made permanent as a vow.

III

THE SUPERSTITION OF DIVORCE (3)

There has long been a curiously consistent attempt to conceal the
fact that France is a Christian country. There have been Frenchmen
in the plot, no doubt, and no doubt there have been Frenchmen —
though I have myself only found Englishmen — in the derivative attempt to conceal the fact that Balzac was a Christian writer. I began
to read Balzac long after I had read the admirers of Balzac; and they
had never given me a hint of this truth. I had read that his books
were bound in yellow and "quite impudently French"; though I
may have been cloudy about why being French should be impudent
in a Frenchman. I had read the truer description of "the grimy wizard of the *Comedie Humaine*," and have lived to learn the truth of it;
Balzac certainly is a genius of the type of that artist he himself describes, who could draw a broomstick so that one knew it had swept
the room after a murder. The furniture of Balzac is more alive than
the figures of many dramas. For this I was prepared; but not for a
certain spiritual assumption which I recognised at once as a historical
phenomenon. The morality of a great writer is not the morality he
teaches, but the morality he takes for granted. The Catholic type of
Christian ethics runs through Balzac's books, exactly as the Puritan
type of Christian ethics runs through Bunyan's books. What his
professed opinions were I do not know, any more than I know
Shakespeare's; but I know that both those great creators of a multitudinous world made it, as compared with other and later writers,
on the same fundamental moral plan as the universe of Dante. There
can be no doubt about it for any one who can apply as a test the
truth I have mentioned; that the fundamental things in a man are
not the things he explains, but rather the things he forgets to explain. But here and there Balzac does explain; and with that intellectual concentration Mr. George Moore[1] has acutely observed in that
novelist when he is a theorist. And the other day I found in one of

[1] George Moore (1852–1932), Irish novelist, critic and dramatist.

Balzac's novels this passage; which, whether or no it would precisely hit Mr. George Moore's mood at this moment, strikes me as a perfect prophecy of this epoch, and might also be a motto for this book: "With the solidarity of the family society has lost that elemental force which Montesquieu defined and called 'honour.' Society has isolated its members the better to govern them, and has divided in order to weaken."

Throughout our youth and the years before the War, the current criticism followed Ibsen in describing the domestic system as a doll's house and the domestic woman as a doll. Mr. Bernard Shaw varied the metaphor by saying that mere custom kept the woman in the home as it keeps the parrot in the cage; and the plays and tales of the period made vivid sketches of a woman who also resembled a parrot in other particulars, rich in raiment, shrill in accent and addicted to saying over and over again what she had been taught to say. Mr. Granville Barker,[2] the spiritual child of Mr. Bernard Shaw, commented in his clever play of "The Voysey Inheritance" on tyranny, hypocrisy and boredom, as the constituent elements of a "happy English home." Leaving the truth of this aside for the moment, it will be well to insist that the conventionality thus criticised would be even more characteristic of a happy French home. It is not the Englishman's house, but the Frenchman's house that is his castle. It might be further added, touching the essential ethical view of the sexes at least, that the Irishman's house is his castle; though it has been for some centuries a besieged castle. Anyhow, those conventions which were remarked as making domesticity dull, narrow and unnaturally meek and submissive, are particularly powerful among the Irish and the French. From this it will surely be easy, for any lucid and logical thinker, to deduce the fact that the French are dull and narrow, and that the Irish are unnaturally meek and submissive. Mr. Bernard Shaw, being an Irishman who lives among Englishmen, may be conveniently taken as the type of the difference; and it will no doubt be found that the political friends of Mr. Shaw, among Englishmen, will be of a wilder revolutionary type than those whom

[2] Harley Granville Barker (1877–1946), English actor, manager and playwright.

he would have found among Irishmen. We are in a position to compare the meekness of the Fenians[3] with the fury of the Fabians.[4] This deadening monogamic ideal may even, in a larger sense, define and distinguish all the flat subserviency of Clare from all the flaming revolt of Clapham. Nor need we now look far to understand why revolutions have been unknown in the history of France; or why they happen so persistently in the vaguer politics of England. This rigidity and respectability must surely be the explanation of all that incapacity for any civil experiment or explosion, which has always marked that sleepy hamlet of very private houses, which we call the city of Paris. But the same things are true not only of Parisians but of peasants; they are even true of other peasants in the great Alliance. Students of Serbian traditions tell us that the peasant literature lays a special and singular curse on the violation of marriage; and this may well explain the prim and sheepish pacifism complained of in that people.

In plain words, there is clearly something wrong in the calculation by which it was proved that a housewife must be as much a servant as a housemaid; or which exhibited the domesticated man as being as gentle as the primrose or as conservative as the Primrose League.[5] It is precisely those who have been conservative about the family who have been revolutionary about the state. Those who are blamed for the bigotry or *bourgeois* smugness of their marriage conventions are actually those blamed for the restlessness and violence of their political reforms. Nor is there seriously any difficulty in discovering the cause of this. It is simply that in such a society the government, in dealing with the family, deals with something almost as permanent and self-renewing as itself. There can be a continuous family policy, like a continuous foreign policy. In peasant countries the family fights, it may almost be said that the farm fights. I do not mean merely that it riots in evil and exceptional times; though this is not unimportant. It was a savage but a sane feature when, in the Irish evictions, the women poured hot water from the windows; it

[3] A member of the Irish revolutionary party advocating Irish Republican independence.

[4] See footnote 1, page 153.

[5] See footnote 10, page 178.

was part of a final falling back on private tools as public weapons. That sort of thing is not only war to the knife, but almost war to the fork and spoon. It was in this grim sense perhaps that Parnell,[6] in that mysterious pun, said that Kettle was a household word in Ireland (it certainly ought to be after its subsequent glories), and in a more general sense it is certain that meddling with the housewife will ultimately mean getting into hot water. But it is not of such crises of bodily struggle that I speak, but of a steady and peaceful pressure from below of a thousand families upon the framework of government. For this a certain spirit of defence and enclosure is essential; and even feudalism was right in feeling that any such affair of honour must be a family affair. It was a true artistic instinct that pictured the pedigree on a coat that protects the body. The free peasant has arms if he has not armorial bearings. He has not an escutcheon; but he has a shield. Nor do I see why, in a freer and happier society than the present, or even the past, it should not be a blazoned shield. For that is true of pedigree which is true of property; the wrong is not in its being imposed on men, but rather in its being denied to them. Too much capitalism does not mean too many capitalists, but too few capitalists; and so aristocracy sins, not in planting a family tree, but in not planting a family forest.

Anyhow, it is found in practice that the domestic citizen can stand a siege, even by the State; because he has those who will stand by him through thick and thin—especially thin. Now those who hold that the State can be made fit to own all and adminster all, can consistently disregard this argument; but it may be said with all respect that the world is more and more disregarding them. If we could find a perfect machine, and a perfect man to work it, it might be a good argument for State Socialism, though an equally good argument for personal despotism. But most of us, I fancy, are now agreed that something of that social pressure from below which we call freedom is vital to the health of the State; and this it is which cannot be fully exercised by individuals, but only by groups and traditions. Such groups have been many; there have been monasteries;

6 Charles Parnell (1846–1891), Irish political leader.

there may be guilds; but there is only one type among them which all human beings have a spontaneous and omnipresent inspiration to build for themselves; and this type is the family.

I had intended this article to be the last of those outlining the elements of this debate; but I shall have to add a short concluding section on the way in which all this is missed in the practical (or rather unpractical) proposals about divorce. Here I will only say that they suffer from the modern and morbid weaknesses of always sacrificing the normal to the abnormal. As a fact the "tyranny, hypocrisy and boredom" complained of are not domesticity, but the decay of domesticity. The case of that particular complaint, in Mr. Granville Barker's play, is itself a proof. The whole point of "The Voysey Inheritance" was that there was no Voysey inheritance. The only heritage of that family was a highly dishonourable debt. Naturally their family affections had decayed when their whole ideal of property and probity had decayed; and there was little love as well as little honour among thieves. It has yet to be proved that they would have been as much bored if they had had a positive and not a negative heritage; and had worked a farm instead of a fraud. And the experience of mankind points the other way.

IV

THE SUPERSTITION OF DIVORCE (4)

I have touched before now on a famous or infamous Royalist who suggested that the people should eat grass; an unfortunate remark perhaps for a Royalist to make; since the regimen is only recorded of a Royal Personage. But there was certainly a simplicity in the solution worthy of a sultan or even a savage chief; and it is this touch of autocratic innocence on which I have mainly insisted touching the social reforms of our day, and especially the social reform known as divorce. I am primarily more concerned with the arbitrary method than with the anarchic result. Very much as the old tyrant would turn any number of men out to grass, so the new tyrant would turn any number of women into grass-widows. Anyhow, to vary the legendary symbolism, it never seems to occur to the king in this fairy tale that the gold crown on his head is a less, and not a more, sacred and settled ornament than the gold ring on the woman's finger. This change is being achieved by the summary and even secret government which we now suffer; and this would be the first point against it, even if it were really an emancipation; and it is only in form an emancipation. I will not anticipate the details of its defence, which can be offered by others, but I will here conclude for the present by roughly suggesting the practical defences of divorce, as generally given just at present, under four heads. And I will only ask the reader to note that they all have one thing in common; the fact that each argument is also used for all that social reform which plain men are already calling slavery.

First, it is very typical of the latest practical proposals that they are concerned with the case of those who are already separated, and the steps they must take to be divorced. There is a spirit penetrating all our society to-day by which the exception is allowed to alter the rule; the exile to deflect patriotism, the orphan to depose parenthood, and even the widow or, in this case as we have seen the grass-widow, to destroy the position of the wife. There is a sort of symbol of this tendency in that mysterious and unfortunate nomadic nation which has been allowed to alter so many things, from a crusade in Russia to a cottage in South Bucks. We have been told to treat the wandering Jew as a pilgrim, while we still treat the wandering Christian as a vagabond. And yet the latter is at least trying to get home, like Ulysses; whereas the former is, if anything, rather fleeing from home, like Cain. He who is detached, disgruntled, non-descript, intermediate, is everywhere made the excuse for altering what is common, corporate, traditional and popular. And the alteration is always for the worse. The mermaid never becomes more womanly, but only more fishy. The centaur never becomes more manly, but only more horsy. The Jew cannot really internationalise Christendom; he can only denationalise Christendom. The proletarian does not find it easy to become a small proprietor; he is finding it far easier to become a slave. So the unfortunate man, who cannot tolerate the woman he has chosen from all the women in the world, is not encouraged to return to her and tolerate her, but encouraged to choose another woman whom he may in due course refuse to tolerate. And in all these cases the argument is the same; that the man in the intermediate state is unhappy. Probably he is unhappy, since he is abnormal; but the point is that he is permitted to loosen the universal bond which has kept millions of others normal. Because he has himself got into a hole, he is allowed to burrow in it like a rabbit and undermine a whole countryside.

Next we have, as we always have touching such crude experiments, an argument from the example of other countries, and especially of new countries. Thus the Eugenists tell me solemnly that there have been very successful Eugenic experiments in America. And they rigidly retain their solemnity (while refusing with many rebukes to believe in mine) when I tell them that one of the Eugenic experiments in America is a chemical experiment; which consists of changing a black man into the allotropic form of white ashes. It is really an exceedingly Eugenic experiment; since its chief object is to discourage an inter-racial mixture of blood which is not desired. But I do not like this American experiment, however American; and I trust and believe that it is not typically American at all. It represents,

I conceive, only one element in the complexity of the great democracy; and goes along with other evil elements; so that I am not at all surprised that the same strange social sections, which permit a human being to be burned alive, also permit the exalted science of Eugenics. It is the same in the milder matter of liquor laws; and we are told that certain rather crude colonials have established prohibition laws, which they try to evade; just as we are told they have established divorce laws, which they are now trying to repeal. For in this case of divorce, at least, the argument from distant precedents has recoiled crushingly upon itself. There is already an agitation for less divorce in America, even while there is an agitation for more divorce in England.

Again, when an argument is based on a need of population, it will be well if those supporting it realise where it may carry them. It is exceedingly doubtful whether population is one of the advantages of divorce; but there is no doubt that it is one of the advantages of polygamy. It is already used in Germany as an argument for polygamy. But the very word will teach us to look even beyond Germany for something yet more remote and repulsive. Mere population, along with a sort of polygamous anarchy, will not appear even as a practical ideal to any one who considers, for instance, how consistently Europe has held the headship of the human race, in face of the chaotic myriads of Asia. If population were the chief test of progress and efficiency, China would long ago have proved itself the most progressive and efficient state. De Quincey[1] summed up the whole of that enormous situation in a sentence which is perhaps more impressive and even appalling than all the perspectives of orient architecture and vistas of opium vision in the midst of which it comes. "Man is a weed in those regions." Many Europeans, fearing for the garden of the world, have fancied that in some future fatality those weeds may spring up and choke it. But no Europeans have really wished that the flowers should become like the weeds. Even if it were true, therefore, that the loosening of the tie necessarily increased the population; even if this were not contradicted, as it is, by the facts of many countries, we should have strong historical grounds for not

[1] Thomas de Quincey (1785–1859), English essayist.

accepting the deduction. We should still be suspicious of the paradox that we may encourage large families by abolishing the family.

Lastly, I believe it is part of the defence of the new proposal that even its defenders have found its principle a little too crude. I hear they have added provisions which modify the principle; and which seem to be in substance, first, that a man shall be made responsible for a money payment to the wife he deserts, and second, that the matter shall once again be submitted in some fashion to some magistrate. For my purpose here, it is enough to note that there is something of the unmistakable savour of the sociology we resist, in these two touching acts of faith, in a cheque-book and in a lawyer. Most of the fashionable reformers of marriage would be faintly shocked at any suggestion that a poor old charwoman might possibly refuse such money, or that a good kind magistrate might not have the right to give such advice. For the reformers of marriage are very respectable people, with some honourable exceptions; and nothing could fit more smoothly into the rather greasy groove of their respectability than the suggestion that treason is best treated with the damages, gentlemen, heavy damages, of Mr. Serjeant Buzfuz; or that tragedy is best treated by the spiritual arbitrament of Mr. Nupkins.[2]

One word should be added to this hasty sketch of the elements of the case. I have deliberately left out the loftiest aspect and argument, that which sees marriage as a divine institution; and that for the logical reason that those who believe in this would not believe in divorce; and I am arguing with those who do believe in divorce. I do not ask them to assume the worth of my creed or any creed; and I could wish they did not so often ask me to assume the worth of their worthless, poisonous plutocratic modern society. But if it could be shown, as I think it can, that a long historical view and a patient political experience can at last accumulate solid scientific evidence of the vital need of such a vow, then I can conceive no more tremendous tribute than this, to any faith, which made a flaming affirmation from the darkest beginnings, of what the latest enlightenment can only slowly discover in the end.

[2] In Charles Dickens' *Pickwick Papers*, Serjeant Buzfuz is the counsel for Mrs. Bardell in the Bardell-Pickwick breach-of-promise suit (chapter 34) and George Nupkins, Esq., is the mayor of Ipswich (chapter 25).

V

THE STORY OF THE FAMILY

The most ancient of human institutions has an authority that may seem as wild as anarchy. Alone among all such institutions it begins with a spontaneous attraction; and may be said strictly and not sentimentally to be founded on love instead of fear. The attempt to compare it with coercive institutions complicating later history has led to infinite illogicality in later times. It is as unique as it is universal. There is nothing in any other social relations in any way parallel to the mutual attraction of the sexes. By missing this simple point, the modern world has fallen into a hundred follies. The idea of a general revolt of women against men has been proclaimed with flags and processions, like a revolt of vassals against their lords, of niggers against nigger-drivers, of Poles against Prussians or Irishmen against Englishmen; for all the world as if we really believed in the fabulous nation of the Amazons. The equally philosophical idea of a general revolt of men against women has been put into a romance by Sir Walter Besant,[1] and into a sociological book by Mr. Belfort Bax.[2] But at the first touch of this truth of an aboriginal attraction, all such comparisons collapse and are seen to be comic. A Prussian does not feel from the first that he can only be happy if he spends his days and nights with a Pole. An Englishman does not think his house empty and cheerless unless it happens to contain an Irishman. A white man does not in his romantic youth dream of the perfect beauty of a black man. A railway magnate seldom writes poems about the personal fascination of a railway porter. All the other revolts against all the other relations are reasonable and even inevitable, because those relations are originally only founded upon force or self-interest. Force can abolish what force can establish; self-interest can terminate a contract when self-interest has dictated the contract. But the love of man and woman is not an institution that

[1] Walter Besant (1836–1901), English writer and novelist.
[2] Belfort Bax (1854–1926), English philosopher, socialist and sociologist.

can be abolished, or a contract that can be terminated. It is something older than all institutions or contracts, and something that is certain to outlast them all. All the other revolts are real, because there remains a possibility that the things may be destroyed, or at least divided. You can abolish capitalists; but you cannot abolish males. Prussians can go out of Poland or negroes can be repatriated to Africa; but a man and a woman must remain together in one way or another; and must learn to put up with each other somehow.

These are very simple truths; that is why nobody nowadays seems to take any particular notice of them; and the truth that follows next is equally obvious. There is no dispute about the purpose of Nature in creating such an attraction. It would be more intelligent to call it the purpose of God; for Nature can have no purpose unless God is behind it. To talk of the purpose of Nature is to make a vain attempt to avoid being anthropomorphic, merely by being feminist. It is believing in a goddess because you are too sceptical to believe in a god. But this is a controversy which can be kept apart from the question, if we content ourselves with saying that the vital value ultimately found in this attraction is, of course, the renewal of the race itself. The child is an explanation of the father and mother; and the fact that it is a human child is the explanation of the ancient human ties connecting the father and mother. The more human, that is the less bestial, is the child, the more lawful and lasting are the ties. So far from any progress in culture or the sciences tending to loosen the bond, any such progress must logically tend to tighten it. The more things there are for the child to learn, the longer he must remain at the natural school for learning them; and the longer his teachers must at least postpone the dissolution of their partnership. This elementary truth is hidden to-day in vast masses of vicarious, indirect and artificial work, with the fundamental fallacy of which I shall deal in a moment. Here I speak of the primary position of the human group, as it has stood through unthinkable ages of waxing and waning civilisations; often unable to delegate any of its work, always unable to delegate all of it. In this, I repeat, it will always be necessary for the two teachers to remain together, in proportion as they have anything to teach. One of the shapeless sea-beasts, that merely detaches itself from its offspring and floats away, could float away to a submarine divorce court, or an advanced club founded on free-love for fishes. The sea-beast might do this, precisely because the sea-beast's offspring need do nothing; because it has not got to learn the polka or the multiplication table. All these are truisms but they are also truths, and truths that will return; for the present tangle of semi-official substitutes is not only a stop-gap, but one that is not big enough to stop the gap. If people cannot mind their own business, it cannot possibly be more economical to pay them to mind each other's business; and still less to mind each other's babies. It is simply throwing away a natural force and then paying for an artificial force; as if a man were to water a plant with a hose while holding up an umbrella to protect it from the rain. The whole really rests on a plutocratic illusion of an infinite supply of servants. When we offer any other system as a "career for women," we are really proposing that an infinite number of them should become servants, of a plutocratic or bureaucratic sort. Ultimately, we are arguing that a woman should not be a mother to her own baby, but a nursemaid to somebody else's baby. But it will not work, even on paper. We cannot all live by taking in each other's washing, especially in the form of pinafores. In the last resort, the only people who either can or will give individual care, to each of the individual children, are their individual parents. The expression as applied to those dealing with changing crowds of children is a graceful and legitimate flourish of speech.

This triangle of truisms, of father, mother and child, cannot be destroyed; it can only destroy those civilisations which disregard it. Most modern reformers are merely bottomless sceptics, and have no basis on which to rebuild; and it is well that such reformers should realise that there is something they cannot reform. You can put down the mighty from their seat; you can turn the world upside down, and there is much to be said for the view that it may then be the right way up. But you cannot create a world in which the baby carries the mother. You cannot create a world in which the mother has not authority over the baby. You can waste your time in trying; by giving votes to babies or proclaiming a republic of infants in arms. You can say, as an educationist said the other day, that small children should "criticise, question authority and suspend their judgment." I do not know why he did not go on to say that they should earn their own living, pay income tax to the state, and die in battle for the fatherland; for the proposal evidently is that children shall have no childhood. But you can, if you find entertainment in such games, organise "representative government" among little boys and girls, and tell them to take their legal and constitutional responsibilities as seriously as possible. In short, you can be crazy; but you cannot be consistent. You cannot really carry your own principle back to the aboriginal group, and really apply it to the mother and the baby. You will not act on your own theory in the simplest and most practical of all possible cases. You are not quite so mad as that.

This nucleus of natural authority has always existed in the midst of more artificial authorities. It has always been regarded as something in the literal sense individual; that is, as an absolute that could not really be divided. A baby was not even a baby apart from its mother; it was something else, most probably a corpse. It was always recognised as standing in a peculiar relation to government; simply because it was one of the few things that had not been made by government; and could to some extent come into existence without the support of government. Indeed the case for it is too strong to be stated. For the case for it is that there is nothing like it; and we can only find faint parallels to it in those more elaborate and painful powers and institutions that are its inferiors. Thus the only way of conveying it is to compare it to a nation; although, compared to it, national divisions are as modern and formal as national anthems. Thus I may often use the metaphor of a city; though in its presence a citizen is as recent as a city clerk. It is enough to note here that everybody does know by intuition and admit by implication that a family is a solid fact, having a character and colour like a nation. The truth can be tested by the most modern and most daily experiences. A man does say "That is the sort of thing the Browns will like"; however tangled and interminable a psychological novel he might compose on the shades of difference between Mr. and Mrs. Brown. A woman does say "I don't like Jemima seeing so much of the Robinsons"; and she does not always, in the scurry of her social or domestic duties, pause to distinguish the optimistic materialism of Mrs. Robinson from the more acid cynicism which tinges the hedonism of Mr. Robinson. There is a colour of the household inside, as conspicuous as the colour of the house outside. That colour is a blend, and if any tint in it predominate it is generally that preferred by Mrs. Robinson. But, like all composite colours, it is a separate colour; as separate as green is from blue and yellow. Every marriage is a sort of wild balance; and in every case the compromise is as unique as an eccentricity. Philanthropists walking in the slums often see the compromise in the street, and mistake it for a fight. When they interfere, they are thoroughly thumped by both parties; and serve them right, for not respecting the very institution that brought them into the world.

The first thing to see is that this enormous normality is like a mountain; and one that is capable of being a volcano. Every abnormality that is now opposed to it is like a mole-hill; and the earnest sociological organisers of it are exceedingly like moles. But the mountain is a volcano in another sense also; as suggested in that tradition of the southern fields fertilised by lava. It has a creative as well as a destructive side; and it only remains, in this part of the analysis, to note the political effect of this extra-political institution, and the political ideals of which it has been the champion; and perhaps the only permanent champion.

The ideal for which it stands in the state is liberty. It stands for liberty for the very simple reason with which this rough analysis started. It is the only one of these institutions that is at once necessary and voluntary. It is the only check on the state that is bound to renew itself as eternally as the state, and more naturally than the state. Every sane man recognises that unlimited liberty is anarchy, or rather is nonentity. The civic idea of liberty is to give the citizen a province of liberty; a limitation within which a citizen is a king. This is the only way in which truth can ever find refuge from public persecution, and the good man survive the bad government. But the good man by himself is no match for the city. There must be balanced against it another ideal institution, and in that sense an immortal institution. So long as the state is the only ideal institution the state will call on the citizen to sacrifice

himself, and therefore will not have the smallest scruple in sacrificing the citizen. The state consists of coercion; and must always be
justified from its own point of view in extending the bounds of coercion; as, for instance, in the case of conscription. The only thing
that can be set up to check or challenge this authority is a voluntary
law and a voluntary loyalty. That loyalty is the protection of liberty,
in the only sphere where liberty can fully dwell. It is a principle of
the constitution that the King never dies. It is the whole principle of
the family that the citizen never dies. There must be a heraldry and
heredity of freedom; a tradition of resistance to tyranny. A man
must be not only free, but free-born.

Indeed, there is something in the family that might loosely be
called anarchist; and more correctly called amateur. As there seems
something almost vague about its voluntary origin, so there seems
something vague about its voluntary organisation. The most vital
function it performs, perhaps the most vital function that anything
can perform, is that of education; but its type of early education is
far too essential to be mistaken for instruction. In a thousand things
it works rather by rule of thumb than rule of theory. To take a commonplace and even comic example, I doubt if any text-book or code
of rules has ever contained any directions about standing a child in a
corner. Doubtless when the modern process is complete, and the coercive principle of the state has entirely extinguished the voluntary element of the family, there will be some exact regulation or restriction
about the matter. Possibly it will say that the corner must be an angle
of at least ninety-five degrees. Possibly it will say that the converging
line of any ordinary corner tends to make a child squint. In fact I am
certain that if I said casually, at a sufficient number of tea-tables, that
corners made children squint, it would rapidly become a universally
received dogma of popular science. For the modern world will accept
no dogmas upon any authority; but it will accept any dogmas on no
authority. Say that a thing is so, according to the Pope or the Bible,
and it will be dismissed as a superstition without examination. But
preface your remark merely with "they say" or "don't you know
that?" or try (and fail) to remember the name of some professor mentioned in some newspaper; and the keen rationalism of the modern

mind will accept every word you say. This parenthesis is not so irrelevant as it may appear, for it will be well to remember that when a rigid officialism breaks in upon the voluntary compromises of the home, that officialism itself will be only rigid in its action and will be exceedingly limp in its thought. Intellectually it will be at least as vague as the amateur arrangements of the home, and the only difference is that the domestic arrangements are in the only real sense practical; that is, they are founded on experiences that have been suffered. The others are what is now generally called scientific; that is, they are founded on experiments that have not yet been made. As a matter of fact, instead of invading the family with the blundering bureaucracy that mismanages the public services, it would be far more philosophical to work the reform the other way round. It would be really quite as reasonable to alter the laws of the nation so as to resemble the laws of the nursery. The punishments would be far less horrible, far more humorous, and far more really calculated to make men feel they had made fools of themselves. It would be a pleasant change if a judge, instead of putting on the black cap, had to put on the dunce's cap; or if we could stand a financier in his own corner.

Of course this opinion is rare, and reactionary — whatever that may mean. Modern education is founded on the principle that a parent is more likely to be cruel than anybody else. It passes over the obvious fact that he is *less* likely to be cruel than anybody else. Anybody may happen to be cruel; but the first chances of cruelty come with the whole colourless and indifferent crowd of total strangers and mechanical mercenaries, whom it is now the custom to call in as infallible agents of improvement; policemen, doctors, detectives, inspectors, instructors, and so on. They are automatically given arbitrary power because there are here and there such things as criminal parents; as if there were no such things as criminal doctors or criminal school-masters. A mother is not always judicious about her child's diet; so it is given into the control of Dr. Crippen.[3] A father is thought not to teach his sons the purest

[3] Hawley Harvey Crippen (1861–1910), American murderer who studied medicine and dentistry in Michigan and London.

morality; so they are put under the tutorship of Eugene Aram.[4] These celebrated criminals are no more rare in their respective professions than the cruel parents are in the profession of parenthood. But indeed the case is far stronger than this; and there is no need to rely on the case of such criminals at all. The ordinary weaknesses of human nature will explain all the weaknesses of bureaucracy and business government all over the world. The official need only be an ordinary man to be more indifferent to other people's children than to his own; and even to sacrifice other people's family prosperity to his own. He may be bored; he may be bribed; he may be brutal, for any one of the thousand reasons that ever made a man a brute. All this elementary common sense is entirely left out of account in our educational and social systems of today. It is assumed that the hireling will *not* flee, and that solely because he is a hireling. It is denied that the shepherd will lay down his life for the sheep; or for that matter, even that the she-wolf will fight for the cubs. We are to believe that mothers are inhuman; but not that officials are human. There are unnatural parents, but there are no natural passions; at least, there are none where the fury of King Lear dared to find them — in the beadle. Such is the latest light on the education of the young; and the same principle that is applied to the child is applied to the husband and wife. Just as it assumes that a child will certainly be loved by anybody except his mother, so it assumes that a man can be happy with anybody except the one woman he has himself chosen for his wife.

Thus the coercive spirit of the state prevails over the free promise of the family, in the shape of formal officialism. But this is not the most coercive of the coercive elements in the modern commonwealth. An even more rigid and ruthless external power is that of industrial employment and unemployment. An even more ferocious enemy of the family is the factory. Between these modern mechanical things the ancient natural institution is not being reformed or

---

[4] Eugene Aram (1704-1759), English schoolmaster suspected of fraud in the company of shoemaker Daniel Clark. When Clark suddenly disappeared and was later found to have been murdered, Aram was arrested, convicted of murder and later executed.

modified or even cut down; it is being torn in pieces. It is not only being torn in pieces in the sense of a true metaphor, like a living thing caught in a hideous clockwork of manufacture. It is being literally torn in pieces, in that the husband may go to one factory, the wife to another, and the child to a third. Each will become the servant of a separate financial group, which is more and more gaining the political power of a feudal group. But whereas feudalism received the loyalty of families, the lords of the new servile state will receive only the loyalty of individuals; that is, of lonely men and even of lost children.

It is sometimes said that Socialism attacks the family; which is founded on little beyond the accident that some Socialists believe in free-love. I have been a Socialist, and I am no longer a Socialist, and at no time did I believe in free-love. It is true, I think in a large and unconscious sense, that State Socialism encourages the general coercive claim I have been considering. But if it be true that Socialism attacks the family in theory, it is far more certain that Capitalism attacks it in practice. It is a paradox, but a plain fact, that men never notice a thing as long as it exists in practice. Men who will note a heresy will ignore an abuse. Let any one who doubts the paradox imagine the newspapers formally printing along with the Honours' List a price list, for peerages and knighthoods; though everybody knows they are bought and sold. So the factory is destroying the family in fact; and need depend on no poor mad theorist who dreams of destroying it in fancy. And what is destroying it is nothing so plausible as free-love; but something rather to be described as an enforced fear. It is economic punishment more terrible than legal punishment, which may yet land us in slavery as the only safety.

From its first days in the forest this human group had to fight against wild monsters; and so it is now fighting against these wild machines. It only managed to survive then, and it will only manage to survive now, by a strong internal sanctity; a tacit oath or dedication deeper than that of the city or the tribe. But though this silent promise was always present, it took at a certain turning point of our history a special form which I shall try to sketch in the next chapter. That turning point was the creation of Christendom by the religion which created it. Nothing will destroy the sacred triangle; and even the Christian faith, the most amazing revolution that ever took place in the mind, served only in a sense to turn that triangle upside down. It held up a mystical mirror in which the order of the three things was reversed; and added a holy family of child, mother and father to the human family of father, mother and child.

VI

THE STORY OF THE VOW

Charles Lamb,[1] with his fine fantastic instinct for combinations that are also contrasts, has noted somewhere a contrast between St. Valentine and valentines. There seems a comic incongruity in such lively and frivolous flirtations still depending on the date and title of an ascetic and celibate bishop of the Dark Ages. The paradox lends itself to his treatment, and there is a truth in his view of it. Perhaps it may seem even more of a paradox to say there is no paradox. In such cases unification appears more provocative than division; and it may seem idly contradictory to deny the contradiction. And yet in truth there is no contradiction. In the deepest sense there is a very real similarity, which puts St. Valentine and his valentines on one side, and most of the modern world on the other. I should hesitate to ask even a German professor to collect, collate and study carefully all the valentines in the world, with the object of tracing a philosophical principle running through them. But if he did, I have no doubt about the philosophic principle he would find. However trivial, however imbecile, however vulgar or vapid or stereotyped the imagery of such things might be, it would always involve one idea, the same idea that makes lovers laboriously chip their initials on a tree or a rock, in a sort of monogram of monogamy. It may be a cockney trick to tie one's love on a tree; though Orlando did it, and would now doubtless be arrested by the police for breaking the bye-laws of the Forest of Arden. I am not here concerned especially to commend the habit of cutting one's own name and private address in large letters on the front of the Parthenon, across the face of the Sphinx, or in any other nook or corner where it may chance to arrest the sentimental interest of posterity. But like many other popular things, of the sort that can generally be found in Shakespeare, there is a meaning in it that would probably be missed by a less popular poet, like Shelley. There is a very permanent truth in the fact that

[1] Charles Lamb (1775–1834), English essayist and critic.

two free persons deliberately tie themselves to a log of wood. And it is the idea of tying oneself to something that runs through all this old amorous allegory like a pattern of fetters. There is always the notion of hearts chained together, or skewered together, or in some manner secured; there is a security that can only be called captivity. That it frequently fails to secure itself has nothing to do with the present point. The point is that every philosophy of sex must fail, which does not account for its ambition of fixity, as well as for its experience of failure. There is nothing to make Orlando commit himself on the sworn evidence of the nearest tree. He is not bound to be bound; he is under constraint, but nobody constrains him to be under constraint. In short, Orlando took a vow to marry precisely as Valentine took a vow not to marry. Nor could any ascetic, without being a heretic, have asserted in the wildest reactions of asceticism, that the vow of Orlando was not lawful as well as the vow of Valentine. But it is a notable fact that even when it was not lawful, it was still a vow. Through all that mediaeval culture, which has left us the legend of romance, there ran this pattern of a chain, which was felt as binding even where it ought not to bind. The lawless loves of mediaeval legends all have their own law, and especially their own loyalty, as in the tales of Tristram or Lancelot. In this sense we might say that mediaeval profligacy was more fixed than modern marriage. I am not here discussing either modern or mediaeval ethics, in the matter of what they did say or ought to say of such things. I am only noting as a historical fact the insistence of the mediaeval imagination, even at its wildest, upon one particular idea. That idea is the idea of the vow. It might be the vow which St. Valentine took; it might be a lesser vow which he regarded as lawful; it might be a wild vow which he regarded as quite lawless. But the whole society which made such festivals and bequeathed to us such traditions was full of the idea of vows; and we must recognise this notion, even if we think it nonsensical, as the note of the whole civilisation. And Valentine and the valentine both express it for us; even more if we feel them both as exaggerated, or even as exaggerating opposites. Those extremes meet; and they meet in the same place. Their trysting place is by the tree on which the lover hung his love-letters. And even if the lover hung himself on the tree, instead of his literary compositions, even that act had about it also an indefinable flavour of finality.

It is often said by the critics of Christian origins that certain ritual feasts, processions or dances are really of pagan origin. They might as well say that our legs are of pagan origin. Nobody ever disputed that humanity was human before it was Christian; and no Church manufactured the legs with which men walked or danced, either in a pilgrimage or a ballet. What can really be maintained, so as to carry not a little conviction, is this: that where such a Church has existed it has *preserved* not only the processions but the dances; not only the cathedral but the carnival. One of the chief claims of Christian civilisation is to have preserved things of pagan origin. In short, in the old religious countries men *continue* to dance; while in the new scientific cities they are often content to drudge.

But when this saner view of history is realised, there does remain something more mystical and difficult to define. Even heathen things are Christian when they have been preserved by Christianity. Chivalry is something recognisably different even from the *virtus* of Virgil. Charity is something exceedingly different from the plain city of Homer. Even our patriotism is something more subtle than the undivided lover of the city; and the change is felt in the most permanent things, such as the love of landscape or the love of woman. To define the differentiation in all these things will always be hopelessly difficult. But I would here suggest one element in the change which is perhaps too much neglected; which at any rate ought not to be neglected; the nature of a vow. I might express it by saying that pagan antiquity was the age of status; that Christian mediaevalism was the age of vows; and that sceptical modernity has been the age of contracts; or rather has tried to be, and has failed.

The outstanding example of status was slavery. Needless to say slavery does not mean tyranny; indeed it need only be regarded relatively to other things to be regarded as charity. The idea of slavery is that large numbers of men are meant and made to do the heavy work of the world, and that others, while taking the margin of profits, must nevertheless support them while they do it. The point is not whether the work is excessive or moderate, or whether the condition is comfortable or uncomfortable. The point is that his work is chosen for the man, his status fixed for the man; and this status is forced on him by law. As Mr. Balfour[2] said about Socialism, that is slavery and nothing else is slavery. The slave might well be, and often was, far more comfortable than the average free labourer; and certainly far more lazy than the average peasant. He was a slave because he had not reached his position by choice, or promise, or bargain, but merely by status.

It is admitted that when Christianity had been for some time at work in the world, this ancient servile status began in some mysterious manner to disappear. I suggest here that one of the forms which the new spirit took was the importance of the vow. Feudalism, for instance, differed from slavery chiefly because feudalism was a vow. The vassal put his hands in those of his lord, and vowed to be his man; but there was an accent on the noun substantive as well as on the possessive pronoun. By swearing to be his man, he proved he was not his chattel. Nobody exacts a promise from a pickaxe, or expects a poker to swear everlasting friendship with the tongs. Nobody takes the word of a spade; and nobody ever took the word of a slave. It marks at least a special stage of transition that the form of freedom was essential to the fact of service, or even of servitude. In this way it is not a coincidence that the word homage actually means manhood. And if there was vow instead of status even in the static parts of Feudalism, it is needless to say that there was a wilder luxuriance of vows in the more adventurous part of it. The whole of what we call chivalry was one great vow. Vows of chivalry varied infinitely from the most solid to the most fantastic; from a vow to give all the spoils of conquest to the poor to a vow to refrain from shaving until the first glimpse of Jerusalem. As I have remarked, this rule of loyalty, even in the unruly exceptions which proved the rule, ran through all the romances and songs of the troubadours; and there were always vows even when they were very far from being marriage vows. The idea is as much present in what they called the Gay Science, of love, as in what they called the Divine Science, of theology.

[2] Arthur Balfour (1848–1930), British statesman and writer.

The modern reader will smile at the mention of these things as sciences; and will turn to the study of sociology, ethnology and psycho-analysis; for if these are sciences (about which I would not divulge a doubt) at least nobody would insult them by calling them either gay or divine.

I mean here to emphasise the presence, and not even to settle the proportion, of this new notion in the middle ages. But the critic will be quite wrong if he thinks it enough to answer that all these things affected only a cultured class, not corresponding to the servile class of antiquity. When we come to workmen and small tradesmen, we find the same vague yet vivid presence of the spirit that can only be called the vow. In this sense there was a chivalry of trades as well as a chivalry of orders of knighthood; just as there was a heraldry of shop-signs as well as a heraldry of shields. Only it happens that in the enlightenment and liberation of the sixteenth century, the heraldry of the rich was preserved, and the heraldry of the poor destroyed. And there is a sinister symbolism in the fact that almost the only emblem still hung above a shop is that of the three balls of Lombardy. Of all those democratic glories nothing can now glitter in the sun; except the sign of the golden usury that has devoured them all. The point here, however, is that the trade or craft had not only something like the crest, but something like the vow of knighthood. There was in the position of the guildsman the same basic notion that belonged to knights and even to monks. It was the notion of the free choice of a fixed estate. We can realise the moral atmosphere if we compare the system of the Christian guilds, not only with the status of the Greek and Roman slaves, but with such a scheme as that of the Indian castes. The oriental caste has some of the qualities of the occidental guild; especially the valuable quality of tradition and the accumulation of culture. Men might be proud of their castes, as they were proud of their guilds. But they had never chosen their castes, as they have chosen their guilds. They had never, within historic memory, even collectively created their castes, as they collectively created their guilds. Like the slave system, the caste system was older than history. The heathens of modern Asia, as much as the heathens of ancient Europe, lived by the very spirit of status. Status in a trade has been accepted like status in a tribe; and that in a tribe of beasts and birds rather than men. The fisherman continued to be a fisherman as the fish continued to be a fish; and the hunter would no more turn into a cook than his dog would try its luck as a cat. Certainly his dog would not be found prostrated before the mysterious altar of Pasht,[3] barking or whining a wild, lonely, and individual vow that he at all costs would become a cat. Yet that was the vital revolt and innovation of vows, as compared with castes or slavery; as when a man vowed to be a monk, or the son of a cobbler saluted the shrine of St. Joseph, the patron saint of carpenters. When he had entered the guild of the carpenters he did indeed find himself responsible for a very real loyalty and discipline; but the whole social atmosphere surrounding his entrance was full of the sense of a separate and personal decision. There is one place where we can still find this sentiment; the sentiment of something at once free and final. We can feel it, if the service is properly understood, before and after the marriage vows at any ordinary wedding in any ordinary church.

Such, in very vague outline, has been the historical nature of vows; and the unique part they played in that mediaeval civilisation out of which modern civilisation rose — or fell. We can now consider, a little less cloudily than it is generally considered nowadays, whether we really think vows are good things; whether they ought to be broken; and (as would naturally follow) whether they ought to be made. But we can never judge it fairly till we face, as I have tried to suggest, this main fact of history; that the personal pledge, feudal or civic or monastic, was the way in which the world did escape from the system of slavery in the past. For the modern breakdown of mere contract leaves it still doubtful if there be any other way of escaping it in the future.

The idea, or at any rate the ideal, of the thing called a vow is fairly obvious. It is to combine the fixity that goes with finality with the self-respect that only goes with freedom. The man is a slave who is his own master, and a king who is his own ancestor. For all kinds of

[3] The Egyptian lioness-headed goddess of life and fertility.

social purposes he has the calculable orbit of the man in the caste or the servile state; but in the story of his own soul he is still pursuing, at great peril, his own adventure. As seen by his neighbours, he is as safe as if immured in a fortress; but as seen by himself he may be for ever careering through the sky or crashing towards the earth in a flying-ship. What is socially humdrum is produced by what is individually heroic; and a city is made not merely of citizens but knight-errants. It is needless to point out the part played by the monastery in civilising Europe in its most barbaric interregnum; and even those who still denounce the monasteries will be found denouncing them for these two extreme and apparently opposite eccentricities. They are blamed for the rigid character of their collective routine; and also for the fantastic character of their individual fanaticism. For the purposes of this part of the argument, it would not matter if the marriage vow produced the most austere discomforts of the monastic vow. The point for the present is that it was sustained by a sense of free will; and the feeling that its evils were not accepted but chosen. The same spirit ran through all the guilds and popular arts and spontaneous social systems of the whole civilisation. It had all the discipline of an army; but it was an army of volunteers.

The civilisation of vows was broken up when Henry the Eighth broke his own vow of marriage. Or rather, it was broken up by a new cynicism in the ruling powers of Europe, of which that was the almost accidental expression in England. The monasteries, that had been built by vows, were destroyed. The guilds, that had been regiments of volunteers, were dispersed. The sacramental nature of marriage was denied; and many of the greatest intellects of the new movement, like Milton, already indulged in a very modern idealisation of divorce. The progress of this sort of emancipation advanced step by step with the progress of that aristocratic ascendancy which has made the history of modern England; with all its sympathy with personal liberty, and all its utter lack of sympathy with popular life. Marriage not only became less of a sacrament but less of a sanctity. It threatened to become not only a contract, but a contract that could not be kept. For this one question has retained a strange symbolic supremacy amid all the similar questions, which seems to perpetuate the coincidence of the origin. It began with divorce for a king; and it is now ending in divorces for a whole kingdom.

The modern era that followed can be called the era of contract; but it can still more truly be called the era of leonine contract. The nobles of the new time first robbed the people, and then offered to bargain with them. It would not be an exaggeration to say that they first robbed the people, and then offered to cheat them. For their rents were competitive rents, their economics competitive economics, their ethics competitive ethics; they applied not only legality but pettifogging. No more was heard of the customary rents of the mediaeval estates; just as no more was heard of the standard wages of the mediaeval guilds. The object of the whole process was to isolate the individual poor man in his dealings with the individual rich man; and then offer to buy and sell with him, though it must necessarily be himself that was bought and sold. In the matter of labour, that is, though a man was supposed to be in the position of a seller, he was more and more really in the possession of a slave. Unless the tendency be reversed, he will probably become admittedly a slave. That is to say, the word slave will never be used; for it is always easy to find an inoffensive word; but he will be admittedly a man legally bound to certain social service, in return for economic security. In other words, the modern experiment of mere contract has broken down. Trusts as well as Trades' Unions express the fact that it has broken down. Social reform, Socialism, Guild Socialism, Syndicalism, even organised philanthropy, are so many ways of saying that it has broken down. The substitute for it may be the old one of status; but it must be something having some of the stability of status. So far history has found only one way of combining that sort of stability with any sort of liberty. In this sense there is a meaning in the much misused phrase about the army of industry. But the army must be stiffened either by the discipline of conscripts or by the vows of volunteers.

If we may extend the doubtful metaphor of an army of industry to cover the yet weaker phrase about captains of industry, there is no doubt about what those captains at present command. They work for a centralised discipline in every department. They erect a vast apparatus of supervision and inspection; they support all the modern restrictions touching drink and hygiene. They may be called the friends of temperance or even of happiness; but even their friends would not call them the friends of freedom. There is only one form of freedom which they tolerate; and that is the sort of sexual freedom which is covered by the legal fiction of divorce. If we ask why this liberty is alone left, when so many liberties are lost, we shall find the answer in the summary of this chapter. They are trying to break the vow of the knight as they broke the vow of the monk. They recognise the vow as the vital antithesis to servile status; the alternative and therefore the antagonist. Marriage makes a small state within the state, which resists all such regimentation. That bond breaks all other bonds; that law is found stronger than all later and lesser laws. They desire the democracy to be sexually fluid, because the making of small nuclei is like the making of small nations. Like small nations, they are a nuisance to the mind of imperial scope. In short, what they fear, in the most literal sense, is home rule.

Men can always be blind to a thing so long as it is big enough. It is so difficult to see the world in which we live, that I know that many will see all I have said here of slavery as a nonsensical nightmare. But if my association of divorce with slavery seems only a far-fetched and theoretical paradox, I should have no difficulty in replacing it by a concrete and familiar picture. Let them merely remember the time when they read "Uncle Tom's Cabin," and ask themselves whether the oldest and simplest of the charges against slavery has not always been the breaking up of families.

VII

THE TRAGEDIES OF MARRIAGE

There is one view very common among the liberal-minded which is exceedingly fatiguing to the clear-headed. It is symbolised in the sort of man who says, "These ruthless bigots will refuse to bury me in consecrated ground, because I have always refused to be baptised." A clear-headed person can easily conceive his point of view, in so far as he happens to think that baptism does not matter. But the clear-headed will be completely puzzled when they ask themselves why, if he thinks that baptism does not matter, he should think that burial does matter. If it is in no way imprudent for a man to keep himself from a consecrated font, how can it be inhuman for other people to keep him from a consecrated field? It is surely much nearer to mere superstition to attach importance to what is done to a dead body than to a live baby. I can understand a man thinking both superstitious, or both sacred; but I cannot see why he should grumble that other people do not give him as sanctities what he regards as superstitions. He is merely complaining of being treated as what he declares himself to be. It is as if a man were to say, "My persecutors still refuse to make me king, out of mere malice because I am a strict republican." Or it is as if he said, "These heartless brutes are so prejudiced against a teetotaler, that they won't even give him a glass of brandy."

The fashion of divorce would not be a modern fashion if it were not full of this touching fallacy. A great deal of it might be summed up as a most illogical and fanatical appetite for getting married in churches. It is as if a man should practice polygamy out of sheer greed for wedding cake. Or it is as if he provided his household with new shoes, entirely by having them thrown after the wedding carriage when he went off with a new wife. There are other ways of procuring cake or purchasing shoes; and there are other ways of setting up a human establishment. What is unreasonable is the request which the modern man really makes of the religious institutions of his fathers. The modern man wants to buy one shoe without the other; to obtain one half of a supernatural revelation without the other. The modern man wants to eat his wedding cake and have it, too.

I am not basing this book on the religious argument, and therefore I will not pause to inquire why the old Catholic institutions of Christianity seem to be especially made the objects of these unreasonable complaints. As a matter of fact nobody does propose that some ferocious Anti-Semite like M. Drumont should be buried as a Jew with all the rites of the Synagogue. But the broad-minded were furious because Tolstoi, who had denounced Russian orthodoxy quite as ferociously, was not buried as orthodox, with all the rites of the Russian Church. Nobody does insist that a man who wishes to have fifty wives when Mahomet allowed him five, must have his fifty with the full approval of Mahomet's religion. But the broad-minded are extremely bitter because a Christian who wishes to have several wives when his own promise bound him to one, is not allowed to violate his vow at the same altar at which he made it. Nobody does insist on Baptists totally immersing people who totally deny the advantages of being totally immersed. Nobody ever did expect Mormons to receive the open mockers of the Book of Mormon, nor Christian Scientists to let their churches be used for exposing Mrs. Eddy as an old fraud. It is only of the forms of Christianity making the Catholic claim that such inconsistent claims are made. And even the inconsistency is, I fancy, a tribute to the acceptance of the Catholic idea in a catholic fashion. It may be that men have an obscure sense that nobody need belong to the Mormon religion and every one does ultimately belong to the Church; and though he may have made a few dozen Mormon marriages in a wandering and entertaining life, he will really have nowhere to go to if he does not somehow find his way back to the churchyard. But all this concerns the general theological question and not the matter involved here, which is merely historical and social. The point here is that it is at least superficially inconsistent to ask institutions for a formal approval, which they can only give by inconsistency.

I have put first the question of what is marriage. And we are now in a position to ask more clearly what is divorce. It is not merely the negation or neglect of marriage; for any one can always neglect marriage. It is not the dissolution of the legal obligation of marriage, or even the legal obligation of monogamy; for the simple reason that no such obligation exists. Any man in modern London may have a hundred wives if he does not call them wives; or rather, if he does not go through certain more or less mystical ceremonies in order to assert that they are wives. He might create a certain social coolness round his household, a certain fading of his general popularity. But that is not created by law, and could not be prevented by law. As the late Lord Salisbury very sensibly observed about boycotting in Ireland, "How can you make a law to prevent people going out of the room when somebody they don't like comes into it?" We cannot be forcibly introduced to a polygamist by a policeman. It would not be an assertion of social liberty, but a denial of social liberty, if we found ourselves practically obliged to associate with all the profligates in society. But divorce is not in this sense mere anarchy. On the contrary divorce is in this sense respectability; and even a rigid excess of respectability. Divorce in this sense might indeed be not unfairly called snobbery. The definition of divorce, which concerns us here, is that it is the attempt to give respectability, and not liberty. It is the attempt to give a certain social status, and not a legal status. It is indeed supposed that this can be done by the alteration of certain legal forms; and this will be more or less true according to the extent to which law as such overawed public opinion, or was valued as a true expression of public opinion. If a man divorced in the large-minded fashion of Henry the Eighth pleaded his legal title among the peasantry of Ireland, for instance, I think he would find a difference still existing between respectability and religion. But the peculiar point here is that many are claiming the sanction of religion as well as of respectability. They would attach to their very natural and sometimes very pardonable experiments a certain atmosphere, and even glamour, which has undoubtedly belonged to the status of marriage in historic Christendom. But before they make this attempt, it would be well to ask why such a dignity ever appeared or in what it consisted. And I fancy we shall find ourselves confronted with the very simple truth, that the dignity arose wholly and entirely out of the fidelity; and that the glamour merely came from the vow. People were regarded as having a certain dignity because they were dedicated in a certain way; as bound to certain duties and, if it be preferred, to certain discomforts. It may be irrational to endure these discomforts; it may even be irrational to respect them. But it is certainly much more irrational to respect them, and then artificially transfer the same respect to the absence of them. It is as if we were to expect uniforms to be saluted when armies were disbanded; and ask people to cheer a soldier's coat when it did not contain a soldier. If you think you can abolish war, abolish it; but do not suppose that when there are no wars to be waged, there will still be warriors to be worshipped. If it was a good thing that the monasteries were dissolved, let us say so and dismiss them. But the nobles who dissolved the monasteries did not shave their heads, and ask to be regarded as saints solely on account of that ceremony. The nobles did not dress up as abbots and ask to be credited with a potential talent for working miracles, because of the austerity of their vows of poverty and chastity. They got inside the houses, but not the hoods, and still less the haloes. They at least knew that it is not the habit that makes the monk. They were not so superstitious as those moderns, who think it is the veil that makes the bride.

What is respected, in short, is the fidelity to the ancient flag of the family, and a readiness to fight for what I have noted as its unique type of freedom. I say readiness to fight, for fortunately the fight itself is the exception rather than the rule. The soldier is not respected because he is doomed to death, but because he is ready for death; and even ready for defeat. The married man or woman is not doomed to evil, sickness or poverty; but is respected for taking a certain step for better for worse, for richer for poorer, in sickness or in health. But there is one result of this line of argument which should correct a danger in some arguments on the same side.

It is very essential that a stricture on divorce, which is in fact simply a defence of marriage, should be independent of sentimentalism, especially in the form called optimism. A man justifying a fight for national independence or civic freedom is neither sentimental nor optimistic. He explains the sacrifice, but he does not explain it away. He does not say that bayonet wounds are pin-pricks, or mere scratches of the thorns on a rose of pleasure. He does not say that the whole display of firearms is a festive display of fireworks. On the contrary, when he praises it most, he praises it as pain rather than pleasure. He increases the praise with the pain; it is his whole boast that militarism, and even modern science, can produce no instrument of torture to tame the soul of man. It is idle, in speaking of war, to pit the realistic against the romantic, in the sense of the heroic; for all possible realism can only increase the heroism; and therefore, in the highest sense, increase the romance. Now I do not compare marriage with war, but I do compare marriage with law or liberty or patriotism or popular government, or any of the human ideals which have often to be defended by war. Even the wildest of those ideals, which seem to escape from all the discipline of peace, do not escape from the discipline of war. The Bolshevists may have aimed at pure peace and liberty; but they have been compelled, for their own purpose, first to raise armies and then to rule armies. In a word, however beautiful you may think your own visions of beatitude, men must suffer to be beautiful, and even suffer a considerable interval of being ugly. And I have no notion of denying that mankind suffers much from the maintenance of the standard of marriage; as it suffers much from the necessity of criminal law or the recurrence of crusades and revolutions. The only question here is whether marriage is indeed, as I maintain, an ideal and an institution making for popular freedom; I do not need to be told that anything making for popular freedom has to be paid for in vigilance and pain, and a whole army of martyrs.

Hence I am far indeed from denying the hard cases which exist here, as in all matters involving the idea of honour. For indeed I could not deny them without denying the whole parallel of militant morality on which my argument rests. But this being first understood, it will be well to discuss in a little more detail what are described as the tragedies of marriage. And the first thing to note about the most tragic of them is that they are not tragedies of marriage at all. They are tragedies of sex; and might easily occur in a highly modern romance in which marriage was not mentioned at all. It is generally summarised by saying that the tragic element is the absence of love. But it is often forgotten that another tragic element is often the presence of love. The doctors of divorce, with an air of the frank and friendly realism of men of the world, are always recommending and rejoicing in a sensible separation by mutual consent. But if we are really to dismiss our dreams of dignity and honour, if we are really to fall back on the frank realism of our experience as men of the world, then the very first thing that our experience will tell us is that it very seldom is a separation by mutual consent; that is, that the consent very seldom is sincerely and spontaneously mutual. By far the commonest problem in such cases is that in which one party wishes to end the partnership and the other does not. And of that emotional situation you can make nothing but a tragedy, whichever way you turn it. With or without marriage, with or without divorce, with or without any arrangements that anybody can suggest or imagine, it remains a tragedy. The only difference is that by the doctrine of marriage it remains both a noble and a fruitful tragedy; like that of a man who falls fighting for his country, or dies testifying to the truth. But the truth is that the innovators have as much sham optimism about divorce as any romanticist can have had about marriage. They regard their story, when it ends in the divorce court, through as rosy a mist of sentimentalism as anybody ever regarded a story ending with wedding bells. Such a reformer is quite sure that when once the prince and princess are divorced by the fairy godmother, they will live happily ever after. I enjoy romance, but I like it to be rooted in reality; and any one with a touch of reality knows that nine couples out of ten, when they are divorced, are left in an exceedingly different state. It will be safe to say in most cases that one partner will fail to find happiness in an infatuation, and the other will from the first accept a tragedy. In the realm of reality and not romance, it is commonly a case of breaking hearts as well as breaking promises; and even dishonour is not always a remedy for remorse.

The next limitation to be laid down in the matter affects certain practical forms of discomfort, on a level rather lower than love or hatred. The cases most commonly quoted concern what is called "drink" and what is called "cruelty." They are always talked about as matters of fact; though in practice they are very decidedly matters of opinion. It is not a flippancy, but a fact, that the misfortune of the woman who has married a drunkard may have to be balanced against the misfortune of the man who has married a teetotaler. For the very definition of drunkenness may depend on the dogma of teetotalism. Drunkenness, it has been very truly observed,[1] "may mean anything from *delirium tremens* to having a stronger head than the official appointed to conduct the examination." Mr. Bernard Shaw once professed, apparently seriously, that any man drinking wine or beer at all was incapacitated from managing a motorcar; and still more, therefore, one would suppose, from managing a wife. The scales are weighted here, of course, with all those false weights of snobbishness which are the curse of justice in this country. The working class is forced to conduct almost in public a normal and varying festive habit, which the upper class can afford to conduct in private; and a certain section of the middle class, that which happens to concern itself most with local politics and social reforms, really has or affects a standard quite abnormal and even alien. They might go any lengths of injustice in dealing with the working man or working woman accused of too hearty a taste in beer. To mention but one matter out of a thousand, the middle class reformers are obviously quite ignorant of the hours at which working people begin to work. Because they themselves, at eleven o'clock in the morning, have only recently finished breakfast and the full moral digestion of the *Daily Mail*, they think a char-woman drinking beer at that hour is one of those arising early in the morning to follow after strong drink. Most of them really do not know that she has already done more than half a heavy day's work, and is partaking of a very reasonable luncheon. The whole problem of proletarian drink is entangled in a network of these misunderstandings; and there is no doubt whatever that, when judged by these generalisations, the poor will be taken in a net of injustices. And this truth is as certain in the case of what is called cruelty as of what is called drink. Nine times out of ten the judgment

[1] The late Cecil Chesterton, in the "New Witness."

on a navvy for hitting a woman is about as just as a judgment on him for not taking off his hat to a lady. It is a class test; it may be a class superiority; but it is not an act of equal justice between the classes. It leaves out a thousand things; the provocation, the atmosphere, the harassing restrictions of space, the nagging which Dickens described as the terrors of "temper in a cart," the absence of certain taboos of social training, the tradition of greater roughness even in the gestures of affection. To make all marriage or divorce, in the case of such a man, turn upon a blow is like blasting the whole life of a gentleman because he has slammed the door. Often a poor man cannot slam the door; partly because the model villa might fall down; but more because he has nowhere to go to; the smoking-room, the billiard-room and the peacock music-room not being yet attached to his premises.

I say this in passing, to point out that while I do not dream of suggesting that there are only happy marriages, there will quite certainly, as things work nowadays, be a very large number of unhappy and unjust divorces. They will be cases in which the innocent partner will receive the real punishment of the guilty partner, through being in fact and feeling the faithful partner. For instance, it is insisted that a married person must at least find release from the society of a lunatic; but it is also true that the scientific reformers, with their fuss about "the feeble-minded," are continually giving larger and looser definitions of lunacy. The process might begin by releasing somebody from a homicidal maniac, and end by dealing in the same way with a rather dull conversationalist. But in fact nobody does deny that a person should be allowed some sort of release from a homicidal maniac. The most extreme school of orthodoxy only maintains that anybody who has had that experience should be content with that release. In other words, it says he should be content with that experience of matrimony, and not seek another. It was put very wittily, I think, by a Roman Catholic friend of mine, who said he approved of release so long as it was not spelt with a hyphen.

To put it roughly, we are prepared in some cases to listen to the man who complains of having a wife. But we are not prepared to listen, at such length, to the same man when he comes back and complains that he has not got a wife. Now in practice at this moment the great mass of the complaints are precisely of this kind. The reformers insist particularly on the pathos of a man's position when he has obtained a separation without a divorce. Their most tragic figure is that of the man who is already free of all those ills he had, and is only asking to be allowed to fly to others that he knows not of. I should be the last to deny that, in certain emotional circumstances, his tragedy may be very tragic indeed. But his tragedy is of the emotional kind which can never be entirely eliminated; and which he has himself, in all probability, inflicted on the partner he has left. We may call it the price of maintaining an ideal or the price of making a mistake; but anyhow it is the point of our whole distinction in the matter; it is here that we draw the line, and I have nowhere denied that it is a line of battle. The battle joins on the debatable ground, not of the man's doubtful past but of his still more doubtful future. In a word, the divorce controversy is not really a controversy about divorce. It is a controversy about re-marriage; or rather about whether it is marriage at all.

And with that we can only return to the point of honour which I have compared here to a point of patriotism; since it is both the smallest and the greatest kind of patriotism. Men have died in torments during the last five years for points of patriotism far more dubious and fugitive. Men like the Poles or the Serbians, through long periods of their history, may be said rather to have lived in torments. I will never admit that the vital need of the freedom of the family, as I have tried to sketch it here, is not a cause as valuable as the freedom of any frontier. But I do willingly admit that the cause would be a dark and terrible one, if it really asked these men to suffer torments. As I have stated it, on its most extreme terms, it only asks them to suffer abnegations. And those negative sufferings I do think they may honourably be called upon to bear, for the glory of their own oath and the great things by which the nations live. In relation to their own nation most normal men will feel that this distinction between release and "re-lease" is neither fanciful nor harsh, but very rational and human. A patriot may be an exile in another country; but he will not be a patriot of another country. He will be as cheerful as he can in an abnormal position; he may or may not sing his country's songs in a strange land; but he will not sing the strange songs as his own. And such may fairly be also the attitude of the citizen who has gone into exile from the oldest of earthly cities.

VIII

THE VISTA OF DIVORCE

The case for divorce combines all the advantages of having it both ways; and of drawing the same deduction from right or left, and from black or white. Whichever way the programme works in practice, it can still be justified in theory. If there are few examples of divorce, it shows how little divorce need be dreaded; if there are many, it shows how much it is required. The rarity of divorce is an argument in favor of divorce; and the multiplicity of divorce is an argument against marriage. Now, in truth, if we were confined to considering this alternative in a speculative manner, if there were no concrete facts but only abstract probabilities, we should have no difficulty in arguing our case. The abstract liberty allowed by the reformers is as near as possible to anarchy, and gives no logical or legal guarantee worth discussing. The advantages of their reform do not accrue to the innocent party, but to the guilty party; especially if he be sufficienty guilty. A man has only to commit the crime of desertion to obtain the reward of divorce. And if they are entitled to take as typical the most horrible hypothetical cases of the abuse of the marriage laws, surely we are entitled to take equally extreme possibilities in the abuse of their own divorce laws. If they, when looking about for a husband, so often hit upon a homicidal maniac, surely we may politely introduce them to the far more human figure of the gentleman who marries as many women as he likes and gets rid of them as often as he pleases. But in fact there is no necessity for us to argue thus in the abstract; for the amiable gentleman in question undoubtedly exists in the concrete. Of course, he is no new figure; he is a very recurrent type of rascal; his name has been Lothario or Don Juan; and he has often been represented as a rather romantic rascal. The point of divorce reform, it cannot be too often repeated, is that the rascal should not only be regarded as romantic, but regarded as respectable. He is not to sow his wild oats and settle down; he is merely to settle down to sowing his wild oats. They are to be regarded as tame and inoffensive oats; almost, if one may say so, as Quaker oats. But there is no need, as I say, to speculate about whether the looser view of divorce might prevail; for it is already prevailing. The newspapers are full of an astonishing hilarity about the rapidity with which hundreds or thousands of human families are being broken up by the lawyers; and about the undisguised haste of the "hustling judges" who carry on the work. It is a form of hilarity which would seem to recall the gaiety of a grave-digger in a city swept by a pestilence. But a few details occasionally flash by in the happy dance; from time to time the court is moved by a momentary curiosity about the causes of the general violation of oaths and promises; as if there might, here and there, be a hint of some sort of reason for ruining the fundamental institution of society. And nobody who notes those details, or considers those faint hints of reason, can doubt for a moment that masses of these men and women are now simply using divorce in the spirit of free-love. They are very seldom the sort of people who have once fallen tragically into the wrong place, and have now found their way triumphantly to the right place. They are almost always people who are obviously wandering from one place to another, and will probably leave their last shelter exactly as they have left their first. But it seems to amuse them to make again, if possible in a church, a promise they have already broken in practice and almost avowedly disbelieve in principle.

In face of this headlong fashion, it is really reasonable to ask the divorce reformers what is their attitude towards the old monogamous ethic of our civilisation; and whether they wish to retain it in general, or to retain it at all. Unfortunately even the sincerest and most lucid of them use language which leaves the matter a little doubtful. Mr. E. S. P. Haynes[1] is one of the most brilliant and most fair-minded controversialists on that side; and he has said, for instance, that he agrees with me in supporting the ideal of indissoluble or, at least, of undissolved marriage. Mr. Haynes is one of the few friends of divorce who are also real friends of democracy; and I am sure that in practice this stands for a real sympathy with the home, especially

[1] E. S. P. Haynes (1877–1949), English writer and lawyer.

the poor home. Unfortunately, on the theoretic side, the word "ideal" is far from being an exact term, and is open to two almost opposite interpretations. For many would say that marriage is an ideal as some would say that monasticism is an ideal, in the sense of a counsel of perfection. Now certainly we might preserve a conjugal ideal in this way. A man might be reverently pointed out in the street as a sort of saint, merely because he was married. A man might wear a medal for monogamy; or have letters after his name similar to V.C. or D.D.; let us say L.W. for "Lives With His Wife, " or "N.D.Y. for "Not Divorced Yet." We might, on entering some strange city, be struck by a stately column erected to the memory of a wife who never ran away with a soldier, or the shrine and image of a historical character, who had resisted the example of the man in the "New Witness" ballade in bolting with the children's nurse. Such high artistic hagiology would be quite consistent with Mr. Haynes' divorce reform; with re-marriage after three years, or three hours. It would also be quite consistent with Mr. Haynes' phrase about preserving an ideal of marriage. What it would not be consistent with is the perfectly plain, solid, secular and social usefulness which I have here attributed to marriage. It does not create or preserve a natural institution, normal to the whole community, to balance the more artificial and even more arbitrary institution of the state; which is less natural even if it is equally necessary. It does not defend a voluntary association, but leaves the only claim on life, death and loyalty with a more coercive institution. It does not stand, in the sense I have tried to explain, for the principle of liberty. In short, it does not do any of the things which Mr. Haynes himself would especially desire to see done. For humanity to be thus spontaneously organised from below, it is necessary that the organisation should be almost as universal as the official organisation from above. The tyrant must find not one family but many families defying his power; he must find mankind not a dust of atoms, but fixed in solid blocks of fidelity. And those human groups must support not only themselves but each other. In this sense what some call individualism is as corporate as communism. It is a thing of volunteers; but volunteers must be soldiers. It is a defence of private persons; but we might say that the private persons must be private soldiers. The family must be recognised as well as real; above all, the family must be recognised by the families. To expect individuals to suffer successfully for a home apart from the home, that is for something which is an incident but not an institution, is really a confusion between two ideas; it is a verbal sophistry almost in the nature of a pun. Similarly, for instance, we cannot prove the moral force of a peasantry by pointing to one peasant; we might almost as well reveal the military force of infantry by pointing to one infant.

I take it, however, that the advocates of divorce do not mean that marriage is to remain ideal only in the sense of being almost impossible. They do not mean that a faithful husband is only to be admired as a fanatic. The reasonable men among them do really mean that a divorced person shall be tolerated as something unusually unfortunate, not merely that a married person shall be admired as something unusually blessed and inspired. But whatever they desire, it is as well that they should realise exactly what they do; and in this case I should like to hear their criticisms in the matter of what they see. They must surely see that in England at present, as in many parts of America in the past, the new liberty is being taken in the spirit of licence as if the exception were to be the rule, or, rather, perhaps the absence of rule. This will especially be made manifest if we consider that the effect of the process is accumulative like a snowball, and returns on itself like a snowball. The obvious effect of frivolous divorce will be frivolous marriage. If people can be separated for no reason they will feel it all the easier to be united for no reason. A man might quite clearly foresee that a sensual infatuation would be fleeting, and console himself with the knowledge that the connection could be equally fleeting. There seems no particular reason why he should not elaborately calculate that he could stand a particular lady's temper for ten months; or reckon that he would have enjoyed and exhausted her repertoire of drawing-room songs in two years. The old joke about choosing the wife to fit the furniture or the fashions might quite logically return, not as an old joke but as a new solemnity; indeed, it will be found that a new religion is generally the return of an old joke. A man might quite consistently see a woman as suited to the period of the hobble skirt, and as less suited to the threatened recurrence of the crinoline. These fancies are fantastic enough, but they are not a shade more fantastic than the facts of many a divorce controversy as urged in the divorce courts. And this is to leave out altogether the most fantastic fact of all: the winking at widespread and conspicuous collusion. Collusion has become not so much an illegal evasion as a legal fiction, and even a legal institution, as it is admirably satirised in Mr. Somerset Maugham's brilliant play of "Home and Beauty." The fact was very frankly brought before the public, by a man who was eminently calculated to disarm satire by sincerity. Colonel Wedgewood[2] is a man who can never be too much honoured, by all who have any hope of popular liberties still finding champions in the midst of parliamentary corruption. He is one of the very few men alive who have shown both military and political courage; the courage of the camp and the courage of the forum. And doubtless he showed a third type of social courage, in avowing the absurd expedient which so many others are content merely to accept and employ. It is admittedly a frantic and farcical thing that a good man should find or think it necessary to pretend to commit a sin. Some of the divorce moralists seem to deduce from this that he ought really to commit the sin. They may possibly be aware, however, that there are some who do not agree with them.

For this latter fact is the next step in the speculative progress of the new morality. The divorce advocates must be well aware that modern civilisation still contains strong elements, not the least intelligent and certainly not the least vigorous, which will not accept the new respectability as a substitute for the old religious vow. The Roman Catholic Church, the Anglo-Catholic school, the conservative peasantries, and a large section of the popular life everywhere, will regard the riot of divorce and re-marriage as they would any other riot of irresponsibility. The consequence would appear to be that two different standards will appear in ordinary morality, and even in ordinary society. Instead of the old social distinction between those who are married and those who are unmarried, there

[2] Colonel Wedgewood (1872–1945), British writer, soldier and statesman.

will be a distinction between those who are married and those who are really married. Society might even become divided into two societies; which is perilously approximate to Disraeli's[3] famous exaggeration about England divided into two nations. But whether England be actually so divided or not, this note of the two nations is the real note of warning in the matter. It is in this connection, perhaps, that we have to consider most gravely and doubtfully the future of our own country.

Anarchy cannot last, but anarchic communities cannot last either. Mere lawlessness cannot live, but it can destroy life. The nations of the earth always return to sanity and solidarity; but the nations which return to it first are the nations which survive. We in England cannot afford to allow our social institutions to go to pieces, as if this ancient and noble country were an ephemeral colony. We cannot afford it comparatively, even if we could afford it positively. We are surrounded by vigorous nations mainly rooted in the peasant or permanent ideals; notably in the case of France and Ireland. I know that the detested and detestably undemocratic parliamentary clique, which corrupts France as it does England, was persuaded or bribed by a Jew named Naquet[4] to pass a crude and recent divorce law, which was full of the hatred of Christianity. But only a very superficial critic of France can be unaware that French parliamentarism is superficial. The French nation as a whole, the most rigidly respectable nation in the world, will certainly go on living by the old standards of domesticity. When Frenchmen are not Christians they are heathens; the heathens who worshipped the household gods. It might seem strange to say, for instance, that an atheist like M. Clemenceau[5] has for his chief ideal a thing called piety. But to understand this it is only necessary to know a little Latin — and a little French.

A short time ago, as I am well aware, it would have sounded very strange to represent the old religious and peasant communities either as a model or a menace. It was counted a queer thing to say, in the days

[3] Benjamin Disraeli (1804–1881), British statesman, novelist and Prime Minister.

[4] Alfred S. Naquet (1834–1916), French socialist writer and chemist.

[5] Georges Clemenceau (1841–1929), French statesman, journalist and Premier.

when my friends and I first said it; in the days of my youth when the republic of France and the religion of Ireland were regarded as alike ridiculous and decadent. But many things have happened since then; and it will not now be so easy to persuade even newspaper readers that Foch[6] is a fool, either because he is a Frenchman or because he is a Catholic. The older tradition, even in the most unfashionable forms, has found champions in the most unexpected quarters. Only the other day Dr. Saleeby,[7] a distinguished scientific critic who had made himself the special advocate of all the instruction and organisation that is called social science, startled his friends and foes alike by saying that the peasant families in the West of Ireland were far more satisfactory and successful than those brooded over by all the benevolent sociology of Bradford.[8] He gave his testimony from an entirely rationalistic and even materialistic point of view; indeed, he carried rationalism so far as to give the preference to Roscommon because the women are still mammals. To a mind of the more traditional type it might seem sufficient to say they are still mothers. To a memory that lingers over the legends and lyrical movements of mankind, it might seem no great improvement to imagine a song that ran "My mammal bids me bind my hair," or "I'm to be Queen of the May, mammal, I'm to be Queen of the May." But indeed the truth to which he testified is all the more arresting, because for him it was materialistic and not mystical. The brute biological advantage, as well as other advantages, was with those for whom that truth was a truth; and it was all the more instinctive and automatic where that truth was a tradition. The sort of place where mothers are still something more than mammals is the only sort of place where they still are mammals. There the people are still healthy animals; healthy enough to hit you if you call them animals. I also have, on this merely

[6] Ferdinand Foch (1851–1929), French army commander who became commander in chief of the Allied armies during the last year of World War I, halted the German spring and summer offensives of 1918, directed the Allied victory offensive and received the German surrender.

[7] See footnote 3, page 40.

[8] Possibly a reference to Edward R. Bradford (1836–1911), English soldier, police official and former official in India.

controversial occasion, used throughout the rationalistic and not the religious appeal. But it is not unreasonable to note that the materialistic advantages are really found among those who most repudiate materialism. This one stray testimony is but a type of a thousand things of the same kind, which will convince any one with the sense of social atmospheres that the day of the peasantries is not passing, but rather arriving. It is the more complex types of society that are now entangled in their own complexities. Those who tell us, with a monotonous metaphor, that we cannot put the clock back, seem to be curiously unconscious of the fact that their own clock has stopped. And there is nothing so hopeless as clockwork when it stops. A machine cannot mend itself; it requires a man to mend it; and the future lies with those who can make living laws for men and not merely dead laws for machinery. Those living laws are not to be found in the scatter-brained scepticism which is busy in the great cities, dissolving what it cannot analyse. The primary laws of man are to be found in the permanent life of man; in those things that have been common to it in every time and land, though in the highest civilisation they have reached an enrichment like that of the divine romance of Cana in Galilee. We know that many critics of such a story say that its elements are not permanent; but indeed it is the critics who are not permanent. A hundred mad dogs of heresy have worried man from the beginning; but it was always the dog that died. We know there is a school of prigs who disapprove of the wine; and there may now be a school of prigs who disapprove of the wedding. For in such a case as the story of Cana, it may be remarked that the pedants are prejudiced against the earthly elements as much as, or more than, the heavenly elements. It is not the supernatural that disgusts them, so much as the natural. And those of us who have seen all the normal rules and relations of humanity uprooted by random speculators, as if they were abnormal abuses and almost accidents, will understand why men have sought for something divine if they wished to preserve anything human. They will know why common sense, cast out from some academy of fads and fashions conducted on the lines of a luxurious madhouse, has age after age sought refuge in the high sanity of a sacrament.

IX

CONCLUSION

This is a pamphlet and not a book; and the writer of a pamphlet not only deals with passing things, but generally with things which he hopes will pass. In that sense it is the object of a pamphlet to be out of date as soon as possible. It can only survive when it does not succeed. The successful pamphlets are necessarily dull; and though I have no great hopes of this being successful, I dare say it is dull enough for all that. It is designed merely to note certain fugitive proposals of the moment, and compare them with certain recurrent necessities of the race; but especially the necessity for some spontaneous social formation freer than that of the state. If it were more in the nature of a work of literature, with anything like an ambition of endurance, I might go deeper into the matter, and give some suggestions about the philosophy or religion of marriage, and the philosophy or religion of all these rather random departures from it. Some day perhaps I may try to write something about the spiritual or psychological quarrel between faith and fads. Here I will only say, in conclusion, that I believe the universal fallacy here is a fallacy of being universal. There is a sense in which it is really a human if heroic possibility to love everybody; and the young student will not find it a bad preliminary exercise to love somebody. But the fallacy I mean is that of a man who is not even content to love everybody, but really wishes to be everybody. He wishes to walk down a hundred roads at once; to sleep in a hundred houses at once; to live a hundred lives at once. To do something like this in the imagination is one of the occasional visions of art and poetry; to attempt it in the art of life is not only anarchy but inaction. Even in the arts it can only be the first hint and not the final fulfillment; a man cannot work at once in bronze and marble, or play the organ and the violin at the same time. The universal vision of being such a Briareus is a nightmare of nonsense even in the merely imaginative world; and ends in mere nihilism in the social world. If a man had a hundred houses, there would still be more houses than he had days in which to dream of them; if a man had a hundred wives, there would still be more women than he could ever know. He would be an insane sultan jealous of the whole human race, and even of the dead and the unborn. I believe that behind the art and philosophy of our time there is a considerable element of this bottomless ambition and this unnatural hunger; and since in these last words I am touching only lightly on things that would need much larger treatment, I will admit that the rending of the ancient roof of man is probably only a part of such an endless and empty expansion. I asked in the last chapter what those most wildly engaged in the mere dance of divorce, as fantastic as the dance of death, really expected for themselves or for their children. And in the deepest sense I think this is the answer; that they expect the impossible, that is the universal. They are not crying for the moon, which is a definite and therefore a defensible desire. They are crying for the world; and when they had it, they would want another one. In the last resort they would like to try every situation, not in fancy but in fact; but they cannot refuse any and therefore cannot resolve on any. In so far as this is the modern mood, it is a thing so deadly as to be already dead. What is vitally needed everywhere, in art as much as in ethics, in poetry as much as in politics, is choice; a creative power in the will as well as in the mind. Without that self-limitation of somebody, nothing living will ever see the light.

EUGENICS
AND OTHER EVILS

1922

TO THE READER

I publish these essays at the present time for a particular reason connected with the present situation; a reason which I should like briefly to emphasize and make clear.

Though most of the conclusions, especially towards the end, are conceived with reference to recent events, the actual bulk of preliminary notes about the science of Eugenics were written before the war. It was a time when this theme was the topic of the hour; when eugenic babies (not visibly very distinguishable from other babies) sprawled all over the illustrated papers; when the evolutionary fancy of Nietzsche was the new cry among the intellectuals; and when Mr. Bernard Shaw and others were considering the idea that to breed a man like a cart-horse was the true way to attain that higher civilization, of intellectual magnanimity and sympathetic insight, which may be found in cart-horses. It may therefore appear that I took the opinion too controversially, and it seems to me that I sometimes took it too seriously. But the criticism of Eugenics soon expanded of itself into a more general criticism of a modern craze for scientific officialism and strict social organization.

And then the hour came when I felt, not without relief, that I might well fling all my notes into the fire. The fire was a very big one, and was burning up bigger things than such pedantic quackeries. And, anyhow, the issue itself was being settled in a very different style. Scientific officialism and organization in the State which had specialized in them, had gone to war with the older culture of Christendom. Either Prussianism would win and the protest would be hopeless, or Prussianism would lose and the protest would be needless. As the war advanced from poison gas to piracy against neutrals, it grew more and more plain that the scientifically organized State was not increasing in popularity. Whatever happened, no Englishmen would ever again go nosing round the stinks of that low laboratory. So I thought all I had written irrelevant, and put it out of my mind.

I am greatly grieved to say that it is not irrelevant. It has gradually grown apparent, to my astounded gaze, that the ruling classes in England are still proceeding on the assumption that Prussia is a pattern for the whole world. If parts of my book are nearly nine years old most of their principles and proceedings are a great deal older. They can offer us nothing but the same stuffy science, the same bullying bureaucracy and the same terrorism by tenth-rate professors that have led the German Empire to its recent conspicuous triumph. For that reason, three years after the war with Prussia, I collect and publish these papers.

G. K. C.

PART ONE

THE FALSE THEORY

I

WHAT IS EUGENICS?

The wisest thing in the world is to cry out before you are hurt. It is no good to cry out after you are hurt; especially after you are mortally hurt. People talk about the impatience of the populace; but sound historians know that most tyrannies have been possible because men moved too late. It is often essential to resist a tyranny before it exists. It is no answer to say, with a distant optimism, that the scheme is only in the air. A blow from a hatchet can only be parried while it is in the air.

There exists to-day a scheme of action, a school of thought, as collective and unmistakable as any of those by whose grouping alone we can make any outline of history. It is as firm a fact as the Oxford Movement, or the Puritans of the Long Parliament; or the Jansenists; or the Jesuits. It is a thing that can be pointed out; it is a thing that can be discussed; and it is a thing that can still be destroyed. It is called for convenience "Eugenics"; and that it ought to be destroyed I propose to prove in the pages that follow. I know that it means very different things to different people; but that is only because evil always takes advantage of ambiguity. I know it is praised with high professions of idealism and benevolence; with silver-tongued rhetoric about purer motherhood and a happier posterity. But that is only because evil is always flattered, as the Furies were called "The Gracious Ones." I know that it numbers many disciples whose intentions are entirely innocent and humane; and who would be sincerely astonished at my describing it as I do. But that is only because evil always wins through the strength of its splendid dupes; and there has in all ages been a disastrous alliance between abnormal innocence and abnormal sin. Of these who are deceived I shall speak of course as we all do of such instruments; judging them by the good they think they are doing, and not by the evil which they really do. But Eugenics itself does exist for those who have sense enough to see that ideas exist; and Eugenics itself, in large quantities or small, coming quickly or coming slowly, urged from good motives or bad, applied to a thousand people

297

or applied to three, Eugenics itself is a thing no more to be bargained about than poisoning.

It is not really difficult to sum up the essence of Eugenics: though some of the Eugenists seem to be rather vague about it. The movement consists of two parts: a moral basis, which is common to all, and a scheme of social application which varies a good deal. For the moral basis, it is obvious that man's ethical responsibility varies with his knowledge of consequences. If I were in charge of a baby (like Dr. Johnson[1] in that tower of vision), and the baby was ill through having eaten the soap, I might possibly send for a doctor. I might be calling him away from much more serious cases, from the bedsides of babies whose diet has been far more deadly; but I should be justified. I could not be expected to know enough about his other patients to be obliged (or even entitled) to sacrifice to them the baby for whom I was primarily and directly responsible. Now the Eugenic moral basis is this; that the baby for whom we are primarily and directly responsible is the babe unborn. That is, that we know (or may come to know) enough of certain inevitable tendencies in biology to consider the fruit of some contemplated union in that direct and clear light of conscience which we can now only fix on the other partner in that union. The one duty can conceivably be as definite as or more definite than the other. The baby that does not exist can be considered even before the wife who does. Now it is essential to grasp that this is a comparatively new note in morality. Of course sane people always thought the aim of marriage was the procreation of children to the glory of God or according to the plan of Nature; but whether they counted such children as God's reward for service or Nature's premium on sanity, they always left the reward to God or the premium to Nature, as a less definable thing. The only person (and this is the point) towards whom one could have precise duties was the partner in the process. Directly considering the partner's claims was the nearest one could get to indirectly considering the claims of posterity. If the women of the harem sang praises of the hero as the Moslem mounted his horse, it was because this was the

---

[1] Samuel Johnson (1709–1784), English lexographer, writer, critic, dramatist, poet and conversationalist.

due of a man; if the Christian knight helped his wife off her horse, it was because this was the due of a woman. Definite and detailed dues of this kind they did not predicate of the babe unborn; regarding him in that agnostic and opportunist light in which Mr. Browdie[2] regarded the hypothetical child of Miss Squeers[3]. Thinking these sex relations healthy, they naturally hoped they would produce healthy children; but that was all. The Moslem woman doubtless expected Allah to send beautiful sons to an obedient wife; but she would not have allowed any direct vision of such sons to alter the obedience itself. She would not have said, "I will now be a disobedient wife; as the learned leech informs me that great prophets are often children of disobedient wives." The knight doubtless hoped that the saints would help him to strong children, if he did all the duties of his station, one of which might be helping his wife off her horse; but he would not have refrained from doing this because he had read in a book that a course of falling off horses often resulted in the birth of a genius. Both Moslem and Christian would have thought such speculations not only impious but utterly unpractical. I quite agree with them; but that is not the point here.

The point here is that a new school believes Eugenics *against* Ethics. And it is proved by one familiar fact: that the heroisms of history are actually the crimes of Eugenics. The Eugenists' books and articles are full of suggestions that non-eugenic unions should and may come to be regarded as we regard sins; that we should really feel that marrying an invalid is a kind of cruelty to children. But history is full of the praises of people who have held sacred such ties to invalids; of cases like those of Colonel Hutchinson[4] and Sir William Temple[5], who remained faithful to betrothals when beauty and health had been apparently blasted. And though the illnesses of

[2] A character in Charles Dickens' *Nicholas Nickelby*.

[3] Also a character in Dickens' *Nicholas Nickelby*.

[4] John Hutchinson (1615–1664), English puritan soldier and regicide. He met and fell in love with Lucy Apsley; on the day of their wedding she contracted smallpox and was badly deformed by the effects of the illness. Hutchinson was untroubled by her shattered beauty and married her as soon as she was able to leave her bed chamber.

[5] Sir William Temple (1628–1699), English essayist and diplomat. He fell in love with Dorothy Osborne, but due to the disapproval of the match on the part of

Dorothy Osborne and Mrs. Hutchinson may not fall under the Eugenic speculations (I do not know), it is obvious that they might have done so; and certainly it would not have made any difference to men's moral opinion of the act. I do not discuss here which morality I favour; but I insist that they are opposite. The Eugenist really sets up as saints the very men whom hundreds of families have called sneaks. To be consistent, they ought to put up statues to the men who deserted their loves because of bodily misfortune; with inscriptions celebrating the good Eugenist who, on his fiancée falling off a bicycle, nobly refused to marry her; or to the young hero who, on hearing of an uncle with erysipelas, magnanimously broke his word. What is perfectly plain is this: that mankind have hitherto held the bond between man and woman so sacred, and the effect of it on the children so incalculable, that they have always admired the maintenance of honour more than the maintenance of safety. Doubtless they thought that even the children might be none the worse for not being the children of cowards and shirkers; but this was not the first thought, the first commandment. Briefly, we may say that while many moral systems have set restraints on sex almost as severe as any Eugenist could set, they have almost always had the character of securing the fidelity of the two sexes to each other, and leaving the rest to God. To introduce an ethic which makes that fidelity or infidelity vary with some calculation about heredity is that rarest of all things, a revolution that has not happened before.

It is only right to say here, though the matter should only be touched on, that many Eugenists would contradict this, in so far as to claim that there was a consciously Eugenic reason for the horror of those unions which begin with the celebrated denial to man of the privilege of marrying his grandmother. Dr. S. R. Steinmetz,[6] with that creepy simplicity of mind with which the Eugenists chill

---

both families, the couple was prevented from marrying. After seven years, Dorothy contracted smallpox and was left permanently scarred. This destroyed her family's hopes for a better match and Sir William's faithfulness to Dorothy proved his love for her; consequently, the couple was allowed to marry in 1655.

[6] Sebald Rudolf Steinmetz (1862–1940), Dutch ethnologist, social philosopher and author of *Endocannibalism* (1896).

the blood, remarks that "we do not yet know quite certainly" what were "the motives for the horror of" that horrible thing which is the agony of Oedipus. With entirely amiable intention, I ask Dr. S. R. Steinmetz to speak for himself. I know the motives for regarding a mother or a sister as separate from other women; nor have I reached them by any curious researches. I found them where I found an analogous aversion to eating a baby for breakfast. I found them in a rooted detestation in the human soul to liking a thing in one way, when you already like it in another quite incompatible way. Now it is perfectly true that this aversion may have acted eugenically; and so had a certain ultimate confirmation and basis in the laws of procreation. But there really cannot be any Eugenist quite so dull as not to see that this is not a defence of Eugenics but a direct denial of Eugenics. If something which has been discovered at last by the lamp of learning is something which has been acted on from the first by the light of nature, this (so far as it goes) is plainly not an argument for pestering people, but an argument for letting them alone. If men did not marry their grandmothers when it was, for all they knew, a most hygienic habit; if we know now that they instinctively avoided scientific peril; that, so far as it goes, is a point in favour of letting people marry anyone they like. It is simply the statement that sexual selection, or what Christians call falling in love, is a part of man which in the rough and in the long run can be trusted. And that is the destruction of the whole of this science at a blow.

The second part of the definition, the persuasive or coercive methods to be employed, I shall deal with more fully in the second part of this book. But some such summary as the following may here be useful. Far into the unfathomable past of our race we find the assumption that the founding of a family is the personal adventure of a free man. Before slavery sank slowly out of sight under the new climate of Christianity, it may or may not be true that slaves were in some sense bred like cattle, valued as a promising stock for labour. If it was so it was so in a much looser and vaguer sense than the breeding of the Eugenists; and such modern philosophers read into the old paganism a fantastic pride and cruelty which are wholly modern. It may be, however, that pagan slaves had some shadow of the blessings of the Eugenist's care. It is quite certain that the pagan freemen would have killed the first man that suggested it. I mean suggested it seriously; for Plato was only a Bernard Shaw who unfortunately made his jokes in Greek. Among free men, the law, more often the creed, most commonly of all the custom, have laid all sorts of restrictions on sex for this reason or that. But law and creed and custom have never concentrated heavily except upon fixing and keeping the family when once it had been made. The act of founding the family, I repeat, was an individual adventure outside the frontiers of the State. Our first forgotten ancestors left this tradition behind them; and our own latest fathers and mothers a few years ago would have thought us lunatics to be discussing it. The shortest general definition of Eugenics on its practical side is that it does, in a more or less degree, propose to control some families at least as if they were families of pagan slaves. I shall discuss later the question of the people to whom this pressure may be applied; and the much more puzzling question of what people will apply it. But it is to be applied at the very least by somebody to somebody, and that on certain calculations about breeding which are affirmed to be demonstrable. So much for the subject itself. I say that this thing exists. I define it as closely as matters involving moral evidence can be defined; I call it Eugenics. If after that anyone chooses to say that Eugenics is not the Greek for this—I am content to answer that "chivalrous" is not the French for "horsy"; and that such controversial games are more horsy than chivalrous.

II

THE FIRST OBSTACLES

Now before I set about arguing these things, there is a cloud of skirmishers, of harmless and confused modern sceptics, who ought to be cleared off or calmed down before we come to debate with the real doctors of the heresy. If I sum up my statement thus: "Eugenics, as discussed, evidently means the control of some men over the marriage and unmarriage of others; and probably means the control of the few over the marriage and unmarriage of the many," I shall first of all receive the sort of answers that float like skim on the surface of teacups and talk. I may very roughly and rapidly divide these preliminary objectors into five sects; whom I will call the Euphemists, the Casuists, the Autocrats, the Precedenters, and the Endeavourers. When we have answered the immediate protestation of all these good, shouting, short-sighted people, we can begin to do justice to those intelligences that are really behind the idea.

Most Eugenists are Euphemists. I mean merely that short words startle them, while long words soothe them. And they are utterly incapable of translating the one into the other, however obviously they mean the same thing. Say to them "The persuasive and even coercive powers of the citizen should enable him to make sure that the burden of longevity in the previous generations does not become disproportionate and intolerable, especially to the females"; say this to them and they sway slightly to and fro like babies sent to sleep in cradles. Say to them "Murder your mother," and they sit up quite suddenly. Yet the two sentences, in cold logic, are exactly the same. Say to them "It is not improbable that a period may arrive when the narrow if once useful distinction between the anthropoid *homo* and the other animals, which has been modified on so many moral points, may be modified also even in regard to the important question of the extension of human diet"; say this to them, and beauty born of murmuring sound will pass into their faces. But say to them, in a simple, manly, hearty way "Let's eat a man!" and their surprise is quite surprising. Yet the sentences say just the same thing. Now, if anyone thinks these two instances extravagant, I will refer to two actual cases from the Eugenic discussions. When Sir Oliver Lodge[1] spoke of the methods "of the stud-farm" many Eugenists exclaimed against the crudity of the suggestion. Yet long before that one of the ablest champions in the other interest had written "What nonsense this education is! Who could educate a racehorse or a greyhound?" Which most certainly either means nothing, or the human stud-farm. Or again, when I spoke of people "being married forcibly by the police," another distinguished Eugenist almost achieved high spirits in his hearty assurance that no such thing had ever come into their heads. Yet a few days after I saw a Eugenist pronouncement, to the effect that the State ought to extend its powers in this area. The State can only be that corporation which men permit to employ compulsion; and this area can only be the area of sexual selection. I mean somewhat more than an idle jest when I say that the policeman will generally be found in that area. But I willingly admit that the policeman who looks after weddings will be like the policeman who looks after wedding-presents. He will be in plain clothes. I do not mean that a man in blue with a helmet will drag the bride and bridegroom to the altar. I do mean that nobody that man in blue is told to arrest will even dare to come near the church. Sir Oliver did not mean that men would be tied up in stables and scrubbed down by grooms. He meant that they would undergo a loss of liberty which to men is even more infamous. He meant that the only formula important to Eugenists would be "by Smith out of Jones." Such a formula is one of the shortest in the world; and is certainly the shortest way with the Euphemists.

The next sect of superficial objectors is even more irritating. I have called them, for immediate purposes, the Casuists. Suppose I say "I, dislike this spread of Cannibalism in the West End restaurants." Somebody is sure to say "Well, after all, Queen Eleanor when she sucked blood from her husband's arm was a cannibal." What is one to say to such people? One can only say "Confine yourself to sucking poisoned blood from people's arms, and I permit you to call yourself

---

[1] Sir Oliver Lodge (1851–1940), British statesman and philosopher.

by the glorious title of Cannibal." In this sense people say of
Eugenics, "After all, whenever we discourage a schoolboy from
marrying a mad negress with a hump back, we are really Eugenists."
Again one can only answer, "Confine yourselves strictly to such
schoolboys as are naturally attracted to hump-backed negresses; and
you may exult in the title of Eugenist, all the more proudly because
that distinction will be rare." But surely anyone's common-sense
must tell him that if Eugenics dealt only with such extravagant
cases, it would be called common-sense—and not Eugenics. The
human race has excluded such absurdities for unknown ages; and has
never yet called it Eugenics. You may call it flogging when you hit a
choking gentleman on the back; you may call it torture when a man
unfreezes his fingers at the fire; but if you talk like that a little longer
you will cease to live among living men. If nothing but this mad
minimum of accident were involved, there would be no such thing
as a Eugenic Congress, and certainly no such thing as this book.

I had thought of calling the next sort of superficial people the
Idealists; but I think this implies a humility towards impersonal
good they hardly show; so I call them the Autocrats. They are those
who give us generally to understand that every modern reform will
"work" all right, because they will be there to see. Where they will
be, and for how long, they do not explain very clearly. I do not
mind their looking forward to numberless lives in succession; for
that is the shadow of a human or divine hope. But even a theos-
ophist does not expect to be a vast number of people at once. And
these people most certainly propose to be responsible for a whole
movement after it has left their hands. Each man promises to be about a
thousand policemen. If you ask them how this or that will work, they
will answer, "Oh, I would certainly insist on this"; or "I would never
go so far as that"; as if they could return to this earth and do what no
ghost has ever done quite successfully—force men to forsake their sins.
Of these it is enough to say that they do not understand the nature of a
law any more than the nature of a dog. If you let loose a law, it will do
as a dog does. It will obey its own nature, not yours. Such sense as you
have put into the law (or the dog) will be fulfilled. But you will not be
able to fulfill a fragment of anything you have forgotten to put into it.

Along with such idealists should go the strange people who seem to think that you can consecrate and purify any campaign for ever by repeating the names of the abstract virtues that its better advocates had in mind. These people will say "So far from aiming at *slavery*, the Eugenists are seeking *true* liberty; liberty from disease and degeneracy, etc." Or they will say "We can assure Mr. Chesterton that the Eugenists have *no* intention of segregating the harmless; justice and mercy are the very motto of——"etc. To this kind of thing perhaps the shortest answer is this. Many of those who speak thus are agnostic or generally unsymphathetic to official religion. Suppose one of them said "The Church of England is full of hypocrisy." What would he think of me if I answered, "I assure you that hypocrisy is condemned by every form of Christianity; and is particularly repudiated in the Prayer Book"? Suppose he said that the Church of Rome had been guilty of great cruelties. What would he think of me if I answered, "The Church is expressly bound to meekness and charity; and therefore cannot be cruel"? This kind of people need not detain us long. Then there are others whom I may call the Precedenters; who flourish particularly in Parliament. They are best represented by the solemn official who said the other day that he could not understand the clamour against the Feeble-Minded Bill as it only extended the "principles" of the old Lunacy Laws. To which again one can only answer "Quite so. It only extends the principles of the Lunacy Laws to persons without a trace of lunacy." This lucid politician finds an old law, let us say, about keeping lepers in quarantine. He simply alters the word "lepers" to "long-nosed people," and says blandly that the principle is the same.

Perhaps the weakest of all are those helpless persons whom I have called the Endeavourers. The prize specimen of them was another M. P. who defended the same Bill as "an honest attempt" to deal with a great evil: as if one had a right to dragoon and enslave one's fellow citizens as a kind of chemical experiment; in a state of reverent agnosticism about what would come of it. But with this fatuous notion that one can deliberately establish the Inquisition or the Terror, and then faintly trust the larger hope, I shall have to deal more seriously in a subsequent chapter. It is enough to say here that the best thing the honest Endeavourer could do would be to make an honest attempt to know what he is doing. And not to do anything else until he has found out. Lastly, there is a class of controversialists so hopeless and futile that I have really failed to find a name for them. But whenever anyone attempts to argue rationally for or against any existent and recognizable *thing*, such as the Eugenic class of legislation, there are always people who begin to chop hay about Socialism and Individualism; and say "*You* object to all State interference; I am in favour of State interference. *You* are an Individualist; I, on the other hand," etc. To which I can only answer, with heart-broken patience, that I am not an Individualist, but a poor fallen but baptized journalist who is trying to write a book about Eugenists, several of whom he has met; whereas he never met an Individualist and is by no means certain he would recognize him if he did. In short, I do not deny, but strongly affirm, the right of the State to interfere to cure a great evil. I say in this case it would interfere to create a great evil; and I am not going to be turned from the discussion of that direct issue to bottomless botherations about Socialism and Individualism, or the relative advantages of always turning to the right and always turning to the left.

And for the rest, there is undoubtedly an enormous mass of sensible, rather thoughtless people, whose rooted sentiment it is that any deep change in our society must be in some way infinitely distant. They cannot believe that men in hats and coats like themselves can be preparing a revolution; all their Victorian philosophy has taught them that such transformations are always slow. Therefore, when I speak of Eugenic legislation, or the coming of the Eugenic State, they think of it as something like *The Time Machine* or *Looking Backward*: a thing that, good or bad, will have to fit itself to their great-great-great-grandchild, who may be very different and may like it; and who in any case is rather a distant relative. To all this I have, to begin with, a very short and simple answer. The Eugenic State has begun. The first of the Eugenic Laws has already been adopted by the Government of this country; and passed with the applause of both parties through the dominant House of Parliament. This first Eugenic Law clears the ground and may be said to proclaim negative Eugenics; but it cannot be defended, and nobody has attempted to defend it, except on the Eugenic theory. I will call it the Feeble-Minded Bill, both for brevity and because the description is strictly accurate. It is, and quite simply and literally, a Bill for incarcerating as madmen those whom no doctor will consent to call mad. It is enough if some doctor or other may happen to call them weak-minded. Since there is scarcely any human being to whom this term has not been conversationally applied by his own friends and relatives on some occasion or other (unless his friends and relatives have been lamentably lacking in spirit), it can be clearly seen that this law, like the early Christian Church (to which, however, it presents points of dissimilarity), is a net drawing in of all kinds. It must not be supposed that we have a stricter definition incorporated in the Bill. Indeed, the first definition of "feeble-minded" in the Bill was much looser and vaguer than the phrase "feeble-minded" itself. It is a piece of yawning idiocy about "persons who though capable of earning their living under favourable circumstances" (as if anyone could earn his living if circumstances were directly unfavourable to his doing so), are nevertheless "incapable of managing their affairs with proper prudence"; which is exactly what all the world and his wife are saying about their neighbours all over this planet. But as an incapacity for any kind of thought is now regarded as statesmanship, there is nothing so very novel about such slovenly drafting. What is novel and what is vital is this: that the *defence* of this crazy Coercion Act is a Eugenic defence. It is not only openly said, it is eagerly urged, that the aim of the measure is to prevent any person whom these propagandists do not happen to think intelligent from having any wife or children. Every tramp who is sulky, every labourer who is shy, every rustic who is eccentric, can quite easily be brought under such conditions as were designed for homicidal maniacs. That is the situation; and that is the point. England has forgotten the Feudal State; it is in the last anarchy of the Industrial State; there is much in Mr. Belloc's theory that it is approaching the Servile State; it cannot at present get at the Distributive State; it has almost certainly missed the Socialist State. But we are already under the Eugenist State; and nothing remains to us but rebellion.

III

THE ANARCHY FROM ABOVE

A silent anarchy is eating out our society. I must pause upon the expression; because the true nature of anarchy is mostly misapprehended. It is not in the least necessary that anarchy should be violent; nor is it necessary that it should come from below. A government may grow anarchic as much as a people. The more sentimental sort of Tory uses the word anarchy as a mere term of abuse for rebellion; but he misses a most important intellectual distinction. Rebellion may be wrong and disastrous; but even when rebellion is wrong, it is never anarchy. When it is not self-defence, it is usurpation. It aims at setting up a new rule in place of the old rule. And while it cannot be anarchic in essence (because it has an aim), it certainly cannot be anarchic in method; for men must be organized when they fight; and the discipline in a rebel army has to be as good as the discipline in the royal army. This deep principle of distinction must be clearly kept in mind. Take for the sake of symbolism those two great spiritual stories which, whether we count them myths or mysteries, have so long been the two hinges of all European morals. The Christian who is inclined to sympathize generally with constituted authority will think of rebellion under the image of Satan, the rebel against God. But Satan, though a traitor, was not an anarchist. He claimed the crown of the cosmos; and had he prevailed, would have expected his rebel angels to give up rebelling. On the other hand, the Christian whose sympathies are more generally with just self-defence among the oppressed will think rather of Christ Himself defying the High Priests and scourging the rich traders. But whether or no Christ was (as some say) a Socialist, He most certainly was not an Anarchist. Christ, like Satan, claimed the throne. He set up a new authority against an old authority; but He set it up with positive commandments and a comprehensible scheme. In this light all mediaeval people—indeed, all people until a little while ago —would have judged questions involving revolt.

John Ball[1] would have offered to pull down the government because it was a bad government, not because it was a government. Richard II. would have blamed Bolingbroke[2] not as a disturber of the peace, but as a usurper. Anarchy, then, in the useful sense of the word, is a thing utterly distinct from any rebellion, right or wrong. It is not necessarily angry; it is not, in its first stages, at least, even necessarily painful. And, as I said before, it is often entirely silent.

Anarchy is that condition of mind or methods in which you cannot stop yourself. It is the loss of that self-control which can return to the normal. It is not anarchy because men are permitted to begin uproar, extravagance, experiment, peril. It is anarchy when people cannot *end* these things. It is not anarchy in the home if the whole family sits up all night on New Year's Eve. It is anarchy in the home if members of the family sit up later and later for months afterwards. It was not anarchy in the Roman villa when, during the Saturnalia, the slaves turned masters or the masters slaves. It was (from the slave-owners' point of view) anarchy if, after the Saturnalia, the slaves continued to behave in a Saturnalian manner; but it is historically evident that they did not. It is not anarchy to have a picnic; but it is anarchy to lose all memory of mealtimes. It would, I think, be anarchy if (as is the disgusting suggestion of some) we all took what we liked off the sideboard. That is the way swine would eat if swine had sideboards; they have no immovable feasts; they are uncommonly progressive, are swine. It is this inability to return within rational limits after a legitimate extravagance that is the really dangerous disorder. The modern world is like Niagara. It is magnificent, but it is not strong. It is as weak as water—like Niagara. The objection to a cataract is not that it is deafening or dangerous or even destructive; it is that it cannot stop. Now it is plain that this sort of chaos can possess the powers that rule a society as easily as the society so ruled. And in modern England it is the powers that rule

---

[1] John Ball (d. 1381), English priest, one of the leaders in Wat Tyler's rebellion, 1381.

[2] Henry of Lancaster (1367–1413). He became King Henry IV of England in 1399 by forcing Richard II to renounce his claim to the throne. During his reign, rebellion and lawlessness were widespread.

who are chiefly possessed by it—who are truly possessed by devils. The phrase, in its sound old psychological sense, is not too strong. The State has suddenly and quietly gone mad. It is talking nonsense; and it can't stop.

Now it is perfectly plain that government ought to have, and must have, the same sort of right to use exceptional methods occasionally that the private householder has to have a picnic or to sit up all night on New Year's Eve. The State, like the householder, is sane if it can treat such exceptions as exceptions. Such desperate remedies may not even be right; but such remedies are endurable as long as they are admittedly desperate. Such cases, of course, are the communism of food in a besieged city; the official disavowal of an arrested spy; the subjection of a patch of civil life to martial law; the cutting of communication in a plague; or that deepest degradation of the commonwealth, the use of national soldiers not against foreign soldiers, but against their own brethren in revolt. Of these exceptions some are right and some wrong; but all are right in so far as they are taken as exceptions. The modern world is insane, not so much because it admits the abnormal as because it cannot recover the normal.

We see this in the vague extension of punishments like imprisonment; often the very reformers who admit that prison is bad for people propose to reform them by a little more of it. We see it in panic legislation like that after the White Slave scare, when the torture of flogging was revived for all sorts of ill-defined and vague and variegated types of men. Our fathers were never so mad, even when they were torturers. They stretched the man out on the rack. They did not stretch the rack out, as we are doing. When men went witch-burning they may have seen witches everywhere—because their minds were fixed on witchcraft. But they did not see things to burn everywhere, because their minds were unfixed. While tying some very unpopular witch to the stake, with the firm conviction that she was a spiritual tyranny and pestilence, they did not say to each other, "A little burning is what my Aunt Susan wants, to cure her of her back-biting," or "Some of these faggots would do your Cousin James good, and teach him to play with poor girls' affections."

Now the name of all this is Anarchy. It not only does not know what it wants, but it does not even know what it hates. It multiplies excessively in the more American sort of English newspapers. When this new sort of New Englander burns a witch the whole prairie catches fire. These people have not the decision and detachment of the doctrinal ages. They cannot do a monstrous action and still see it is monstrous. Wherever they make a stride they make a rut. They cannot stop their own thoughts, though their thoughts are pouring into the pit

A final instance, which can be sketched much more briefly, can be found in this general fact: that the definition of almost every crime has become more and more indefinite, and spreads like a flattening and thinning cloud over larger and larger landscapes. Cruelty to children, one would have thought, was a thing about as unmistakable, unusual and appalling as parricide. In its application it has come to cover almost every negligence that can occur in a needy household. The only distinction is, of course, that these negligences are punished in the poor, who generally can't help them, and not in the rich, who generally can. But that is not the point I am arguing just now. The point here is that a crime we all instinctively connect with Herod on the bloody night of Innocents has come precious near being attributable to Mary and Joseph when they lost their child in the Temple. In the light of a fairly recent case (the confessedly kind mother who was lately jailed because her confessedly healthy children had no water to wash in) no one, I think, will call this an illegitimate literary exaggeration. Now this is exactly as if all the horror and heavy punishment, attached in the simplest tribes to parricide, could now be used against my son who had done any act that could colourably be supposed to have worried his father, and so affected his health. Few of us would be safe.

Another case out of hundreds is the loose extension of the idea of libel. Libel cases bear no more trace of the old and just anger against the man who bore false witness against his neighbour than "cruelty" cases do of the old and just horror of the parents that hated their own flesh. A libel case has become one of the sports of the less athletic rich — a variation on *baccarat*, a game of chance. A music-hall actress got damages for a song that was called "vulgar," which is as if I could fine or imprison my neighbour for calling my handwriting "rococo." A politician got huge damages because he was said to have spoken to children about Tariff Reform; as if that seductive topic would corrupt their virtue, like an indecent story. Sometimes libel is defined as anything calculated to hurt a man in his business; in which case any new tradesman calling himself a grocer slanders the grocer opposite. All this, I say, is Anarchy; for it is clear that its exponents possess no power of distinction, or sense of proportion, by which they can draw the line between calling a woman a popular singer and calling her a bad lot; or between charging a man with leading infants to Protection and leading them to sin and shame. But the vital point to which to return is this. That it is not necessarily nor even specially, an anarchy in the populace. It is an anarchy in the organ of government. It is the magistrates — voices of the governing class — who cannot distinguish between cruelty and carelessness. It is the judges (and their very submissive special juries) who cannot see the difference between opinion and slander. And it is the highly placed and highly paid experts who have brought in the first Eugenic Law, the Feeble-Minded Bill — thus showing that they can see no difference between a mad and a sane man.

That, to begin with, is the historic atmosphere in which this thing was born. It is a peculiar atmosphere, and luckily not likely to last. Real progress bears the same relation to it that a happy girl laughing bears to an hysterical girl who cannot stop laughing. But I have described this atmosphere first because it is the only atmosphere in which such a thing as the Eugenist legislation could be proposed among men. All other ages would have called it to some kind of logical account, however academic or narrow. The lowest sophist in the Greek schools would remember enough of Socrates to force the Eugenist to tell him (at least) whether Midias was segregated because he was curable or because he was incurable. The meanest Thomist of the mediaeval monasteries would have the sense to see that you cannot discuss a madman when you have not discussed a man. The most owlish Calvinist commentator in the seventeenth century would ask the Eugenist to reconcile such Bible texts as derided fools with the other Bible texts that praised them. The dullest shopkeeper in Paris in 1790 would have asked what were the Rights of Man, if they did not include the rights of the lover, the husband, and the father. It is only in our own London Particular (as Mr. Guppy[3] said of the fog) that small figures can loom so large in the vapour, and even mingle with quite different figures, and have the appearance of a mob. But, above all, I have dwelt on the telescopic quality in these twilight avenues, because unless the reader realizes how elastic and unlimited they are, he simply will not believe in the abominations we have to combat.

One of those wise old fairy tales, that come from nowhere and flourish everywhere, tells how a man came to own a small magic machine like a coffee-mill, which would grind anything he wanted when he said one word and stop when he said another. After performing marvels (which I wish my conscience would let me put into this book for padding) the mill was merely asked to grind a few grains of salt at an officers' mess on board ship; for salt is the type everywhere of small luxury and exaggeration, and sailors' tales should be taken with a grain of it. The man remembered the word that started the salt mill, and then, touching the word that stopped it, suddenly remembered that he forgot. The tall ship sank, laden and sparkling to the topmasts with salt like Arctic snows; but the mad mill was still grinding at the ocean bottom, where all the men lay drowned. And that (so says this fairy tale) is why the great waters about our world have a bitter taste. For the fairy tales knew what the modern mystics don't — that one should not let loose either the supernatural or the natural.

[3] A clerk in Dickens' *Bleak House* (1852).

IV

THE LUNATIC AND THE LAW

The modern evil, we have said, greatly turns on this: that people do not see that the exception proves the rule. Thus it may or may not be right to kill a murderer; but it can only conceivably be right to kill a murderer because it is wrong to kill a man. If the hangman, having got his hand in, proceeded to hang friends and relatives to his taste and fancy, he would (intellectually) unhang the first man, though the first man might not think so. Or thus again, if you say an insane man is irresponsible, you imply that a sane man is responsible. He is responsible for the insane man. And the attempt of the Eugenists and other fatalists to treat all men as irresponsible is the largest and flattest folly in philosophy. The Eugenist has to treat everybody, including himself, as an exception to a rule that isn't there.

The Eugenists, as a first move, have extended the frontiers of the lunatic asylum; let us take this as our definite starting point, and ask ourselves what lunacy is, and what is its fundamental relation to human society. Now that raw juvenile scepticism that clogs all thought with catchwords may often be heard to remark that the mad are only the minority, the sane only the majority. There is a neat exactitude about such people's nonsense; they seem to miss the point by magic. The mad are not a minority because they are not a corporate body; and that is what their madness means. The sane are not a majority; they are mankind. And mankind (as its name would seem to imply) is a *kind*, not a degree. In so far as the lunatic differs, he differs from all minorities and majorities in kind. The madman who thinks he is a knife cannot go into partnership with the other who thinks he is a fork. There is no trysting place outside reason; there is no inn on those wild roads that are beyond the world.

The madman is not he that defies the world. The saint, the criminal, the martyr, the cynic, the nihilist may all defy the world quite sanely. And even if such fanatics would destroy the world the world owes them a strictly fair trial according to proof and public law. But the madman is not the man who defies the world; he is the man who *denies* it. Suppose we are all standing round a field and looking at a tree in the middle of it. It is perfectly true that we all see it (as the decadents say) in infinitely different aspects: that is not the point; the point is that we all say it is a tree. Suppose, if you will, that we are all poets, which seems improbable; so that each of us could turn his aspect into a vivid image distinct from a tree. Suppose one says it looks like a green cloud and another like a green fountain, and a third like a green dragon and the fourth like a green cheese. The fact remains: that they all say it *looks* like these things. It is a tree. Nor are any of the poets in the least mad because of any opinions they may form, however frenzied, about the functions or future of the tree. A conservative poet may wish to clip the tree; a revolutionary poet may wish to burn it. An optimist poet may want to make it a Christmas tree and hang candles on it. A pessimist poet may want to hang himself on it. None of these are mad, because they are all talking about the same thing. But there is another man who is talking horribly about something else. There is a monstrous exception to mankind. Why he is so we know not; a new theory says it is heredity; an older theory says it is devils. But in any case, the spirit of it is the spirit that denies, the spirit that really denies realities. This is the man who looks at the tree and does not say it looks like a lion, but says that it *is* a lamp-post.

I do not mean that all mad delusions are as concrete as this, though some are more concrete. Believing your own body is glass is a more daring denial of reality than believing a tree is a glass lamp at the top of a pole. But all true delusions have in them this unalterable assertion—that what is not is. The difference between us and the maniac is not about how things look or how things ought to look, but about what they self-evidently are. The lunatic does not say that he ought to be King; Perkin Warbeck[1] might say that. He says he is King. The lunatic does not say he is as wise as Shakespeare; Bernard Shaw might say that. The lunatic says he *is* Shakespeare. The lunatic does not say he is divine in the same sense as Christ; Mr. R. J.

[1] Perkin Warbeck (1474?–1499), Flemish pretender to English throne, claimed to be son of English king.

Campbell[2] would say that. The lunatic says he *is* Christ. In all cases the difference is a difference about what is there; not a difference touching what should be done about it.

For this reason, and for this alone, the lunatic is outside public law. This is the abysmal difference between him and the criminal. The criminal admits the facts, and therefore permits us to appeal to the facts. We can so arrange the facts around him that he may really understand that agreement is in his own interests. We can say to him, "Do not steal apples from this tree, or we will hang you on that tree." But if the man really thinks one tree is a lamp-post and the other tree a Trafalgar Square fountain, we simply cannot treat with him at all. It is obviously useless to say, "Do not steal apples from this lamp-post, or I will hang you on that fountain." If a man denies the facts, there is no answer but to lock him up. He cannot speak our language: not that varying verbal language which often misses fire even with us, but that enormous alphabet of sun and moon and green grass and blue sky in which alone we meet, and by which alone we can signal to each other. That unique man of genius, George Macdonald, described in one of his weird stories two systems of space co-incident; so that where I knew there was a piano standing in a drawing-room you knew there was a rose-bush growing in a garden. Something of this sort is in small or great affairs the matter with the madman. He cannot have a vote, because he is the citizen of another country. He is a foreigner. Nay, he is an invader and an enemy; for the city he lives in has been super-imposed on ours.

Now these two things are primarily to be noted in his case. First, that we can only condemn him to a *general* doom, because we only know his *general* nature. All criminals, who do particular things for particular reasons (things and reasons which, however criminal, are always comprehensible), have been more and more tried for such separate actions under separate and suitable laws ever since Europe began to become a civilization—and until the rare and recent reincursions of barbarism in such things as the Indeterminate Sentence. Of that I shall speak later; it is enough for this argument to point out the plain facts.

---

[2] Reginald John Campbell (1867–1956), British clergyman and writer.

It is the plain fact that every savage, every sultan, every outlawed baron, every brigand-chief has always used this instrument of the In-determinate Sentence, which has been recently offered us as some-thing highly scientific and humane. All these people, in short, being barbarians, have always kept their captives until they (the barbarians) chose to think the captives were in a fit frame of mind to come out. It is also the plain fact that all that has been called civilization or progress, justice or liberty, for nearly three thousand years, has had the general direction of treating even the captive as a free man, in so far as some clear case of some defined crime had to be shown against him. All law has meant allowing the criminal, within some limits or other, to argue with the law: as Job was allowed, or rather challenged, to argue with God. But the criminal is, among civilized men, tried by one law for one crime for a perfectly simple reason: that the motive of the crime like the meaning of the law, is conceivable to the common intelligence. A man is punished specially as a burglar, and not generally as a bad man, because a man may be a burglar and in many other respects not be a bad man. The act of burglary is pun-ishable because it is intelligible. But when acts are unintelligible, we can only refer them to a general untrustworthiness, and guard against them by a general restraint. If a man breaks into a house to get a piece of bread, we can appeal to his reason in various ways. We can hang him for housebreaking; or again (as has occurred to some daring thinkers) we can give him a piece of bread. But if he breaks in, let us say, to steal the parings of other people's finger nails, then we are in a difficulty: we cannot imagine what he is going to do with them, and therefore cannot easily imagine what we are going to do with him. If a villain comes in, in cloak and mask, and puts a little arsenic in the soup, we can collar him and say to him distinctly, "You are guilty of Murder; and I will now consult the code of tribal law, under which we live, to see if this practice is not forbidden." But if a man in the same cloak and mask is found at midnight put-ting a little soda-water in the soup, what can we say? Our charge necessarily becomes a more general one. We can only observe, with a moderation almost amounting to weakness, "You seem to be the sort of person who will do this sort of thing." And then we can lock him up. The principle of the indeterminate sentence is the creation of the indeterminate mind. It does apply to the incomprehensible creature, the lunatic. And it applies to nobody else.

The second thing to be noted is this: that it is only by the unanimity of sane men that we can condemn this man as utterly separate. If he says a tree is a lamp-post he is mad; but only because all other men say it is a tree. If some men thought it was a tree with a lamp on it, and others thought it was a lamp-post wreathed with branches and vegetation, then it would be a matter of opinion and degree; and he would not be mad, but merely extreme. Certainly he would not be mad if nobody but a botanist could see it was a tree. Certainly his enemies might be madder than he, if nobody but a lamplighter could see it was not a lamp-post. And similarly a man is not an imbecile if only a Eugenist thinks so. The question then raised would not be his sanity, but the sanity of one botanist or one lamplighter or one Eugenist. That which can condemn the abnormally foolish is not the abnormally clever, which is obviously a matter in dispute. That which can condemn the abnormally foolish is the normally foolish. It is when he begins to say and do things that even stupid people do not say or do, that we have a right to treat him as the exception and not the rule. It is only because we none of us profess to be anything more than man that we have authority to treat him as something less.

Now the first principle behind Eugenics becomes plain enough. It is the proposal that somebody or something should criticize men with the same superiority with which men criticize madmen. It might exercise this right with great moderation; but I am not here talking about the exercise, but about the right. Its *claim* certainly is to bring all human life under the Lunacy Laws.

Now this is the first weakness in the case of the Eugenists: that they cannot define who is to control whom; they cannot say by what authority they do these things. They cannot see the exception is different from the rule—even when it is misrule, even when it is an unruly rule. The sound sense in the old Lunacy Law was this: that you cannot deny that a man is a citizen until you are practically prepared to deny that he is a man. Men, and only men, can be the judges of whether he is a man. But any private club of prigs can be judges of whether he ought to be a citizen. When once we step down from that tall and splintered peak of pure insanity we step on to a tableland where one man is not so widely different from another. Outside the exception, what we find is the average. And the practical, legal shape of the quarrel is this: that unless the normal men have the right to expel the abnormal, what particular sort of abnormal men have the right to expel the normal men? If sanity is not good enough, what is there that is saner than sanity?

Without any grip of the notion of a rule and an exception, the general idea of judging people's heredity breaks down and is useless. For this reason: that if everything is the result of a doubtful heredity, the judgment itself is the result of a doubtful heredity also. Let it judge not that it be not judged. Eugenists, strange to say, have fathers and mothers like other people; and our opinion about their fathers and mothers is worth exactly as much as their opinions about ours. None of the parents were lunatics, and the rest is mere likes and dislikes. Suppose Dr. Saleeby[3] had gone to Byron and said, "My lord, I perceive you have a club-foot and inordinate passions: such are the hereditary results of a profligate soldier marrying a hot-tempered woman." The poet might logically reply (with characteristic lucidity and impropriety), "Sir, I perceive you have a confused mind and an unphilosophic theory about other people's love affairs. Such are the hereditary delusions bred by a Syrian doctor marrying a Quaker lady from New York." Suppose Dr. Karl Pearson[4] had said to Shelley, "From what I see of your temperament, you are running great risks in forming a connection with the daughter of a fanatic and eccentric like Godwin."[5] Shelley would be employing the strict rationalism of the older and stronger free thinkers, if he answered, "From what I observe of your mind, you are rushing on destruction in marrying the great-niece of an old corpse of a courtier and dilettante like Samuel

[3] See footnote 3, page 40.

[4] Karl Pearson (1857–1936), writer and Professor of Eugenics who married Maria Sharpe, great-niece of Samuel Rogers.

[5] Mary Godwin (Mary Wollstonecraft), (1759–1797), early feminist writer, wife of William Godwin and second wife of the poet Percy Shelley.

Rogers."[6] It is only opinion for opinion. Nobody can pretend that either Mary Godwin or Samuel Rogers was mad; and the general view a man may hold about the healthiness of inheriting their blood or type is simply the same sort of general view by which men do marry for love or liking. There is no reason to suppose that Dr. Karl Pearson is any better judge of a bridegroom than the bridegroom is of a bride.

An objection may be anticipated here, but it is very easily answered. It may be said that we do, in fact, call in medical specialists to settle whether a man is mad; and that these specialists go by technical and even secret tests that cannot be known to the mass of men. It is obvious that this is true; it is equally obvious that it does not affect our argument. When we ask the doctor whether our grandfather is going mad, we still mean mad by our own common human definition. We mean, is he going to be a certain sort of person whom men recognize when once he exists. That certain specialists can detect the approach of him, before he exists, does not alter the fact that it is of the practical and popular madman that we are talking, and of him alone. The doctor merely sees a certain fact potentially in the future, while we, with less information, can only see it in the present; but his fact is our fact and everybody's fact, or we should not bother about it at all. Here is no question of the doctor bringing an entirely new sort of person under coercion, as in the Feeble-Minded Bill. The doctor can say, "Tobacco is death to you," because the dislike of death can be taken for granted, being a highly democratic institution; and it is the same with the dislike of the indubitable exception called madness. The doctor can say, "Jones has that twitch in the nerves, and he may burn down the house." But it is not the medical detail we fear, but the moral upshot. We should say, "Let him twitch, as long as he doesn't burn down the house." The doctor may say "He has that look in the eyes, and he may take the hatchet and brain you all." But we do not object to the look in the eyes as such; we object to consequences which, once come, we should all call insane if there were no doctors in the world.

---

[6] Samuel Rogers (1763–1855), English poet and patron of artists and men of letters.

We should say, "Let him look how he likes; as long as he does not look for the hatchet."

Now, that specialists are valuable for this particular and practical purpose, of predicting the approach of enormous and admitted human calamities, nobody but a fool would deny. But that does not bring us one inch nearer to allowing them the right to define what is a calamity; or to call things calamities which common-sense does not call calamities. We call in the doctor to save us from death; and, death being admittedly an evil, he has the right to administer the queerest and most recondite pill which he may think is a cure for all such menaces of death. He has not the right to administer death as the cure for all human ills. And as he has no moral authority to enforce a new conception of happiness, so he has no moral authority to enforce a new conception of sanity. He may know I am going mad; for madness is an isolated thing like leprosy; and I know nothing about leprosy. But if he merely thinks my mind is weak, I may happen to think the same of his. I often do.

In short, unless pilots are to be permitted to ram ships on to the rocks and then say that heaven is the only true harbour; unless judges are to be allowed to let murderers loose, and explain afterwards that the murder had done good on the whole; unless soldiers are to be allowed to lose battles and then point out that true glory is to be found in the valley of humiliation; unless cashiers are to rob a bank in order to give it an advertisement; or dentists to torture people to give them a contrast to their comforts; unless we are prepared to let loose all these private fancies against the public and accepted meaning of life or safety or prosperity or pleasure—then it is as plain as Punch's nose that no scientific man must be allowed to meddle with the public definition of madness. We call him in to tell us where it is or when it is. We could not do so, if we had not ourselves settled what it is.

As I wish to confine myself in this chapter to the primary point of the plain existence of sanity and insanity, I will not be led along any of the attractive paths that open here. I shall endeavor to deal with them in the next chapter. Here I confine myself to a sort of summary. Suppose a man's throat has been cut, quite swiftly and suddenly, with a table knife, at a small table where we sit. The whole of civil law rests on the supposition that we are witnesses; that we saw it; and if we do not know about it, who does? Now suppose all the witnesses fall into a quarrel about degrees of eyesight. Suppose one says he had brought his reading-glasses instead of his usual glasses; and therefore did not see the man fall across the table and cover it with blood. Suppose another says he could not be certain it was blood, because a slight colour-blindness was hereditary in his family. Suppose a third says he cannot swear to the uplifted knife, because his oculist tells him he is astigmatic, and vertical lines do not affect him as do horizontal lines. Suppose another says that dots have often danced before his eyes in very fantastic combinations, many of which were very like one gentleman cutting another gentleman's throat at dinner. All these things refer to real experiences. There is such a thing as myopia; there is such a thing as colour-blindness; there is such a thing as astigmatism; there is such a thing as shifting shapes swimming before the eyes. But what should we think of a whole dinner party that could give nothing except these highly scientific explanations when found in company with a corpse? I imagine there are only two things we could think: either that they were all drunk, or they were all murderers.

And yet there is an exception. If there were one man at table who was admittedly *blind*, should we not give him the benefit of the doubt? Should we not honestly feel that he was the exception that proved the rule? The very fact that he could not have seen would remind us that the other men must have seen. The very fact that he had no eyes must remind us of eyes. A man can be blind; a man can be dead: a man can be mad. But the comparison is necessarily weak, after all. For it is the essence of madness to be unlike anything else in the world: which is perhaps why so many men wiser than we have traced it to another.

Lastly, the literal maniac is different from all other persons in dispute in this vital respect: that he is the only person whom we can, with a final lucidity, declare that we do not want. He is almost always miserable himself, and he always makes others miserable. But this is not so with the mere invalid. The Eugenists would probably answer all my examples by taking the case of marrying into a family with consumption (or some such disease which they are fairly sure is hereditary) and asking whether such cases at least are not clear cases for a Eugenic intervention. Permit me to point out to them that they once more make a confusion of thought. The sickness or soundness of a consumptive may be a clear and calculable matter. The happiness or unhappiness of a consumptive is quite another matter, and is not calculable at all. What is the good of telling people that if they marry for love, they may be punished by being the parents of Keats or the parents of Stevenson? Keats died young; but he had more pleasure in a minute than a Eugenist gets in a month. Stevenson had lung-trouble; and it may, for all I know, have been perceptible to the Eugenic eye even a generation before. But who would perform that illegal operation: the stopping of Stevenson? Intercepting a letter bursting with good news, confiscating a hamper full of presents and prizes, pouring torrents of intoxicating wine into the sea, all this is a faint approximation for the Eugenic inaction of the ancestors of Stevenson. This, however, is not the essential point; with Stevenson it is not merely a case of the pleasure we get, but of the pleasure he got. If he had died without writing a line, he would have had more red-hot joy than is given to most men. Shall I say of him, to whom I owe so much, let the day perish wherein he was born? Shall I pray that the stars of the twilight thereof be dark and it be not numbered among the days of the year, because it shut not up the doors of his mother's womb? I respectfully decline; like Job, I will put my hand upon my mouth.

V

THE FLYING AUTHORITY

It happened one day that an atheist and a man were standing together on a doorstep; and the atheist said, "It is raining." To which the man replied, "What is raining?": which question was the beginning of a violent quarrel and a lasting friendship. I will not touch upon any heads of the dispute, which doubtless included Jupiter, Pluvius, the Neuter Gender, Pantheism, Noah's Ark, Mackintoshes, and the Passive Mood; but I will record the one point upon which the two persons emerged in some agreement. It was that there is such a thing as an atheistic literary style; that materialism may appear in the mere diction of a man, though he be speaking of clocks or cats or anything quite remote from theology. The mark of the atheistic style is that it instinctively chooses the word which suggests that things are dead things; that things have no souls. Thus they will not speak of waging war, which means willing it; they speak of the "outbreak of war," as if all the guns blew up without the men touching them. Thus those Socialists that are atheist will not call their international sympathy, sympathy; they will call it "solidarity," as if the poor men of France and Germany were physically stuck together like dates in a grocer's shop. The same Marxian Socialists are accused of cursing the Capitalists inordinately; but the truth is that they let the Capitalists off much too easily. For instead of saying that employers pay less wages, which might pin the employers to some moral responsibility, they insist on talking about the "rise and fall" of wages; as if a vast silver sea of sixpences and shillings was always going up and down automatically like the real sea at Margate. Thus they will not speak of reform, but of development; and they spoil their one honest and virile phrase, "the class war," by talking of it as no one in his wits can talk of a war, predicting its finish and final result as one calculates the coming of Christmas Day or the taxes. Thus, lastly (as we shall see touching our special subject-matter here) the atheist syle in letters always avoids talking of love or lust, which are things alive, and calls marriage or concubinage "the relations of the sexes"; as if a man and a woman were two wooden objects standing in a certain angle and attitude to each other, like a table and a chair.

Now the same anarchic mystery that clings round the phrase, "*il pleut*," clings round the phrase, "*il faut*." In English it is generally represented by the passive mood in grammar, and the Eugenists and their like deal especially in it; they are as passive in their statements as they are active in their experiments. Their sentences always enter tail first, and have no subject, like animals without heads. It is never "the doctor should cut off this leg" or "the policeman should collar that man." It is always "Such limbs should be amputated," or "Such men should be under restraint." Hamlet said, "I should have fatted all the region kites with this slave's offal." The Eugenist would say, "The region kites should, if possible, be fattened; and the offal of this slave is available for the dietetic experiment." Lady Macbeth said, "Give me the daggers; I'll let his bowels out." The Eugenist would say, "In such cases the bowels should, etc." Do not blame me for the repulsiveness of the comparisons. I have searched English literature for the most decent parallels to Eugenist language.

The formless god that broods over the East is called "Om." The formless god who has begun to brood over the West is called "On." But here we must make a distinction. The impersonal word *on* is French, and the French have a right to use it, because they are a democracy. And when a Frenchman says "one" he does not mean himself, but the normal citizen. He does not mean merely "one," but one and all. "*On n'a que sa parole*" does not mean "*Noblesse oblige*," or "I am the Duke of Billingsgate and must keep my word." It means: "One has a sense of honour as one has a backbone: every man, rich or poor, should feel honourable"; and this, whether possible or no, is the purest ambition of the republic. But when the Eugenists say, "Conditions must be altered" or "Ancestry should be investigated," or what not, it seems clear that they do not mean that the democracy must do it, whatever else they may mean. They do not mean that any man not evidently mad may be trusted with these tests and rearrangements as the French democratic system trusts such a man with a vote or a farm or the control of a family. That would mean that Jones and Brown, being both ordinary men, would set about arranging each other's marriages. And this state of affairs would seem a little elaborate, and it might occur even to the Eugenic mind that if Jones and Brown are quite capable of arranging each other's marriages, it is just possible that they might be capable of arranging their own.

This dilemma, which applies in so simple a case, applies equally to any wide and sweeping system of Eugenist voting; for though it is true that the community can judge more dispassionately than a man can judge in his own case, this particular question of the choice of a wife is so full of disputable shades in every conceivable case, that it is surely obvious that almost any democracy would simply vote the thing out of the sphere of voting, as they would any proposal of police interference in the choice of walking weather or of children's names. I should not like to be the politician who should propose a particular instance of Eugenics to be voted on by the French people. Democracy dismissed, it is here hardly needful to consider the other old models. Modern scientists will not say that George III., in his lucid intervals, should settle who is mad; or that the aristocracy that introduced gout shall supervise diet.

I hold it clear, therefore, if anything is clear about the business, that the Eugenists do not merely mean that the mass of common men should settle each other's marriages between them; the question remains, therefore, whom they do instinctively trust when they say that this or that ought to be done. What is this flying and evanescent authority that vanishes wherever we seek to fix it? Who is the man who is the lost subject that governs the Eugenist's verb? In a large number of cases I think we can simply say that the individual Eugenist means himself, and nobody else. Indeed one Eugenist, Mr. A. H. Huth, actually had a sense of humour, and admitted this. He thinks a great deal of good could be done with a surgical knife, if we would only turn him loose with one. And this may be true. A great deal of good could be done with a loaded revolver, in the hands of a judicious student of human nature. But it is imperative that the Eugenist should perceive that on that principle we can never get beyond a perfect balance of different sympathies and antipathies. I mean that I should differ from Dr. Saleeby or Dr. Karl Pearson not only in a vast majority of individual cases, but in a vast majority of cases in which they would be bound to admit that such a difference was natural and reasonable. The chief victim of these famous doctors would be a yet more famous doctor: that eminent though unpopular practitioner, Dr. Fell.[1]

To show that such rational and serious differences do exist, I will take one instance from that Bill which proposed to protect families and the public generally from the burden of feeble-minded persons. Now, even if I could share the Eugenic contempt for human rights, even if I could start gaily on the Eugenic campaign, I should not begin by removing feeble-minded persons. I have known as many families in as many classes as most men; and I cannot remember meeting any very monstrous human suffering arising out of the presence of such insufficient and negative types. There seems to be comparatively few of them; and those few by no means the worst burdens upon domestic happiness. I do not hear of them often; I do not hear of them doing much more harm than good; and in the few cases I know well they are not only regarded with human affection, but can be put to certain limited forms of human use. Even if I were a Eugenist, then I should not personally elect to waste my time locking up the feeble-minded. The people I should lock up would be the strong-minded. I have known hardly any cases of mere mental weakness making a family a failure; I have known eight or nine cases of violent and exaggerated force of character making a family a hell. If the strong-minded could be segregated it would quite certainly be better for their friends and families. And if there is really anything in heredity, it would be better for posterity too. For the kind of egoist I mean is a madman in a much more plausible sense than the mere harmless "deficient"; and to hand on the horrors of his anarchic and insatiable temperament is a much graver responsibility than to leave a mere inheritance of childishness. I would not arrest such tyrants, because I think that even moral tyranny in a few homes is better

[1] Possibly John Fell (d. 1686), who is satirized by Tom Brown in his famous line: "I do like thee, Dr. Fell."

than a medical tyranny turning the state into a madhouse. I would not segregate them, because I respect a man's free-will and his front-door and his right to be tried by his peers. But since free-will is believed by Eugenists no more than by Calvinists, since front-doors are respected by Eugenists no more than by house-breakers, and since the Habeas Corpus is about as sacred to Eugenists as it would be to King John, why do not *they* bring light and peace into so many human homes by removing a demoniac from each of them? Why do not the promoters of the Feeble-Minded Bill call at the many grand houses in town or country where such nightmares notoriously are? Why do they not knock at the door and take the bad squire away? Why do they not ring the bell and remove the dipsomaniac prize-fighter? I do not know; and there is only one reason I can think of, which must remain a matter of speculation. When I was at school, the kind of boy who liked teasing halfwits was not the sort that stood up to bullies.

That, however it may be, does not concern my argument. I mention the case of the strong-minded variety of the monstrous merely to give one out of the hundred cases of the instant divergence of individual opinions the moment we begin to discuss who is fit or unfit to propagate. If Dr. Saleeby and I were setting out on a segregating trip together, we should separate at the very door; and if he had a thousand doctors with him, they would all go different ways. Everyone who has known as many kind and capable doctors as I have, knows that the ablest and sanest of them have a tendency to possess some little hobby or half-discovery of their own, as that oranges are bad for children, or that trees are dangerous in gardens, or that many more people ought to wear spectacles. It is asking too much of human nature to expect them not to cherish such scraps of originality in a hard, dull, and often heroic trade. But the inevitable result of it, as exercised by the individual Saleebys, would be that each man would have his favourite kind of idiot. Each doctor would be mad on his own madman. One would have his eyes on devotional curates; another would wander about collecting obstreperous majors; a third would be the terror of animal-loving spinsters, who would flee with all their cats and dogs before him. Short of sheer literal anarchy, therefore, it seems plain that the Eugenist must find some authority other than his own implied personality. He must, once and for all, learn the lesson which is hardest for him and me and for all our fallen race—the fact that he is only himself.

We now pass from mere individual men who obviously cannot be trusted, even if they are individual medical men, with such despotism over their neighbours; and we come to consider whether the Eugenists have at all clearly traced any more imaginable public authority, any apparatus of great experts or great examinations to which such risks of tyranny could be trusted. They are not very precise about this either; indeed, the great difficulty I have throughout in considering what are the Eugenist's proposals is that they do not seem to know themselves. Some philosophic attitude which I cannot myself connect with human reason seems to make them actually proud of the dimness of their definitions and the uncompleteness of their plans. The Eugenic optimism seems to partake generally of the nature of that dazzled and confused confidence, so common in private theatricals, that it will be all right on the night. They have all the ancient despotism, but none of the ancient dogmatism. If they are ready to reproduce the secrecies and cruelties of the Inquisition, at least we cannot accuse them of offending us with any of that close and complicated thought, that arid and exact logic which narrowed the minds of the Middle Ages; they have discovered how to combine the hardening of the heart with a sympathetic softening of the head. Nevertheless, there is one large, though vague, idea of the Eugenists, which is an idea, and which we reach when we reach this problem of a more general supervision.

It was best presented perhaps by the distinguished doctor who wrote the article on these matters in that composite book which Mr. Wells edited, and called "The Great State." He said the doctor should no longer be a mere plasterer of paltry maladies, but should be, in his own words, "the health adviser of the community." The same can be expressed with even more point and simplicity in the proverb that prevention is better than cure. Commenting on this, I said that it amounted to treating all people who are well as if they were ill. This the writer admitted to be true, only adding that everyone is ill. To which I rejoin that if everyone is ill the health adviser is ill too, and therefore cannot know how to cure that minimum of illness. This is the fundamental fallacy in the whole business of preventive medicine. Prevention is not better than cure. Cutting off a man's head is not better than curing his headache; it is not even better than failing to cure it. And it is the same if a man is in revolt, even a morbid revolt. Taking the heart out of him by slavery is not better than leaving the heart in him, even if you leave it a broken heart. Prevention is not only not better than cure; prevention is even worse than disease. Prevention means being an invalid for life, with the extra exasperation of being quite well. I will ask God, but certainly not man, to prevent me in all my doings. But the decisive and discussable form of this is well summed up in that phrase about the health adviser of society. I am sure that those who speak thus have something in their minds larger and more illuminating than the other two propositions we have considered. They do not mean that all citizens should decide, which would mean merely the present vague and dubious balance. They do not mean that all medical men should decide, which would mean a much more unbalanced balance. They mean that a few men might be found who had a consistent scheme and vision of a healthy nation, as Napoleon had a consistent scheme and vision of an army. It is cold anarchy to say that all men are to meddle in all men's marriages. It is cold anarchy to say that any doctor may seize and segregate anyone he likes. But it is not anarchy to say that a few great hygienists might enclose or limit the life of all citizens, as nurses do with a family of children. It is not anarchy, it is tyranny; but tyranny is a workable thing. When we ask by what process such men could be certainly chosen, we are back again on the old dilemma of despotism, which means a man, or democracy which means men, or aristocracy which means favouritism. But as a vision the thing is plausible and even rational. It is rational, and it is wrong.

It is wrong, quite apart from the suggestion that an expert on health cannot be chosen. It is wrong because an expert on health cannot exist. An expert on disease can exist, for the very reason we have already considered in the case of madness, because experts can only arise out of exceptional things. A parallel with any of the other learned professions will make the point plain. If I am prosecuted for trespass, I will ask my solicitor which of the local lanes I am forbidden to walk in. But if my solicitor, having gained my case, were so elated that he insisted on settling what lanes I should walk in; if he asked me to let him map out all my country walks, because he was the perambulatory adviser of the community — then that solicitor would solicit in vain. If he will insist on walking behind me through woodland ways, pointing out with his walking-stick likely avenues and attractive short-cuts, I shall turn on him with passion, saying: "Sir, I pay you to know one particular puzzle in Latin and Norman-French, which they call the law of England; and you do know the law of England. I have never had any earthly reason to suppose that you know England. If you did, you would leave a man alone when he was looking at it." As are the limits of the lawyer's special knowledge about walking, so are the limits of the doctor's. If I fall over the stump of a tree and break my leg, as is likely enough, I shall say to the lawyer, "Please go and fetch the doctor." I shall do it because the doctor really has a larger knowledge of a narrower area. There are only a certain number of ways in which a leg can be broken; I know none of them, and he knows all of them. There is such a thing as being a specialist in broken legs. There is no such thing as being a specialist in legs. When unbroken, legs are a matter of taste. If the doctor has really mended my leg, he may merit a colossal equestrian statue on the top of an eternal tower of brass. But if the doctor has really mended my leg he has no more rights over it. He must not come and teach me how to walk; because he and I learnt that in the same school, the nursery. And there is no more abstract likelihood of the doctor walking more elegantly than I do than there is of the barber or the bishop or the burglar walking more elegantly than I do. There cannot be a general specialist; the specialist can have no kind of authority, unless he has avowedly limited his range. There cannot be such a thing as the health adviser of the community, because there cannot be such a thing as one who specialises in the universe.

Thus when Dr. Saleeby says that a young man about to be married should be obliged to produce his health-book as he does his

bank-book, the expression is neat; but it does not convey the real respects in which the two things agree, and in which they differ. To
begin with, of course, there is a great deal too much of the bank-
book for the sanity of our commonwealth; and it is highly probable
that the health-book, as conducted in modern conditions, would
rapidly become as timid, as snobbish, and as sterile as the money side
of marriage has become. In the moral atmosphere of modernity the
poor and the honest would probably get as much the worst of it if
we fought with health-books as they do when we fight with bank-
books. But that is a more general matter; the real point is in the difference between the two. The difference is in this vital fact; that a
monied man generally thinks about money, whereas a healthy man
does not think about health. If the strong young man cannot produce his health-book, it is for the perfectly simple reason that he has
not got one. He can mention some extraordinary malady he has; but
every man of honour is expected to do that now, whatever may be
the decision that follows on the knowledge.

Health is simply Nature, and no naturalist ought to have the impudence to understand it. Health, one may say, is God; and no agnostic has any right to claim His acquaintance. For God must mean,
among other things, that mystical and multitudinous balance of all
things, by which they are at least able to stand up straight and endure; and any scientist who pretends to have exhausted this subject
of ultimate sanity, I will call the lowest of religious fanatics. I will
allow him to understand the madman, for the madman is an exception. But if he says he understands the sane man, then he says he has
the secret of the Creator. For whenever you and I feel fully sane, we
are quite incapable of naming the elements that make up that mysterious simplicity. We can no more analyse such peace in the soul
than we can conceive in our heads the whole enormous and dizzy
equilibrium by which, out of suns roaring like infernos and heavens
toppling like precipices, He has hanged the world upon nothing.

We conclude, therefore, that unless Eugenic activity be restricted
to monstrous things like mania, there is no constituted or con-
stitutable authority that can really over-rule men in a matter in
which they are so largely on a level. In the matter of fundamental

human rights, nothing can be above Man, except God. An institution claiming to come from God might have such authority; but this is the last claim the Eugenists are likely to make. One caste or one profession seeking to rule men in such matters is like a man's right eye claiming to rule him, or his left leg to run away with him. It is madness. We now pass on to consider whether there is really anything in the way of Eugenics to be done, with such cheerfulness as we may possess after discovering that there is nobody to do it.

VI

THE UNANSWERED CHALLENGE

Dr. Saleeby did me the honour of referring to me in one of his addresses on this subject, and said that even I cannot produce any but a feeble-minded child from a feeble-minded ancestry. To which I reply, first of all, that he cannot produce a feeble-minded child. The whole point of our contention is that this phrase conveys nothing fixed and outside opinion. There is such a thing as mania, which has always been segregated; there is such a thing as idiotcy, which has always been segregated; but feeble-mindedness is a new phrase under which you might segregate anybody. It is essential that this fundamental fallacy in the use of statistics should be got somehow into the modern mind. Such people must be made to see the point, which is surely plain enough, that it is useless to have exact figures if they are exact figures about an inexact phrase. If I say, "There are five fools in Action," it is surely quite clear that, though no mathematician can make five the same as four or six, that will not stop you or anyone else from finding a few more fools in Action. Now weak-mindedness, like folly, is a term divided from madness in this vital manner—that in one sense it applies to all men, in another to most men, in another to very many men, and so on. It is as if Dr. Saleeby were to say, "Vanity, I find, is undoubtedly hereditary. Here is Mrs. Jones, who was very sensitive about her sonnets being criticized, and I found her little daughter in a new frock looking in the glass. The experiment is conclusive, the demonstration is complete; there in the first generation is the artistic temperament—that is vanity; and there in the second generation is dress—and that is vanity." We should answer, "My friend, all is vanity, vanity and vexation of spirit—especially when one has to listen to logic of your favourite kind. Obviously all human beings must value themselves; and obviously there is in all such valuation an element of weakness, since it is not the valuation of eternal justice. What is the use of your finding by experiment in some people a thing we know by reason must be in all of them?"

335

Here it will be as well to pause a moment and avert one possible misunderstanding. I do not mean that you and I cannot and do not practically see and personally remark on this or that eccentric or intermediate type, for which the word "feeble-minded" might be a very convenient word, and might correspond to a genuine though indefinable fact of experience. In the same way we might speak, and do speak, of such and such a person being "mad with vanity" without wanting two keepers to walk in and take the person off. But I ask the reader to remember always that I am talking of words, not as they are used in talk or novels, but as they will be used, and have been used, in warrants and certificates, and Acts of Parliament. The distinction between the two is perfectly clear and practical. The difference is that a novelist or a talker can be trusted to try and hit the mark; it is all to his glory that the cap should fit, that the type should be recognized; that he should, in a literary sense, hang the right man. But it is by no means always to the interest of governments or officials to hang the right man. The fact that they often do stretch words in order to cover cases is the whole foundation of having any fixed laws or free institutions at all. My point is not that I have never met anyone whom I should call feeble-minded, rather than mad or imbecile. My point is that if I want to dispossess a nephew, oust a rival, silence a blackmailer, or get rid of an importunate widow, there is nothing in logic to prevent my calling them feeble-minded too. And the vaguer the charge is the less they will be able to disprove it.

One does not, as I have said, need to deny heredity in order to resist legislation, any more than one needs to deny the spiritual world in order to resist an epidemic of witch-burning. I admit there may be such a thing as hereditary feeble-mindedness; I believe there is such a thing as witchcraft. Believing that there are spirits, I am bound in mere reason to suppose that there are probably evil spirits; believing that there are evil spirits, I am bound in mere reason to suppose that some men grow evil by dealing with them. All that is mere rationalism; the superstition (that is the unreasoning repugnance and terror) is in the person who admits there can be angels but denies there can be devils. The superstition is in the person who admits there can be devils but denies there can be diabolists. Yet I should certainly resist any effort to search for witches, for a perfectly simple reason, which is the key of the whole of this controversy. The reason is that it is one thing to believe in witches and quite another to believe in witch-smellers. I have more respect for the Eugenists, who go about persecuting the fool of the family; because the witch-finders, according to their own conviction, ran a risk. Witches were not the feeble-minded, but the strong-minded—the evil mesmerists, the rulers of the elements. Many a raid on a witch, right or wrong, seemed to the villagers who did it a righteous popular rising against a vast spritiual tyranny, a papacy of sin. Yet we know that the thing degenerated into a rabid and despicable persecution of the feeble or the old. It ended by being a war upon the weak. It ended by being what Eugenics begins by being.

When I said above that I believed in witches, but not in witch-smellers, I stated my full position about that conception of heredity, that half-formed philosophy of fears and omens; of curses and weird recurrence and darkness and the doom of blood, which, as preached to humanity to-day, is often more inhuman than witchcraft itself. I do not deny that this dark element exists; I only affirm that it is dark; or, in other words, that its most strenuous students are evidently in the dark about it. I would no more trust Dr. Karl Pearson on a heredity-hunt than on a heresy-hunt. I am perfectly ready to give my reasons for thinking this; and I believe any well-balanced person, if he reflects on them, will think as I do. There are two senses in which a man may be said to know or not know a subject. I know the subject of arithmetic, for instance; that is, I am not good at it, but I know what it is. I am sufficiently familiar with its use to see the absurdity of anyone who says, "So vulgar a fraction cannot be mentioned before ladies," or "This unit is Unionist, I hope." Considering myself for one moment as an arithmetician, I may say that I know next to nothing about my subject: but I know my subject. I know it in the street. There is the other kind of man, like Dr. Karl Pearson, who undoubtedly knows a vast amount about his subject; who undoubtedly lives in great forests of facts concerning kinship and inheritance. But it is not, by any means, the same thing to have searched the forests and to have recognized the frontiers. Indeed, the two things generally belong to two very different types of mind. I gravely doubt whether the Astronomer-Royal would write the best essay on the relations between astronomy and astrology. I doubt whether the President of the Geographical Society could give the best definition and the history of the words "geography" and "geology."

Now the students of heredity, especially, understand all of their subject except their subject. They were, I suppose, bred and born in that brier-patch, and have really explored it without coming to the end of it. That is, they have studied everything but the question of what they are studying. Now I do not propose to rely merely on myself to tell them what they are studying. I propose, as will be seen in a moment, to call the testimony of a great man who has himself studied it. But to begin with, the domain of heredity (for those who see its frontiers) is a sort of triangle, enclosed on its three sides by three facts. The first is that heredity undoubtedly exists, or there would be no such thing as a family likeness, and every marriage might suddenly produce a small negro. The second is that even simple heredity can never be simple; its complexity must be literally unfathomable, for in that field fight unthinkable millions. But yet again it never is simple heredity: for the instant anyone is, he experiences. The third is that these innumerable ancient influences, these instant inundations of experiences, come together according to a combination that is unlike anything else on this earth. It is a combination that does combine. It cannot be sorted out again, even on the Day of Judgment. Two totally different people have become in the sense most sacred, frightful, and unanswerable, one flesh. If a golden-haired Scandinavian girl has married a very swarthy Jew, the Scandinavian side of the family may say till they are blue in the face that the baby has his mother's nose or his mother's eyes. They can never be certain the black-haired Bedouin is not present in every feature, in every inch. In the person of the baby he may have gently pulled his wife's nose. In the person of the baby he may have partly blacked his wife's eyes.

Those are the three first facts of heredity. That it exists; that it is subtle and made of a million elements; that it is simple, and cannot be unmade into those elements. To summarize: you know there is wine in the soup. You do not know how many wines there are in the soup, because you do not know how many wines there are in the world. And you never will know, because all chemists, all cooks, and all common-sense people tell you that the soup is of such a sort that it can never be chemically analysed. That is a perfectly fair parallel to the hereditary element in the human soul. There are many ways in which one can feel that there is wine in the soup, as in suddenly tasting a wine specially favoured; that corresponds to seeing suddenly flash on a young face the image of some ancestor you have known. But even then the taster cannot be certain he is not tasting one familiar wine among many unfamiliar ones — or seeing one known ancestor among a million unknown ancestors. Another way is to get drunk on the soup, which corresponds to the case of those who say they are driven to sin and death by hereditary doom. But even then the drunkard cannot be certain it was the soup, any more than the traditional drunkard who is certain it was the salmon.

Those are the facts about heredity which anyone can see. The upshot of them is not only that a miss is as good as a mile, but a miss is as good as a win. If the child has his parents' nose (or noses) that may be heredity. But if he has not, that may be heredity too. And as we need not take heredity lightly because two generations differ — so we need not take heredity a scrap more seriously because two generations are similar. The thing is there, in what cases we know not, in what proportion we know not, and we cannot know.

Now it is just here that the decent difference of function between Dr. Saleeby's trade and mine comes in. It is his business to study human health and sickness as a whole, in a spirit of more or less enlightened guesswork; and it is perfectly natural that he should allow for heredity here, there, and everywhere, as a man climbing a mountain or sailing a boat will allow for weather without even explaining it to himself. An utterly different attitude is incumbent on any conscientious man writing about what laws should be enforced or about how commonwealths should be governed. And when we consider how plain a fact is murder, and yet how hesitant and even hazy we all grow about the guilt of a murderer, when we consider how simple an act is stealing, and yet how hard it is to convict and punish those rich commercial pirates who steal the most, when we consider how cruel and clumsy the law can be even about things as old and plain as the Ten Commandments—I simply cannot conceive any responsible person proposing to legislate on our broken knowledge and bottomless ignorance of heredity.

But though I have to consider this dull matter in its due logical order, it appears to me that this part of the matter has been settled, and settled in a most masterly way, by somebody who has infinitely more right to speak on it than I have. Our press seems to have a perfect genius for fitting people with caps that don't fit; and affixing the wrong terms of eulogy and even the wrong terms of abuse. And just as people will talk of Bernard Shaw as a naughty winking Pierrot,[1] when he is the last great Puritan and really believes in respectability; just as (si parva licet, etc.) they will talk of my own paradoxes, when I pass my life in preaching that the truisms are true; so an enormous number of newspaper readers seem to have it fixed firmly in their heads that Mr. H. G. Wells is a harsh and horrible Eugenist in great goblin spectacles who wants to put us all into metallic microscopes and dissect us with metallic tools. As a matter of fact, of course, Mr. Wells, so far from being too definite, is generally not definite enough. He is an absolute wizard in the appreciation of atmospheres and the opening of vistas; but his answers are more agnostic than his questions. His books will do everything except shut. And so far from being the sort of man who would stop a man from propagating, he cannot even stop a full stop. He is not Eugenic enough to prevent the black dot at the end of a sentence from breeding a line of little dots.

But this is not the clear-cut blunder of which I spoke. The real blunder is this. Mr. Wells deserves a tiara of crowns and a garland of medals for all kinds of reasons. But if I were restricted, on grounds of public economy, to giving Mr. Wells only one medal *ob cives servatos*, I would give him a medal as the Eugenist who destroyed Eugenics. For everyone spoke of him rightly or wrongly, as a Eugenist; and he certainly had, as I have not, the training and type

[1] A male character in certain French pantomimes, with a white face and wearing loose, white, fancy costume.

of culture required to consider the matter merely in a biological and not in a generally moral sense. The result was that in that fine book, "Mankind in the Making," where he inevitably came to grips with the problem, he threw down to the Eugenists an intellectual challenge which seems to me unanswerable, but which, at any rate, is unanswered. I do not mean that no remote Eugenist wrote upon the subject; for it is impossible to read all writings, especially Eugenist writings. I do not mean that the leading Eugenists write as if this challenge had never been offered. The gauntlet lies unlifted on the ground.

Having given honour for the idea where it is due, I may be permitted to summarize it myself for the sake of brevity. Mr. Wells' point was this. That we cannot be certain about the inheritance of health, because health is not a quality. It is not a thing like darkness in the hair or length in the limbs. It is a relation, a balance. You have a tall, strong man; but his very strength depends on his not being too tall for his strength. You catch a healthy, full-blooded fellow; but his very health depends on his being not too full of blood. A heart that is strong for a dwarf will be weak for a giant; a nervous system that would kill a man with a trace of a certain illness will sustain him to ninety if he has no trace of that illness. Nay, the same nervous system might kill him if he had an excess of some other comparatively healthy thing. Seeing, therefore, that there are apparently healthy people of all types, it is obvious that if you mate two of them, you may even then produce a discord out of two inconsistent harmonies. It is obvious that you can no more be certain of a good offspring than you can be certain of a good tune if you play two fine airs at once on the same piano. You can be even less certain of it in the more delicate case of beauty, of which the Eugenists talk a great deal. Marry two handsome people whose noses tend to the aquiline, and their baby (for all you know) may be a goblin with a nose like an enormous parrot's. Indeed, I actually know a case of this kind. The Eugenist has to settle, not the result of fixing one steady thing to a second steady thing; but what will happen when one toppling and dizzy equilibrium crashes into another.

This is the interesting conclusion. It is on this degree of knowledge that we are asked to abandon the universal morality of mankind. When we have stopped the lover from marrying the unfortunate woman he loves, when we have found him another uproariously healthy female whom he does not love in the least, even then we have no logical evidence that the result may not be as horrid and dangerous as if he had behaved like a man of honour.

VII

THE ESTABLISHED CHURCH OF DOUBT

Let us now finally consider what the honest Eugenists do mean, since it has become increasingly evident that they cannot mean what they say. Unfortunately, the obstacles to any explanation of this are such as to insist on a circuitous approach. The tendency of all that is printed and much that is spoken to-day is to be, in the only true sense, behind the times. It is because it is always in a hurry that it is always too late. Give an ordinary man a day to write an article, and he will remember the things he has really heard latest; and may even, in the last glory of the sunset, begin to think of what he thinks himself. Give him an hour to write it, and he will think of the nearest text-book on the topic, and make the best mosaic he may out of classical quotations and old authorities. Give him ten minutes to write it and he will run screaming for refuge to the old nursery where he learnt his stalest proverbs, or the old school where he learnt his stalest politics. The quicker goes the journalist the slower go his thoughts. The result is the newspaper of our time, which every day can be delivered earlier and earlier, and which, every day, is less worth delivering at all. The poor panting critic falls farther behind the motor-car of modern fact. Fifty years ago he was barely fifteen years behind the times. Fifteen years ago he was not more than fifty years behind the times. Just now he is rather more than a hundred years behind the times: and the proof of it is that the things he says, though manifest nonsense about our society to-day, really were true about our society some hundred and thirty years ago. The best instance of his belated state is his perpetual assertion that the supernatural is less and less believed. It is a perfectly true and realistic account — of the eighteenth century. It is the worst possible account of this age of psychics and spirit-healers and fakirs and fashionable fortune-tellers. In fact, I generally reply in eighteenth century language to this eighteenth century language to this eighteenth century illusion. If somebody says to me, "The creeds are crumbling," I reply,

343

"And the King of Prussia, who is himself a Freethinker, is certainly capturing Silesia from the Catholic Empress." If somebody says, "Miracles must be reconsidered in the light of rational experience," I answer affably, "But I hope that our enlightened leader, Hébert, will not insist on guillotining that poor French queen." If somebody says, "We must watch for the rise of some new religion which can commend itself to reason," I reply, "But how much more necessary is it to watch for the rise of some military adventurer who may destroy the Republic; and, to my mind, that young Major Bonaparte has rather a restless air." It is only in such language from the Age of Reason that we can answer such things. The age we live in is something more than and age of superstition — it is an age of innumerable superstitions. But it is only with one example of this that I am concerned here.

I mean the error that still sends men marching about disestablishing churches and talking of the tyranny of compulsory church teaching or compulsory church tithes. I do not wish for an irrelevant misunderstanding here; I would myself certainly disestablish any church that had a numerical minority, like the Irish or the Welsh; and I think it would do a great deal of good to genuine churches that have a partly conventional majority, like the English, or even the Russian. But I should only do this if I had nothing else to do; and just now there is very much else to do. For religion, orthodox, or unorthodox, is not just now relying on the weapon of State establishment at all. The Pope practically made no attempt to preserve the Concordat; but seemed rather relieved at the independence his Church gained by the destruction of it: and it is common talk among the French clericalists that the Church has gained by the change. In Russia the one real charge brought by religious people (especially Roman Catholics) against the Orthodox Church is not its orthodoxy or heterodoxy, but its abject dependence on the State. In England we can almost measure an Anglican's fervour for his Church by his comparative coolness about its establishment — that is, its control by a Parliament of Scotch Presbyterians like Balfour, or Welsh Congregationalists like Lloyd George. In Scotland the powerful combination of the two great sects outside the establishment have left it in a position in which it feels no disposition to boast of being called by mere lawyers the Church of Scotland. I am not here arguing that Churches should not depend on the State; nor that they do not depend upon much worse things. It may be reasonably maintained that the strength of Romanism, though it be not in any national police, is in a moral police more rigid and vigilant. It may be reasonably maintained that the strength of Anglicanism, though it be not in establishment, is in aristocracy, and its shadow, which is called snobbishness. All I assert here is that the Churches are not now leaning heavily on their political establishment; they are not using heavily the secular arm. Almost everywhere their legal tithes have been modified, their legal boards of control have been mixed. They may still employ tyranny, and worse tyranny: I am not considering that. They are not specially using that special tyranny which consists in using the government.

The thing that really is trying to tyrannize through government is Science. The thing that really does use the secular arm is Science. And the creed that really is levying tithes and capturing schools, the creed that really is enforced by fine and imprisonment, the creed that really is proclaimed not in sermons but in statutes, and spread not by pilgrims but by policemen—that creed is the great but disputed system of thought which began with Evolution and has ended in Eugenics. Materialism is really our established Church; for the Government will really help it to persecute its heretics. Vaccination, in its hundred years of experiment, has been disputed almost as much as baptism in its approximate two thousand. But it seems quite natural to our politicians to enforce vaccination; and it would seem to them madness to enforce baptism.

I am not frightened of the word "persecution" when it is attributed to the churches; nor is it in the least as a term of reproach that I attribute it to the men of science. It is as a term of legal fact. If it means the imposition by the police of a widely disputed theory, incapable of final proof—then our priests are not now persecuting, but our doctors are. The imposition of such dogmas constitutes a State Church—in an older and stronger sense than any that can be applied to any supernatural Church to-day. There are still places where the religious minority is forbidden to assemble or to teach in this way or that; and yet more where it is excluded from this or that public post. But I cannot now recall any place where it is compelled by the criminal law to go through the rite of the official religion. Even the Young Turks did not insist on all Macedonians being circumcised.

Now here we find ourselves confronted with an amazing fact. When, in the past, opinions so arguable have been enforced by State violence, it has been at the instigation of fanatics who held them for fixed and flaming certainties. If truths could not be evaded by their enemies, neither could they be altered even by their friends. But what are the certain truths that the secular arm must now lift the sword to enforce? Why, they are that very mass of bottomless questions and bewildered answers that we have been studying in the last chapters—questions whose only interest is that they are trackless and mysterious; answers whose only glory is that they are tentative and new. The devotee boasted that he would never abandon the faith; and therefore he persecuted for the faith. But the doctor of science actually boasts that he will always abandon a hypothesis; and yet he persecutes for the hypothesis. The Inquisitor violently enforced his creed, because it was unchangeable. The *savant* enforces it violently because he may change it the next day.

Now this is a new sort of persecution; and one may be permitted to ask if it is an improvement on the old. The difference, so far as one can see at first, seems rather favourable to the old. If we are to be at the merciless mercy of man, most of us would rather be racked for a creed that existed intensely in somebody's head, rather than vivisected for a discovery that had not yet come into anyone's head, and possibly never would. A man would rather be tortured with a thumbscrew until he chose to see reason than tortured with a vivisecting knife until the vivisector chose to see reason. Yet that is the real difference between the two types of legal enforcement. If I gave in to the Inquisitors, I should at least know what creed to profess. But even if I yelled out a *credo* when the Eugenists had me on the rack, I should not know what creed to yell. I might get an extra turn of the rack for confessing to the creed they confessed quite a week ago.

Now let not light-minded persons say that I am here taking extravagant parallels; for the parallel is not only perfect, but plain. For this reason: that the difference between torture and vivisection is not in any way affected by the fierceness or mildness of either. Whether they gave the rack half a turn or half a hundred, they were, by hypothesis, dealing with a truth which they knew to be there. Whether they vivisect painfully or painlessly, they are trying to find out whether the truth is there or not. The old Inquisitors tortured to put their own opinions into somebody. But the new Inquisitors torture to get their own opinions out of him. They do not know what their own opinions are, until the victim of vivisection tells them. The division of thought is a complete chasm for anyone who cares about thinking. The old persecutor was trying to *teach* the citizen, with fire and sword. The new persecutor is trying to *learn* from the citizen, with scalpel and germ-injector. The master was meeker than the pupil will be.

I could prove by many practical instances that even my illustrations are not exaggerated, by many placid proposals I have heard for the vivisection of criminals, or by the filthy incident of Dr. Neisser.[1] But I prefer here to stick to a strictly logical line of distinction, and insist that whereas in all previous persecutions the violence was used to end *our* indecision, the whole point here is that the violence is used to end the indecision of the persecutors. This is what the honest Eugenists really mean, so far as they mean anything. They mean that the public is to be given up, not as a heathen land for conversion, but simply as a *pabulum* for a experiment. That is the real, rude, barbaric sense behind this Eugenic legislation. The Eugenist doctors are not such fools as they look in the light of any logical inquiry about what they want. They do not know what they want, except that they want your soul and body and mine in order to find out. They are quite seriously, as they themselves might say, the first religion to be experimental instead of doctrinal. All other established Churches have been based on somebody having found the truth. This is the first Church that was ever based on not having found it.

[1] Albert Ludwig Siegmund Neisser (1855–1916), German physician who discovered the bacillus which produced gonorrhea and researched both syphilis and leprosy. In his attempt to discover the cause of syphilis, he performed some inoculation experiment upon prostitutes which resulted in charges that he "maliciously inoculated innocent children with syphilis poison".

There is in them a perfectly sincere hope and enthusiasm; but it is not for us, but for what they might learn from us, if they could rule us as they can rabbits. They cannot tell us anything about heredity, because they do not know anything about it. But they do quite honestly believe that they would know something about it, when they had married and mismarried us for a few hundred years. They cannot tell us who is fit to wield such authority, for they know that nobody is; but they do quite honestly believe that when that authority has been abused for a very long time, somebody somehow will be evolved who is fit for the job. I am no Puritan, and no one who knows my opinions will consider it a mere criminal charge if I say that they are simply gambling. The reckless gambler has no money in his pockets; he has only the ideas in his head. These gamblers have no idea in their heads; they have only the money in their pockets. But they think that if they could use the money to buy a big society to experiment on, something like an idea might come to them at last. That is Eugenics.

I confine myself here to remarking that I do not like it. I may be very stingy, but I am willing to pay the scientist for what he does know; I draw the line at paying him for everything he doesn't know. I may be very cowardly, but I am willing to be hurt for what I think or what he thinks—I am not willing to be hurt, or even inconvenienced, for whatever he might happen to think after he had hurt me. The ordinary citizen may easily be more magnanimous than I, and take the whole thing on trust; in which case his career may be happier in the next world, but (I think) sadder in this. At least, I wish to point out to him that he will not be giving his glorious body as soldiers give it, to the glory of a fixed flag, or martyrs to the glory of a deathless God. He will be, in the strict sense of the Latin phrase, giving his vile body for an experiment—an experiment of which even the experimentalist knows neither the significance nor the end.

VIII

A SUMMARY OF A FALSE THEORY

I have up to this point treated the Eugenists, I hope, as seriously as they treat themselves. I have attempted an analysis of their theory as if it were an utterly abstract and disinterested theory; and so considered, there seems to be very little left of it. But before I go on, in the second part of this book, to talk of the ugly things that really are left, I wish to recapitulate the essential points in their essential order, lest any personal irrelevance or over-emphasis (to which I know myself to be prone) should have confused the course of what I believe to be a perfectly fair and consistent argument. To make it yet clearer, I will summarize the thing under chapters, and in quite short paragraphs.

In the first chapter I attempted to define the essential point in which Eugenics can claim, and does claim, to be a new morality. That point is that it is possible to consider the baby in considering the bride. I do not adopt the ideal irresponsibility of the man who said, "What has posterity done for us?" But I do say, to start with, "What can we do for posterity, except deal fairly with our contemporaries?" Unless a man love his wife whom he has seen, how shall he love his child whom he has not seen?

In the second chapter I point out that this division in the conscience cannot be met by mere mental confusions, which would make any woman refusing any man a Eugenist. There will always be something in the world which tends to keep outrageous unions exceptional; that influence is not Eugenics, but laughter.

In the third chapter I seek to describe the quite extraordinary atmosphere in which such things have become possible. I call that atmosphere anarchy; but insist that it is an anarchy in the centres where there should be authority. Government has become ungovernable; that is, it cannot leave off governing. Law has become lawless; that is, it cannot see where laws should stop. The chief feature of our time is the meekness of the mob and the madness of the government. In this atmosphere it is natural enough that medical experts, being authorities, should go mad, and attempt so crude and random and immature a dream as this of petting and patting (and rather spoiling) the babe unborn.

In chapter four I point out how this impatience has burst through the narrow channel of the Lunacy Laws, and has obliterated them by extending them. The whole point of the madman is that he is the exception that prove the rule. But Eugenics seeks to treat the whole rule as a series of exceptions—to make all men mad. And on that ground there is hope for nobody; for all opinions have an author, and all authors have a heredity. The mentality of the Eugenist makes him believe in Eugenics as much as the mentality of the reckless lover makes him violate Eugenics; and both mentalities are, on the materialist hypothesis, equally the irresponsible product of more or less unknown physical causes. The real security of the man against any logical Eugenics is like the false security of Macbeth. The only Eugenist that could rationally attack him must be a man of no woman born.

In the chapter following this, which is called "The Flying Authority," I try in vain to locate and fix any authority that could rationally rule men in so rooted and universal a matter; little would be gained by ordinary men doing it to each other; and if ordinary practitioners did it they would very soon show, by a thousand whims and quarrels, that they were ordinary men. I then discussed the enlightened despotism of a few general professors of hygiene, and found it unworkable, for an essential reason: that while we can always get men intelligent enough to know more than the rest of us about this or that accident or pain or pest, we cannot count on the appearance of great cosmic philosophers; and only such men can be even supposed to know more than we do about normal conduct and common sanity. Every sort of man, in short, would shirk such a responsibility, except the worst sort of man, who would accept it.

I pass on, in the next chapter, to consider whether we know enough about heredity to act decisively, even if we were certain who ought to act. Here I refer the Eugenists to the reply of Mr. Wells, which they have never dealt with to my knowledge or satisfaction— the important and primary objection that health is not a quality but a proportion of qualities; so that even health married to health might produce the exaggeration called disease. It should be noted here, of course, that an individual biologist may quite honestly believe that he has found a fixed principle with the help of Weissmann[1] or Mendel. But we are not discussing whether he knows enough to be justified in thinking (as is somewhat the habit of the anthropoid *Homo*) that he is right. We are discussing whether *we* know enough, as responsible citizens, to put such powers into the hands of men who may be deceived or who may be deceivers. I conclude that we do not.

In the last chapter of the first half of the book I give what is, I believe, the real secret of this confusion, the secret of what the Eugenists really want. They want to be allowed to find out what they want. Not content with the endowment of research, they desire the establishment of research; that is the making of it a thing official and compulsory, like education or state insurance; but still it is only research and not discovery. In short, they want a new kind of State Church, which shall be an Established Church of Doubt—instead of Faith. They have no Science of Eugenics at all, but they do really mean that if we will give ourselves up to be vivisected they may very probably have one some day. I point out, in more dignified diction, that this is a bit thick.

And now, in the second half of this book, we will proceed to the consideration of things that really exist. It is, I deeply regret to say, necessary to return to realities, as they are in your daily life and mine. Our happy holiday in the land of nonsense is over; we shall see no more its beautiful city, with the almost Biblical name of Bosh, nor the forests full of mares' nests, nor the fields of tares that are ripened only by moonshine. We shall meet no longer those delicious monsters that might have talked in the same wild club with the Snark[2] and the Jabberwock[3] or the Pobble[4] or the Dong with the

[1] August Weissmann (1834–1914), German biologist and theoretician on heredity.

[2] The imaginary animal invented by Lewis Carroll as the central figure in his mock-heroic poem "The Hunting of Snark" (1876).

[3] The central figure of a strange, almost gibberish poem in Lewis Carroll's *Through the Lookingglass.*

[4] The Pobble Who Has No Toes is the central character in a poem written by Edward Lear (*Nonsense Omnibus*, 1843). The Pobble, whose feet were once "garnished with toes so neat", lost all ten of them while swimming across the Bristol Channel.

Luminous Nose;[5] the father who can't make head or tail of the mother, but thoroughly understands the child she will some day bear; the lawyer who has to run after his own laws almost as fast as the criminals run away from them; the two mad doctors who might discuss for a million years which of them has the right to lock up the other; the grammarian who clings convulsively to the Passive Mood, and says it is the duty of something to get itself done without any human assistance; the man who would marry giants to giants until the back breaks, as children pile brick upon brick for the pleasure of seeing the staggering tower tumble down; and, above all, the superb man of science who wants you to pay him and crown him because he has so far found out nothing. These fairy-tale comrades must leave us. They exist, but they have no influence in what is really going on. They are honest dupes and tools, as you and I were very nearly being honest dupes and tools. If we come to think coolly of the world we live in, if we consider how very practical is the practical politician, at least where cash is concerned, how very dull and earthy are most of the men who own millions and manage the newspaper trusts, how very cautious and averse from idealist upheaval are those that control this capitalist society—when we consider all this, it is frankly incredible that Eugenics should be a front bench fashionable topic and almost an Act of Parliament, if it were in practice only the unfinished fantasy which it is, as I have shown, in pure reason. Even if it were a just revolution, it would be much too revolutionary a revolution for modern statesmen, if there were not something else behind. Even if it were a true ideal, it would be much too idealistic an ideal for our "practical men," if there were not something real as well. Well, there is something real as well. There is no reason in Eugenics, but there is plenty of motive. Its supporters are highly vague about its theory, but they will be painfully practical about its practice. And while I reiterate that many of its more eloquent agents are probably quite innocent instruments, there *are* some, even among Eugenists, who by this time know what they are doing. To them we shall not say, "What is Eugenics?" or "Where on earth are you going?" but only "Woe unto you, hypocrites, that devour widows' houses and for a pretence use long words."

[5] See footnote 6, page 49.

PART TWO
THE REAL AIM

I

THE IMPOTENCE OF IMPENITENCE

The root formula of an epoch is always an unwritten law, just as the law that is the first of all laws, that which protects life from the murderer, is written nowhere in the Statute Book. Nevertheless there is all the difference between having and not having a notion of this basic assumption in an epoch. For instance, the Middle Ages will simply puzzle us with their charities and cruelties, their asceticism and bright colours, unless we catch their general eagerness for building and planning, dividing this from that by walls and fences — the spirit that made architecture their most successful art. Thus even a slave seemed sacred; the divinity that did hedge a king, did also, in one sense, hedge a serf, for he could not be driven out from behind his hedges. Thus even liberty became a positive thing like a privilege; and even, when most men had it, it was not opened like the freedom of a wilderness, but bestowed, like the freedom of a city. Or again, the seventeenth century may seem a chaos of contradictions, with its almost priggish praise of parliaments and its quite barbaric massacre of prisoners, until we realize that, if the Middle Ages was a house half built, the seventeenth century was a house on fire. Panic was the note of it, and that fierce fastidiousness and exclusiveness that comes from fear. Calvinism was its charateristic religion, even in the Catholic Church, the insistence on the narrowness of the way and the fewness of the chosen. Suspicion was the note of its politics — "put not you trust in princes." It tried to thrash everything out by learned, virulent, and ceaseless controversy; and it weeded its population by witch-burning. Or yet again: the eighteenth century will present pictures that seem utterly opposite, and yet seem singularly typical of the time: the sack of Versailles and the "Vicar of Wakefield"; the pastorals of Watteau and the dynamite speeches of Danton. But we shall understand them all better if we once catch sight of the idea of *tidying up* which ran through the

355

whole period, the quietest people being prouder of their tidiness, civilization, and sound taste than of any of their virtues; and the wildest people having (and this is the most important point) no love of wildness for its own sake, like Nietzsche or the anarchic poets, but only a readiness to employ it to get rid of unreason or disorder. With these epochs it is not altogether impossible to say that some such form of words is a key. The epoch for which it is almost impossible to find a form of words is our own.

Nevertheless, I think that with us the key-word is "inevitability," or, as I should be inclined to call it, "impenitence." We are subconsciously dominated in all departments by the notion that there is no turning back, and it is rooted in materialism and the denial of free-will. Take any handful of modern facts and compare them with the corresponding facts a few hundred years ago. Compare the modern Party System with the political factions of the seventeenth century. The difference is that in the older time the party leaders not only really cut off each other's heads, but (what is much more alarming) really repealed each other's laws. With us it has become traditional for one party to inherit and leave untouched the acts of the other when made, however bitterly they were attacked in the making. James II. and his nephew William were neither of them very gay specimens; but they would both have laughed at the idea of "a continuous foreign policy." The Tories were not Conservatives; they were, in the literal sense, reactionaries. They did not merely want to keep the Stuarts; they wanted to bring them back.

Or again, consider how obstinately the English mediaeval monarchy returned again and again to its vision of French possessions, trying to reverse the decision of fate; how Edward III. returned to the charge after the defeats of John and Henry III., and Henry V. after the failure of Edward III.; and how even Mary had that written on her heart which was neither her husband nor her religion. And then consider this: that we have comparatively lately known a universal orgy of the thing called Imperialism, the unity of the Empire the only topic, colonies counted like crown jewels, and the Union Jack waved across the world. And yet no one so much as dreamed, I will not say of recovering, the American colonies for the Imperial unity (which would have been too dangerous a task for modern empire-builders), but even of re-telling the story from an Imperial standpoint. Henry V. justified the claims of Edward III. Joseph Chamberlain would not have dreamed of justifying the claims of George III. Nay, Shakespeare justifies the French War, and sticks to Talbot[1] and defies the legend of Joan of Arc. Mr. Kipling would not dare to justify the American War, stick to Burgoyne, and defy the legend of Washington. Yet there really was much more to be said for George III. than there ever was for Henry V. It was not said, much less acted upon, by the modern Imperialists; because of this basic modern sense, that as the future is inevitable, so is the past irrevocable. Any fact so complete as the American exodus from the Empire must be considered as final for aeons, though it hardly happened more than a hundred years ago. Merely because it has managed to occur it must be called first, a necessary evil, and then an indispensable good. I need not add that I do not want to reconquer America; but then I am not an Imperialist.

Then there is another way of testing it: ask yourself how many people you have met who grumbled at a thing as incurable, and how many who attacked it as curable? How many people we have heard abuse the British elementary schools, as they would abuse the British climate? How few have we met who realized that British education can be altered, but British weather cannot? How few there were that knew that the clouds were more immortal and more solid than the schools? For a thousand that regret compulsory education, where is the hundred, or the ten, or the one, who would repeal compulsory education? Indeed, the very word proves my case by its unpromising and unfamiliar sound. At the beginning of our epoch men talked with equal ease about Reform and Repeal. Now everybody talks about reform; but nobody talks about repeal. Our fathers did not talk of Free Trade, but of the Repeal of the Corn Laws. They did not talk of Home Rule, but of the Repeal of the Union. In those days people talked of a "Repealer" as the most practical of all politicians, the kind of politician that carries a club. Now the Repealer

[1] Charles Talbot, Duke of Shrewsbury (1660–1718), British statesman and Prime Minister in 1714.

is flung far into the province of an impossible idealism: and the leader of one of our great parties, having said, in a heat of temporary sincerity, that he would repeal an Act, actually had to write to all the papers to assure them that he would only amend it. I need not multiply instances, though they might be multiplied almost to a million. The note of the age is to suggest that the past may just as well be praised, since it cannot be mended. Men actually in that past have toiled like ants and died like locusts to undo some previous settlement that seemed secure; but we cannot do so much as repeal an Act of Parliament. We entertain the weak-minded notion that what is done can't be undone. Our view was well summarized in a typical Victorian song with the refrain: "The mill will never grind with the water that is past." There are many answers to this. One (which would involve a disquisition on the phenomena of Evaporation and Dew) we will here avoid. Another is, that to the minds of simple country folk, the object of a mill is not to grind water, but to grind corn, and that (strange as it may seem) there really have been societies sufficiently vigilant and valiant to prevent their corn perpetually flowing away from them, to the tune of a sentimental song.

Now this modern refusal to undo what has been done is not only an intellectual fault; it is a moral fault also. It is not merely our mental inability to understand the mistake we have made. It is also our spiritual refusal to admit that we have made a mistake. It was mere vanity in Mr. Brummell[2] when he sent away trays full of imperfectly knotted neckcloths, lightly remarking, "These are our failures." It is a good instance of the nearness of vanity to humility, for at least he had to admit that they were failures. But it would have been spiritual pride in Mr. Brummell if he had tied on all the cravats, one on top of the other, lest his valet should discover that he had ever tied one badly. For in spiritual pride there is always an element of secrecy and solitude. Mr. Brummell would be satanic; also (which I fear would affect him more) he would be badly dressed. But he would be a perfect presentation of the modern publicist, who cannot do anything right, because he must not admit that he ever did anything wrong.

---

[2] Beau Brummell (1778–1840), English dandy who set standards of fashion for men.

This strange, weak obstinacy, this persistence in the wrong path of progress, grows weaker and worse, as do all such weak things. And by the time in which I write its moral attitude has taken on something of the sinister and even the horrible. Our mistakes have become our secrets. Editors and journalists tear up with a guilty air all that reminds them of the party promises unfulfilled, or the party ideals reproaching them. It is true of our statesmen (much more than of our bishops, of whom Mr. Wells said it), that socially in evidence they are intellectually in hiding. The society is heavy with uncon-fessed sins; its mind is sore and silent with painful subjects; it has a constipation of conscience. There are many things it has done and al-lowed to be done which it does not really dare to think about; it calls them by other names and tries to talk itself into faith in a false past, as men make up the things they would have said in a quarrel. Of these sins one lies buried deepest but most noisome, and though it is stifled, stinks; the true story of the relations of the rich man and the poor in England. The half-starved English proletarian is not only nearly a skeleton, but he is a skeleton in a cupboard.

It may be said, in some surprise, that surely we hear to-day on every side the same story of the destitute proletariat and the social problem, of the sweating in the unskilled trades or the over-crowding in the slums. It is granted; but I said the true story. Un-true stories there are in plenty, on all sides of the discussion. There is the interesting story of the Class Conscious Proletarian of All Lands, the chap who has "solidarity," and is always just going to abolish war. The Marxian Socialists will tell you all about him; only he isn't there. A common English workman is just as incapable of thinking of a German as anything but a German as he is of thinking of himself as anything but an Englishman. Then there is the opposite story; the story of the horrid man who is an atheist and wants to destroy the home, but who, for some private reason, prefers to call this Social-ism. He isn't there either. The prosperous Socialists have homes ex-actly like yours and mine; and the poor Socialists are not allowed by the Individualists to have any at all. There is the story of the Two Workmen, which is a very nice and exciting story, about how one passed all the public houses in Cheapside and was made Lord Mayor on arriving at the Guildhall, while the other went into all the public houses and emerged quite ineligible for such a dignity. Alas! for this also is vanity. A thief might become Lord Mayor, but an honest workman certainly couldn't. Then there is the story of "The Relentless Doom" by which rich men were, by economic laws, forced to go on taking away money from poor men, although they simply longed to leave off: this is an unendurable thought to a free and Christian man, and the reader will be relieved to hear that it never happened. The rich could have left off stealing whenever they wanted to leave off, only this never happened either. Then there is the story of the cunning Fabian[3] who sat on six comittees at once and so coaxed the rich man to become quite poor. By simply repeating in a whisper, that there are "wheels within wheels," this talented man managed to take away the millionaire's motor car, one wheel at a time, till the millionaire had quite forgotten that he ever had one. It was very clever of him to do this, only he has not done it. There is not a screw loose in the millionaire's motor, which is capable of running over the Fabian and leaving him a flat corpse in the road at a moment's notice. All these stories are very fascinating stories to be told by the Individualist and Socialist in turn to the great Sultan of Capitalism, because if they left off amusing him for an instant he would cut off their heads. But if they once began to tell the true story of the Sultan to the Sultan, he would boil them in oil; and this they wish to avoid.

The true story of the sin of the Sultan he is always trying, by listening to these stories, to forget. As we have said before in this chapter, he would prefer not to remember, because he has made up his mind not to repent. It is a curious story, and I shall try to tell it truly in the two chapters that follow. In all ages the tyrant is hard because he is soft. If his car crashes over bleeding and accusing crowds, it is because he has chosen the path of least resistance. It is because it is much easier to ride down a human race than ride up a moderately steep hill. The fight of the oppressor is always a pillow-fight; commonly a war with cushions — always a war for cushions. Saladin, the great Sultan, if I remember rightly, accounted it the

[3] A reference to the Roman general Fabius; Fabian came to be applied to a movement within the British socialist movement advocating a gradual passage to socialism.

greatest feat of swordsmanship to cut a cushion. And so indeed it is, as all of us can attest who have been for years past trying to cut into the swollen and windy corpulence of the modern compromise, that is at once cosy and cruel. For there is really in our world to-day the colour and silence of the cushioned divan; and that sense of palace within palace and garden within garden which makes the rich irresponsibility of the East. Have we not already the wordless dance, the wineless banquet, and all that strange unchristian conception of luxury without laughter? Are we not already in an evil Arabian Nights, and walking the nightmare cities of an invisible despot? Does not our hangman strangle secretly, the bearer of the bow string? Are we not already eugenists—that is, eunuch-makers? Do we not see the bright eyes, the motionless faces, and all the presence of something that is dead and yet sleepless? It is the presence of the sin that is sealed with pride and impenitence; the story of how the Sultan got his throne. But it is not the story he is listening to just now, but another story which has been invented to cover it—the story called "Eugenius: or the Adventures of One Not Born," a most varied and entrancing tale, which never fails to send him to sleep.

II

TRUE HISTORY OF A TRAMP

He awoke in the Dark Ages and smelt dawn in the dark, and knew he was not wholly a slave. It was as if, in some tale of Hans Andersen, a stick or a stool had been left in the garden all night and had grown alive and struck root like a tree. For this is the truth behind the old legal fiction of the servile countries, that the slave is a "chattel," that is a piece of furniture like a stick or a stool. In the spiritual sense, I am certain is was never so unwholesome a fancy as the spawn of Nietzsche suppose to-day. No human being, pagan or Christian, I am certain, ever thought of another human being as a chair or a table. The mind cannot base itself on the idea that a comet is a cabbage; not can it on the idea that a man is a stool. No man was ever unconscious of another's presence — or even indifferent to another's opinion. The lady who is said to have boasted her indifference to being naked before male slaves was showing off — or she meant something different. The lord who fed fishes by killing a slave was indulging in what most cannibals indulge in — a satanist affectation. The lady was consciously shameless and the lord was consciously cruel. But it simply is not in the human reason to carve men like wood or examine women like ivory, just as it is not the human reason to think that two and two make five.

But there was this truth in the legal simile of furniture: that the slave, though certainly a man, was in one sense a dead man; in the sense that he was *moveable*. His locomotion was not his own: his master moved his arms and legs for him as if he were a marionette. Now it is important in the first degree to realize here what would be involved in such a fable as I have imagined, of a stool rooting itself like a shrub. For the general modern notion certainly is that life and liberty are in some way to be associated with novelty and not standing still. But it is just because the stool is lifeless that it moves about. It is just because the tree is alive that it does stand still. That was the main difference between the pagan slave and the Christian serf. The serf still belonged to the lord, as the stick that struck root in the garden; would have still belonged to the owner of the garden; but it would have become a *live* possession. Therefore the owner is forced, by the laws of nature, to treat it with *some* respect; something becomes due from him. He cannot pull it up without killing it; it has gained a *place* in the garden—or the society. But the moderns are quite wrong in supposing that mere change and holiday and variety have necessarily any element of this life that is the only seed of liberty. You may say if you like that an employer, taking all his workpeople to a new factory in a Garden City, is giving them the greater freedom of forest landscapes and smokeless skies. If it comes to that, you can say that the slave-traders took negroes from their narrow and brutish African hamlets, and gave them the polish of foreign travel and medicinal breezes of a sea-voyage. But the tiny seed of citizenship and independence there already was in the serfdom of the Dark Ages, had nothing to do with what nice things the lord might do to the serf. It lay in the fact that there were some nasty things he could not do to the serf—there were not many, but there were some, and one of them was eviction. He could not make the serf utterly landless and desperate utterly without access to the means of production, though doubtless it was rather the field that owned the serf, than the serf that owned the field. But even if you call the serf a beast of the field, he was not what we have tried to make the town workman—a beast with no field. Foulon[1] said of the French peasants, "Let them eat grass." If he had said it of the modern London proletariat, they might well reply, "You have not left us even grass to eat."

There was, therefore, both in theory and practice, *some* security for the serf, because he had come to life and rooted. The seigneur could not wait in the field in all weathers with a battle-ax to prevent the serf scratching any living out of the ground, any more than the man in my fairy-tale could sit out in the garden all night with an umbrella to prevent the shrub getting any rain. The relation of lord and serf, therefore, involves a combination of two things: inequality and security. I know there are people who will at once point wildly

[1] See footnote 3, page 217.

to all sorts of examples, true and false, of insecurity of life in the Middle Ages; but these are people who do not grasp what we mean by the characteristic institutions of a society. For the matter of that, there are plenty of examples of equality in the Middle Ages, as the craftsmen in their guild or the monks electing their abbot. But just as modern England is not a feudal country, though there is a quaint survival called Heralds' College—or Ireland is not a commercial country, though there is a quaint survival called Belfast—it is true of the bulk and shape of that society that came out of the Dark Ages and ended at the Reformation, that it did not care about giving everybody an equal position, but did care about giving everybody a position. So that by the very beginning of that time even the slave had become a slave one could not get rid of, like the Scotch servant who stubbornly asserted that if his master didn't know a good servant he knew a good master. The free peasant, in ancient or modern times, is free to go or stay. The slave, in ancient times, was free neither to go nor stay. The serf was not free to go; but he was free to stay.

Now what have we done with this man? It is quite simple. There is no historical complexity about it in that respect. We have taken away his freedom to stay. We have turned him out of his field, and whether it was injustice, like turning a free farmer out of his field, or only cruelty to animals, like turning a cow out of its field, the fact remains that he is out in the road. First and last, we have simply destroyed the security. We have not in the least destroyed the inequality. All classes, all creatures, kind or cruel, still see this lowest stratum of society as separate from the upper strata and even the middle strata; he is as separate as the serf. A monster fallen from Mars, ignorant of our simplest word, would know the tramp was at the bottom of the ladder, as well as he would have known it of the serf. The walls of mud are no longer round his boundaries, but only round his boots. The coarse bristling hedge is at the end of his chin, and not of his garden. But mud and bristles still stand out round him like a horrific halo, and separate him from his kind. The Martian would have no difficulty in seeing he was the poorest person in the nation. It is just as impossible that he should marry an heiress, or fight a duel with a duke, or contest a seat at Westminster, or enter a club in Pall Mall, or take a scholarship at Balliol, or take a seat at an opera, or propose a good law, or protest against a bad one, as it was impossible to the serf. Where he differs is in something very different. He has lost what was possible to the serf. He can no longer scratch the bare earth by day or sleep on the bare earth by night, without being collared by a policeman.

Now when I say this man has been oppressed as hardly any other man on this earth has been oppressed, I am not using rhetoric: I have a clear meaning which I am confident of explaining to any honest reader. I do not say he has been treated worse: I say he has been treated differently from the unfortunate in all ages. And the difference is this: that all the others were told to do something, and killed or tortured if they did anything else. This man is not told to do something: he is merely forbidden to do anything. When he was a slave, they said to him, "Sleep in this shed; I will beat you if you sleep anywhere else." When he was a serf, they said to him, "Let me find you in this field: I will hang you if I find you in anyone else's field." But now he is a tramp they say to him, "You shall be jailed if I find you in anyone else's field: *but I will not give you a field.*" They say, "You shall be punished if you are caught sleeping outside your shed: *but there is no shed.*" If you say that modern magistracies could never say such mad contradictions, I answer with entire certainty that they do say them. A little while ago two tramps were summoned before a magistrate, charged with sleeping in the open air when they had nowhere else to sleep. But this is not the full fun of the incident. The real fun is that each of them eagerly produced about twopence, to prove that they could have got a bed, but deliberately didn't. To which the policeman replied that twopence would not have got them a bed: they could not possibly have got a bed: and *therefore* (argued that thoughtful officer) they ought to be punished for not getting one. The intelligent magistrate was much struck with the argument: and proceeded to imprison these two men for not doing a thing they could not do. But he was careful to explain that if they had sinned needlessly and in wanton lawlessness, they would have left the court without a stain on their characters; but as they could not avoid it, they were very much to blame. These things are being done in every part of England every day. They have their parallels even in every daily paper; but they have no parallel in any other earthly people or period; except in that insane command to make bricks without straw which brought down all the plagues of Egypt. For the common historical joke about Henry VIII. hanging a man for being Catholic and burning him for being Protestant is a symbolic joke only. The sceptic in the Tudor time could do something: he could always agree with Henry VIII. The desperate man to-day can do nothing. For you cannot agree with a maniac who sits on the bench with the straws sticking out of his hair and says, "Procure three-pence from nowhere and I will give you leave to do without it."

If it be answered that he can go to the work-house, I reply that such an answer is founded on confused thinking. It is true that he is free to go to the workhouse, but only in the same sense in which he is free to go to jail, only in the same sense in which the serf under the gibbet was free to find peace in the grave. Many of the poor greatly prefer the grave to the workhouse, but that is not at all my argument here. The point is this: that it could not have been the general policy of a lord towards serfs to kill them all like wasps. It could not have been his standing "Advice to Serfs" to say, "Get hanged." It cannot be the standing advice of magistrates to citizens to go to prison. And, precisely as plainly, it cannot be the standing advice of rich men to very poor men to go to the workhouses. For that would mean the rich raising their own poor rates enormously to keep a vast and expensive establishment of slaves. Now it may come to this, as Mr. Belloc maintains, but it is not the theory on which what we call the workhouse does in fact rest. The very shape (and even the very size) of a workhouse expresses the fact that it was found for certain quite exceptional human failures—like the lunatic asylum. Say to a man, "Go to the madhouse," and he will say, "Wherein am I mad?" Say to a tramp under a hedge, "Go to the house of exceptional failures," and he will say with equal reason, "I travel because I have no house; I walk because I have no horse; I sleep out because I have no bed. Wherein have I failed?" And he may have the intelligence to add, "Indeed, your worship, if somebody has failed, I think it is not I." I concede, with all due haste, that he might perhaps say "me."

The specialty then of this man's wrong is that it is the only historic wrong that has in it the quality of *nonsense*. It could only happen in a nightmare; not in a clear and rational hell. It is the top point of that anarchy in the governing mind which, as I said at at the beginning, is the main trait of modernity, especially in England. But if the first note in our policy is madness, the next note is certainly meanness. There are two peculiarly mean and unmanly legal man-traps in which this wretched man is tripped up. The first is that which prevents him from doing what any ordinary savage or nomad would do — take his chance of an uneven subsistence on the rude bounty of nature.

There is something very abject about forbidding this; because it is precisely this adventurous and vagabond spirit which the educated classes praise most in their books, poems and speeches. To feel the drag of the roads, to hunt in nameless hills and fish in secret streams, to have no address save "Over the Hills and Far Away," to be ready to breakfast on berries and the daybreak and sup on the sunset and a sodden crust, to feed on wild things and be a boy again, all this is the heartiest and sincerest impulse in recent culture, in the songs and tales of Stevenson, in the cult of George Borrow[2] and in the delightful little books published by Mr. E. V. Lucas.[3] It is the one true excuse in the core of Imperialism; and it faintly softens the squalid prose and wooden-headed wickedness of the Self-Made Man who "came up to London with twopence in his pocket." But when a poorer but braver man with less that twopence in his pocket does the very thing we are always praising, makes the blue heavens his house, we send him to a house built for infamy and flogging. We take poverty itself and only permit it with a property qualification; we only allow a man to be poor if he is rich. And we do this most savagely if he has sought to snatch his life by that particular thing of which our boyish adventure stories are fullest — hunting and fishing. The extremely severe English game laws hit most heavily what the highly reckless English romances praise most irresponsibly. All our literature is full of praise of the chase — especially of the wild goose chase. But if a poor man followed, as Tennyson says, "far as the wild

[2] Georges Borrow (1803–1881), British writer, novelist, hygiene enthusiast.
[3] E. V. Lucas (1868–1938), British writer and publisher.

swan wings to where the world dips down to sea and sands,"
Tennyson would scarcely allow him to catch it. If he found the
wildest goose in the wildest fenland in the wildest regions of the
sunset, he would very probably discover that the rich never sleep;
and that there are no wild things in England.

In short, the English ruler is always appealing to a nation of
sportsmen and concentrating all his efforts on preventing them from
having any sport. The Imperialist is always pointing out with ex-
ultation that the common Englishman can live by adventure
anywhere on the globe, but if the common Englishmen tries to live
by adventure in England, he is treated as harshly as a thief, and
almost as harshly as an honest journalist. This is hypocrisy: the
magistrate who gives his son "Treasure Island" and then imprisons a
tramp is a hypocrite; the squire who is proud of English colonists
and indulgent to English schoolboys, but cruel to English poachers,
is drawing near that deep place wherein all liars have their part. But
out point here is that the baseness is in the idea of *bewildering* the
tramp; of leaving him no place for repentance. It is quite true, of
course, that in the days of slavery or of serfdom the needy were
fenced by yet fiercer penalties from spoiling the hunting of the rich. But
in the older case there were two very important differences, the second
of which is our main subject in this chapter. The first is that in a
comparatively wild society, however fond of hunting, it seems impossible that enclosing and game-keeping can have been so omnipresent and
efficient as in a society full of maps and policemen. The second difference is the one already noted: that if the slave or semi-slave was forbidden to get his food in the green wood, he was told to get it somewhere
else. The note of unreason was absent.

This is the first meanness; and the second is like unto it. If there is
one thing of which cultivated modern letters is full besides adventure it is altruism. We are always being told to help others, to regard
our wealth as theirs, to do what good we can, for we shall not pass
this way again. We are everywhere urged by humanitarians to help
lame dogs over stiles — though some humanitarians, it is true, seem
to feel a colder interest in the case of lame men and women. Still, the
chief fact of our literature, among all historic literatures, is human

charity. But what is the chief fact of our legislation? The great out-standing fact of modern legislation, among all historic legislations, is the forbidding of human charity. It is this astonishing paradox, a thing in the teeth of all logic and conscience, that a man that takes another man's money with his leave can be punished as if he had taken it without his leave. All through those dark or dim ages be-hind us, through times of servile stagnation, of feudal insolence, of pestilence and civil strife and all else that can wear down the weak, for the weak to ask for charity was counted lawful, and to give that charity, admirable. In all other centuries, in short, the casual bad deeds of bad men could be partly patched and mended by the casual good deeds of good men. But this is now forbidden; for it would leave the tramp a last chance if he could beg.

Now it will be evident by this time that the interesting scientific ex-periment on the tramp entirely depends on leaving him *no* chance, and not (like the slave) one chance. Of the economic excuses offered for the persecution of beggars it will be more natural to speak in the next chap-ter. It will suffice here to say that they are mere excuses, for a policy that has been persistent while probably largely unconscious, with a selfish and atheistic unconsciousness. That policy was directed towards something — or it could never have cut so cleanly and cruelly across the sentimental but sincere modern trends to adventure and altruism. Its object is soon stated. It was directed towards making the very poor man work for the capitalist, for any wages or none. But all this, which I shall also deal with in the next chapter, is here only important as introducing the last truth touching the man of despair. The game laws have taken from him his human command of Nature. The mendicancy laws have taken from him his human demand on Man. There is one human thing left it is much harder to take from him. Debased by him and his betters, it is still something brought out of Eden, where God made him a demigod: it does not depend on money and but little on time. He can create in his own image. The terrible truth is in the heart of a hundred legends and mysteries. As Jupiter could be hidden from all-devouring Time, as the Christ Child could be hidden from Herod — so the child unborn is still hidden from the omniscient oppressor. He who lives not yet, he and he alone is left; and they seek his life to take it away.

III

TRUE HISTORY OF A EUGENIST

He does not live in a dark lonely tower by the sea, from which are heard the screams of vivisected men and women. On the contrary, he lives in Mayfair. He does not wear great goblin spectacles that magnify his eyes to moons or diminish his neighbours to beetles. When he is more dignified he wears a single eyeglass; when more intelligent, a wink. He is not indeed wholly without interest in heredity and Eugenical biology; but his studies and experiments in this science have specialized almost exclusively in *equus celer*, the rapid or running horse. He is not a doctor; though he employes doctors to work up a case for Eugenics, just as he employs doctors to correct the errors of his dinner. He is not a lawyer, though unfortunately often a magistrate. He is not an author or a journalist; though he not infrequently owns a newspaper. He is not a soldier, though he may have a commission in the yeomanry; nor is he generally a gentleman, though often a nobleman. His wealth now commonly comes from a large staff of employed persons who scurry about in big buildings while he is playing golf. But he very often laid the foundations of his fortune in a very curious and poetical way, the nature of which I have never fully understood. It consisted in his walking about the street without a hat and going up to another man and saying, "Suppose I have two hundred whales out of the North Sea." To which the other man replied, "And let us imagine that I am in possession of two thousand elephants' tusks." They then exchange, and the first man goes up to a third man and says, "Supposing me to have lately come into the possession of two thousand elephants' tusks, would you, etc.?" If you play this game well, you become very rich; if you play it badly you have to kill yourself or try your luck at the Bar. The man I am speaking about must have played it well, or at any rate successfully.

He was born about 1860; and has been a Member of Parliament since about 1890. For the first half of his life he was a Liberal; for the second half he has been a Conservative; but his actual policy in Parliament has remained largely unchanged and consistent. His policy in Parliament is as follows: he takes a seat in a room downstairs at Westminster, and takes from his breast pocket an excellent cigarcase, from which in turn he takes an excellent cigar. This he lights, and converses with other owners of such cigars on *equus celer* or such matters as may afford him entertainment. Two or three times in the afternoon a bell rings; whereupon he deposits the cigar in an ashtray with great particularity, taking care not to break the ash, and proceeds to an upstairs room, flanked with two passages. He then walks into whichever of the two passages shall be indicated to him by a young man of the upper classes, holding a slip of paper. Having gone into this passage he comes out of it again, is counted by the young man and proceeds downstairs again; where he takes up the cigar once more, being careful not to break the ash. This process, which is known as Representative government, has never called for any great variety in the manner of his life. Nevertheless, while his Parliamentary policy is unchanged, his change from one side of the House to the other did correspond with a certain change in his general policy in commerce and social life. The change of the party label is by this time quite a trifling matter; but there was in his case a change of philosophy or at least a change of project; though it was not so much becoming a Tory, as becoming rather the wrong kind of Socialist. He is a man with a history. It is a sad history, for he is certainly a less good man than he was when he started. That is why he is the man who is really behind Eugenics. It is because he has degenerated that he has come to talking of Degeneration.

In his Radical days (to quote from one who corresponded in some ways to this type) he was a much better man, because he was a much less enlightened one. The hard impudence of his first Manchester Individualism was softened by two relatively humane qualities; the first was a much great manliness in his pride; the second was a much greater sincerity in his optimism. For the first point, the modern capitalist is merely industrial; but this man was also industrious. He was proud of hard work; nay, he was even proud of low work—if he could speak of it in the past and not the present. In fact, he invented a new kind of Victorian snobbishness, an inverted snobbishness. While the snobs of Thackeray turned Muggins into De Mogyns, while the snobs of Dickens wrote letters describing themselves as officers' daughters "accustomed to every luxury—except spelling," the Individualist spent his life in hiding his prosperous parents. He was more like an American plutocrat when he began; but he has since lost the American simplicity. The Frenchman works until he can't play; and then thanks the devil, his master, that he is donkey enough to die in harness. But the Englishman, as he has since become, works until he can pretend that he never worked at all. He becomes as far as possible another person—a country gentleman who has never heard of his shop; one whose left hand holding a gun knows not what his right hand doeth in a ledger. He uses a peerage as an alias, and a large estate as a sort of alibi. A stern Scotch minister remarked concerning the game of golf, with a terrible solemnity of manner, "the man who plays golf—he neglects his business, he forsakes his wife, he forgets his God." He did not seem to realize that it is the chief aim of many a modern capitalist's life to forget all three.

This abandonment of a boyish vanity in work, this substitution of a senile vanity in indolence, this is the first respect in which the rich Englishman has fallen. He was more of a man when he was at least a master-workman and not merely a master. And the second important respect in which he was better at the beginning is this: that he did then, in some hazy way, half believe that he was enriching other people as well as himself. The optimism of the early Victorian Individualists was not wholly hypocritical. Some of the clearest-headed and blackest-hearted of them, such as Malthus, saw where things were going, and boldly based their Manchester city on pessimism instead of optimism. But this was not the general case; most of the decent rich of the Bright[1] and Cobden[2] sort did have a kind of confused faith that the economic conflict would work well in the long run for everybody. They thought the troubles of the poor were incurable by State action (they thought that of all troubles), but they

[1] John Bright (1811–1889), British writer and economist.

[2] Richard Cobden (1804–1865), English economist, manufacturer and statesman.

did not cold-bloodedly contemplate the prospect of those troubles growing worse and worse. By one of those tricks or illusions of the brain to which the luxurious are subject in all ages, they sometimes seemed to feel as if the populace had triumphed symbolically in their own persons. They blasphemously thought about their thrones of gold what can only be said about a cross—that they, being lifted up, would draw all men after them. They were so full of the romance that anybody could be Lord Mayor, that they seemed to have slipped into thinking that everybody could. It seemed as if a hundred Dick Whittingtons,[3] accompanied by a hundred cats, could all be accommodated at the Mansion House. It was all nonsense; but it was not (until later) all humbug.

Step by step, however, with a horrid and increasing clearness, this man discovered what he was doing. It is generally one of the worst discoveries a man can make. At the beginning, the British plutocrat was probably quite as honest in suggesting that every tramp carried a magic cat like Dick Whittington, as the Bonapartist patriot was in saying that every French soldier carried a marshal's *baton* in his knapsack. But it is exactly here that the difference and the danger appears. There is no comparison between a well-managed thing like Napoleon's army and an unmanageable thing like modern competition. Logically, doubtless, it was impossible that every soldier should carry a marshal's *baton*; they could not all be marshals any more than they could all be mayors. But if the French soldier did not always have a *baton* in his knapsack, he always had a knapsack. But when that Self-Helper who bore the adorable name of Smiles[4] told the English tramp that he carried a coronet in his bundle, the English tramp had an unanswerable answer. He pointed out that he had no bundle. The powers that ruled him had not fitted him with a knapsack, any more than they had fitted him with a future—or even a present. The destitute Englishman, so far from hoping to become

[3] Dick Whittington (c. 1358–1423), Mayor of London, later became a subject of legends and tales. He was said to have sent a cat he owned to a country with lots of rats but no cats, so he made a fortune.

[4] Samuel Smiles (1812–1904), Scottish writer and physician who became famous for promoting the ideas of self-help.

anything, had never been allowed even to be anything. The French soldier's ambition may have been in practice not only a short, but even a deliberately shortened ladder, in which the top rungs were knocked out. But for the English it was the bottom rungs that were knocked out, so that they could not even begin to climb. And sooner or later, in exact proportion to his intelligence, the English plutocrat began to understand not only that the poor were impotent, but that their impotence had been his only power. The truth was not merely that his riches had left them poor; it was that nothing but their poverty could have been strong enough to make him rich. It is this paradox, as we shall see, that creates the curious difference between him and every other kind of robber.

I think it is no more than justice to him to say that the knowledge, where it has come to him, has come to him slowly; and I think it came (as most things of common-sense come) rather vaguely and as in a vision—that is, by the mere look of things. The old Cobdennite employer was quite within his rights in arguing that earth is not heaven, that the best obtainable arrangement might contain many necessary evils; and that Liverpool and Belfast might be growing more prosperous as a whole in spite of pathetic things that might be seen there. But I simply do not believe he has been able to look at Liverpool and Belfast and continue to think this: that is why he has turned himself into a sham country gentleman. Earth is not heaven, but the nearest we can get to heaven ought not to *look* like hell; and Liverpool and Belfast look like hell, whether they are or not. Such cities might be growing prosperous as a whole, though a few citizens were more miserable. But it was more and more broadly apparent that it was exactly and precisely *as a whole* that they were not growing more prosperous, but only the few citizens who were growing more prosperous by their increasing misery. You could not say a country was becoming a white man's country when there were more and more black men in it every day. You could not say a community was more and more masculine when it was producing more and more women. Nor can you say that a city is growing richer and richer when more and more of its inhabitants are very poor men. There might be a false agitation founded on the pathos of individual cases in a community pretty normal in bulk. But the fact is that no one can take a cab across Liverpool without having a quite complete and unified impression that the pathos is not a pathos of individual cases, but a pathos in bulk. People talk of the Celtic sadness; but there are very few things in Ireland that look so sad as the Irishman in Liverpool. The desolation of Tara[5] is cheery compared with the desolation of Belfast. I recommend Mr. Yeats and his mournful friends to turn their attention to the pathos of Belfast. I think if they hung up the harp that once in Lord Furness's[6] factory, there would be a chance of another string breaking.

Broadly, and as things bulk to the eye, towns like Leeds, if placed beside towns like Rouen or Florence, or Chartres, or Cologne, do actually look like beggars walking among burghers. After that over-powering and unpleasant impression it is really useless to argue that they are richer because a few of their parasites get rich enough to live somewhere else. The point may be put another way, thus: that it is not so much that these more modern cities have this or that monopoly of good or evil; it is that they have every good in its fourth-rate form and every evil in its worst form. For instance, that interesting weekly paper *The Nation* amiably rebuked Mr. Belloc and myself for suggesting that revelry and the praise of fermented liquor were more characteristic of Continental and Catholic communities than of communities with the religion and civilization of Belfast. It said that if we would "cross the border" into Scotland, we should find out our mistake. Now, not only have I crossed the border, but I have had considerable difficulty in crossing the road in a Scotch town on a festive evening. Men were literally lying like piled-up corpses in the gutters, and from broken bottles whisky was pouring down the drains. I am not likely, therefore, to attribute a total and arid abstinence to the whole of industrial Scotland. But I never said that drinking was a mark rather of the Catholic countries. I said that *moderate* drinking was a mark rather of the Catholic countries. In other words, I say of the common type of Continental citizen, not that he is the only person who is drinking, but that he is the only

[5] A village in the NE Republic of Ireland, home of ancestral Irish kings.

[6] Sir Stephen Wilson Furness (1872–1914), British industrialist and shipbuilder.

person who knows how to drink. Doubtless gin is as much a feature of Hoxton as beer is a feature of Munich. But who is the connoisseur who prefers the gin of Hoxton to the beer of Munich? Doubtless the Protestant Scotch ask for "Scotch," as the men of Burgundy ask for Burgundy. But do we find them lying in heaps on each side of the road when we walk through a Burgundian village? Do we find the French peasant ready to let Burgundy escape down a drain-pipe? Now this one point, on which I accept *The Nation's* challenge, can be exactly paralleled on almost every point by which we test a civilization. It does not matter whether we are for alcohol or against it. On either argument Glasgow is more objectionable than Rouen. The French abstainer makes less fuss; the French drinker gives less offence. It is so with property, with war, with everything. I can understand a teetotaller being horrified, on his principles, at Italian wine-drinking. I simply cannot believe he could be *more* horrified at it than at Hoxton gin-drinking. I can understand a Pacifist, with his special scruples, disliking the militarism of Belfort. I flatly deny that he can dislike it more than the militarism of Berlin. I can understand a good Socialist hating the petty cares of the distributed peasant property. I deny that any good Socialist can hate them *more* than he hates the large cares of Rockefeller. That is the unique tragedy of the plutocratic state to-day; it has *no* successes to hold up against the failures it alleges to exist in Latin or other methods. You can (if you are well out of his reach) call the Irish rustic debased and superstitious. I defy you to contrast his debasement and superstition with the citizenship and enlightenment of the English rustic.

To-day the rich man knows in his heart that he is a cancer and not an organ of the State. He differs from all other thieves or parasites for this reason: that the brigand who takes by force wishes his victims to be rich. But he who wins by a one-sided contract actually wishes them to be poor. Rob Roy in a cavern, hearing a company approaching, will hope (or if in a pious mood, pray) that they may come laden with gold or goods. But Mr. Rockefeller, in his factory, knows that if those who pass are laden with goods they will pass on. He will therefore (if in a pious mood) pray that they may be destitute, and so be forced to work his factory for him for a starvation wage. It is said (and also, I believe, disputed) that Blücher[7] riding through the richer parts of London exclaimed, "What a city to sack!" But Blücher was a soldier if he was a bandit. The true sweater feels quite otherwise. It is when he drives through the poorest parts of London that he finds the streets paved with gold, being paved with prostrate servants; it is when he sees the grey lean leagues of Bow and Poplar that his soul is uplifted and he knows he is secure. This is not rhetoric, but economics.

I repeat that up to a point the profiteer was innocent because he was ignorant; he had been lured on by easy and accommodating events. He was innocent as the new Thane of Glamis was innocent, as the new Thane of Cawdor was innocent; but the King — the modern manufacturer, like Macbeth, decided to march on, under the mute menace of the heavens. He knew that the spoil of the poor was in his houses; but he could not, after careful calculation, think of any way in which they could get it out of his houses without being arrested for housebreaking. He faced the future with a face flinty with pride and impenitence. This period can be dated practically by the period when the old and genuine Protestant religion of England began to fail; and the average business man began to be agnostic, not so much because he did not know where he was, as because he wanted to forget. Many of the rich took to scepticism exactly as the poor took to drink; because it was a way out. But in any case, the man who had made a mistake not only refused to unmake it, but decided to go on making it. But in this he made yet another most amusing mistake, which was the beginning of all Eugenics.

[7] Gebhart Blücher (1742–1819), Prussian Field Marshal.

IV

THE VENGEANCE OF THE FLESH

By a quaint paradox, we generally miss the meaning of simple stories because we are not subtle enough to understand their simplicity. As long as men were in sympathy with some particular religion or other romance of things in general, they saw the thing solid and swollowed it whole, knowing that it could not disagree with them. But the moment men have lost the instinct of being simple in order to understand it, they have to be very subtle in order to understand it. We can find, for instance, a very good working case in those old puritanical nursery tales about the terrible punishment of trivial sins; about how Tommy was drowned for fishing on the Sabbath, or Sammy struck by lightning for going out after dark. Now these moral stories are immoral, because Calvanism is immoral. They are wrong, because Puritanism is wrong. But they are not quite so wrong, they are not a quarter so wrong, as many superficial sages have supposed.

The truth is that everything that ever came out of a human mouth had a human meaning; and not one of the fixed fools of history was such a fool as he looks. And when our great-uncles or great-grandmothers told a child he might be drowned by a breaking of the Sabbath, their souls (though undoubtedly, as Touchstone said, in a parlous state) were not in quite so simple a state as is suggested by supposing that their god was a devil who dropped babies into the Thames for a trifle. This form of religious literature is a morbid form if taken by itself; but it did correspond to certain reality in psychology which most people of any religion, or even of none, have felt a touch of at some time or other. Leaving out theological terms as far as possible, it is the subconscious feeling that one can be wrong with Nature as well as right with Nature; that the point of wrongness may be a detail (in the superstitions of heathens this is often quite a triviality); but that if one is really wrong with Nature, there is no particular reason why all her rivers should not drown or all her storm-bolts strike one who is, by this vague yet vivid hypothesis, her enemy. This may be a mental sickness, but it is too human or too mortal a sickness to be called solely a superstition. It is not solely a superstition; it is not simply superimposed upon human nature by something that has got on top of it. It flourishes without check among non-Christian systems, and it flourishes especially in Calvinism, because Calvinism is the most non-Christian of Christian systems. But like everything else that inheres in the natural senses and spirit of man, it has something in it; it is not stark unreason. If it is an ill (and it generally is), it is one of the ills that flesh is heir to, but he is the lawful heir. And like many other dubious or dangerous human instincts or appetites, it is sometimes useful as a warning against worse things.

Now the trouble of the nineteenth century very largely came from the loss of this; the loss of what we may call the natural and heathen mysticism. When modern critics say that Julius Caesar did not believe in Jupiter, or that Pope Leo did not believe in Catholicism, they overlook an essential difference between those ages and ours. Perhaps Julius did not believe in Jupiter; but he did not disbelieve in Jupiter. There was nothing in his philosophy, or the philosophy of that age, that could forbid him to think that there was a spirit personal and predominant in the world. But the modern materialists are not permitted to doubt; they are forbidden to believe. Hence, while the heathen might avail himself of accidental omens, queer coincidences or casual dreams, without knowing for certain whether they were really hints from heaven or premonitory movements in his own brain, the modern Christian turned heathen must not entertain such notions at all, but must reject the oracle as the altar. The modern sceptic was drugged against all that was natural in the supernatural. And this was why the modern tyrant marched upon his doom, as a tyrant literally pagan might possibly not have done.

There is one idea of this kind that runs through most popular tales (those, for instance, on which Shakespeare is so often based) — an idea that is profoundly moral even if the tales are immoral. It is what may be called the flaw in the deed: the idea that, if I take my advantage to the full, I shall hear of something to my disadvantage. Thus

Midas fell into a fallacy about the currency; and soon had reason to become something more than a Bimetallist. Thus Macbeth had a fallacy about forestry; he could not see the trees for the wood. He forgot that, though a place cannot be moved, the trees that grow on it can. Thus Shylock had a fallacy of physiology; he forgot that, if you break into the house of life, you find it a bloody house in the most emphatic sense. But the modern capitalist did not read fairy-tales, and never looked for the little omens at the turnings of the road. He (or the most intelligent section of him) had by now realized his position, and knew in his heart it was a false position. He thought a margin of men out of work was good for his business; he could no longer really think it was good for his country. He could no longer be the old "hard-headed" man who simply did not understand things; he could only be the hard-hearted man who faced them. But he still marched on; he was sure he had made no mistake.

However, he had made a mistake—as definite as a mistake in multiplication. It may be summarized thus: that the same inequality and insecurity that makes cheap labour may make bad labour, and at last no labour at all. It was as if a man who wanted something from an enemy, should at last reduce the enemy to come knocking at his door in the despair of winter, should keep him waiting in the snow to sharpen the bargain; and then come out to find the man dead upon the doorstep.

He had discovered the divine boomerang; his sin had found him out. The experiment of Individualism—the keeping of the worker half in and half out of work—was far too ingenious not to contain a flaw. It was too delicate a balance to work entirely with the strength of the starved and the vigilance of the benighted. It was too desperate a course to rely wholly on desperation. And as time went on the terrible truth slowly declared itself; the degraded class was really degenerating. It was right and proper enough to use a man as a tool; but the tool, ceaselessly used, was being used up. It was quite reasonable and respectable, of course, to fling a man away like a tool; but when it was flung away in the rain the tool rusted. But the comparison to a tool was insufficient for an awful reason that had already begun to dawn upon the master's mind. If you pick up a hammer, you do not find a whole family of nails clinging to it. If you fling away a chisel by the roadside, it does not litter and leave a lot of little chisels. But the meanest of the tools, Man, had still this strange privilege which God had given him, doubtless by mistake. Despite all improvements in machinery, the most important part of the machinery (the fittings technically described in the trade as "hands") were apparently growing worse. The firm was not only encumbered with one useless servant, but he immediately turned himself into five useless servants. "The poor should not be emancipated," the old reactionaries used to say, "until they are fit for freedom." But if this downrush went on, it looked as if the poor would not stand high enough to be fit for slavery.

So at least it seemed, doubtless in a great degree subconsciusly, to the man who had wagered all his wealth on the usefulness of the poor to the rich and the dependence of the rich on the poor. The time came at last when the rather reckless breeding in the abyss below ceased to be a supply, and began to be something like a wastage; ceased to be something like keeping foxhounds, and began alarmingly to resemble a necessity of shooting foxes. The situation was aggravated by the fact that these sexual pleasures were often the only ones the very poor could obtain, and were, therefore, disproportionately pursued, and by the fact that their conditions were often such that prenatal nourishment and such things were utterly abnormal. The consequences began to appear. To a much less extent than the Eugenists assert, but still to a notable extent, in a much looser sense than the Eugenists assume, but still in some sort of sense, the types that were inadequate or incalculable or uncontrollable began to increase. Under the hedges of the country, on the seats of the parks, loafing under the bridges or leaning over the Embankment, began to appear a new race of men—men who are certainly not mad, whom we shall gain no scientific light by calling feeble-minded, but who are, in varying individual degrees, dazed or drink-sodden, or lazy or tricky or tired in body and spirit. In a far less degree than the teetotallers tell us, but still in a large degree, the traffic in gin and bad beer (itself a capitalist enterprise) fostered the evil, though it had not begun it. Men who had no human bond with the instructed man, men who seemed to him monsters and creatures without mind, became an eyesore in the market-place and a terror on the empty roads. The rich were afraid.

Moreover, as I have hinted before, the act of keeping the destitute out of public life, and crushing them under confused laws, had an effect on their intelligences which paralyses them even as a proletariat. Modern people talk of "Reason versus Authority"; but authority itself involves reason, or its orders would not even be understood. If you say to your valet, "Look after the buttons on my waistcoat," he may do it, even if you throw a boot at his head. But if you say to him, "Look after the buttons on my tophat," he will not do it, though you empty a bootshop over him. If you say to a schoolboy, "Write out that Ode to Horace from memory in the original Latin," he may do it without a flogging. If you say, "Write out that Ode of Horace in the original German," he will not do it with a thousand floggings. If you will not learn logic, he certainly will not learn Latin. And the ludicrous laws to which the needy are subject (such as that which punishes the homeless for not going home) have really, I think, a great deal to do with a certain increase in their sheepishness and short-wittedness, and, therefore, in their industrial inefficiency. By one of the monstrosities of the feeble-minded theory, a man actually acquitted by judge and jury could *then* be examined by doctors as to the state of his mind—presumably in order to discover by what diseased eccentricity he had refrained from the crime. In other words, when the police cannot jail a man who is innocent of doing something, they jail him for being too innocent to do anything. I do not suppose the man is an idiot at all, but I can believe he feels more like one after the legal process than before. Thus all the factors—the bodily exhaustion, the harassing fear of hunger, the reckless refuge in sexuality, and the black botheration of bad laws—combined to make the employee more unemployable.

Now, it is very important to understand here that there were two courses of action still open to the disappointed capitalist confronted by the new peril of this real or alleged decay. First, he might have reversed his machine, so to speak, and started unwinding the long rope of dependence by which he had originally dragged the proletarian to his feet. In other words, he might have seen that the workmen had more money, more leisure, more luxuries, more status in the community, and then trusted to the normal instincts of reasonably happy human beings to produce a generation better born, bred and cared for than these tortured types that were less and less use to him. It might still not be too late to rebuild the human house upon such an architectural plan that poverty might fly out of the window, with the reasonable prospect of love coming in at the door. In short, he might have let the English poor, the mass of whom were not weak-minded, though more of them were growing weaker, a reasonable chance, in the form of more money, of achieving their eugenical resurrection themselves. It has never been shown, and it cannot be shown, that the method would have failed. But it can be shown, and it must be closely and clearly noted, that the method had very strict limitations from the employers' own point of view. If they made the worker too comfortable, he would not work to increase another's comforts; if they made him too independent, he would not work like a dependent. If, for instance, his wages were so good that he could save out of them, he might cease to be a wage-earner. If his house or garden were his own, he might stand an economic siege in it. The whole capitalist experiment had been built on his dependence; but now it was getting out of hand, not in the direction of freedom, but of frank helplessness. One might say that his dependence had got independent of control.

But there was another way. And towards this the employer's ideas began, first darkly and unconsciously, but now more and more clearly, to drift. Giving property, giving leisure, giving status costs money. But there is one human force that costs nothing. As it does not cost the beggar a penny to indulge, so it would not cost the employer a penny to employ. He could not alter or improve the tables or the chairs on the cheap. But there were two pieces of furniture (labelled respectively "the husband" and "the wife") whose relations were much cheaper. He could alter the *marriage* in the house in such a way as to promise himself the largest possible number of the kind of children he did want, with the smallest number of the kind he did not. He could divert the force of sex from producing vagabonds.

And he could harness to his high engines unbought the red un-broken river of the blood of a man in his youth, as he has already harnessed to them all the wild waste rivers of the world.

V

THE MEANNESS OF THE MOTIVE

Now, if any ask whether it be imaginable that an ordinary man of the wealthier type should analyse the problem or conceive the plan, the in-humanly far-seeing plan, as I have set it forth, the answer is: "Certainly not." Many rich employers are too generous to do such a thing; many are too stupid to know what they are doing. The eugenical opportunity I have described is but an ultimate analysis of a whole drift of thoughts in the type of man who does not analyse his thoughts. He sees a slouching tramp, with a sick wife and a string of rickety children, and honestly wonders what he can do with them. But prosperity does not favour self-examination; and he does not even ask himself whether he means "How can I help them?" or "How can I use them?"—what he can still do for them, or what they could still do for him. Probably he sincerely means both, but the latter much more than the former; he laments the breaking of the tools of Mammon much more than the breaking of the images of God. It would be almost impossible to grope in the limbo of what he does think; but we can assert that there is one thing he doesn't think. He doesn't think, "This man might be as jolly as I am, if he need not come to me for work or wages."

That this is so, that at root the Eugenist is the Employer, there are multitudinous proofs on every side, but they are of necessity miscellaneous, and in many cases negative. The most enormous is in a sense the most negative: that no one seems able to imagine capitalist industrialism being sacrificed to any other object. By a curious recurrent slip in the mind, as irritating as a catch in a clock, people miss the main thing and concentrate on the mean thing. "Modern conditions" are treated as fixed, though the very word "modern" implies that they are fugitive. "Old ideas" are treated as impossible, though their very antiquity often proves their permanence. Some years ago some ladies petitioned that the platforms of our big railway stations should be raised, as it was more convenient for the hobble skirt. It never occurred to them to change to a sensible skirt. Still less did it occur to them that, compared with all the female fashions that have fluttered about on it, by this time St. Pancras[1] is as historic as St. Peter's.

I could fill this book with examples of the universal, unconscious assumption that life and sex must live by the laws of "business" or industrialism, and not *vice versa*; examples from all the magazines, novels, and newspapers. In order to make it brief and typical, I take one case of a more or less Eugenist sort from a paper that lies open in front of me — a paper that still bears on its forehead the boast of being peculiarly an organ of democracy in revolt. To this a man writes to say that the spread of destitution will never be stopped until we have educated the lower classes in the methods by which the upper classes prevent procreation. The man had the horrible playfulness to sign his letter "Hopeful." Well, there are certainly many methods by which people in the upper classes prevent procreation; one of them is what used to be called "platonic friendship," till they found another name for it at the Old Bailey.[2] I do not suppose the hopeful gentleman hopes for this; but some of us find the abortion he does hope for almost as abominable. That, however, is not the curious point. The curious point is that the hopeful one concludes by saying, "When people have large families and small wages, not only is there a high infantile death-rate, but often those who do live to grow up are stunted and weakened by having had to share the family income for a time with those who died early. There would be less unhappiness if there were no unwanted children." You will observe that he tacitly takes it for granted that the small wages and the income, desperately shared, are the fixed points, like day and night, the conditions of human life. Compared with them marriage and maternity are luxuries, things to be modified to suit the wage-market. There are unwanted children; but unwanted by whom? This man does not really mean that the parents do not want to have them. He means that the employers do not want to pay them properly.

[1] A London railroad station.

[2] The central criminal court of the city of London and of the greater London area.

Doubtless, if you said to him directly, "Are you in favour of low wages?" he would say, "No." But I am not, in this chapter, talking about the effect on such modern minds of a cross-examination to which they do not subject themselves. I am talking about the way their minds work, the instinctive trick and turn of their thoughts, the things they assume before argument, and the way they faintly feel that the world is going. And, frankly, the turn of their mind is to tell the child he is not wanted, as the turn of my mind is to tell the profiteer he is not wanted. Motherhood, they feel, and a full childhood, and the beauty of brothers and sisters, are good things in their way, but not so good as a bad wage. About the mutilation of womanhood and the massacre of men unborn, he signs himself "Hopeful." He is hopeful of female indignity, hopeful of human annihilation. But about improving the small bad wage he signs himself "Hopeless."

This is the first evidence of motive: the ubiquitous assumption that life and love must fit into a fixed framework of employment, even (as in this case) of bad employment. The second evidence is the tacit and total neglect of the scientific question in all the departments in which it is not an employment question; as, for instance, the marriages of the princely, patrician, or merely plutocratic houses. I do not mean, of course, that no scientific men have rigidly tackled these, though I do not recall any cases. But I am not talking of the merits of individual men of science, but of the push and power behind this movement, the thing that is able to make it fashionable and politically important. I say, if this power were an interest in truth, or even in humanity, the first field in which to study would be in the weddings of the wealthy. Not only would the records be more lucid, and the examples more in evidence, but the cases would be more interesting and more decisive. For the grand marriages have presented both extremes of the problem of pedigree—first the "breeding in and in," and later the most incongruous cosmopolitan blends. It would really be interesting to note which worked the best, or what point of compromise was safest. For the poor (about whom the newspaper Eugenists are always talking) cannot offer any test cases so complete. Waiters never had to marry waitresses, as princes had to marry princesses. And (for the other extreme) housemaids seldom marry Red Indians. It may be because there are none to marry. But to the millionaires the continents are flying railway stations, and the most remote races can be rapidly linked together. A marriage in London or Paris may chain Ravenna to Chicago, or Ben Cruachan to Bagdad. Many European aristocrats marry Americans, notoriously the most mixed stock in the world; so that the disinterested Eugenist, with a little trouble, might reveal rich stores of negro or Asiatic blood to his delighted employer. Instead of which he dulls our ears and distresses our refinement by tedious denunciations of the monochrome marriages of the poor.

For there is something really pathetic about the Eugenist's neglect of the aristocrat and his family affairs. People still talk about the pride of pedigree; but it strikes me as the one point on which the aristocrats are almost morbidly modest. We should be learned Eugenists if we were allowed to know half as much of their heredity as we are of their hairdressing. We see the modern aristocrat in the most human poses in the illustrated papers, playing with his dog or parrot—nay, we see him playing with his child, or with his grandchild. But there is something heartrending in his refusal to play with his grandfather. There is often something vague and even fantastic about the antecedents of our most established families, which would afford the Eugenist admirable scope not only for investigation but for experiment. Certainly, if he could obtain the necessary powers, the Eugenist might bring off some startling effects with the mixed materials of the governing class. Suppose, to take wild and hypothetical examples, he were to marry a Scotch earl, say, to the daughter of a Jewish banker, or an English duke to an American parvenu of semi-Jewish extraction? What would happen? We have here an unexplored field.

It remains unexplored not merely through snobbery and cowardice, but because the Eugenist (at least the influential Eugenist) half-consciously knows it is no part of his job; what he is really wanted for is to get the grip of the governing classes on to the unmanageable output of poor people. It would not matter in the least if all Lord Cowdray's[3]

[3] Lord Cowdray (1856–1927), British educator and industrialist.

decendants grew up too weak to hold a tool or turn a wheel. It would matter very much, especially to Lord Cowdray, if all his employees grew up like that. The oligarch can be unemployable, because he will not be employed. Thus the practical and popular exponent of Eugenics has his face always turned towards the slums, and instinctively thinks in terms of them. If he talks of segregating some incurably vicious type of the sexual sort, he is thinking of a ruffian who assaults girls in lanes. He is not thinking of a millionaire like White, the victim of Thaw.[4] If he speaks of the hopelessness of feeble-mindedness, he is thinking of some stunted creature gaping at hopeless lessons in a poor school. He is not thinking of a millionaire like Thaw, the slayer of White. And this not because he is such a brute as to like people like White or Thaw any more than we do, but because he knows that *his* problem is the degeneration of the useful classes; because he knows that White would never have been a millionaire if all his workers had spent themselves on women as White did, that Thaw would never have been a millionaire if all his servants had been Thaws. The ornaments may be allowed to decay, but the machinery *must* be mended. That is the second proof of the plutocratic impulse behind all Eugenics: that no one thinks of applying it to the prominent classes. No one thinks of applying it where it could most easily be applied.

A third proof is the strange new disposition to regard the poor as a *race*; as if they were a colony of Japs or Chinese coolies. It can be most clearly seen by comparing it with the old, more individual, charitable, and (as the Eugenists might say) sentimental view of poverty. In Goldsmith or Dickens or Hood there is a basic idea that the particular poor person ought not to be so poor: it is some accident or some wrong. Oliver Twist or Tiny Tim are fairy princes waiting for their fairy godmother. They are held as slaves, but rather as the hero and heroine of a Spanish or Italian romance were held as slaves by the Moors. The modern poor are getting to be regarded as slaves in the separate and sweeping sense of the negroes in the plantations. The bondage of the white hero to the black master was regarded as abnormal; the bondage of the black to the white master

4 See footnote 1, page 426.

as normal. The Eugenist, for all I know, would regard the mere existence of Tiny Tim as a sufficient reason for massacring the whole family of Cratchit; but, as a matter of fact, we have here a very good instance of how much more practically true to life is sentiment than cynicism. The poor are *not* a race or even a type. It is senseless to talk about breeding them; for they are not a breed. They are, in cold fact, what Dickens describes: "a dustbin of individual accidents," of damaged dignity, and often of damaged gentility. The class very largely consists of perfectly promising children, lost like Oliver Twist, or crippled like Tiny Tim. It contains very valuable things, like most dustbins. But the Eugenist delusion of the barbaric breed in the abyss affects even those more gracious philanthropists who almost certainly do want to assist the destitute and not merely to exploit them. It seems to affect not only their minds, but their very eye-sight. Thus, for instance, Mrs. Alec Tweedie almost scornfully asks, "When we go through the slums, do we see beautiful children?" The answer is, "Yes, very often indeed." I have seen children in the slums quite pretty enough to be Little Nell or the outcast whom Hood called "young and so fair." Nor has the beauty anything necessarily to do with health; there are beautiful healthy children, beautiful dying children, ugly dying children, ugly uproarious children in Petticoat Lane or Park Lane. There are people of every physical and mental type of every sort of health and breeding, in a single back street. They have nothing in common but the wrong we do them.

The important point is, however, that there is more fact and realism in the wildest and most elegant old fictions about disinherited dukes and long-lost daughters than there is in this Eugenist attempt to make the poor all of a piece—a sort of black fungoid growth that is ceaselesly increasing in chasm. There is a cheap sneer at poor landladies: that they always say they have seen better days. Nine times out of ten they say it because it is true. What can be said of the great mass of Englishmen, by anyone who knows any history, except that they have seen better days? And the landlady's claim is not snobbish, but rather spirited; it is her testimony to the truth in the old tales of which I spoke: that she *ought not* to be so poor or so servile in status; that a normal person ought to have more property and more power in the State than *that*. Such dreams of lost dignity are perhaps the only things that stand between us and the cattle-breeding paradise now promised. Nor are such dreams by any means impotent. I remember Mr. T. P. O'Connor[5] wrote an interesting article about Madame Humbert[6], in the course of which he said that Irish peasants, and probably most peasants, tended to have a half-fictitious family legend about an estate to which they were entitled. This was written in the time when Irish peasants were landless in their land; and the delusion doubtless seemed all the more entertaining to the landlords who ruled them and the money-lenders who ruled the landlords. But the dream has conquered the realities. The phantom farms have materialized. Merely by tenaciously affirming the kind of pride that comes after a fall, by remembering the old civilization and refusing the new, by recurring to an old claim that seemed to most Englishmen like the lie of a broken-down lodging-house keeper at Margate—by all this the Irish have got what they want, in solid mud and turf. That imaginary estate has conquered the Three Estates of the Realm.

But the homeless Englishman must not even remember a home. So far from his house being his castle, he must not have even a castle in the air. He must have no memories; that is why he is taught no history. Why is he told none of the truth about the mediaeval civilization except a few cruelties and mistakes in chemistry? Why does a mediaeval burgher never appear till he can appear in a shirt and a halter? Why does a mediaeval monastery never appear till it is "corrupt" enough to shock the innocence of Henry VIII.? Why do we hear of one charter—that of the barons—and not a word of the charters of the carpenters, smiths, shipwrights and all the rest? The reason is that the English peasant is not only not allowed to have an

---

[5] T. P. O'Connor (1848–1929), British journalist and politician.

[6] The wife of a former deputy for Seine-et-Marne. She had maintained a luxurious establishment for many years on the basis of her assertion that she had inherited several million pounds sterling from an Englishman. She borrowed large amounts of money on the basis of this legend. The fraud was exposed, she fled the country and was arrested in Spain.

estate, he is not even allowed to have lost one. The past has to be painted pitch black, that it may be worse than the present.

There is one strong, startling, outstanding thing about Eugenics, and that is its meanness. Wealth, and the social science supported by wealth, had tried an inhuman experiment. The experiment had entirely failed. They sought to make wealth accumulate — and they made men decay. Then instead of confessing the error, and trying to restore the wealth, or attempting to repair the decay, they are trying to cover their first cruel experiment with a more cruel experiment. They put a poisonous plaster on a poisonous wound. Vilest of all, they actually quote the bewilderment produced among the poor by their first blunder as a reason for allowing them to blunder again. They are apparently ready to arrest all the opponents of their system as mad, merely because the system was maddening. Suppose a captain had collected volunteers in a hot, waste country by the assurance that he could lead them to water, and knew where to meet the rest of his regiment. Suppose he led them wrong, to a place where the regiment could not be for days, and there was no water. And suppose sunstroke struck them down on the sand man after man, and they kicked and danced and raved. And, when at last the regiment came, suppose the captain successfully concealed his mistake because all his men had suffered too much from it to testify to its ever having occurred. What would you think of the gallant captain? It is pretty much what I think of this particular captain of industry.

Of course, nobody supposes that all Capitalists, or most Capitalists, are conscious of any such intellectual trick. Most of them are as much bewildered as the battered proletariat; but there are some who are less well-meaning and more mean. And these are leading their more generous colleagues towards the fulfilment of this ungenerous evasion, if not towards the comprehension of it. Now a ruler of the Capitalist civilization, who had come to consider the idea of ultimately herding and breeding the workers like cattle, has certainly contemporary problems to review. He has to consider what forces still exist in the modern world for the frustration of his design. The first question is how much remains of the old ideal of individual liberty. The second question is how far the modern mind is committed to such egalitarian ideas as may be implied in Socialism. The third is whether there is any power of resistance in the tradition of the populace itself. These three questions for the future I shall consider in their order in the final chapters that follow. It is enough to say here that I think the progress of these ideals has broken down at the precise point where they will fail to prevent the experiment. Briefly, the progress will have deprived the Capitalist of his old Individualist scruples, without committing him to his new Collectivist obligations. He is in a very perilous position; for he has ceased to be a Liberal without becoming a Socialist, and the bridge by which he was crossing has broken above an abyss of Anarchy.

VI

THE ECLIPSE OF LIBERTY

If such a thing as the Eugenic sociology had been suggested in the period from Fox to Gladstone, it would have been far more fiercely repudiated by the reformers than by the Conservatives. If Tories had regarded it as an insult to marriage, Radicals would have far more resolutely regarded it as an insult to citizenship. But in the interval we have suffered from a process resembling a sort of mystical parricide, such as is told of so many gods, and is true of so many great ideas. Liberty has produced scepticism, and scepticism has destroyed liberty. The lovers of liberty thought they were leaving it unlimited, when they were only leaving it undefined. They thought they were only leaving it undefined, when they were really leaving it undefended. Men merely finding themselves free found themselves free to dispute the value of freedom. But the important point to seize about this reactionary scepticism is that as it is bound to be unlimited in theory, so it is bound to be unlimited in practice. In other words, the modern mind is set in an attitude which would enable it to advance, not only towards Eugenic legislation, but towards any conceivable or inconceivable extravagances of Eugenics.

Those who reply to any plea for freedom invariably fall into a certain trap. I have debated with numberless different people on these matters, and I confess I find it amusing to see them tumbling into it one after another. I remember discussing it before a club of very active and intelligent Suffragists, and I cast it here for convenience in the form which it there assumed. Suppose, for the sake of argument, that I say that to take away a poor man's pot of beer is to take away a poor man's personal liberty, it is very vital to note what is the usual or almost universal reply. People hardly ever do reply, for some reason or other, by saying that a man's liberty consists of such and such things, but that beer is an exception that cannot be classed among them, for such and such reasons. What they almost invariably do say is something like this: "After all, what is liberty?

394

Man must live as a member of a society, and must obey those laws which, etc., etc." In other words, they collapse into a complete confession that they *are* attacking all liberty and any liberty; that they *do* deny the very existence or the very possibility of liberty. In the very form of the answer they admit the full scope of the accusation against them. In trying to rebut the smaller accusation, they plead guilty to the larger one.

This distinction is very important, as can be seen from any practical parallel. Suppose we wake up in the middle of the night and find that a neighbor has entered the house not by the front-door but by the skylight; we may suspect that he has come after the fine old family jewellery. We may be reassured if he can refer it to a really exceptional event; as that he fell on to the roof out of an aeroplane, or climbed on to the roof to escape from a mad dog. Short of the incredible, the stranger the story the better the excuse; for an extraordinary event requires an extraordinary excuse. But we shall hardly be reassured if he merely gazes at us in a dreamy and wistful fashion and says, "After all, what is property? Why should material objects be thus artificially attached, etc., etc.?" We shall merely realize that his attitude allows of his taking the jewellery and everything else. Or if the neighbour approaches us carrying a large knife dripping with blood, we may be convinced by his story that he killed another neighbour in self-defence, that the quiet gentleman next door was really a homicidal maniac. We shall know that homicidal mania is exceptional and that we ourselves are so happy as not to suffer from it; and being free from the disease may be free from the danger. But it will not soothe us for the man with the gory knife to say softly and pensively, "After all, what is human life? Why should we cling to it? Brief at the best, sad at the brightest, it is itself but a disease from which, etc., etc." We shall perceive that the sceptic is in a mood not only to murder us but to massacre everybody in the street. Exactly the same effect which would be produced by the questions of "What is property?" and "What is life?" is produced by the question of "What is liberty?" It leaves the questioner free to disregard any liberty, or in other words to take any liberties. The very thing he says is an anticipatory excuse for anything he may choose to do. If he gags a man to prevent him from indulging in profane swearing, or locks him in the coal cellar to guard against his going on the spree, he can still be satisfied with saying, "After all, what is liberty? Man is a member of, etc., etc."

That is the problem, and that is why there is now no protection against Eugenic or any other experiments. If the men who took away beer as an unlawful pleasure had paused for a moment to define the lawful pleasures, there might be a different situation. If the men who had denied one liberty had taken the opportunity to affirm other liberties, there might be some defence for them. But it never occurs to them to admit any liberties at all. It never so much as crosses their minds. Hence the excuse for the last oppression will always serve as well as for the next oppression; and to that tyranny there can be no end.

Hence the tyranny has taken but a single stride to reach the secret and sacred place of personal freedom, where no sane man ever dreamed of seeing it; and especially the sanctuary of sex. It is as easy to take away a man's wife or baby as to take away his beer when you can say "What is liberty?"; just as it is easy to cut off his head as to cut off his hair if you are free to say "What is life?" There is no rational philosophy of human rights generally disseminated among the populace, to which we can appeal in defence even of the most intimate or individual things that anybody can imagine. For so far as there was a vague principle in these things, that principle has been wholly changed. It used to be said that a man could have liberty, so long as it did not interfere with the liberty of others. This did afford some rough justification for the ordinary legal view of the man with the pot of beer. For instance, it was logical to allow some degree of distinction between beer and tea, on the ground that a man may be moved by excess of beer to throw the pot at somebody's head. And it may be said that the spinster is seldom moved by excess of tea to throw the tea-pot at anybody's head. But the whole ground of argument is now changed. For people do not consider what the drunkard does to others by throwing the pot, but what he does to himself by drinking the beer. The argument is based on health; and it is said that the Government must safeguard the health of the community.

And the moment that is said, there ceases to be the shadow of a difference between beer and tea. People can certainly spoil their health with tea or with tobacco or with twenty other things. And there is no escape for the hygienic logician except to restrain and regulate them all. If he is to control the health of the community, he must necessarily control all the habits of all the citizens, and among the rest their habits in the matter of sex.

But there is more than this. It is not only true that it is the last liberties of man that are being taken away; and not merely his first or most superficial liberties. It is also inevitable that the last liberties should be taken first. It is inevitable that the most private matters should be most under public coercion. This inverse variation is very important, though very little realized. If a man's personal health is a public concern, his most private acts are *more* public than his most public acts. The official must deal *more* directly with his cleaning his teeth in the morning than with his using his tongue in the marketplace. The inspector must interfere *more* with how he sleeps in the middle of the night than with how he works in the course of the day. The private citizen must have much *less* to say about his bath or his bedroom window than about his vote or his banking account. The policeman must be in a new sense a private detective; and shadow him in private affairs rather than in public affairs. A policeman must shut doors behind him for fear he should sneeze, or shove pillows under him for fear he should snore. All this and things far more fantastic follow from the simple formula that the State must make itself responsible for the health of the citizen. But the point is that the policeman must deal primarily and promptly with the citizen in his relation to his home, and only indirectly and more doubtfully with the citizen in his relation to his city. By the whole logic of this test, the king must hear what is said in the inner chamber and hardly notice what is proclaimed from the house-tops. We have heard of a revolution that turns everything upside down. But this is almost literally a revolution that turns everything inside out.

If a wary reactionary of the tradition of Metternich had wished in the nineteenth century to reverse the democratic tendency, he would naturally have begun by depriving the democracy of its margin of

more dubious powers over more distant things. He might well begin, for instance, by removing the control of foreign affairs from
popular assemblies; and there is a case for saying that a people may
understand its own affairs, without knowing anything whatever
about foreign affairs. Then he might centralize great national questions, leaving a great deal of local government in local questions.
This would proceed so for a long time before it occurred to the
blackest terrorist of the despotic ages to interfere with a man's own
habits in his own house. But the new sociologists and legislators are,
by the nature of their theory, bound to begin where the despots
leave off, even if they leave off where the despots begin. For them, as
they would put it, the first things must be the very fountains of life,
love and birth and babyhood; and these are always covered fountains, flowing in the quiet courts of the home. For them, as Mr.
H. G. Wells put it, life itself may be regarded merely as a tissue of
births. Thus they are coerced by their own rational principle to begin all coercion at the other end; at the inside end. What happens to
the outside end, the external and remote powers of the citizen, they
do not very much care; and it is probable that the democratic institutions of recent centuries will be allowed to decay in undisturbed dignity for a century or two more. Thus our civilization will find itself
in an interesting situation, not without humour; in which the citizen is still supposed to wield imperial powers over the ends of the
earth, but has admittedly no power over his own body and soul at
all. He will still be consulted by politicians about whether opium is
good for Chinamen, but not whether ale is good for him. He will be
cross-examined for his opinions about the danger of allowing Kam-
skatka[1] to have a war-fleet, but not about allowing his own child to
have a wooden sword. Above all, he will be consulted about the
delicate diplomatic crisis created by the proposed marriage of the
Emperor of China, and not allowed to marry as he pleases.

Part of this prophecy or probability has already been accomplished;
the rest of it, in the absence of any protest, is in process of accomplishment. It would be easy to give an almost endless catalogue

[1] Probably Kamchatka, a Russian area and peninsula jutting into the Bering Sea.

of examples, to show how, in dealing with the poorer classes at least, coercion has already come near to a direct control of the relations of the sexes. But I am much more concerned in this chapter to point out that all these things have been adopted in principle, even where they have not been adopted in practice. It is much more vital to realize that the reformers have possessed themselves of a *principle*, which will cover all such things if it be granted, and which is not sufficiently comprehended to be contradicted. It is a principle whereby the deepest things of flesh and spirit must have the most direct relation with the dictatorship of the the State. They must have it, by the whole reason and rationale upon which the thing depends. It is a system that might be symbolized by the telephone from headquarters standing by a man's bed. He must have a relation to Government like his relation to God. That is, the more he goes into the inner chambers, and the more he closes the doors, the more he is alone with the law. The social machinery which makes such a State uniform and submissive will be worked outwards from the household as from a handle, or a single mechanical knob or button. In a horrible sense, loaded with fear and shame and every detail of dishonour, it will be true to say that charity begins at home.

Charity will begin at home in the sense that all home children will be like charity children. Philanthropy will begin at home, for all householders will be like paupers. Police administration will begin at home, for all citizens will be like convicts. And when health and the humours of daily life have passed into the domain of this social discipline, when it is admitted that the community must primarily control the primary habits, when all law begins, so to speak, next to the skin or nearest the vitals — then indeed it will appear absurd that marriage and maternity should not be similarly ordered. Then indeed it will seem to be illogical, and it will be illogical, that love should be free when life has lost its freedom.

So passed, to all appearance, from the minds of men the strange dream and fantasy called freedom. Whatever be the future of these evolutionary experiments and their effect on civilization, there is one land at least that has something to mourn. For us in England something will have perished which our fathers valued all the more because they hardly troubled to name it; and whatever be the stars of a more universal destiny, the great star of our night has set. The English had missed many other things that men of the same origins had achieved or retained. Not to them was given, like the French, to establish eternal communes and clear codes of equality; not to them, like the South Germans, to keep the popular culture of their songs; not to them, like the Irish, was it given to die daily for a great religion. But a spirit had been with them from the first which fenced, with a hundred quaint customs and legal fictions, the way of a man who wished to walk nameless and alone. It was not for nothing that they forgot all their laws to remember the name of an outlaw, and filled the green heart of England with the figure of Robin Hood. It was not for nothing that even their princes of art and letters had about them something of kings incognito, undiscovered by formal or academic fame; so that no eye can follow the young Shakespeare as he came up the green lanes from Stratford, or the young Dickens when he first lost himself among the lights of London. It is for nothing that the very roads are crooked and capricious, so that a man looking down on a map like a snaky labyrinth, could tell that he was looking on the home of a wandering people. A spirit at once wild and familiar rested upon its woodlands like a wind at rest. If that spirit be indeed departed, it matters little that it has been driven out by perversions it had itself permitted, by monsters it had idly let loose. Industrialism and Capitalism and the rage for physical science were English experiments in the sense that the English lent themselves to their encouragement; but there was something else behind them and within them that was not they—its name was liberty, and it was our life. It may be that this delicate and tenacious spirit has at last evaporated. If so, it matters little what becomes of the external experiments of our nation in later time. That at which we look will be a dead thing alive with its own parasites. The English will have destroyed England.

VII

THE TRANSFORMATION OF SOCIALISM

Socialism is one of the simplest ideas in the world. It has always puzzled me how there came to be so much bewilderment and misunderstanding and miserable mutual slander about it. At one time I agreed with Socialism, because it was simple. Now I disagree with Socialism, because it is too simple. Yet most of its opponents still seem to treat it, not merely as an iniquity but as a mystery of iniquity, which seems to mystify them even more than it maddens them. It may not seem strange that its antagonists should be puzzled about what it is. It may appear more curious and interesting that its admirers are equally puzzled. Its foes used to denounce Socialism as Anarchy, which is its opposite. Its friends seemed to suppose that it is a sort of optimism, which is almost as much of an opposite. Friends and foes alike talked as if it involved a sort of faith in ideal human nature; why I could never imagine. The Socialist system, in a more special sense than any other, is founded not on optimism but on original sin. It proposes that the State, as the conscience of the community, should possess all primary forms of property; and that obviously on the ground that men cannot be trusted to own or barter or combine or compete without injury to themselves. Just as a State might own all the guns lest people should shoot each other, so this State would own all the gold and land lest they should cheat or rackrent or exploit each other. It seems extraordinarily simple and even obvious; and so it is. It is too obvious to be true. But while it is obvious, it seems almost incredible that anybody ever though it optimistic.

I am myself primarily opposed to Socialism, or Collectivism or Bolshevism or whatever we call it, for a primary reason not immediately involved here: the ideal of property. I say the ideal and not merely the idea; and this alone disposes of the moral mistake in the matter. It disposes of all the dreary doubts of the Anti-Socialists about men not yet being angels, and all the yet drearier hopes of the Socialists about men soon being supermen. I do not admit that private property is a concession to baseness and selfishmess; I think it is a point of honour. I think it is the most truly popular of all points of honour. But this, though it has everything to do with my plea for a domestic dignity, has nothing to do with this passing summary of the situation of Socialism. I only remark in passing that it is vain for the more vulgar sort of Capitalists, sneering at ideals, to say to me that in order to have Socialism "You must alter human nature." I answer "Yes. You must alter it for the worse."

The clouds were considerably cleared away from the meaning of Socialism by the Fabians of the 'nineties; by Mr. Bernard Shaw, a sort of anti-romantic Quixote, who charged chivalry as chivalry charged windmills, with Sidney Webb[1] for his Sancho Panza. In so far as these paladins had a castle to defend, we may say that their castle was the Post Office. The red pillar-box was the immovable post against which the irresistible force of Capitalist individualism was arrested. Business men who said that nothing could be managed by the State were forced to admit that they trusted all their business letters and business telegrams to the State.

After all, it was not found necessary to have an office competing with another office, trying to send out pinker postage-stamps or more picturesque postmen. It was not necessary to efficiency that the post-mistress should buy a penny stamp for a halfpenny and sell it for two-pence; or that she should haggle and beat customers down about the price of a postal order; or that she should always take tenders for tel-egrams. There was obviously nothing actually impossible about the State management of national needs; and the Post Office was at least tolerably managed. Though it was not always a model employer, by any means, it might be made so by similar methods. It was not impos-sible that equitable pay, and even equal pay, could be given to the Post-master-General and the postman. We had only to extend this rule of public responsibility, and we should escape from all the terror of inse-curity and torture of compassion, which hag-rides humanity in the in-sane extremes of economic inequality and injustice. As Mr. Shaw put it, "A man must save Society's honour before he can save his own."

[1] Sidney Webb (1859–1947), English writer, economist and socialist theoretician.

That was one side of the argument: that the change would remove inequality; and there was an answer on the other side. It can be stated most truly by putting another model institution and edifice side by side with the Post Office. It is even more of an ideal republic, or commonwealth without competition or private profit. It supplies its citizens not only with the stamps but with clothes and food and lodging, and all they require. It observes considerable level of equality in these things; notably in the clothes. It not only surpervises the letters but all the other human communications; notable the sort of evil communications that corrupt good manners. This twin model to the Post Office is called the Prison. And much of the scheme for a model State was regarded by its opponents as a scheme for a model prison; good because it fed men equally, but less acceptable since it imprisoned them equally.

It is better to be in a bad prison than in a good one. From the standpoint of the prisoner this is not at all a paradox; if only because in a bad prison he is more likely to escape. But apart from that, a man was in many ways better off in the old dirty and corrupt prison, where he could bribe turnkeys to bring him drink and meet fellow-prisoners to drink with. Now that is exactly the difference between the present system and the proposed system. Nobody worth talking about respects the present system. Capitalism is a corrupt prison. That is the best that can be said for Capitalism. But it is something to be said for it; for a man is a little freer in that corrupt prison than he would be in a complete prison. As a man can find one jailer more lax than another, so he could find one employer more kind than another; he has at least a choice of tyrants. In the other case he finds the same tyrant at every turn. Mr. Shaw and other rational Socialists have agreed that the State would be in practice government by a small group. Any independent man who disliked that group would find his foe waiting for him at the end of every road.

It may be said of Socialism, therefore, very briefly, that its friends recommended it as increasing equality, while its foes resisted it as decreasing liberty. On the one hand it was said that the State could provide homes and meals for all; on the other it was answered that this could only be done by State officials who would inspect houses and regulate meals. The compromise eventually made was one of the most interesting and even curious cases in history. It was decided to do everything that had even been denounced in Socialism, and nothing that had ever been desired in it. Since it was supposed to gain equality at the sacrifice of liberty, we proceeded to prove that it was possible to sacrifice liberty without gaining equality. Indeed, there was not the faintest attempt to gain equality, least of all economic equality. But there was a very spirited and vigourous effort to eliminate liberty, by means of an entirely new crop of crude regulations and interferences. But it was not the Socialist State regulating those whom it fed, like children or even like convicts. It was the Capitalist State raiding those whom it had trampled and deserted in every sort of den, like outlaws or broken men. It occurred to the wiser sociologists that, after all, it would be easy to proceed more promptly to the main business of bullying men, without having gone through the laborious preliminary business of supporting them. After all it was easy to inspect the house without having helped to build it; it was even possible, with luck, to inspect the house in time to prevent it being built. All that is described in the documents of the Housing Problem; for the people of this age loved problems and hated solutions. It was easy to restrict the diet without providing the dinner. All that can be found in the documents of what is called Temperance Reform.

In short, people decided that it was impossible to achieve any of the good of Socialism, but they comforted themselves by achieving all the bad. All that official discipline, about which the Socialists themselves were in doubt or at least on the defensive, was taken over bodily by the Capitalists. They have now added all the bureaucratic tyrannies of a Socialist state to the old plutocratic tyrannies of a Capitalist State. For the vital point is that it did not in the smallest degree diminish the inequalities of a Capitalist State. It simply destroyed such individual liberties as remained among its victims. It did not enable any man to build a better house; it only limited the houses he might live in — or how he might manage to live there; forbidding him to keep pigs or poultry or to sell beer or cider. It did not even add anything to a man's wages; it only took away something from a man's wages and locked it up, whether he liked it or not, in a sort of money-box which was regarded as a medicine-chest. It does not send food into the house to feed the children; it only sends an inspector into the house to punish the parents for having no food to feed them. It does not see that they have got a fire; it only punishes them for not having a fireguard. It does not even occur to it to provide the fireguard.

Now this anomalous situation will probably ultimately evolve into the Servile State of Mr. Belloc's thesis. The poor will sink into slavery; it might as correctly be said that the poor will rise into slavery. That is to say, sooner or later, it is very probable that the rich will take over the philanthropic as well as the tyrannic side of the bargain; and will feed men like slaves as well as hunting them like outlaws. But for the purpose of my own argument it is not necessary to carry the process so far as this, or indeed any farther than it has already gone. The purely negative stage of interference, at which we have stuck for the present, is in itself quite favourable to all these eugenical experiments. The capitalist whose half-conscious thought and course of action I have simplified into a story in the preceding chapters, finds this insufficient solution quite sufficient for his purposes. What he has felt for a long time is that he must check or improve the reckless and random breeding of the submerged race, which is at once outstripping his requirements and failing to fulfil his needs. Now the anomalous situation has already accustomed him to stopping things. The first interferences with sex need only be negative; and there are already negative interferences without number. So that the study of this stage of Socialism brings us to the same conclusion as that of the ideal of liberty as formally professed by Liberalism. The ideal of liberty is lost, and the ideal of Socialism is changed, till it is a mere excuse for the oppression of the poor.

The first movements for intervention in the deepest domestic concerns of the poor all had this note of negative interference. Official papers were sent round to the mothers in poor streets; papers in which a total stranger asked these respectable women questions which a man would be killed for asking, in the class of what we called gentlemen or in the countries of what were called free men. They were questions supposed to refer to the conditions of maternity; but the point is here that the reformers did not begin by building up those economic or material conditions. They did not attempt to pay money or establish property to create those conditions. They never give anything—except orders. Another form of the intervention, and one already mentioned, is the kidnapping of children upon the most fantastic excuses of sham psychology. Some people established an apparatus of tests and trick questions; which might make an amusing game of riddles for the family fireside, but seems an insufficient reason for mutilating and dismembering the family. Others became interested in the hopeless moral condition of children born in the economic condition which they did not attempt to improve. They were great on the fact that crime was a disease; and carried on their criminological studies so successfully as to open the reformatory for little boys who played truant; there was not reformatory for reformers. I need not pause to explain that crime is not a disease. It is criminology that is a disease.

Finally one thing may be added which is at least clear. Whether or no the organization of industry will issue positively in a eugenical reconstruction of the family, it has already issued negatively, as in the negations alredy noted, in a partial destruction of it. It took the form of a propaganda of popular divorce, calculated at least to accustom the masses to a new notion of the shifting and re-grouping of families. I do not discuss the question of divorce here, as I have done elsewhere, in its intrinsic character; I merely note it as one of these negative reforms which have been substituted for positive economic equality. It was preached with a weird hilarity, as if the suicide of love were something not only humane but happy. But it need not be explained, and certainly it need not be denied, that the harassed poor of a diseased industrialism were indeed maintainting marriage under every disadvantage, and often found individual relief in divorce. Industrialism does produce many unhappy marriages, for the same reason that it produces so many unhappy men. But all the reforms were directed to rescuing the industrialism rather than the happiness. Poor couples were to be divorced because they were already divided. Through all this modern muddle there runs the curious principle of sacrificing the ancient uses of things because they do not fit in with the modern abuses. When the tares are found in the wheat, the greatest promptitude and practicality is always shown in burning the wheat and gathering the tares into the barn. And since the serpent coiled about the chalice had dropped his poison in the wine of Cana, analysts were instantly active in the effort to preserve the poison and to pour away the wine.

VIII

THE END OF THE HOUSEHOLD GOD

The only place where it is possible to find an echo of the mind of the English masses is either in conversation or in comic songs. The latter are obviously the more dubious; but they are the only things recorded and quotable that come anywhere near it. We talk about the popular Press; but in truth there is no popular Press. It may be a good thing; but, anyhow, most readers would be mildly surprised if a newspaper leading article were written in the language of a navvy. Sometimes the Press is interested in things in which the democracy is also genuinely interested; such as horse-racing. Sometimes the Press is about as popular as the Press Gang. We talk of Labour leaders in Parliament; but they would be highly unparliamentary if they talked like labourers. The Bolshevists, I believe, profess to promote something that they call "proletarian art," which only shows that the word Bolshevism can sometimes be abbreviated into bosh. That sort of Bolshevist is not a proletarian, but rather the very thing he accuses everybody else of being. The Bolshevist is above all a bourgeois; a Jewish intellectual of the town. And the real case against industrial intellectualism could hardly be put better than in this very comparison. There has never been such a thing as proletarian art; but there has emphatically been such a thing as peasant art. And the only literature which even reminds us of the real tone and talk of the English working classes is to be found in the comic song of the English music-hall.

I first heard one of them on my voyage to America, in the midst of the sea within sight of the New World, with the Statue of Liberty beginning to loom up on the horizon. From the lips of a young Scotch engineer, of all people in the world, I heard for the first time these immortal words from a London music-hall song:—

"Father's got the sack from the water-works
  For smoking of his old cherry-briar;
Father's got the sack from the water-works
  'Cos he might set the water-works on fire."

As I told my friends in America, I think it no part of a patriot to boast; and boasting itself is certainly not a thing to boast of. I doubt the persuasive power of English as exemplified in Kipling, and one can easily force it on foreigners too much, even as exemplified in Dickens. I am no Imperialist, and only on rare and proper occasions a Jingo. But when I hear those words about Father and the water-works, when I hear under far-off foreign skies anything so gloriously English as that, then indeed (I said to them), then indeed: —

> "I thank the goodness and the grace
>   That on my birth have smiled,
> And made me, as you see me here,
>   A little English child."

But that noble stanza about the water-works has other elements of nobility besides nationality. It provides a compact and almost perfect summary of the whole social problem in industrial countries like England and America. If I wished to set forth systematically the elements of the ethical and economic problem in Pittsburgh of Sheffield, I could not do better than take these few words as a text, and divide them up like the heads of a sermon. Let me note the points in some rough fashion here.

1. —*Father.* This word is still in use among the more ignorant and ill-paid of the industrial community; and is the badge of an old convention or unit called the family. A man and woman having vowed to be faithful to each other, the man makes himself responsible for all the children of the woman, and is thus generically called "Father." It must not be supposed that the poet or singer is necessarily one of the children. It may be the wife, called by the same ritual "Mother." Poor English wives say "Father" as poor Irish wives say "Himself," meaning the titular head of the house. The point to seize is that among the ignorant this convention or custom still exists. Father and the family are the foundations of thought; the natural authority still comes natural to the poet; but it is overlaid and thwarted with more artificial authorities; the official, the schoolmaster, the policeman, the employer, and so on. What these forces fighting the family are we shall see, my dear brethren, when we pass to our second heading; which is: —

2.—*Got the Sack.* This idiom marks a later stage of the history of the language than the comparatively primitive word "Father." It is needless to discuss whether the term comes from Turkey or some other servile society. In America they say that Father has been fired. But it involves the whole of the unique economic system under which Father has now to live. Though assumed by family tradition to be a master, he can now, by industrial tradition, only be a particular kind of servant; a servant who has not the security of a slave. If he owned his own shop and tools, he could not get the sack. If his master owned him, he could not get the sack. The slave and the guildsman know where they will sleep every night; it was only the proletarian of individualist industrialism who could get the sack, if not in the style of the Bosphorus, at least in the sense of the Embankment. We pass to the third heading.

3.—*From the Water-works.* This detail of Father's life is very important; for this is the reply to most of the Socialists, as the last section is to so many of the Capitalists. The water-works which employed Father is a very large, official and impersonal institution. Whether it is technically a bureaucratic department or a big business makes little or no change in the feelings of Father in connection with it. The water-works might or might not be nationalized; and it would make no necessary difference to Father being fired, and no difference at all to his being accused of playing with fire. In fact, if the Capitalists are more likely to give him the sack, the Socialists are even more likely to forbid him the smoke. There is no freedom for Father except in some sort of private ownership of things like water and fire. If he owned his own well his water could never be cut off, and while he sits by his own fire his pipe can never be put out. That is the real meaning of property, and the real argument against Socialism; probably the only argument against Socialism.

4.—*For Smoking.* Nothing marks this queer intermediate phase of industrialism more strangely than the fact that, while employers still claim the right to sack him like a stranger, they are already beginning to claim the right to supervise him like a son. Economically he can go and starve on the Embankment; but ethically and hygienically he must be controlled and coddled in the nursery. Government repudiates all responsibility for seeing that he gets bread. But it anxiously accepts all responsibility for seeing that he does not get beer. It passses an Insurance Act to force him to provide himself with medicine; but it is avowedly indifferent to whether he is able to provide himself with meals. Thus while the sack is inconsistent with the family, the supervision is really inconsistent with the sack. The whole thing is a tangled chain of contradictions. It is true that in the special and sacred text of scripture we are here considering, the smoking is forbidden on a general and public and not on a medicinal and private ground. But it is none the less relevant to remember that, as his masters have already proved that alcohol is a poison, they may soon prove that nicotine is a poison. And it is most significant of all that this sort of danger is even greater in what is called the new democracy of America than in what is called the old oligarchy of England. When I was in America, people were already "defending" tobacco. People who defend tobacco are on the road to proving that daylight is defensible, or that it is not really sinful to sneeze. In other words, they are quietly going mad.

5.—*Of his old Cherry-briar.* Here we have the intermediate and anomalous position of the institution of Property. The sentiment still exists, even among the poor, or perhaps especially among the poor. But it is attached to toys rather than tools; to the minor products rather than to the means of production. But something of the sanity of ownership is still to be observed; for instance, the element of custom and continuity. It was an *old* cherry-briar; systematically smoked by Father in spite of all wiles and temptations to Woodbines[1] and gaspers; an old companion possibly connected with various romantic or diverting events in Father's life. It is perhaps a relic as well as a trinket. But because it is not a true tool, because it gives the man no grip on the creative energies of society, it is, with all the rest of his self-respect, at the mercy of the thing called the sack. When he gets the sack from the water-works, it is only too probable that he will have to pawn his old cherry-briar.

6.—*'Cos he might set the water-works on fire.* And that single line,

[1] Any cheap cigarette; derived from Wills "Wild Woodbine" cigarettes which was among the cheapest available.

like the lovely single lines of the great poets, is so full, so final, so perfect a picture of all the laws we pass and all the reasons we give for them, so exact an analysis of the logic of all our precautions at the present time, that the pen falls even from the hand of the commentator; and the masterpiece is left to speak for itself.

Some such analysis as the above gives a better account than most of the anomalous attitude and situation of the English proletarian today. It is the more appropriate because it is expressed in the words he actually uses; which certainly do not include the word "proletarian." It will be noted that everything that goes to make up that complexity is in an unfinished state. Property has not quite vanished; slavery has not quite arrived; marriage exists under difficulties; social regimentation exists under restraints, or rather under subterfuges. The question which remains is which force is gaining on the other, and whether the old forces are capable of resisting the new. I hope they are; but I recognize that they resist under more than one heavy handicap. The chief of these is that the family feeling of the workmen is by this time rather an instinct than an ideal. The obvious thing to protect an ideal is a religion. The obvious thing to protect the ideal of marriage is the Christian religion. And for various reasons, which only a history of England could explain (though it hardly every does), the working classes of this country have been very much cut off from Christianity. I do not dream of denying, indeed I should take every opportunity of affirming, that monogamy and its domestic responsibilities can be defended on rational apart from religious grounds. But a religion is the practical protection of any moral idea which has to be popular and which has to be pugnacious. And our ideal, if it is to survive, will have to be both.

Those who make merry over the landlady who has seen better days, of whom something has been said already, commonly speak, in the same jovial journalese, about her household goods as her household gods. They would be much startled if they discovered how right they are. Exactly what is lacking to the modern materialist is something that can be what the household gods were to the ancient heathen. The household gods of the heathen were not only wood and stone; at least there is always more than that in the stone of the hearth-stone and the wood of the roof-tree. So long as Christianity continued the tradition of patron saints and portable relics, this idea of a blessing on the household could continue. If men had not domestic divinities, at least they had divine domesticities. When Christianity was chilled with Puritanism and rationalism, this inner warmth or secret fire in the house faded on the hearth. But some of the embers still glow or at least glimmer; and there is still a memory among the poor that their material possessions are something sacred. I know poor men for whom it is the romance of their lives to refuse big sums of money for an old copper warming-pan. They do not want it, in any sense of base utility. They do not use it as a warming-pan; but it warms them for all that. It is indeed, as Sergeant Buzfuz[2] humorously observed, a cover for hidden fire. And the fire is that which burned before the strange and uncouth wooden gods, like giant dolls, in the huts of ancient Italy. It is a household god. And I can imagine some such neglected and unlucky English man dying with his eyes on the red gleam of that piece of copper, as happier men have died with their eyes on the golden gleam of a chalice or a cross.

It will thus be noted that there has always been some conection between a mystical belief and the materials of domesticity; that they generally go together; and that now, in a more mournful sense, they are gone together. The working classes have no reserves of property with which to defend their relics of religion. They have no religion with which to sanctify and dignify their property. Above all, they are under the enormous disadvantage of being right without knowing it. They hold their sound principles as if they were sullen prejudices. They almost secrete their small property as if it were stolen property. Often a poor woman will tell a magistrate that she sticks to her husband, with the defiant and desperate air of a wanton resolved to run away from her husband. Often she will cry as hopelessly, and as it were helplessly, when deprived of her child as if she were a child deprived of her doll. Indeed, a child in the street, crying

---

[2] A character in Charles Dickens' *Pickwick Papers.* He was the counsel for Mrs. Bardell in the Bardell-Pickwick breach-of-promise suit. During his opening statement, he asserts that a remark written about a warming-pan in a note from Pickwick to Mrs. Bardell conveyed a hidden message.

for her lost doll, would probably receive more sympathy than she does.

Meanwhile the fun goes on; and many such conflicts are recorded, even in the newspapers, between heart-broken parents and house-breaking philanthropists; always with one issue, of course. There are any number of them that never get into the newspapers. And we have to be flippant about these things as the only alternative to being rather fierce; and I have no desire to end on a note of universal ferocity. I know that many who set such machinery in motion do so from motives of sincere but confused compassion, and many more from a dull but not dishonourable medical or legal habit. But if I and those who agree with me tend to some harshness and abruptness of condemnation, these worthy people need not be altogether impatient with our impatience. It is surely beneath them, in the scope of their great schemes, to complain of protests so ineffectual about wrongs so individual. I have considered in this chapter the chances of general democratic defence of domestic honour, and have been compelled to the conclusion that they are not at present hopeful; and it is at least clear that we cannot be founding on them any personal hopes. If this conclusion leaves us defeated, we submit that it leaves us disinterested. Ours is not the sort of protest, at least, that promises anything even to the demagogue, let alone the sycophant. Those we serve will never rule, and those we pity will never rise. Parliament will never be surrounded by a mob of submerged grandmothers brandishing pawn-tickets. There is no trade union of defective children. It is not very probable that modern government will be overturned by a few poor dingy devils who are sent to prison by mistake, or rather by ordinary accident. Surely it is not for those magnificent Socialists, or those great reformers and reconstructors of Capitalism, sweeping onward to their scientific triumphs and caring for none of these things, to murmur at our vain indignation. At least if it is vain it is the less venal; and in so far as it is hopeless it is also thankless. They have their great campaigns and cosmopolitan systems for the regimentation of millions, and the records of science and progress. They need not be angry with us, who plead for those who will never read our words or reward our effort, even with gratitude. They need surely have no worse mood towards us than mystification, seeing that in recalling these small things of broken hearts or homes, we are but recording what cannot be recorded; trivial tragedies that will fade faster and faster in the flux of time, cries that fail in a furious and infinite wind, wild words of despair that are written only upon running water; unless, indeed, as some so stubbornly and strangely say, they are somewhere cut deep into a rock, in the red granite of the wrath of God.

IX

A SHORT CHAPTER

Round about the year 1913 Eugenics was turned from a fad to a fashion. Then, if I may so summarize the situation, the joke began in earnest. The organizing mind which we have seen considering the problem of slum population, the popular material and the possibility of protests, felt that the time had come to open the campaign. Eugenics began to appear in big headlines in the daily Press, and big pictures in the illustrated papers. A foreign gentleman named Bolce, living at Hampstead, was advertised on a huge scale as having every intention of being the father of the Superman. It turned out to be a Superwoman, and was called Eugenette. The parents were described as devoting themselves to the production of perfect pre-natal conditions. They "eliminated everything from their lives which did not tend towards complete happiness." Many might indeed be ready to do this; but in the voluminous contemporary journalism on the subject I can find no detailed notes about how it is done. Communications were opened with Mr. H. G. Wells, with Dr. Saleeby, and apparently with Dr. Karl Pearson. Every quality desired in the ideal baby was carefully cultivated in the parents. The problem of a sense of humour was felt to be a matter of great gravity. The Eugenist couple, naturally fearing they might be deficient on this side, were so truly scientific as to have resort to specialists. To cultivate a sense of fun, they visited Harry Lauder,[1] and then Wilkie Bard,[2] and afterwards George Robey;[3] but all, it would appear, in vain. To the newspaper reader, however, it looked as if the names of

[1] Harry Lauder (1870–1950), Scottish balladeer and composer whose ballads gave lyric life for the first time to the simple, courageous humor and unabashed sentimentality of the Scottish working people.

[2] Wilkie Bard (Billie Smith) (1870–1944), music-hall performer who popularized the vogue for tongue-twisters with "She Sells Sea-Shells on the Sea-Shore."

[3] George Robey (1869–1954), English music hall singer and composer who performed a vast range of humorous and sometimes pathetic characters in songs and sketches.

Metchnikoff[4] and Steinmetz and Karl Pearson would soon be quite as familiar as those of Robey and Lauder and Bard. Arguments about these Eugenic authorities, reports of the controversies at the Eugenic Congress, filled countless columns. The fact that Mr. Bolce, the creator of perfect prenatal conditions, was afterwards sued in a lawcourt for keeping his own flat in conditions of filth and neglect, cast but a slight and momentary shadow upon the splendid dawn of the science. It would be vain to record any of the thousand testimonies to its triumph. In the nature of things, this should be the longest chapter in the book, or rather the beginning of another book. It should record, in numberless examples, the triumphant popularization of Eugenics in England. But as a matter of fact this is not the first chapter but the last. And this must be a very short chapter, because the whole of this story was cut short. A very curious thing happened. England went to war.

This would in itself have been a sufficiently irritating interruption in the early life of Eugenette, and in the early establishment of Eugenics. But a far more dreadful and disconcerting fact must be noted. With whom, alas, did England go to war? England went to war with the Superman in his native home. She went to war with that very land of scientific culture from which the very ideal of a Superman had come. She went to war with the whole of Dr. Steinmetz, and presumably with at least half of Dr. Karl Pearson. She gave battle to the birthplace of nine-tenths of the professors who were the prophets of the new hope of humanity. In a few weeks the very name of professor was a matter for hissing and low plebeian mirth. The very name of Nietzsche, who had held up this hope of something superhuman to humanity, was laughed at for all the world as if he had been touched with lunacy. A new mood came upon the whole people; a mood of marching, of spontaneous soldierly vigilance and democratic discipline, moving to the faint tune of bugles far away. Men began to talk strangely of old and common things, of the counties of England, of its quiet landscapes, of motherhood and the half-buried religion of the race. Death shone on the land like a new daylight, making all things vivid and visibly

[4] Elie Metchnikoff (d. 1916), French writer and scientist.

dear. And in the presence of this awful actuality it seemed, somehow or other, as if even Mr. Bolce and the Eugenic baby were things unaccountably far-away and almost, if one may say so, funny.

Such a revulsion requires explanation, and it may be briefly given. There was a province of Europe which had carried nearer to perfection than any other the type of order and foresight that are the subject of this book. It had long been the model State of all those more rational moralists who saw in science the ordered salvation of society. It was admittedly ahead of all other States in social reform. All the systematic social reform. All the systematic social reforms were professedly and proudly borrowed from it. Therefore when this province of Prussia found it convenient to extend its imperial system to the neighbouring and neutral State of Belgium, all these scientific enthusiasts had a privilege not always granted to mere theorists. They had the gratification of seeing their great Utopia at work, on a grand scale and very close at hand. They had not to wait, like other evolutionary idealists, for the slow approach of something nearer to their dreams; or to leave it merely as a promise to posterity. They had not to wait for it as for a distant thing like the vision of a future state; but in the flesh they had seen their Paradise. And they were very silent for five years.

The thing died at last, and the stench of it stank to the sky. It might be thought that so terrible a savour would never altogether leave the memories of men; but men's memories are unstable things. It may be that gradually these dazed dupes will gather again together, and attempt again to believe their dreams and disbelieve their eyes. There may be some whose love of slavery is so ideal and disinterested that they are loyal to it even in its defeat. Wherever a fragment of that broken chain is found, they will be found hugging it. But there are limits set in the everlasting mercy to him who has been once deceived and a second time deceives himself. They have seen their paragons of science and organization playing their part on land and sea; showing their love of learning at Louvain and their love of humanity at Lille. For a time at least they have believed the testimony of their senses. And if they do not believe now, neither would they believe though one rose from the dead; though all the millions who died to destroy Prussianism stood up and testified against it.

DIVORCE VERSUS DEMOCRACY

1916

PREFACE

I have been asked to put forward in pamphlet form this rather hasty essay as it appeared in "Nash's Magazine"; and I do so by the kind permission of the editor. The rather chaotic quality of its journalism it is now impossible to alter. The convictions upon which it is based are unaltered and unalterable. Indeed, in so far as circumstances have since affected them, they are greatly strengthened. In so far as there was something sporadic and seemingly irrelevant in the writing, it was partly because I was contending against an evil that was diffused and indefinable, at once tentative and ubiquitous. Since then that disease has come to a head and burst; primarily in the North of Europe. By that historic habit which generally makes one European people the standard bearer of a social tendency, which made the Empire a Roman Empire and the Revolution a French Revolution, the North Germans have become the peculiar champions of that modern change which would make the State infinitely superior to the Family. It is even asserted that Prussian political authority is now encouraging the abandonment of common morality for the support of population; and even if this horrible thing be untrue, it is highly significant that it can be plausibly said of Prussia and certainly of no other Christian State. And in the new light of action it is possible to trace more clearly the trend towards divorce, as also that trend towards the other pagan institution of slavery, which would certainly have accompanied it. But the enslaving force in Europe struck too early; and the whole movement has been brought to a standstill.

The same circumstances have given an importance to a formula of my own which I still think rather important. It may be summarised as the patriotism of the household. In the experience of nationality we do not admit that any excess of despair can come into the same logical world as desertion. No amount of tragedy need amount to treason. The Christian view of marriage conceives of the home as self-governing in a manner analogous to an independent state; that is, that it may include internal reform and even internal rebellion; but because of the bond, not against it. In this way it is itself a sort of standing reformer of the State; for the State is judged by whether its arrangements bear helpfully or bear hardly on the human fulness and fertility of the free family. Thus the Wicked Ten in Rome[1] were condemned and cast down because their public powers permitted a wrong against the purity of a private family. Thus the mediaeval revolt against the Poll Tax began by the authority of an official insulting the authority of a father. Men do not now, any more than then, become sinless by receiving a post in a bureaucracy; and if the domestic affairs of the poor were once put into the hands of mere lawyers and inspectors, the poor would soon find themselves in positions from which there is no exit save by the sword of Virginius[2] and the hammer of Wat Tyler.[3] As for the section of the rich who are still seeking a servile solution, they, of course, are still seeking the extension of divorce. It is only "*divide et impera*"; and they want the division of sex for the division of labour. The very same economic calculation which makes them encourage tyranny in the shop makes them encourage licence in the family. But now the free families of five great nations have risen against them; and their plot has failed.

G. K. Chesterton

[1] The Decemviri, a ten member ruling body in early Rome.

[2] See footnote 2, page 217.

[3] See footnote 1, page 217.

DIVORCE VERSUS DEMOCRACY

On this question of divorce I do not profess to be impartial, for I have never perceived any intelligent meaning in the word. I merely (and most modestly) profess to be right. I also profess to be representative: that is, democratic. Now, one may believe in democracy or disbelieve in it. It would be grossly unfair to conceal the fact that there are difficulties on both sides. The difficulty of believing in democracy is that it is so hard to believe—like God and most other good things. The difficulty of disbelieving in democracy is that there is nothing else to believe in. I mean there is nothing else on earth or in earthly politics. Unless an aristocracy is selected by gods, it must be selected by men. It may be negatively and passively permitted, but either heaven or humanity must permit it; otherwise it has no more moral authority than a lucky pickpocket. It is babytalk to talk about "Supermen" or "Nature's Aristocracy" or "The Wise Few." "The Wise Few" must be either those whom others think wise— who are often fools; or those who think themselves wise —who are always fools.

Well, if one happens to believe in democracy as I do, as a large trust in the active and passive judgment of the human conscience, one can have no hesitation, no "impartiality," about one's view of divorce; and especially about one's view of the extension of divorce among the democracy. A democrat in any sense must regard that extension as the last and vilest of the insults offered by the modern rich to the modern poor. The rich do largely believe in divorce; the poor do mainly believe in fidelity. But the modern rich are powerful and the modern poor are powerless. Therefore for years and decades past the rich have been preaching their own virtues. Now that they have begun to preach their vices too, I think it is time to kick.

There is one enormous and elementary objection to the popularising of divorce, which comes before any consideration of the nature of marriage. It is like an alphabet in letters too large to be seen. It is this: That even if the democracy approved of divorce as strongly and deeply as the democracy does (in fact) disapprove of it—any man of common sense must know that nowadays the thing will be worked probably against the democracy, but quite certainly by the plutocracy. People seem to forget that in a society where power goes with wealth and where wealth is in an extreme state of inequality, extending the powers of the law means something entirely different from extending the powers of the public. They seem to forget that there is a great deal of difference between what laws define and what laws do. A poor woman in a poor public-house was broken with a ruinous fine for giving a child a sip of shandy-gaff. Nobody supposed that the law verbally stigmatised the action for being done by a poor person in a poor public-house. But most certainly nobody will dare to pretend that a rich man giving a boy a sip of champagne would have been punished so heavily — or punished at all. I have seen the thing done frequently in country houses; and my host and hostess would have been very much surprised if I had gone outside and telephoned for the police. The law theoretically condemns any one who tries to frustrate the police or even fails to assist them. Yet the rich motorists are allowed to keep up an organised service of anti-police detectives — wearing a conspicuous uniform — for the avowed purpose of showing motorists how to avoid capture. No one supposes again that the law says in so many words that the right to organise for the evasion of laws is a privilege of the rich but not of the poor. But take the same practical test. What would the police say, what would the world say, if men stood about the streets in green and yellow uniforms, notoriously for the purpose of warning pickpockets of the presence of a plain-clothes officer? What would the world say if recognised officials in peaked caps watched by night to warn a burglar that the police were waiting for him? Yet there is no distinction of principle between the evasion of that police-trap and the other police-trap — the police-trap which prevents a motorist from killing a child like a chicken; which prevents the most frivolous kind of murder, the most piteous kind of sudden death.

Well, the Poor Man's Divorce Law will be applied exactly as all these others are applied. Everybody must know that it would mean in practice that well-dressed men, doctors, magistrates, and inspectors, would have more power over the family lives of the ill-dressed men, navvies, plumbers, and potmen. Nobody can have the impudence to pretend that it would mean that navvies, plumbers, and potmen would (either individually or collectively) have more power over the family lives of doctors, magistrates, and inspectors. Nobody dare assert that because divorce is a State affair, therefore the poor citizen will have any power, direct or indirect, to divorce a duchess from a duke or a banker from a banker's wife. But no one will call it inconceivable that the power of rich families over poor families, which is already great, the power of the duke as landlord, the power of the banker as money-lender, might be considerably increased by arming magistrates with more powers of interference in private life. For the dukes and bankers often are magistrates, always the friends and relatives of magistrates. The navvies are not. The navvy will be the subject of the new experiments; certainly never the experimentalist. It is the poor man who will show to the imaginative eye of science all those horrors which, according to newspaper correspondents, cry aloud for divorce—drunkenness, madness, cruelty, incurable disease. If he is slow in working for his master, he will be "defective." If he is worn out by working for his master, he will be "degenerate." If he, at some particular opportunity, prefers to work for himself to working for his master, he will be obviously insane. If he never has any opportunity of working for any masters he will be "unemployable." All the bitter embarrassments and entanglements incidental to extreme poverty will be used to break conjugal happiness, as they are already used to break parental authority. Marriage will be called a failure wherever it is a struggle; just as parents in modern England are sent to prison for neglecting the children whom they cannot afford to feed.

I will take but one instance of the enormity and silliness which is really implied in these proposals for the extension of divorce. Take the case quoted by many contributors to the discussion in the papers —the case of what is called "cruelty." Now what is the real meaning of this as regards the prosperous and as regards the struggling classes of the community? Let us take the prosperous classes first. Every one knows that those who are really to be described as gentlemen all profess a particular tradition, partly chivalrous, partly merely modern and refined—a tradition against "laying hands upon a woman, save in a way of kindness." I do not mean that a gentleman hates the cowing of a woman by brute force: any one must hate that. I mean he has a ritual, taboo kind of feeling about the laying on of a finger. If a gentleman (real or imitation) has struck his wife ever so lightly, he feels he has done one of those things that thrill the thoughts with the notion of a border-line; something like saying the Lord's Prayer backwards, touching a hot kettle, reversing the crucifix, or "breaking the pledge." The wife may forgive the husband more easily for this than for many things; but the husband will find it hard to forgive himself. It is a purely class sentiment, like the poor folks' dislike of hospitals. What is the effect of this class sentiment on divorce among the higher classes?

The first effect, of course, is greatly to assist those faked divorces so common among the fashionable. I mean that where there is a collusion, a small pat or push can be remembered, exaggerated, or invented; and yet seem to the solemn judges a very solemn thing in people of their own social class. But outside these cases, the test is not wholly inappropriate as applied to the richer classes. For all Gentlemen feeling or affecting this special horror, it does really look bad if a gentleman has broken through it; it does look like madness or a personal hatred and persecution. It may even look like worse things. If a man with luxurious habits, in artistic surroundings, is cruel to his wife, it may be connected with some perversion of sex cruelty, such as was alleged (I know not how truly) in the case of the millionaire Thaw.[1] We need not deny that such cases are cases for separation, if not for divorce.

But this test of technical cruelty, which is rough and ready as applied to the rich, is absolutely mad and meaningless as applied to the poor. A poor woman does not judge her husband as a bully by whether he has ever hit out. One might as well say that a school-boy judges whether another schoolboy is a bully by whether he has ever

[1] Stanford White courted Evelyn Nesbit, the provocative beauty and showgirl who later married railroad millionaire Harry Kendal Thaw. One June 25, 1906, White was shot and killed by Thaw who had learned of White's amorous involvements with Miss Nesbit before their marriage. Thaw claimed that he murdered White in order to avenge his wife's honor. Thaw was tried in two sensational trials, the first ending in a hung jury and the second acquitting him on the grounds of insanity.

hit out. The poor wife, like the schoolboy, judges him as a bully by whether he is a bully. She knows that while wife-beating may really be a crime, wife-hitting is sometimes very like just self-defence. No one knows better than she does that her husband often has a great deal to put up with; sometimes she means him to; sometimes she is justified. She comes and tells this to magistrates again and again; in police court after police court women with black eyes try to explain the thing to judges with no eyes. In street after street women turn in anger on the hapless knight-errant who has interrupted an instantaneous misunderstanding. In these people's lives the rooms are crowded, the tempers are torn to rags, the natural exits are forbidden. In such societies it is as abominable to punish or divorce people for a blow as it would be to punish or divorce a gentleman for slamming a door. Yet who can doubt, if ever divorce is applied to the populace, it would be applied in the spirit which takes the blow quite seriously? If any one doubts it, he does not know what world he is living in.

It is common to meet nowadays men who talk of what they call Free Love as if it were something like Free Silver—a new and ingenious political scheme. They seem to forget that it is as easy to judge what it would be like as to judge of what legal marriage would be like. "Free Love" has been going on in every town and village since the beginning of the world; and the first fact that every man of the world knows about it is plain enough. It never does produce any of the wild purity and perfect freedom its friends attribute to it. If any paper had the pluck to head a column "Is Concubinage a Failure?" instead of "Is Marriage a Failure?" the answer "Yes" would be given by the personal memory of all. Modern people perpetually quote some wild expression of monks in the wilderness (when a whole civilisation was maddened by remorse) about the perilous quality of Woman, about how she was a spectre and a serpent and a destroying fire. Probably the establishment of nuns, situated a few miles off, described Man also as a serpent and a spectre; but their works have not come down to us.

Now all this old-world wit against Benedick the married man was sensible enough. But so was the bachelorhood of the old monks, who said it, sensible enough. It is perfectly true that to entangle yourself with another soul in the most tender and tragic degree is to make, in all rational possibility, a martyr or a fool of yourself. Most of the modern denunciations of marriage might have been copied direct from the maddest of the monkish diaries. The attack on marriage is an argument for celibacy. It is not an argument for divorce. For that entanglement which celibacy avowedly avoids, divorce merely reduplicates and repeats. It may have been a sort of solemn comfort to a gentleman of Africa to reflect that he had no wife. It cannot be anything but a discomfort to a gentleman of America to wonder which wife he really has. If progress means, as in the ludicrous definition of Herbert Spencer, "an advance from the simple to the complex," then certainly divorce is a part of progress. Nothing can be conceived more complex than the condition of a man who has settled down finally four or five times. Nothing can be conceived more complex than the position of a profligate who has not only had ten *liaisons*, but ten legal *liaisons*. There is a real sense in which free love might free men. But freer divorce would catch them in the most complicated net ever woven in this wicked world.

The tragedy of love is in love, not in marriage. There is not unhappy marriage that might not be an equally unhappy concubinage, or a far more unhappy seduction. Whether the tie be legal or no, matters something to the faithless party; it matters nothing to the faithful one. The pathos reposes upon the perfectly simple fact that if any one deliberately provokes either passions or affections, he is responsible for them as long as they go on, as the man is responsible for letting loose a flood or setting fire to a city. His remedy is not to provoke them, like the hermit. His punishment, when he deserves punishment, is to spend the rest of his life in trying to undo any ill he has done. His escape is despair—which is called, in this connection, divorce. For every healthy man feels one fundamental fact in his soul. He feels that he must have a life, and not a series of lives. He would rather the human drama were a tragedy than that it were a series of Music-hall Turns and Potted Plays. A man wishes to save the souls of all the men he has been: of the dirty little schoolboy; of the doubtful and morbid youth; of the lover; of the husband.

Re-incarnation has always seemed to me a cold creed; because each incarnation must forget the other. It would be worse still if this short human life were broken up into yet shorter lives, each of which was in its turn forgotten.

If you are a democrat who likes also to be an honest man—if (in other words) you want to know what the people want and not merely what you can somehow induce them to ask for—then there is no doubt at all that this is what they want. You can only realise it by looking for human nature elsewhere than in election reports; but when you have once looked for it you see it and you never forget it. From the fact that every one thinks it natural that young men and women should carve names on trees, to the fact that every one thinks it unnatural that old men and women should be separated in work-houses, millions and millions of daily details prove that people do regard the relation as normally permanent; not a vision, but as a vow.

Now for the exceptions, true or false. I would note a strange and even silly oversight in the discussion of such exceptions, which has haunted most arguments for further divorce. The ordinary emancipated prig or poet who urges this side of the question always talks to one tune. "Marriage may be the best for most men," he says, "but there are exceptional natures that demand a more undulating experience; constancy will do for the common herd, but there are complex natures and complex cases where no one could recommend constancy. I do not ask (at the present Stage of Progress) for the abolition of marriage; I hereby ask that it may be remitted in such individual and extreme examples."

Now it is perfectly astounding to me that any one who has walked about this world should make such a blunder about the breed we call mankind. Surely it is plain enough that if you ask for dreadful exceptions, you will get them—too many of them. Let me take once again a rough parable. Suppose I advertised in the papers that I had a place for any one who was too stupid to be a clerk. Probably I should receive no replies; possibly one. Possibly also (nay, probably) it would be from the one man who was not stupid at all. But suppose I had advertised that I had a place for any one who was too clever to be a clerk. My office would be instantly besieged by all

the most hopeless fools in the four kingdoms. To advertise for exceptions is simply to advertise for egoists. To advertise for egoists is to advertise for idiots. It is exactly the bore who does think that his case is
interesting. It is precisely the really common person who does think
that his case is uncommon. It is always the dull man who does think
himself rather wild. To ask solely for strange experiences of the soul is
simply to let loose all the imbecile asylums about one's ears. Whatever
other theory is right, this theory of the exceptions is obviously
wrong—or (what matters more to our modern atheists) is obviously
unbusinesslike. It is, moreover, to any one with popular political sympathies, a very deep and subtle sort of treason. By thus putting a premium on the exceptional we grossly deceive the unconsciousness of
the normal. It seems strangely forgotten that the indifference of a nation is sacred as well as its differences. Even public apathy is a kind of
public opinion—and in many cases a very sensible kind. If I ask everybody to vote about Mineral Meals and do not get a single ballot-paper
returned, I may say that the citizens have not voted. But they have.

The principle held by the populace, against which this plutocratic
conspiracy is being engineered, is simply the principle expressed in
the Prayer Book in the words "for better, for worse." It is the principle that all noble things have to be paid for, even if you only pay
for them with a promise. One does not take one's interest out of
England as one takes it out of Consols.[2] A man is not an Englishman
unless he can endure even the decay and death of England. And just
as every citizen is a potential soldier, so every wife or husband is a
potential hospital nurse—or even asylum attendant. For though we
should all approve of certain tragedies being mitigated by a celibate
separation—yet the more real love and honour there has been in the
marriage, the less real mitigation there will be in the parting. But
this sound public instinct both about patriotism and marriage also
insists that the first vow or obligation shall be mitigated, not merely
erased and forgotten. Many a good woman has loved and refused a
doubtful man, with the proviso that she would marry no one else;
the old institution of marriage has the same feeling about the

[2] The abbreviation for the Consolidated Annuities, a form of British government
stock originating in 1751.

tragedy that is post-matrimonial. The thing remains real; it binds one to something. If I am exiled from England I will go and live on an island somewhere and be as jolly as I can. I will not become a patriot of any other land.

SOCIAL REFORM
VERSUS
BIRTH CONTROL

1927

SOCIAL REFORM
VERSUS BIRTH CONTROL

The real history of the world is full of the queerest cases of notions that have turned clean head-over-heels and completely contradicted themselves. The last example is an extraordinary notion that what is called Birth Control is a social reform that goes along with other social reforms favoured by progressive people.

It is rather like saying that cutting off King Charles' head was one of the most elegant of the Cavalier fashions in hair-dressing. It is like saying that decapitation is an advance on dentistry. It may or may not be right to cut off the King's head; it may or may not be right to cut off your own head when you have the toothache. But anybody ought to be able to see that if we once simplify things by head-cutting we can do without hair-cutting; that it will be needless to practise dentistry on the dead or philanthropy on the unborn—or the unbegotten. So it is not a provision for our descendants to say that the destruction of our descendants will render it unnecessary to provide them with anything. It may be that it is only destruction in the sense of negation; and it may be that few of our descendants may be allowed to survive. But it is obvious that the negation is a piece of mere pessimism, opposing itself to the more optimistic notion that something can be done for the whole family of man. Nor is it surprising to anybody who can think, to discover that this is exactly what really happened.

The story began with Godwin,[1] the friend of Shelley, and the founder of so many of the social hopes that are called revolutionary. Whatever we think of his theory in detail, he certainly filled the more generous youth of his time with that thirst for social justice and equality which is the inspiration of Socialism and other ideals. What is even more gratifying, he filled the wealthy old men of his time with pressing and enduring terror; and about three-quarters of

---

[1] William Godwin (1756–1836), English political philosopher, essayist and novelist.

the talk of Tories and Whigs of that time consists of sophistries and excuses invented to patch up a corrupt compromise of oligarchy against the appeal to fraternity and fundamental humanity made by men like Godwin and Shelley.

Malthus: An answer to Godwin

The old oligarchs would use any tool against the new democrats; and one day it was their dismal good luck to get hold of a tool called Malthus.[2] Malthus wrote avowedly and admittedly an answer to Godwin. His whole dreary book was only intended to be an answer to Godwin. Whereas Godwin was trying to show that humanity might be made happier and more humane, Malthus was trying to show that humanity could never by any possiblity be made happier or more humane. The argument he used was this: that if the starving man were made tolerably free or fairly prosperous, he would marry and have a number of children, and there would not be food for all. The inference was, evidently, that he must be left to starve. The point about the increase of children he fortified by a fantastically mathematical formula about geometrical progression, which any living human being can clearly see is inapplicable to any living thing. Nothing depending on the human will can proceed by geometrical progression, and population certainly does not proceed by anything of the sort.

But the point is here, that Malthus meant his argument as an argument against all social reform. He never thought of using it as anything else, except an argument against all social reform. Nobody else ever thought in those more logical days of using it as anything but an argument against social reform. Malthus even used it as an argument against the ancient habit of human charity. He warned people against any generosity in the giving of alms. His theory was always thrown as cold water on any proposal to give the poor man property or a better status. Such is the noble story of the birth of Birth Control.

The only difference is this: that the old capitalists were more sincere

---

[2] Thomas Malthus (1766–1834), English population theorist and clergyman.

and more scientific, while the modern capitalists are more hypocritical and more hazy. The rich man of 1850 used it in theory for the oppression of the poor. The rich man of 1927 will only use it in practice for the oppression of the poor. Being incapable of theory, being indeed incapable of thought, he can only deal in two things: what he calls practicality and what I call sentimentality. Not being so much of a man as Malthus, he cannot bear to be a pessimist, so he becomes a sentimentalist. He mixes up this old plain brutal idea (that the poor must be forbidden to breed) with a lot of slipshod and sickly social ideals and promises which are flatly incompatible with it. But he is after all a practical man, and he will be quite as brutal as his forbears when it comes to practice. And the practical upshot of the whole thing is plain enough. If he can prevent his servants from having families, he need not support those families. Why the devil should he?

A Simple Test

If anybody doubts that this is the very simple motive, let him test it by the very simple statements made by the various Birth-Controllers like the Dean of St. Paul's.[3] They never do say that we suffer from a *too* bountiful supply of bankers or that cosmopolitan financiers must not have such large families. They do not say that the fashionable throng at Ascot wants thinning, or that it is desirable to decimate the people dining at the Ritz or the Savoy. Though, Lord knows, if ever a thing human could look like a sub-human jungle, with tropical flowers and very poisonous weeds, it is the rich crowd that assembles in a modern Americanized hotel.

But the Birth-Controllers have not the smallest desire to control that jungle. It is much too dangerous a jungle to touch. It contains tigers. They never do talk about a danger from the comfortable classes, even from a more respectable section of the comfortable classes. The Gloomy Dean is not gloomy about there being too many Dukes; and naturally not about there being too many Deans. He is not

[3] William R. Inge (1860–1954), Anglican clergyman and writer.

primarily annoyed with a politician for having a whole population of poor relations, though places and public salaries have to be found for all the relations. Political Economy means that everybody except politicians must be economical.

The Birth-Controller does not bother about all these these things, for the perfectly simple reason that it is not such people that he wants to control. What he wants to control is the populace, and he practically says so. He always insists that a workman has no right to have so many children, or that a slum is perilous because it is producing so many children. The question he dreads is "Why has not the workman a better wage? Why has not the slum family a better house?" His way of escaping from it is to suggest, not a larger house but a smaller family. The landlord or the employer says in his hearty and handsome fashion: "You really cannot expect me to deprive myself of my money. But I will make a sacrifice, I will deprive myself of your children."

One of a Class

Meanwhile, as the Malthusian attack on democratic hopes slowly stiffened and strengthened all the reactionary resistance to reform in this country, other forces were already in the field. I may remark in passing that Malthus, and his sophistry against all social reform, did not stand alone. It was one of a whole class of scientific excuses invented by the rich as reasons for denying justice to the poor, especially when the old superstitious glamour about kings and nobles had faded in the nineteenth century. One was talking about the Iron Laws of Political Econonomy, and pretending that somebody had proved somewhere, with figures on a slate, that injustice is incurable. Another was a mass of brutal nonsense about Darwinism and a struggle for life, in which the devil must catch the hindmost. As a fact it was struggle for wealth, in which the devil generally catches the foremost. They all had the character of an attempt to twist the new tool of science to make it a weapon for the old tyranny of money.

But these forces, though powerful in a diseased industrial plutocracy, were not the only forces even in the nineteenth century. Towards the end of that century, especially on the Continent, there was another movement going on, notably among Christian Socialists and those called Catholic Democrats and others. There is no space to describe it here; its interest lies in being the exact reversal of the order of argument used by the Malthusian and the Birth-Controller. This movement was not content with the test of what is called a Living Wage. It insisted specially on what it preferred to call a Family Wage. In other words, it maintained that no wage is just or adequate unless it does envisage and cover the man, not only considered as an individual, but as the father of a normal and reasonably numerous family. This sort of movement is the true contrary of Birth Control and both will probably grow until they come into some tremendous controversial collision. It amuses me to reflect on that big coming battle, and to remember that the more my opponents practise Birth Control, the fewer there will be of them to fight us on that day.

The Conflict

What I cannot get my opponents in this matter to see, in the strange mental confusion that covers the question, is the perfectly simple fact that these two claims, whatever else they are, are contrary claims. At the very beginning of the whole discussion stands the elementary fact that limiting families is a reason for lowering wages and not a reason for raising them. You may like the limitation for other reasons, as you may dislike it for other reasons. You may drag the discussion off to entirely different questions, such as, whether wives in normal homes are slaves. You may compromise out of consideration for the employer or for some other reason, and meet him half-way by taking half a loaf or having half a family. But the claims are in principle opposite. It is the whole truth in that theory of the class war about which the newspapers talk such nonsense. The full claim of the poor would be to have what they considered a full-sized family. If you cut this down to suit wages you make a concession to fit the capitalist conditions. The practical application

I shall mention in a moment; I am talking now about the primary logical contradiction. If the two methods can be carried out, they can be carried out so as to contradict and exclude each other. One has no need of the other; one can dispense with or destroy the other. If you can make the wage larger, there is no need to make the family smaller. If you can make the family small, there is no need to make the wage larger. Anyone may judge which the ruling capitalist will probably prefer to do. But if he does one, he need not do the other.

There is of course a great deal more to be said. I have dealt with only one feature of Birth Control — its exceedingly unpleasant origin. I said it was purely capitalist and reactionary; I venture to say I have proved it was entirely capitalist and reactionary. But there are many other aspects of this evil thing. It is unclean in the light of the instincts; it is unnatural in relation to the affections; it is part of a general attempt to run the populace on a routine of quack medicine and smelly science; it is mixed up with a muddled idea that women are free when they serve their employers but slaves when they help their husbands; it is ignorant of the very existence of real households where prudence comes by free-will and agreement. It has all those aspects, and many of them would be extraordinarily interesting to discuss. But in order not to occupy too much space, I will take as a text nothing more than the title.

A Piece of Humbug

The very name of "Birth Control" is a piece of pure humbug. It is one of those blatant euphemisms used in the headlines of the Trust Press. It is like "Tariff Reform." It is like "Free Labour." It is meant to mean nothing, that it may mean anything, and especially something totally different from what it says. Everybody believes in birth control, and nearly everybody has exercised some control over the conditions of birth. People do not get married as somnambulists or have children in their sleep. But throughout numberless ages and nations, the normal and real birth control is called self control. If anybody says it cannot is possibly work, I say it does. In many classes, in many countries where these quack nostrums are unknown, populations of free men have remained within reasonable limits by sound traditions of thrift and responsibility. In so far as there is a local evil of excess, it comes with all other evils from the squalor and despair of our decaying industrialism. But the thing the capitalist newpapers call birth control is not control at all. It is the idea that people should be, in one respect, completely and utterly uncontrolled, so long as they can evade everything in the function that is positive and creative, and intelligent and worthy of a free man. It is a name given to a succession of different expedients (the one that was used last is always described as having been dreadfully dangerous) by which it is possible to filch the pleasure belonging to a natural process while violently and unnaturally thwarting the process itself.

The nearest and most respectable parallel would be that of the Roman epicure, who took emetics at intervals all day so that he might eat five or six luxurious dinners daily. Now any man's common sense, unclouded by newspaper science and long words, will tell him at once that an operation like that of the epicures is likely in the long run even to be bad for his digestion and pretty certain to be bad for his character. Men left to themselves have sense enough to know when a habit obviously savours of perversion and peril. And if it were the fashion in fashionable circles to call the Roman expedient by the name of "Diet Control," and to talk about it in a lofty fashion as merely "the improvement of life and the service of life" (as if it meant no more than the mastery of man over his meals), we should take the liberty of calling it cant and saying that it had no relation to the reality in debate.

The Mistake

The fact is, I think, that I am in revolt against the conditions of industral capitalism and the advocates of Birth Control are in revolt against the conditions of human life. What their spokesmen can possibly mean by saying that I wage a "class war against mothers" must remain a matter of speculation. If they mean that I do the unpardonable wrong to mothers of thinking they will wish to continue to be mothers, even in a society of greater economic justice and civic equality, then I think they are perfectly right. I doubt whether mothers could escape from motherhood into Socialism. But the advocates of Birth Control seem to want some of them to escape from it into capitalism. They seem to express a sympathy with those who prefer "the right to earn outside the home" or (in other words) the right to be a wage-slave and work under the orders of a total stranger because he happens to be a richer man. By what conceivable contortions of twisted thought this ever came to be considered a freer condition than that of companionship with the man she has herself freely accepted, I never could for the life of me make out. The only sense I can make of it is that the proletarian work, though obviously more servile and subordinate than the parental, is so far safer and more irresponsible because it is not parental. I can easily believe that there are some people who do prefer working in a factory to working in a family; for there are always some people who prefer slavery to freedom, and who especially prefer being governed to governing someone else. But I think their quarrel with motherhood is not like mine, a quarrel with inhuman conditions, but simply a quarrel with life. Given an attempt to escape from the nature of things, and I can well believe that it might lead at last to something like "the nursery school for our children staffed by other mothers and single women of expert training."

I will add nothing to that ghastly picture, beyond speculating pleasantly about the world in which women cannot manage their own children but can manage each other's. But I think it indicates an abyss between natural and unnatural arrangements which would have to be bridged before we approached what is supposed to be the subject of discussion.

The text of this book has been set in Bembo by the Neumann Press of Long Prairie, Minnesota. Printed and bound in Dexter, MI, by Thomson-Shore, Inc. Cover and jacket design by Darlene Lawless.